I0417859

A GIRL WHO WALKED
THROUGH FIRE

a girl who walked through fire

Krys Graf

This novel may be based on true stories, but this book is a work of fiction. Any references to real people, organizations or locales are intended to give the fiction authenticity. Dialogue and names are the product of the author's imagination. Any similarity to real persons living or dead is coincidental.
Copyright © 2021 Krys Graf
All rights reserved.
Library of Congress Control number: 2019903074

ISBN: 0692689591
ISBN 13: 9780692689592

Courage will find you at unexpected moments. It taps on your shoulder and jumpstarts your conscience to stand its ground and right a wrong in this world.

I will let the path of self-destruction implode on those who have chosen to take that road. I will stand aside as karmic energy rains into those who give their worst to others.

Somewhere between the space of calm and chaos is a catalyst, the flash of which ignites an event, and creates a fallout, the cloud of which can linger for a lifetime.

Waves topple like gargantuan dominoes by the breath of a cosmic force, making all entities equal in nature's dimension.

What some lack in knowledge they replace with opinion.

Being in a band in 1975 without being immersed by some kind of drug was like trying to take a bath without water.

Krys Graf – a girl a band a diary

This book is dedicated:
To: all who have been broken, and refuse to let it define them.
To: the memories of: Kenneth E Schroeder, Fred Showalter, and Brian Darabosh.
To: our road crew: Brian Darabosh (Drax), Fred Showalter (Showey), Tom Uthmeier (Hound), Dave Braun, Tim 'O' Waldron, John Borger (Slick), Mike, Derrick, and Fred Spence. You all worked so hard, made many sacrifices, and were appreciated more than you ever knew.

Thank you to: Matt G. and Elle G. for your kind input, Denise S. for your exceptional overview, Laurie W. for your great suggestions, Mark David Anthony Casanova, Karen H., Topher M., Calley S., for your valuable reviews, and Karen Moore for legal recommendations
Chapter 11.

All rights reserved. No part of this publication may be reproduced, stored in a retrieval system, or transmitted in any form or by any means, digital, electronic, mechanical, photocopying, recording, or otherwise, or conveyed via the Internet or a website without prior written permission from the author, except in the case of brief quotations embodied in critical articles and reviews.
A list of characters is provided on the last page.

Prologue

Under a midnight canvas, tall grasses crunched as their feet struck the immense thicket of wilderness, where meadow fragrances lingered in each rustle, break, and snap. The buzz, chirp, and hum of small creatures echoed into the field, as an endless rush of water surged down the Menomonee River near their path. They looked upward at the patterns they had seen since childhood. Ursa Major and Minor, Cassiopeia, Virgo, Leo, and Pegasus glistened in a sky as black as their hair and eyes.

It was an almost daily destination where they viewed the Milky Way which stretched across the heavens. Similar in height and build, at a distance, they looked to be brothers. One of them kicked his foot to the ground as he sat, and thumped a metal object. Dropping both feet rendered the same clang. Curious as to what it was, they dug and unearthed a heavy, corroded canister.

"Who has a match? I want to see what's in here."

They picked up a withered branch and held it over the flame to provide light, and struggled to free the lid on a discolored gray and yellow tin labeled: Meyer Bros. Roasted Coffee.

Inside was an assortment of tarnished nails, candles, a carving knife, a graphite pencil, a bottle of One Night Cough Syrup, a folded, unreadable note, and an old wool sock which contained irregularly-shaped rocks. The nine stones had a bright luster.

"These look like gold."

"They could be pyrite."

"No, they're too yellow, and they have the appearance of chewed gum."

"Judging by how rusty the container is, I think it's been down there for a while. It must have been pushed up to the surface by the winter freezes and thaws. What an incredible find. I doubt if the owner will return for it."

"Let's each keep three of these nuggets, and bury the canister a little deeper. We'll put our names and addresses on the paper, and keep the gold in a safe place. If we're contacted, we give it back. If not, it's ours. I'll be able to buy land near a lake or a river for my family."

"We can't take this. It's not rightfully ours."

"Oh, yes we can, and we will. Come on, start digging."

Three young men tamped the ground down hard. Each sat clasping unexpected treasure, in awe of a find they might have to return.

Out of nowhere, the flash of a fiery blaze consumed the field, causing one of them to bolt upwards and turn away. As he rose to his feet, the inferno vanished.

"Why are you so edgy?"

"Did you see it?"

"See what?"

"I thought I saw something burning out there." He stood motionless for a minute, blinking hard, trying to process the apparition. Around him leaves clapped, and insects, owls and tree frogs sang out reminders that small life forms brimmed through the darkness. Having spent his youth roaming these fields, he bolted between two large flagstone kilns, and down a small hill. To his left, he brushed his hand along an ancient limestone wall, filled with cracks and hollows.

His friends followed him, the torch still glowing.

"What the hell are you doing?"

"You know I sleep in the same room as my two older brothers. If they find these, I'll never seem them again. It's much safer here."

"This will be a pact between us. If no one contacts us, we take no more than our equal share."

Each counted an exact number of craters upward, and hid their valuables inside.

During the night, he was unable to rid his thoughts of the firestorm he had witnessed. Throughout his life, his glimpses into the future had all had come to pass.

In the morning the trio walked to school together, joined the crowd, entered ornate doors, and sat on wooden chairs. Each had been assigned to separate corners. The class was called to attention, and homework papers were collected. As their books opened, smoke swirled under the gap of the door and crept into the room.

Within minutes, the walls burst into flames. Many believe the intense heat of the incinerator chimney ignited the flammable shingles of the cedar roof like dry kindling. Screaming students and teachers used chairs to smash open windows. They ran for their lives as a haze circled through rooms and hallways. The flashover engulfed all that was combustible. Chaos pierced the raging plumes, consuming all who cried out in anguish.

Though the village had a motorized pump and pump connection, no water truck was available. Volunteer firefighters, helpless bystanders, teachers, and the pupils who escaped stood in shock. Chalkboards, artwork, books, and every last desk disintegrated.

An institution of learning sizzled into the summer clouds above. Those who fled were forever changed as flickering ashes rained down around them. The building was devoured within an hour.

As one young man watched the conflagration topple the elaborate structure, his smooth copper skin glistened in the heat. It was what he had seen the previous evening. He wondered if warning someone might have made a difference, but he knew as always, he was not trusted by anyone other than his two close friends.

He found his teacher, and asked if he could obtain a certificate for the classes he had taken, but her narrowed eyes exuded the kind of aloofness that he had witnessed untold times. She ranted that it should not matter to someone like him. At a time like this, how dare he ask for anything whatsoever. His kind never belonged at that school.

As he walked away, a scream grew deep in his lungs, but the only sound he could make was a wheeze as his throat constricted. His fingers tightened into fists which he carried in formidable silence. He dismissed the valuable rocks he hid. His life had been filled with hardships, and the way things tended to go for him, he doubted ever seeing them again.

That day on June 27, 1919, because all contents were destroyed in the two story brick high school in Menomonee Falls, Wisconsin, he received nothing to validate the immeasurable hours he had devoted to his studies.

His parents had no formal schooling. He must push his books aside, they insisted. His education was of no value to them. World War I had ended seven months ago, and the country needed young, hard workers. Employment would be a necessity. His family planned to move within the week, and his assistance was required. His father was elderly, and his mother was in poor health. Ridiculed and bullied by his two older brothers who could neither read nor write, his dream of becoming a doctor swirled into the dry winds that charred the elegant building into cinders. Within hours, a man's destiny was forever changed.

Chapter 1

Bright flashes lit up her bedroom throughout the night as a deluge pounded on her windows and roof. Insomnia tapped on her shoulders with each thunderous boom, and howl through swaying trees.

Tangled in a heap of blankets, grogginess detained her when the luminescence of morning filtered through the blinds. The taste for coffee lured her to the kitchen where she sat beside a percolating brew which bubbled into a glass carafe. She poured a cupful, took a sip, and walked to the doorway. Daylight was as innocent as the night was wicked.

Outside, branches and leaves floated across streaming water, and the house appeared submerged. Strobing blackness had been replaced by clear skies. She opened the door to pick up one of the papers sailing across the ripples, and in the instant it took to step downward, it disappeared. A smooth emerald lawn tickled her feet. She blinked hard and rubbed her eyes.

The aftermath of anything horrific in her life was always followed by dead quiet, and a revision of her perception of the world.

She was startled by the discovery of rainwater down a flight of stairs to her basement. She knew her neighbors were cleaning up similar floods.

Water seeped up concrete walls and flooring, and she dredged into the muck to open a cabinet door and pull out diaries from the bottom of a bookshelf. A half an inch higher than the rainwater, the journals were still intact. They captured the days when she wedged into a narrow space to write. On one side, she had felt the warmth of a heating vent and on the other was a seven foot plank of sanded pine that held shelving together.

When her day ended, time permitting, she penned an entry. Every year, when a datebook was full, it was tossed into a container filled with love letters, fan mail, packets of photos and negatives, newspaper clippings, ticket stubs, and cassette tapes. An inscribed plaque dated 1/1/77 was buried at the bottom. Though the pages of 1970 to 1977 were yellowed, the writing remained legible.

The disinterred diaries which she opened on her upstairs desk, unlocked a vault of memories. Inscribed in folds of paper, cursive script bared itself, and revealed a life she had dissolved like a piece of ice in the warmth of her hand. In a damp box, yellowed parchment drew flashbacks of fans, former bandmates, and road crew.

According to the entries of January 1977, the city of Milwaukee had 6,725 fires the previous year. Of those fires, 2,213 were caused by arson. In 1977, the U.S. Law Enforcement Assistance Administration reported the results of a survey of fire investigators in a publication titled: Arson and Arson Investigation. It was one of the first texts of its kind. By then, her emotional wounds still burned, but she was done being a victim, and ready to take on the world. She opened a page.

Chapter 2

Tuesday, January 4 –
Saturday, January 8

She dreamt she was engulfed in a raging fire, but was startled out of a deep sleep by the ringing phone. She wanted to throw it across the room. Why anyone persisted on a line for so long at 8:00 am, she could not understand. Those who were aware of her occupation and private number knew to wait at least until noon. She reached behind her head to the bedside table, keeping her eyes closed, and fumbled for the handset.

"Miss Loxx, you're abusing my patience. I want the rest of the cash you owe me."

"Wha…what? Who is this?"

"You know who this is, and my rates are higher when I pack heat." Tiny's loud, harsh voice was like a lion's roar, and forced her to hold the speaker away from her ear.

"Why didn't you collect it from me at one of the clubs? I thought you were paid up. I haven't seen any recent invoices from you."

"I sent one to your post office box a month ago," he said.

"I mailed a check out a while ago, but if I still owe you, I'm subtracting twenty bucks for waking me up after three hours of sleep."

"You people in Word Locket think you're so special. You better not," said Tiny.

"Oh yea? A decent bodyguard should know what their client does for a living. I've been up all night doing a show. And why the hell are you waking me up over thirty bucks?" She slammed the handset down, and flung it behind her into the closet, where it beeped loudly.

Wide awake, she combed her fingers through her light-brown hair, and pet her pup who slept beside the wood frame of the waterbed. She let Ebbie outside, where she ran within a three foot tall chicken wire fence, which extended from the house to the garage near the alley, and was set up to protect her from the neighbor who almost poisoned her.

Built into the hallway adjoining the kitchen, Lexa opened the refrigerator which she shared with Sam, who lived in the upper flat. She pulled out strawberries, butter, and an English muffin.

Sunlight streamed through white and green gingham curtains onto pale mint walls. She filled the food and water bowls which sat beside the stove, and took the towel off of the hook near the side door to rub off the snow stuck to Ebbie's wavy, white fur. Last night's snowfall accumulated in the window over the white sink, and the two adjacent windows which face the alleyway and garage.

Ebbie crunched on her brown nuggets, and looked up after each bite as Lexa ate at her white table and four chairs positioned in the corner across from the sink.

Though her bruises were fading, the pain in her back, legs and wrists was a reminder to never count on Sam, her husband. She had searched throughout the Stone Toad night club for him in a panic, when her boot caught the edge of a slick wooden stairway, and she took a hard landing down six steps. He wouldn't leave her behind, would he? Yes he did, and she needed to purge him from her life.

She lay on the waterbed's waves, and turned on the television.

Standing in front of the blackened scraps of a house, a newscaster held a mic up to her mouth. "Numerous properties have been torched in the city of Milwaukee resulting in four men standing trial for conspiracy involving arson, racketeering, and mail fraud. Firefighters have extinguished 6,725 fires over the past year, including buildings, trucks and automobiles. Witnesses have reported a red vehicle in the vicinity during the crimes. Police are seeking information of an arsonist who is a white male, has brown chin-length hair, and is roughly 5'10". He was speculated to have been seen last at..." She changed the channel to a game show.

Tuesday January 4, 1977

There are roughly 19 fires a day in this city. The images of my burnt garage and van still haunt me even though the blaze happened over a year ago. I have dreams where gaping jagged holes open to the sky from the roof above my head, and black glass drips down the charred walls where windows once were.

He may have been called Tiny when he was a toddler, but Thurston Tinsky outgrew the nickname most likely by the time he was six. He could knock most doors down with a swing of his hips, and depending upon the momentum and trajectory, one jolt of his arm will topple most men. Stay clear of him when he is in a bad mood, which seems to be most of the time, and the only reason I didn't hire a new bodyguard is because I'm still alive.

Wednesday January 5, 1977

Sam's secret visits to our upper flat came to an end on the night his mistress went into a rage, and took a bat to the walls and mirrors as her deceitful lover slept downstairs beside me. I never suspected his infidelity while I was at work. Now I hear different women's voices upstairs, and our relationship is held together by a string which we call a band. I had a premonition an hour ago. Blood had drenched my arms, pillow and bedding, but I did not understand why.

Sam knocked on her door at 7:00 pm on Thursday. "Ted, Grant and Karl are here. I'll meet you in the van."

"See you out there." She grabbed her long tan leather coat, her brown suitcase containing clothes, jewelry and boots, locked up the house, and sat in her usual spot on the captain's chair behind the driver.

Whether they spoke or sat in silence prior to a long performance was directly proportional to the amount of sleep each had acquired.

The Globe was an east side music hangout, known for packing in young partiers who could enter on a fake ID. The band waited in the basement dressing room, where they changed ensembles before the show and in between sets.

The dim lighting shone on the short brown wisps of Hound's curly hair, and his bright blue eyes lit up the hallway more than the flashlight he carried. "Listen up Word Locket! The PA speakers are cranked, and the crowd is fired-up for a solid show tonight. I've got your drinks set up on all the amplifiers. Are you ready?"

"Yea, it's time to rock and roll," said Sam as he walked up the steps. "Can you bring me a double scotch?"

"So early?"

"I need to take the edge off."

"What…too many babes fighting over you?"

"Something like that."

A man of many talents, Sam Lynnch graduated near the top of his class at the Milwaukee School of Engineering. He had an uncanny ability to attract women, and his triumphs were as easy as a snap of his long fingers which slid along the neck of a guitar. He loved to grasp all of those beautiful bodies.

Showey, who was referred to as the production designer, secured scaffolding and adjusted the light show during the night. His long brown hair brushed against the heat of one of the PAR lamps which held a 1000 watt bulb.

Drax's wild brown eyes studied the twenty-four channel audio mixer, where he rendered his expertise on the dynamics and distortion of the music as he saw fit. As the sound engineer, his night was spent optimizing the signal-to-noise ratio by adjusting sliders and dials.

The crowd screamed, whistled and held up lighters during the crescendo, and Word Locket returned for a final encore. Since drinks were free for band members and their entourage, when the night came to an end, no one was sober. Groupies offered rides to Grant and Sam, who hustled outside with their arms wrapped around pretty maidens.

Ted left with his wife, Debra. Thick, brown shoulder-length curls framed her full lips and exotic, dark eyes. A strong, 5'3" woman, she cracked a whip to keep her juvenile husband in line.

Streetlights glinted off the snow along the curb sides. Lexa buckled the passenger safety belt, and Karl started the ignition. He drove down the road, and turned left onto Water Street when a lump of clothes and flesh appeared on the road. His foot shot out like a bullet to stomp on the brakes. Both lurched forward, but were whiplashed back by seat restraints.

In the middle of the street, a young brown-haired man was suffused by headlights of the van. They slammed the doors behind them and edged toward the body, whose purple lips stood out against bleached skin.

"He looks dead," said Karl.

She bent down and touched his neck. "His pulse is okay, but this guy smells like booze."

"I'll go to the club and call the police," said Karl.

As he ran to find a phone, she dug through pockets, found a wallet, removed a driver's license, examined and replaced it. The limp twenty-three year old wearing blue jeans and a black jacket lived several miles south of where he had collapsed. *He feels like ice.* She tucked her scarf under his head.

"How's he doing, and did you get his name?" Karl asked when he returned.

"He hasn't budged, and his name is Casey Relmen." She looked up at Karl.

"Hey Casey!" There was no response. "We need to get him out of the line of traffic," said Karl.

He reached under the shoulders of the man's leather jacket, and Lexa clutched his feet. As they moved him, his arms shot upward. His brown eyes blinked and opened.

"Who are you people?" They set him down.

"Casey, what happened to you?" The glow of the headlamps gave Lexa's waist-length hair an angelic shimmer.

"How do you know my name?" His brown hair, wet from the road, was stuck to his face.

"We were sent from above to save you," said Karl who gazed upward. The van's lights saturated his 5'9" outline, and gave his wavy brown hair an ethereal halo. "Your time is not up yet. We're giving you a second chance."

"Who sent you?" Casey sat up and massaged his head. "Man, I had too much to drink. I'm losing it."

"Arise," said Karl. We've come to rescue you."

"I wanted someone to run me over," he mumbled. "My life sucks. I don't want to be saved. Why...why? It wasn't supposed to be this way." Sirens wailed in the distance. "Did you call the cops? You can't leave me here. You don't understand. My life is hell. Get me out of here. Please, please," he cried. He crawled towards the van, his jeans blackened by oil and soot.

"I asked for an ambulance," said Karl. They have my name. They're going to be looking for someone in the road."

"If you're really trying to help me, you can't leave me here."

Karl and Lexa looked at each other, shrugged, and invited him into the warm van.

"Do you have a car?" She turned toward him as Karl revved the engine.

"I hitched a ride to meet up with some people, but they left me," he slurred.

Karl and Lexa again glanced at each other. "Okay, direct us," she said.

He gave them a sketch of his life story as they drove.

8

"Hop on the Thirty-Fifth Street bridge, and head south." They approached National Avenue. "Drop me off at this corner."

She rolled the passenger window partway down as he got out. "Hey, do you want us to put your name on Word Locket's next few guest lists, and see us for free?"

"Miss Loxx, that would be nice," said Casey. He smiled and waved at them as he left.

"He looks a lot like you, Karl. That guy could pass for your brother. It's sad to be so young, and desperate enough to attempt suicide," she said.

"I'm glad the road wasn't iced up. I almost killed him."

"We're all only a heartbeat away from the other side," she said. "Something in his hands is preoccupying him. He's not heading to the address on his ID. Slow down. Let's see where he's going."

"Do we have to? I'm tired and I want to go home." Karl drove a short distance, and they spied on him as he walked long past the spot where they dropped him off. "The guy wants to walk off all the booze he drank. Can we go now?" asked Karl.

"In the dead of night, he's nowhere near where he lives."

Casey approached a red car, got in, and sped off.

"That was odd. He said he hitched a ride, and he wanted us to run him over," she said.

"Maybe he parked by the apartment of one of the friends who dumped him."

As they approached her block, bright, swirling red and blue lights illuminated the darkness. The north and south entrances of her street were barricaded. Worry gnawed at her insides. She and Karl were asked for identification by police who refused to divulge why law enforcement surrounded her neighborhood.

Men and women in uniforms flooded the house bordered by a white picket fence. Karl was scrutinized as he entered his car and left. Eyes followed her as she stepped out of the van and while she fumbled her key into the lock. To get a better view, she kept the lights off, and pushed the curtain aside on the dining room window, where she watched the crowd of officers. When she read 'Coroner' on a van parked at the curb, she knew something terrible had happened, but she had no idea how long it would take for her to find out, if ever at all.

> Thursday January 6, 1977
> *If I had been home this evening, I may have been a victim. The flash of cameras, officers conversing inside and out in the cold night made for an ominous scene at Doris and Roy's house. Though my neighbors never said much to me, I always took their presence for granted.*
>
> *We had a near fatality on the underside of our van. He chattered non-stop about how his classmates tormented him throughout his life. In grade school, he took a daily beating. He hated high school because of the brutality of his classmates. Water was thrown between his legs while he was being punched and kicked. His attackers tossed anything liquid at him on a regular basis, making him walk home in wet clothes on subzero days. His life must have been difficult.*

Chills jolted her to where she nestled under extra blankets. The battered stranger lying on the street, and the death of her neighbor overwhelmed her. Unable to sleep, at 5:00 am, she opened a Nembutal capsule, touched her tongue onto the bitter powder, and swallowed it.

The clank of steel pounding against a wooden post awoke her at noon. She raised the shade, and pushed aside the peach curtain to peer out of the bedroom window, careful not to knock over the lamp and phone on the bedside table below it. A 'For Sale' sign went up on the front lawn of her neighbor lady's property, and furniture was being loaded into a moving van.

Lexa ate, fed Ebbie, and put her coat on to find the woman and wish her well.

"Hello? I wasn't aware you were in a hurry to move." Other than a few scattered boxes, her home was empty.

"My family is afraid of leaving me alone because of the awful things happening to my longtime friends. I don't feel safe anymore."

"What happened?"

"Doris was murdered yesterday. Our neighbor, Earl Blesdin was robbed by some knife-wielding thug, and shoved down the stairs two days ago. He has lived behind us ever since I moved in." She somberly looked through the deserted rooms.

Distress seeped into Lexa like the cold that trailed around the vacant corners by the open doors. She let out a deep sigh. "Is Earl in the hospital?"

The white-haired woman trembled. "He was, but they sent him home. This community is going to hell in a handbasket. Earl used to lend a hand when my husband worked on his engine. When he was younger, he carried our old refrigerator out to the curb. He was able to lift almost anything. Now his poor wife Bessie finds him unconscious, down his stairwell. When our kids were small, they walked to the grocery store, and the parks nearby. They played baseball in the streets until it was dark out. We knew all the kids around here by their first and last names. Nowadays we keep our doors locked, and worry about something bad happening, most likely because it will. Mark my words. Their homes will be going up for sale." Her throat whispered a scratchy sorrow. The glory days of her community had become echoes of a tone arm being set on an old phonograph record.

"Did Earl recall anything about his attacker?" asked Lexa.

"He had a concussion, and a young punk is all he remembers. Then I get the bad news about Doris. I can't believe she's gone. I'll never get over it."

"Who told you?"

"Several neighbors called me. We watch out for each other. They saw her taken out in a body bag, and Roy was crying. None of us has

11

ever seen him do that." Sadness filled the woman's voice. Her lifelong friend was departed, and the once robust Earl was badly injured.

"How is your husband?" asked Lexa.

"Not good. He doesn't recognize me anymore. They're sending him to a long-term care facility."

"I'm sorry," said Lexa.

"I know why you told me you didn't want children. Other than when you first moved in, I rarely saw you and your husband together. I seldom see you smile. You've got the same kind of relationship I have had. Get out while you can."

"Thank you for your insight, said Lexa. "I wish you and your family many happy years together." She gave the elderly woman a hug, and they said their good-byes. It was her last conversation with the lady who detailed the history of her house, and unknowingly helped uncover the malicious plot of emotionally wounded war vets.

It took a year to meet Doris and Roy, her neighbors to the right, because of a white, four foot tall picket fence. It seemed as though anyone on Lexa's side of the slats was invisible. One day she walked up and waved until Roy noticed. His solid build, dark eyes, and almost black hair reminded her of the Hollywood actor Robert Mitchum. He gave her a slight nod.

It took a letter in the wrong mailbox to put a name to their faces several months later. This misplaced letter was her opportunity to knock on their door and introduce herself. She told them she was a nurse, and was glad to offer advice or assistance, but when she was outside, they offered no more than a forced smile which clung to a brief "Hello". Despite their avoidance of her, she felt sadness for a tragic departure, and fear for a crime so close to her doorstep.

The phone rang as she opened the door. It was Tarick Tagan, asking if she was free for dinner on Monday. Three days ago he called to chat and wish her a Happy New Year. Upon hearing his warm voice, she took deep breaths to maintain her composure. "I'd love to see you. Sure, I can be ready by 3:00." She hung up and stared out of her kitchen window at Doris' house, realizing she knew almost nothing about her.

Concerned for her safety, Lexa reached for the civil war sword alongside her waterbed and examined its markings and weightiness. Detectives never found it the day they ransacked her house. It had been left behind on the top shelf of her bedroom closet. Seven rounds remained in the chamber of her 45 caliber Colt. Bitterness ran through her as she picked up her Rapala knife which she used on someone's wrist a few days ago. The 3" hat pin she took from her deceased German grandmother's sewing desk was woven along the outer fabric of her purse.

Lexa held the pin to the light, and remembered how throughout her childhood, countless stories of survival were shared by Oma. Her husband fell victim to the war ten years into their marriage. She and her blonde, blue-eyed child had once taken refuge in a bomb shelter, but she stood no chance against the devastation of cancer.

While packing her bag for tonight's show, Lexa was preoccupied by the one person who made her forget about anything evil. All became pristine, even murky car exhaust over the snow became clouds that drifted into oblivion. The color of the sea in his eyes, his long solid legs, and the way he held her head when he kissed her, always gave her a subtle shiver.

"You look absorbed," said Karl from the seat beside her on their way to Racine. "Are you thinking about that guy who got beat up when he was in high school?"

His words snapped her back to the custom-built van. "I'm falling in lust."

"I can relate," he laughed. "When some sweet young thing looks up at me wearing a skimpy shirt, I get an eyeful of supple breasts, and I'm glad to have my Rickenbacker bass guitar where it belongs."

"If you happen to score some Seconal or Nembutal, keep me in mind," she said.

"I'll see what I can do."

13

Friday January 7, 1977

Morpheus, the Greek God of dreams has forgotten the way to my bedside. Being awakened by constant disruptions has ultimately caused somniphobia, a fear of sleep. Prior to Sam's betrayal, sleep had been as simple as closing my eyes. Now I am a pill seeker.

Sam's blue eyes and blonde hair have become drab; his skin is lined with overuse of alcohol and sun, and his belt is notched by conquests. His brother Ted knows, but his parents think he is an angel.

Every hand that harmed me, every ugly word that has been said to me has formed a hole in which the darkness has settled. Each day I work to fill the hollows with light, but some days are more difficult than others.

She awoke feeling drained, and hesitated in opening her eyes. A bitter taste in her mouth, a metallic smell in her nostrils, her fingers and arms felt sticky, chilled and wet. Disoriented in the swishing waterbed, she looked around as confusion melted into panic. A dark red liquid saturated her arms, and her vision would not focus.

Crimson soaked blankets nudged her shoulder. She raised her hands upward, and inspected her cotton leggings, sleeves, shirt, and bed sheets. Groping her face on the way to the bathroom mirror, she grasped the sink to steady her wooziness. Her reflection increased her heart rate to where she could feel it.

Damn it. Another nosebleed. She turned on the shower, and re-called when she had to run off the stage a little over a month ago. This rupture recurred with a vengeance. *There are no magic pills or remedies for nosebleeds, and I hate doctors.*

She washed and dried her bedding prior to Word Locket's show at 2340 N Farewell Ave. Originally a bowling alley, Century Hall was renovated into a night club. A bar was lit up near the front entrance, and through a doorway in a spacious hall, stood a large concert stage.

14

The most stable roadies over the past year, Hound, Drax, and Showey had finished unloading gear from the truck parked in the alleyway. Proficient in the set-up of amps and positioning of equipment, the monitors were ready in a blink, and sound levels were adjusted on the audio mixing board console. Each choice as to what piece to grab, where to position it and what got plugged into which speaker, mic or amplifier had been well rehearsed. Drax ordered a drink as soon as the bartender arrived.

The club was packed that Saturday when the band went on. At the beginning of their last set, the blast of an explosion was unleashed at the front of the stage near Karl. Lexa dropped her mic and fell. Sam flew sideways; Grant, Karl and Ted fell backwards. Voices were silenced for a second. Screaming began because of what sounded like a gunshot.

"What the hell was that?" Grant yelled.

"Did one of the monitors blow up?" Drax asked in a tone of dread.

In the ensuing clamor, people scattered toward the exit. Shouting voices became deafening.

My ears are ringing," said Grant. He eyed a large blackened area near the mic stands. "It sounded like an M-80 firecracker. Those have about 300 milligrams of flash powder. That's enough to take out a limb or kill someone. "Karl, did you see what happened?"

"It's crammed in here, but I saw a guy who had the hood of a dark gray sweatshirt up. He threw something and ran," said Karl.

Lexa set her mouth on her mic. "We're giving a $20 reward for any information on who launched a cherry bomb on us. We're going to take a short break."

On cue, Drax, flipped on his taped mix of music through the PA, and the crowd settled down. Lexa asked the bartender for two beers. She handed one to Ted, and one to Karl.

"The contract is solid, and we need the cash. We have truck repair bills, and road crew to pay. Twelve more tunes, and we're out of here. We can make it through one more set."

15

"Lexa…" A brown-eyed young man approached her through the crowd. "Lexa Loxx!"

She turned around. "Hey, you're the guy we hauled out of the road. How are you? What's your name again?"

"It's Casey Relmen. Don't you remember?"

"I'm better at faces than I am at names."

"I paid five bucks to get in. You said I'd be on your guest list."

I forgot. "I didn't think you'd take me up on it."

"I saw a man use a lighter on something, and toss it on the stage. It's some Indian man who lives around here. He's a freak, and does weird stuff like that. Those things can blow a hand off. Bullies used to throw 'em at me."

You just earned twenty bucks. Thanks for the info."

"How's Karl doing? Looks like he took the worst of it."

"He's hanging in there."

"Can we meet up later? I'll tell you more about what I saw. There's a restaurant down the street, and the food is decent," he said.

"I'll check if everyone else is up for it."

In the dressing room, Lexa asked her bandmates and roadies if they wanted to meet at a nearby diner after the equipment was packed. Since she handled the ledgers and expenses, she would use part of the night's revenue to treat them to a meal. Though everyone was rattled, they agreed. She found Casey to tell him.

Refusing to disappoint the crowd, she pranced across the stage and garnered two encores. The band changed clothes, snapped up their suitcases, and stashed them under the bed in the back of the van. A nearby explosion rattled the windows. They looked up to see plumes billowing nearby.

"That sounded gruesome," said Lexa, who started sprinting toward the detonation.

"Come on, get in the van," said Grant. "We'll get there faster." He crossed North Ave., headed north on Murray Ave., and took a left on East Thomas. A house was engulfed in flames which shot up twenty

16

feet. The van stopped, and as they each stepped out, sirens began a distant wail. Billows of a backdraft wafted upward from the windows.

The whooshing sizzles and crackles created a cataclysmic hymn under the smoky sky. A squad car's tires screeched and stopped near the middle of the road. Two officers glared at her. The driver held the mic of a CB radio over his mouth, and the second cop walked out, as fire engines arrived.

"What are you doing here at 2:30 am?" He made note of the group's black slacks, boots, and leather jackets.

"We were the band at Century Hall tonight. We heard an explosion and wanted to check it out," said Grant Slanik, whose icy breath became visible by the flashing on the cherry-topped vehicle. Though at 6' he matched the cop's height, years of pounding on drums streamlined his muscles like those of a Greyhound.

"I suppose there's hundreds who saw you afterwards," the man said loudly over the drone of sirens. Another patrol car pulled up, and an ambulance was followed by two more fire trucks. Bright flashes and screeching sirens filled the frigid air.

"We're witnesses, and our roadies are still packing up," shouted Karl. "They're almost finished loading if you want to check it out."

The other officer wrote the van's license plate on his notepad. As emergency vehicles closed in, the noise level pierced their ears. Three more engines arrived, and firefighters in protective gear began their mission to extinguish the intense heat of the whirling flares.

"I'll need all your names, and pertinent information. Miss, you first," he hollered. He darted his gaze up and down at the long-haired suspects, and moved them several houses away to repeat his request.

The inferno sliced the house in half, and as streams of water dampened the dark vapors wafting from it, the remainder of it crumbled.

They were detained until each of them gave their personal data and separate accounts of the incident. Thirty minutes later, the band was given permission to leave.

At the restaurant, Showey, Drax and Hound signaled them to their table. They said the guy in the gray sweatshirt left. He thought the band had ditched him.

"I wanted to ask him who lobbed an explosive at us," said Lexa.

The volume at the table increased about the shock wave on the stage, the fire they had witnessed, and the scrutinizing by the local authorities until the restaurant manager informed them his customers complained about the noise. When the man returned within ten minutes for a second reprimand, Lexa arose, paid the bill, and everyone left.

Saturday January 8, 1977

The police eyed us with so much contempt; I thought we were going to jail. I'm certain we looked suspicious to them. Their zeal for suspects overshadowed their interest in witnesses.

I'm saddened by the bad news about my neighbor Earl Blesdin's injuries and concussion. I will bring something to him and his wife Bessie tomorrow. Maybe they know what happened to Doris, since Roy rarely speaks to me.

Sam had minor damage to his guitar in the fall, and his brother Ted's guitar, though still usable, took a quarter size dent to the lower right side. Karl's bass landed on top of him, and his back is sore. Grant's drum sticks flew out of his hands, and one of his cymbals toppled over.

There's a screeching in my skull from the explosion. Drax said M-80's were once used by the military to simulate gunfire. None of us could determine why we were targeted.

18

Chapter 3

Sunday, January 9 –
Sunday, January 16

At noon, Lexa walked through the alley clutching a large basket of assorted fruits, wrapped in yellow cellophane. A police officer stood beside the chain-linked gate of Mr. and Mrs. Blesdin's back yard. She hesitated. In a second glance, he faded away as he reached out to her.

She shivered on the front porch, and was about to leave after a long wait and pressing the doorbell twice. Earl opened the door cautiously. Barely recognizable, he looked nothing like the pillar of a man he had been when she first moved in. In the dark, it would have been difficult to tell where his blue flannel shirt ended, and his skin began. She smiled and held out the basket as he opened the door.

"Thank you," he said quietly. He once had the kind of beauty that turned heads, and his strong build had been envied. A quiet magnificence still flickered through his dark eyes and lashes. His black and silver hair stood out against the shadowed, dabbled blotches on his swollen face. He invited her into his ranch home, and they sat on his brown plaid sofa across from two yellow velour chairs. Tinsel, lights, and red ornaments hung on an evergreen tree propped in a corner. He set the basket on the coffee table near his knees. "Is the whole neighborhood gossiping about me?"

"I don't know our other neighbors. When I get home in the early hours, I'm exhausted, but I'll try to be more observant."

19

"I was robbed at knifepoint by a punk who looked like one of your stoned-out friends."

"My friends aren't perfect, but they're not violent."

"Your house is visible from my rear windows and door. What has been said about you and your husband or boyfriend or whatever he is, is disgraceful."

"Did you hear things from the man who was sent to a psychiatric ward, or his wife?"

"Both of them gave me an earful. Not to mention Roy and Doris, but she's passed on." He gazed downward, and frowned. "I used to know everyone around here. My wife Bessie and I are going to see Roy later today."

"I once had bruises like you have. Your skin will return to its former color, but you'll never be quite the same again."

"I used to box back in the day, and knocked a few guys out cold. I had fists of steel. We used our strength and wits if someone got out of line. Now, kids point knives at us, and whatever weapons they have on them."

"What is Doris and Roy's last name? I've lived beside them for two and a half years. I should attend her wake."

"Their last name is Kemke. And her wake is tomorrow at 10:00 am."

"Thank you." She opened her purse, scribbled her phone number down, and handed it to him. "I want you to have this. We have to watch out for each other."

Distrust in his face, he grasped the paper as she walked to the doorway.

The wind caught her hair as she stepped outside. She pulled her coat collar up, and ran across the alley to her house.

She slammed the door and surmised that most likely all the nearby gawkers thought of her and her estranged husband, and anyone who came to visit as drug-abusing losers. No wonder it had taken so long for Roy and Doris to speak to her. All the nosey gossipers peering behind curtains had seen the officers who were called to investigate all the loud music rehearsals. Their suspicions and fears must have been aroused when law enforcement searched her house a few months ago. No doubt they saw her get shoved into a squad car, and the large man who used his gun to break the window on her side door. Which one of them spied Tarick's car parked overnight in November? They speculated on what kind of trouble was brewing whenever they picked up a receiver to chatter. Since the newsmonger of the neighborhood was leaving, maybe Lexa's relationships with those around her would improve.

Sunday January 9, 1977

Earl Blesdin's veins are seething with hatred toward me and everyone who he perceives is in my world. He has forgotten the days of his youth, when his fierce dark eyes glistened as though the sand in the hourglass of his life had just begun to pour downward, and time was his to control.

I had another premonition while brushing my teeth. As I looked in the mirror, I wore an orange jumpsuit. It's not something I would ever buy. I stood ghastly pale in a dungeon.

It is said that a person's ability to glimpse into the future has roots in evolution. This brief stance in another dimension beyond the boundaries of physical reality creates a juncture in which one can avoid impending disaster and take corresponding measures, but I don't know what measures I need to take.

Julette, who died in the bedroom where I sleep, appeared to me this morning, smiled, and vanished.

On Monday, she sat elbow to elbow in the back of a church listening to the sermon about the life of Doris Kemke. She learned more about this woman in thirty minutes than she had in all the while they lived beside each other. At age 61, she was an active member of the parish council, the choir, the women's ministry, and the Christian mothers. She had regularly volunteered as a chaperone for school field trips and had been a Girl Scout leader for nine years. She had always been involved in the PTA, and was the president for four years. She worked at the phone company since she was nineteen, and was looking forward to retirement.

Her husband Roy's sobs echoed to the last pew as the priest eloquently recalled what a devoted, loving wife and mother she was to her daughters Marion and Melinda, whose arms were huddled around him from each side. Doris was compassionate, and never hurt a living soul. She adored her eight grandchildren.

Earl Blesdin was easily recognizable by the wispy streaks of gray brushed into his dense black hair. His wife Bessie's silver scarf matched her short, curly hair. Perhaps the man with thick, wavy, light brown hair who sat next to her in a tan wool coat was her son. He placed his arm around her as she sobbed.

If the newly deceased had enemies, they mingled amidst a sea of mulling mourners. Family and friends filtered out at the end of the service. Lexa lacked enough courage to approach any of them.

Outside, she bent her head down, drew in a deep gasp, and released a puff of frosted steam. Every funeral mirrored her losses and memories of the loved ones she would spend her life letting go of. She had sat beside Oma when she took in her last breath, the mother figure who had lived with her since she was an infant. Huddled in the corner of her living room leaning on the bookshelf, Lexa took in the news when her mother had called to inform her of the death of her grandfather, who had been so strong a paternal presence that she compared all fathers to him.

Tarick arrived at 2:55, and she welcomed him in. His face, reddened by the icy wind, was as chiseled as it has been when she had seen him in November, and she pondered on whether it was his high cheekbones that angled to his chin, firm jawline, or the smoothness of his skin that caused her pupils to widen.

"Hi, come in and warm up. Can I get you something to drink?" she asked.

"Thanks, but we have a reservation at The Glass Rainbow restaurant.

"I'll get my coat." She looked up at a man who was eleven inches taller than she was. His wavy hair was a darker shade of brown, but the eyes looking into hers were sparkling, clear-blue ripples in seawater.

In his silver Chevy Camaro, she slid beside him. He turned the radio on, and they sang along to 'Play That Funky Music White Boy' by Wild Cherry, and "You Sexy Thing" by Hot Chocolate, on their short drive.

The hostess seated them, and the waitress detailed the menu items. When the woman left to fill their orders, he announced how excited he was that his band was making arrangements to perform at a club in LA for record execs to showcase their original songs. He asked if she had heard them six months ago when she saw his band.

"I did, but I left your show early. When the women started punching each other and pulling hair, I headed to the exit. There was a blonde there who we threw out of our van because she refused to get out. The way she glared at me, I thought she was going to attack me next."

"That blonde was our bass player's girlfriend. She started the fight, pulled out the main power cord, and killed our electricity. At first, he was madly in love with her. He couldn't say enough about Kalie Deckler. She was fantastic when she bought him a new bass guitar. She bought new clothes for him. She's the best sex he ever had. Kalie this, Kalie that. He never said a sentence without her name in it. Five weeks later, things started missing from the house. She bullied any chick who looked at him. When she threatened his family, he dumped her, and now she harasses us. We are afraid of what she's capable of, and we call her crazy Kalie. We caught her trying to set our house on fire."

"The image of her thrashing like a banshee and screeching when the guys wrestled her out of our van will forever be imprinted in my head. Are you certain it was her?"

"She didn't take the breakup well. She's been stalking us for the past few months, and shows up at almost every gig. Three weeks ago, one of the roadies came home from an errand and saw her car in our driveway. Our back door was on fire. He extinguished it with the hose, and called the police.

"Do you think she'll try it again and do more damage?"

"She's in jail. We'll be away for a few weeks, maybe more depending on how the tapings go. The roadies will watch over our house."

As they waited for their food, she wondered if his sole intent was to tell her he was moving far away to pursue his music career. If her band was offered a recording contract, they would leave as quickly as they could pack. A hard working musician's aspiration was a solid record deal. He was happier and more animated than she had ever seen him.

He buttered warm bread. "You said there was something you wanted to tell me."

"Do you recall when the massive guy broke into my house while we ate breakfast in November?" She used her fork to push noodles around the plate.

"I'll never forget it."

"His best friend needed medical care. They were desperate. He thought the only way I was going to help him was if a gun was pointed at me. He wasn't a bad person. I'm sorry you got in the middle of it. They left the state, and I doubt if I'll ever see them again. So…when are you leaving for LA?"

"The day after tomorrow. I still have a lot to get done."

"So is this a goodbye dinner?" she asked.

"I hope it isn't. We'll give it our best shot, but we have to wait to find out if we get a contract. You know the rest. It's uncertain like everything else."

"Your songs are melodic, the riffs are great, and the beats are solid. I think they will go over really well. How many do you have?" she asked.

"Twelve. Enough for a full album."

"I have no doubt that you can get signed, but make sure you firmly believe it will happen."

"Thanks. It's what my mom said."

They walked up the steps to her kitchen. Lexa made hot cocoa and handed one to him. In the living room, they sat on the sofa.

"I thought you intended to avoid me after all the craziness we've been through," she said, holding the warm cup.

"Don't be too hard on yourself. At first I wasn't sure if I could handle some wild woman in a rock band, but it's hard for me to stop thinking about you. You do keep me guessing."

He set his mug on the square table in front of his long legs, and smoothed her hair back. He trailed his mouth down her neck, to her breasts. His warm lips moistened the flesh alongside her neck. The touch of his kiss was like kindling to her flames.

The clasps that had been sealed by her insecurities snapped open with each kiss. He caressed her forehead, eyes, cheeks and shoulders. She felt it into her toes and finger tips as she wove them through his wavy light-brown hair. She wrapped her legs around his hips. As they embraced, his hands wove behind her head.

The phone began a non-stop ring. They backed away and looked at each other.

"My number is unpublished. It may be urgent." She went to the kitchen to pick up the receiver, and Tarick followed her.

"Yes, this is Lexa."

"I need your help. Come quickly. Earl looks horrible. Please, I'm not sure what to do."

"What do you mean? Is he in pain?"

"No, he can't talk or lift his left arm."

"I'll call an ambulance and I'll be right there."

"Is there anything I can do?" Tarick asked.

"I gave my number to my neighbor yesterday. I'll check out what's going on and return when he's on the way to a hospital."

She dialed, gave the requested information, and headed into the cold darkness toward the Blesdin's residence.

At their back gate, the latch was jammed. She pounded on it, and took her shoe off to give it a few strikes on the underside. No matter how she fumbled on the hardware, the ice held firm, and she was unable to release it. She grabbed onto the mesh of the chain-link fence, and climbed to the top, but when she swung her leg over it, the sharp tips cut into her wrists, hands, and black jeans. As she scrambled downward, her heel got caught in the wires. The fence rattled as she yanked her foot free, and jumped down. The lights of a vehicle sped toward her. She sprinted toward the front entrance. A man emerged from the car, and screamed at her to freeze, but she sped toward the front door.

"Stop!"

She was determined to reach Earl, and put more distance between her and the shouting man.

"Get your hands in the air! Now!" The red light of the cherry top flashed, and a siren blared out a whoop. An officer raced toward her.

"I have to help someone. I've done nothing wrong." She jaunted to Earl's front porch.

"Stop now, and get your hands up." He lunged at her, and clutched her arm.

A spotlight flashed into her face. She was pulled to the squad car by her left wrist.

26

"We have the suspect. Matches the description to a T." She heard the squelch of the CB radio, and the voice of the officer in the patrol car. The cop nearest to her cuffed her wrists, and led her to the back seat, where he pushed her inside.

"What is going on?"

The driver spoke into the mic, "Affirmative. We're bringing her in."

"Please knock on the door of the house we're at. They need help."

"You were told to stop. What are you running from? Do not make the police chase you."

In each passing second, the siren of an emergency vehicle became louder, but the door of the vehicle was banged shut. Cold handcuffs dug into her back, as a monotone voice recited her rights. The unbuttoned lightweight sweater she wore over her satin black low-cut top and jeans did not protect her from the minus six degree night. Her teeth chattered. As she shook heavily, she looked behind the car, and caught a glimpse of Tarick. She wondered if new evidence was discovered to get her imprisoned for the murder she had been accused of. It must have been falsified in some way, since she knew she was innocent.

"Why am I handcuffed? My neighbor may need an aspirin."

"An aspirin? You were running around in the dark to give someone a pill? Now we heard it all. You're going to tell us all about it at the station."

At the Milwaukee county jail, she was taken to a small white room, and questioned by a gray-haired officer. He asked if she knew why she was being detained. When she did not, he became irate, and accused her of playing dumb. She was informed that they were detaining her overnight for a lineup in the morning. They photographed, fingerprinted, and booked her for the misdemeanor charge of fleeing from an officer, and a felony charge of aggravated arson.

"Arson? Someone has made a terrible mistake. I have witnesses who can prove where I was this evening."

27

"Tell it to the judge."

"I thought I was allowed to use a phone."

"Later."

A wrinkled, cold, orange jumpsuit was shoved at her, and she shivered as the cloth pressed against her skin. The room had little heat. She gasped at her pale reflection in the glass of a window they passed. The guard slammed the door to the cell. Nine other inmates looked her up and down, but turned away. Two of them conversed, and the rest were silent. She felt bewildered. *If only I had walked to the front door. Sweet dreams Tarick.* She remembered her visions, and now she understood them. Her head fell downward. On a cold, hard bench, she closed her eyes, and wrapped her arms around her shivering body. Her stomach felt like it was twisting from hunger. It was one of the longest nights of her life.

When her name was called in the morning, she was given a number, and shoved into a lineup. Five women stood beside her. Markers listing heights stretched across the wall behind them. They were instructed to hold their heads up, and look forward. It had been well over twenty-four hours since she had slept, and the food she could not finish at the restaurant was in her refrigerator. Sleep and sustenance preoccupied her as she stood in solemn stillness.

The judge's office was basic. From across a wooden desk, his scripted intonation, like hail pinging on a window, informed her of her charges.

"How do you wish to plead?"

"Not guilty. I have an alibi. Three people can make a statement of my whereabouts. If they were questioned yesterday evening, this could have been cleared up."

"We have an eyewitness who made a positive ID."

"I have witnesses also." She thought about Tarick, the hostess, the wait staff, and the dispatcher.

"A public defender will be assigned if you can't afford a lawyer, and a preliminary hearing will be set for Thursday, January twenty-seventh."

"There's been a mistake." *Why has someone set me up?*

Upon hearing the amount of her bond, she felt faint from hunger, exhaustion, and shock. As she was led down a corridor, she was overcome by a choking sensation. She had no priors, and she was too rattled to scrape up even ten bucks. A few months ago, Sam threatened to let her burn if she got into any trouble. She dared not drag her brother Nathan who had two young children, or her parents who lived over a thousand miles away into her dilemma.

The guard was indifferent to Lexa, who sensed that the multitudes taken through the same pathway had all been absorbed by whom to turn to. Her desire to run from the jail mounted. Anyone who could offer assistance, or have access to resources was her main concern. The name of every person she knew began blinking in her mind like flash cards. No, no, no. All *no* to every name.

A voice floated around her head. Did she want to make a phone call? "Hello, miss. Missy. Hey!" The volume intensified.

"Do you want to make a call?"

"Ph…phone…yes." Sprinting through a highway of faces, she saw the image of her best option, and Karl's face lit up. His dad was a doctor and may be willing to aid the singer of his band. She dialed, and held the receiver to her ear in her right hand, with her left arm around her waist. She rocked her body forward to dull the pain in her stomach. Six rings purred into the receiver. *Please answer.* She closed her eyes.

"This better be good."

"I need your help, and fast. I'm in jail."

"For what? Drunk driving? Serves you right. I've slept about three hours and I can't function."

"I'm locked behind bars. We have a show tonight. I haven't slept in over twenty-four hours. And I need $10,000 to get out of here. Any suggestions?"

"Is this a damn joke?" The moments of silence crackled like a lit fuse.

"Do I strike you as someone crazy enough to wake you at the break of dawn to pretend I've been taken prisoner? If Sam finds out, things will get ugly."

"Stop rambling. What day is it?"

"It's Tuesday the eleventh."

"I'll talk to my dad. He's up by now. I'll see what I can do."

Two hours later, the wintry air stung their faces as they got into Karl's turquoise Chevelle Malibu.

"How was San Quentin?" he asked.

"Like your worst nightmare. Thanks for springing me out. I had always thought if I was ever imprisoned, it would be for some worthy cause like saving the rainforest. Not for something I didn't do. I'll tell you what happened when my brain kicks in. I'm writing a note for Sam, so he can tell everyone that you and I are skipping sound check." She didn't ask, nor did she care where Karl got that amount of cash.

"I have a little present for you," he said.

"How much to I owe you for these?" she said as she cradled the sleeping pills.

She paid Karl, walked up the steps, threw herself onto the bed, and dialed Tarick's number, but no one answered. She closed her eyes. Disoriented when she awoke in the dark, she had no awareness of whether it was 7:00 at night or 7:00 am until she flipped on the television. She called for Tarick again and spoke to a roadie. He had no idea where anyone was. She asked him to take a message. She was in desperate need of help.

"I can't think straight," she said to Karl before they started their first song. "I'm so numb."

30

"Try to hold yourself together. I'll get you a drink after the first set."

She held her mic to her mouth, smiled, raised her arm, and the show began. Vocals and instruments were amplified throughout every inch of space in the club.

Drax tweaked the sound, and raised the volume in increments. His motto was, "Go outside if you want small talk. Inside this club, you party."

Her arrest, hunger, and lack of sleep took hold to where she sat in meditation in the dressing room and sipped on water between sets throughout the night.

"What is wrong with you two? Stop giving me dirty looks." Sam sneered at Karl and Lexa as he locked up his guitar. "I didn't do anything to you guys."

"What are you talking about? I'm tired and hungry. Don't take it personally," said Karl. "Don't expect others to be nicer to you than you are to them."

"Don't go all Aristotle on me," said Sam as he left the dressing room.

"Where do you want to stop to eat?" Karl asked as he started the ignition.

"It doesn't matter, anywhere that's still open." On their drive, she detailed the events of the previous evening.

"The cops were on your tail really fast. It's an odd coincidence. Would Sam call them and make up a story about you?"

"I'm not sure, but police are on thick patrol in my block since my neighbor was murdered on Thursday. The one I was running to was robbed. My most credible witness is out of state, and I can't fathom when he'll be back. I don't know his family, or his friends, or anyone who can contact him in L.A yet. I'll track down which hospital my neighbors are at tomorrow. I also need to find the wait staff at the restaurant to testify," she said.

31

"And in between trying to prove you're innocent, you'll be on rock and roll duty almost every night," said Karl.

"My name may be on a list of suspects because of that fire we drove to on Saturday, and even worse, I'm still a primary suspect in the murder of a local man."

"What? No, we were witnesses. You're a murder suspect?" he asked.

"Being innocent means nothing these days. The guy faked his death and left town. I was the last person to be seen with him," said Lexa.

"You need a decent lawyer. My dad has a lot of contacts. I can give you a few names."

"Do any of them work for free? If not, I'm screwed."

"Get a public defender," he said.

"I can't. I'm not indigent, and I have too many assets. I own a house, a VW, a van, guitars, and I'm part owner of all of our equipment and the truck. I have to prove I am not their suspect."

"Have you seen the papers lately? Something strange is going on. There were two more big fires in the city. Yesterday, a bar on 27th and Clybourn had around $11,000 in damages. And on today's front page, the attorney in the arson for hire trial tried to destroy the government's star witness for the defendant. It seems we live in a culture where anger and aggression are rewarded by media attention," said Karl.

"I'm sure my star witness will get raked over the coals. He's a musician like us. We're thought of as scumbag drug-abusers. And please thank your dad for posting my bond," she said.

She awoke at 1:00 pm on Wednesday, called Tarick's house, and asked if he got her message.

"He told us he couldn't reach you. He gave us the number for his hotel, but he probably checked out by now."

"Thanks."

She dialed the local hospitals to find Bessie and Earl Blesdin, and was informed that he was at Northwest General Hospital in the intensive care unit. She ate, dressed quickly, stopped at a florist, and drove northbound.

Strictly family members were allowed in the ICU. Of course she was his granddaughter. And she was worried about him because Grandma was crying, and Grandad couldn't speak. When she entered the room, she handed the bouquet of mixed flowers to Mrs. Blesdin.

"Call me Bessie. This is Benjamin." She introduced Lexa to her son, who at 6'1" stood near the bedrails. It was the man she had seen in church who most likely had a high-salaried occupation, based on his tailored gray wool suit, black Italian leather shoes and matching overcoat.

Though his voice said a quiet, "Hello," his Rolex watch and diamond ring screamed of success. "Please call me Ben." He reached to shake her hand. His mom's steel blue eyes and dad's firm jaw line had given him a magnetic pull. His smile gestured, 'I like me, and I know you will too.'

"Pleased to meet you," said Lexa.

"Why didn't you come over on Monday evening?" asked the elderly woman.

"Your gate was frozen. My hands got cut on the sharp tips when I tried to climb the fence. As I got down, a car approached me, so I ran to the front of your house. The police arrested me."

"For what? Climbing my fence?" asked Bessie.

"No, I was accused of arson, and I have no idea what they're talking about. I asked them to knock on your door to check if you called me, but they refused." Lexa glanced over to Earl, who looked agitated. She walked up to him, and he became more disturbed. His eyes widened. He searched for the right words, but his mouth could not convey them.

"Did he did," said Earl, who began thrashing. "He did...." His movements became more distressed as Lexa neared his bedside.

"What's the matter, Earl?" asked Bessie.

33

"Did di...did...," he said enlarging his dark eyes, and rolling side to side.

Bessie and her son glared at Lexa, who shook her head in confusion. Earl hyperventilated and repeated his fearful message. His heart monitor raced, and electronic beeping bounced off the walls in the room. A nurse ran in.

"What's going on in here?"

"He...he...did...he," said a terrified Earl. He scowled at Lexa, who opened her palms upward.

"Miss, I must ask you to leave," the nurse said sternly.

"I'm not sure what he is trying to tell us, but I'll go, so he can rest."

As she backed out of the small, glass-enclosed room, his writhing and reciting persisted. Bessie and her son appeared confused. The nurse said she would give Earl an injection to calm him down.

Bewildered over Earl's frenzy, she was anxious to locate the servers and door hostess at the Glass Rainbow restaurant.

While she ate a peanut butter sandwich, she thumbed through the phone book. At 3:30, she asked if the manager was available. He was expected to arrive at 5:00 pm. Tonight she had to skip another sound check. Someone should recognize her from two days ago.

At the crowded restaurant, she asked the hostess to allow her to speak to the manager on an urgent matter. It took twenty minutes before she was allowed to approach him. In trying to converse, Lexa exaggerated a compliment regarding the waitress on Monday.

"Great job?" He walked away. "She isn't reliable. Because of her, I'm waiting on tables. She knows we have specials every Wednesday, and she blew her hours off. I'm firing her, so keep your compliments."

"I need her name and address."

"What? No. We don't want any trouble here."

"She's a witness for someone who has a court date at the end of January. If you don't give it to me now, I'll ask the police to come for it. So if you'd rather have a subpoena..."

"Ordinarily I don't give that out, but today she can jump off a cliff for all I care. I'll give it to you, but good luck getting her to show up."

When the performance had ended, the raspy assertions of a stricken man wove throughout the voices in the dressing room. Her eyes singled out Karl. She toyed with the suspicion that he could harm someone, maybe push them down a flight of stairs.

He turned toward her stare. "What?"

"The latch on my suitcase is jammed," she said.

"Try my pocket knife," he said.

She searched his soft, hazel eyes for signs of guilt. Bags were snapped shut as everyone filtered out of the crowded room.

Tomorrow, she had to visit the ICU again. She knew Mr. Blesdin's agitation must be a fluke. He was confused.

Friday January 14, 1977

I visited Earl today, but I did not stay long. His bed was ripped up by his anxiety. His dark eyes conveyed a message I was not able to understand. Bessie looked at me as though I am guilty of something but she's not sure what. I explained why I need her assistance, and asked her to attend my hearing. I offered her a ride, and she accepted. I don't have high hopes of an appearance by the waitress.

And somewhere in this city, a lit cigarette was tossed, an ash fell onto a sofa cushion, a sleeve caught fire over a stovetop, and a child discovered a lighter.

She paced the stage at Headliners night club in Madison, between Karl and Sam. Grant's cymbal crashes, snare, toms and bass drum pulsated behind her. It was during the last song of the first set before she noticed Tiny, her former bodyguard. A massive man at six feet five, his blue eyes locked onto hers, and the matching gang beside him followed suit. His backup team clad in blue jeans and vests, she pictured them shopping together.

She had last seen him in July. His wavy, blonde hair had grown to chin length, and was slicked behind his ears. His dark blonde beard was full again, and his belt was concealed by the white t-shirt which hung over his belly. She wondered why he traveled as far as Madison to collect the measly amount she owed him.

Another cold stare was focused on her. Casey Relmen stood near the bar sipping on a beer. She slid into the dressing room behind the stage when the set ended.

"Karl, guess who's here? The abused guy who we almost hit in the road," said Lexa. "He's giving me dirty looks. I didn't tell him we'd put him on the guest list for of all our shows. Did you?"

"No, but I'll buy him a beer to calm him down."

"I wonder if he gets hammered whenever he goes out. It's a long way to his house, and I don't want to be his chauffer service."

Karl walked in the opposite direction as she headed to Tiny, who sat at the bar.

"Lexa Loxx. Imagine finding you here," Tiny said, widening his blue eyes.

"Yea, I'm thrilled to see you too. What's a mug like yours doing in a club like this?"

"Huh?"

"I suppose you're here to get your funds," she said.

"We came to hear some tunes, and yea, you can hand over the rest of those bills. My friends who live here have some fine cannabis. They grow it in their basements." Tiny pushed a tendril of his blonde hair back and pointed to his counterparts who sat beside him.

"Cannabis?" *It's no surprise that Tiny and his gang make a few extra bucks selling pot.* She turned to face the other men. "Nice to meet you." She shook their massive hands.

"Tell the guys in your band we've got high quality stuff."

"How about you do it while your friend and I settle things up?"

The large men laughed and threw out obscene comments, as Tiny followed her to the dressing room.

Showey, who stood nearby, came close to the stature of these men. He pulled his thick, shoulder-length brown hair into a pony tail, and frowned at their remarks. Their cackles were cut short.

"Are they your old high school buddies?" she asked Tiny.

"No, they're from the Dependable Security branch in Madison. They usually do concert venues. They're trying to talk me into moving here so we can work together, but they don't know I make more than they do," he said as he closed his wallet.

She was relieved to have Tiny off her back as they crawled into the van. He was a man who had the capability of getting his dues one way or another.

Ted crept to the built-in bed. "I had too much to drink," he said.

"So what else is new?" asked Grant.

"Casey said if I'm sick, he can sub for me," said Karl. "He memorized all of our songs. He used to play the bass guitar in another band, and he wants to join our next rehearsal."

"Don't tell me you said yes. I'm not doing a gig if you're not there. If some chick subs for me, is it still Word Locket? Is the onstage chemistry the same? You have a fan club. Some girls pay just to see you. Some women want Sam, and some want Grant."

"What about me?" asked Ted. "I have my own fan club too. You guys always ignore me. I'm sick of it." He combed his brown hair, and his slurred rambles continued for the entire drive.

Saturday January 15, 1977
The agitation in each of us was in direct proportion to the amount of alcohol consumed. We all wanted to tape up Ted's mouth. I told him that just because you whine about things, it doesn't make you worse off than everyone. It just makes you a whiner.

He called me a bitch. Grant screamed at him to shut up and looked hostile enough to smack him. I thought they were going to get into it again like they did in the dressing room last year. Sam pulled over, stopped the van, and shouted, "Whoever throws the first punch will be outside walking."

Ted said, "Yes, Mom." When Sam turned around and took a swing at Ted, the van got knocked out of gear, and began to roll into a ditch. He grabbed the wheel, and hit the brakes just before we tipped over. The rest of the ride was pandemonium.

At 3 am Sam stormed up to his flat. Grant and Karl's engines fired-up, and their tires squealed down the alley. Ted slammed the door of his car. Twice. He banged his hand on the horn for a few minutes, and his foot hit the floor of the gas petal, revving the engine to the red line, before he screeched off through a thick cloud of smoke. Our popularity in the neighborhood is improving every day.

She had little desire to get out of bed, and ruminated as to why Earl Blesdin became so hysterical around her.

At the hospital, she checked in at the desk, and again said she was his granddaughter. Alone in his room, he snored in a serene sleep. The feeding tube inserted into his nostril was taped to his cheek. Murmured voices in the hallway, bleeps, ticking, a bubbling humidifier, and the hiss of the oxygen filled the small room. Monitors pinged in a steady rhythm, and intravenous lines dangled around him.

She pushed a chair up to the bed rails and watched him breathe. *Am I doing the right thing by sitting beside him? I don't know. Is human behavior recorded in some karmic realm that keeps tabs on the great, the good, the bad and the ugly deeds?*

She touched his hand. A transparent film secured thin clear tubes to his arms, and white blankets covered his legs. His facial bruises had begun to fade, and his washed out blue gown was held together by snaps. She looked up as his wife and son entered the room.

"He looks so peaceful, doesn't he?" asked Bessie.

"Yes, he does. I wonder why he gets so upset when he sees me. Didn't he like the fruit I brought over?"

"He did. I don't understand what is affecting him like this. Five days ago, his left arm became paralyzed. Next thing, his speech was garbled. I couldn't think straight, and dialed the phone number on the note you wrote. It was right by my phone, and it said nurse Lexa. I trust nurses. Thank you for calling an ambulance."

"You're welcome."

Earl opened his resigned eyes, and looked around. Lexa thought his condition may have worsened, as he gave no response to his surroundings. Bessie leaned over and kissed his cheek. His son gave him a nod, and waited for any kind of response, but Earl seemed distant, and as he closed his eyes, a tear trickled down his cheek.

Sunday January 16, 1977

Oma often used to say, "Why are you always sad, sweetheart?" She said if I always look forlorn, my face will become locked like that forever, and I won't be able to stop even when I want to. I suppose the adults in my life got used to the sad-eyed child, and it became who I was to them. It eventually defined me. Living on army bases, and moving almost every year dissolved every acquaintance along the way.

My best memories were when I ran through wild forests of towering trees and tall grasses, hopped over stones on a rolling brook, or sat on a swing, closed my eyes and imagined that I was far away in some exotic land.

39

Chapter 4

Monday, January 17 –
Sunday, January 23

She stared at the ceiling early Monday morning, retracing the events leading up to her arrest. Tiny's visit to squeeze the balance of his cash annoyed her. If she refused to pay him, she could count on Showey to come to her rescue, or she could use the long pin which was still woven along the side of her purse, and run. She grabbed the phone off of her bedside table on the second ring.

"Hello?"

"It's Tarick. What happened to you?" He sounded annoyed. "I went outside to make sure you were okay. I saw a police car and an ambulance, but you were gone."

"I never made it home because I got arrested, and spent the night in a cellblock."

"I'm confused. You went to your neighbors."

"I never got past the alley. Apparently I fit the description of an arsonist, and was picked out of a lineup. Karl posted my bail. I have a preliminary hearing on January twenty-seventh. I need to get the waitress from the restaurant to testify where I was until almost 6:00. The lady whose husband had the stroke is willing to help me, but your testimony would be better."

"I want to help you, but I can't get out of any of our shows. We need to be obedient little puppets. We have a string of signed contracts for clubs here. I'm really sorry."

"How's it going in LA?" she asked.

"We are ninety-nine percent sure we are getting a contract. We nailed our set for the execs. They said they loved our music."

"Fantastic. Your band has serious talent and the potential to be big stars," she said.

"I wish I could share all the sights out here with you. I miss you."

"Same here. So what's next?"

"The guys from ABC-Paramount records want a meeting later this week. They talked about recording us at The Record Plant in Sausalito. If things go well, we're going to rent a car, and take Hwy 1 up there."

"You're living my dream. Take lots of pictures. You'll want to remember it all," she said.

His life's ambition and all of his dreams depend on what transpires in the weeks that lie ahead. They each had their own challenges.

She rolled out of bed, and opened the window shade. On the shoveled sidewalk near the 'for sale' sign, two six foot, broad-shouldered men followed a well-dressed man into the vacant house. She guessed the larger men to be either brothers, or a father and son, due to the older man with long silver and black hair being so similar in appearance to the younger black-haired man. She pulled the shade down, and went to the kitchen for coffee.

The itineraries for Word Locket's February appearances took an hour to design. She delivered the template to a print shop. The 525 copies were ready for pick-up the week before the new month, and address labels were attached by Ted's wife Debra, who transported them to the post office.

Lexa deposited the band's take for the week at the bank, collected mail from the post office box, and during bites of spaghetti, she practiced her guitar.

At 7:00 pm, the band gathered in Sam's flat for a low decibel rehearsal. Karl walked in carrying two six-packs of beer, trailed by Casey, whose silver watch glistened as he popped open a beer, and said, "To the people who saved my life. You guys are incredible." Both in black shirts under leather jackets, dark jeans, and black ankle-height boots, other than Casey being an inch taller, they looked eerily similar.

Drax, Grant, Karl, Sam and Ted popped off tabs, and took long gulps. Casey rolled a joint to share, and amplifiers hummed as guitars were strummed. The session became a loose jam. At midnight, a suggestion was made to see what band was at Teddy's Nightclub on Farwell Avenue, and all agreed except for Lexa. The upper door slammed. Revving engines squealed through the alleyway.

She was sitting on her waterbed holding her guitar when the doorbell rang. A fist pounded on her door. She pulled her arms into a sweater and switched on the back porch light. Across the silvery snow, a room lit up behind opaque curtains, and a man peeked out.

Casey banged on the door until she opened it. "You should come along. It'll be fun."

"No thanks. I spend too much time in clubs."

He stared into her eyes. "I'll buy you a drink. You're gonna miss some good music, and a lot of laughs. Grab your coat."

"No, but thanks anyway."

"Karl wants you to join us. He doesn't want you to feel left out."

No he doesn't. He knows me. "You lost a bet, didn't you?"

"Maybe," he said as he walked away.

Roy disappeared behind his curtain.

Lexa arrived at the hospital at 10:30 am to visit Earl Blesdin, and gave her name at the ICU desk.

"He's not here any longer, Miss. He went to the rehab unit," said the receptionist who wrote out and handed her his new location.

"Thank you." She entered his room, and found his wife sitting on a chair reading a magazine. Earl's bed was empty.

"It's nice of you to visit him. He's in therapy. They're trying some simple strengthening exercises, and it's not going well. He's fighting them, but he has always been a fighter."

"Have the doctors informed you of what his outcome will be?"

"They said it's too soon to tell, but I'm hoping for the best. Ben said he'd help us. He also mentioned that we're going to have new neighbors. Yesterday, when he checked on the house, he saw the realtor and they had a chat."

"That was a fast sale." Lexa leaned forward.

"Their house was decimated by a fire, and they needed somewhere to live," said Bessie.

"There have been so many fires over this past year. When my van burned up, I lost a lot of valuable things. But losing a home is devastating. After my house was broken into a few weeks ago, I had deadbolt locks installed. It makes me feel a little safer, especially after what happened to Doris. Have you heard how Roy Kemke is doing?"

"Roy said Doris was struck on her head by a heavy object. There was no forced entry. The door was unlocked, so either she let someone in, or they followed her, hit her, and dragged her into the house. He isn't sure if anything is missing yet. The house wasn't vandalized, and three dollars was in her wallet."

"So, he doesn't know if money was taken, and some was left behind on purpose?"

"No he doesn't." Bessie's eyes squinted into blue mosaic opal stones. She stared at Lexa as though she knew more than she should.

Earl was wheeled into the room slumped forward, gaunt and colorless. He had no intravenous lines, but the nasogastric tube remained taped to his nose and cheek. He lifted his head, enlarged his eyes, and began panting. His weak, hoarse voice stammered out, "Did it, he did it he," over and over. Bessie mustered up the dirtiest look she could give to Lexa until she said she would leave.

43

On her drive home, she wondered if she would always trigger this response from him. Did he see a woman who resembled her before his stroke? A witness identified her as an arson suspect, and it made her angry that this criminal was wreaking havoc in her neighborhood and in her life.

Preoccupied by events from the past two weeks, she had difficulty concentrating on stage. Karl, Sam, Ted and Grant conversed in the dressing room when the first set ended.

"Casey doesn't care what anyone thinks about him. When the juke box blared, 'Get Down Tonight', he got up on the bar to dance," said Karl. "Then he stripped down to his undies and socks, and grabbed his beer."

"When his drink splashed onto the folks sitting below, the bouncer pulled him down and got a beer shower when Casey landed on top of him," said Grant.

"When Casey swung his boots at the bouncer he ducked, but the people at the bar got smacked in the heads. They all jumped up to punch him, and he hurled out a few heavy swings. He got tossed outside, and now he's permanently banned," said Ted.

"He chased after cars in the middle of the road. I'm amazed no one hit him," said Karl.

"How much did it take to get him so drunk?" Lexa asked.

"We all shared two pitchers, but I think he had a few shots at the bar. He passed out in my car, and I walked him and his things into his dad's house. I'm not sure how much he'll remember, said Karl."

"You guys got to Teddy's at around 12:30. How fast did two pitchers go down?"

"I dunno. We all left at around 1:30," said Ted. "Well maybe it was around 1:00."

"I'm glad you don't dance half naked on bars," said Lexa as they crawled into the van to head home.

"Yea, but he's such a great guy," said Karl.

"He had us laughing long before he kissed the bouncer," said Grant who insisted it was his turn to drive.

She awoke thinking it was an act of goodwill to bring a meal to Roy, and prepared Oma's recipe for beef rouladen, baked potatoes and vegetables. When she knocked on his door, no one answered. She made another attempt before leaving, but got no response.

Casey Relmen made his presence known upon their arrival at 'Hanna's' night club on East Locust Street, and gravitated to Ted, Grant, and Karl. He handed each of them a beer, and made a few callous remarks, followed by howling laughter. Why he attended so many of their shows made her assume he was the consummate admirer. Throughout the night, he brought drinks to the band, and joined the roadies as they unplugged and hauled equipment to the truck.

When everyone went their separate ways at 3:00 am, she noticed a light on in Roy's home. Inside, a distraught, lonely man was rethinking his life.

> Wednesday January 19, 1977
> *A section of the daily newspaper lists names of the newly deceased, and those who are mourning for them, who have been left behind to brush the dust under the carpet, piece their lives back together, and move forward if they're able to. Doris Kemke had been surrounded by friends and family, but she had an enemy. She may have known who pushed Earl down the stairs. Most don't survive the hard fall he took. Perhaps more was more taken from them than their families are aware of. Earl fears that someone from my band robbed him. What if he's right?*

She awoke feeling chilled and clammy. Breathing was strenuous. Light filtered through the shade, and her hands were sticky and red. Blood covered her arms. She sat up, feeling lightheaded, and turned her bedside light on. She had another nosebleed. Rising slowly, she staggered to the bathroom, took a few deep breaths, and squeezed the bridge of her nose. Woozy and dizzy, she lowered her body to the cold tile floor, rested her head and spine against the wall, and waited.

She sat on the floor pinching her nose shut for fifteen minutes. She arose, ran cold water over a cloth, and wiped off her face and arms. She needed more than three hours of sleep to get through tonight's show. Four bandmates and three roadies depended on her role in the performance. She cleaned up, changed clothes, and crawled into the opposite side of the bed where she slept a few more hours. Lacking the strength to pull bedding apart to wash sheets, she turned on the television. Jimmy Carter was being sworn in as president on every station. Ebbie licked Lexa's cheek, and she stroked her pup's soft fur before letting her out and giving her clean water and food.

She dressed and secured her seat in the van.

"You look wiped out," said Karl. "You worried about the prelim hearing?"

"Yes, but my neighbor Bessie is my witness. I should be able to get everything straightened out. I'm going to nap on the way to the club."

Upon returning from Joliet, Illinois, Lexa entered a cold, dark house. Because of her nosebleed, her bed and bathroom looked as though someone was murdered in it, and unopened mail sat on her kitchen and dining room tables. Floors needed vacuuming, dirty dishes were scattered in the sink, and Ebbie was almost out of food. She wrote a note to Sam, shoved it under his upstairs door, fell onto the waterbed, and into a sound sleep.

The drawn shades and peach curtains could not stop the trickles of sunlight on the walls. She stretched and reached for the clock on the bedside table. Her priorities were to take care of her pup, and to make sure Mrs. Blesdin would join her in the courtroom next Thursday. She dressed and left for the hospital. The receptionist at the front desk informed her that Earl Blesdin was discharged a few hours ago.

"Has he gone home?"

"We don't have that information."

At the nurse's station she was able to milk a receptionist for his whereabouts. She ran from her VW into Doctor's Nursing Home on 27th and Wisconsin Avenue where she was given his room number.

Scattered throughout hallways and stark rooms, frail men and women clung to canes, walkers, and wheelchairs, lacking enough stamina to leave the locked doors which secured them, and return to their past freedom and lives. Some picked at transparent flowers, as though their eyes were fixed upon a window to another dimension.

When she entered his room, Earl and Bessie looked up in disbelief. Their frightened stares were unwelcoming. He was crumpled, drooling on his chest, and restrained to a chair near a narrow bed. His dignity stripped, his gown was poorly snapped, and his bare legs bowed outwards. Bessie had lost weight, and her gray dress sagged on her 5'4" frame. Deep circles hung under her soft blue eyes.

"He needs a blanket," said Lexa. She took one off of the bed.

"Who told you where we were?" asked Bessie.

"A secretary told me. How is Earl doing?" Lexa covered Earl's legs.

"He's not improving, so they sent him here. They don't have much hope for him. The doctor said he probably won't get better. I can't take care of him alone."

"You told me Ben would help you."

"Yes, but on his own terms."

"No one suggested home care? A nurse and an aide can come to your house. He can get bed baths. I can teach you how to hook up his tube feedings. It's got to be hard for you to rush over here every day."

"They never said anything about it."

"Nursing agencies provide those services if you're interested."

Bessie seemed to revive. "It sounds like a good option."

"Give it some thought. I can help you make arrangements." Lexa moved a chair to face them. Earl's dark eyes appeared vacant, and his drool fell onto the blanket.

"It's got to be heartbreaking for you to see him this way."

"You have no idea." Bessie took a deep breath to blink away tears.

Lexa handed her a tissue, and patted her hand. "I'm sorry. I wish we could turn time back." The room was silent as Bessie sobbed.

"Is there any news about Roy? I tried to bring a meal to him but he didn't answer his door."

Bessie dabbed at the tears streaming down her neck. "They think he did it. The police said Doris was hit on the side of her head with a hammer, and Roy's fingerprints were the only ones on the handle."

"No! Not once have I heard him raise his voice to her." Lexa realized that neither she nor Sam quarreled publicly. *No wonder his parents think we're still a couple. Perhaps the neighbors argued behind closed doors. Maybe under their pleasant appearances lurked a couple ready to kill each other, and two weeks ago he snapped.* "How long were they married?"

"They've been together for thirty-eight years. Their daughter Marion was born in 1939. I had Ben a month later. We became so close. Roy was a caring husband, and he adored Doris. If she didn't like someone, he didn't like someone. When she joined church groups, he got involved in similar organizations. They were like peas in a pod for all the years I've known them."

"I didn't start a fire any more than Roy killed Doris," said Lexa. "If I pick you up, will you come to my court hearing next week?"

"Of course dear, of course."

"Thank you. I need to leave, but if you give me your number, we can discuss home care for Earl." Relief overcame her as she clutched the paper that Bessie had given her.

She took her usual route through the alley, and as she approached the garage, she felt confused as to why a squad car was parked behind her home. She exited her VW to see a second police vehicle in the street. In his winter jacket, Roy stood beside his fence. His dark, puzzled eyes were glued on her, and his graying, wavy hair whipped in the wind. Fear caused her to shake as she gave him a crooked smile, and she kept a brisk pace to the door.

What the hell happened? This insanity has to stop. She ran inside. The house was occupied by uniformed men and women.

"Miss, what's your name?"

"Where is Sam? Did something happen to him?"

"What is your name?" A tall, male officer looked annoyed.

She refused to answer, and avoided the staring faces. Sam forced his way toward her. "Where were you? We thought you were dead."

"Dead? Why?" asked Lexa.

"Your…your bloody bed. The bathroom floor looks like someone was slaughtered. I imagined the worst."

"Oh. It was a bad…nosebleed. I didn't have time to clean it up. I had to find…someone. I'm fine, really. There's been a mistake."

"False alarm, folks." The officers finished filling out their forms. Each gave Lexa a malicious look before trickling down the stairs, and in particular the large man she had seen once too often last year.

Officer Humphrey's badge was freshly polished. He had ransacked her house three months ago. His contemptuous eyes like little black beetles, bore through her in not finding what he was searching for. Despite his grin, she sensed a scheme underway to get her accused of some heinous crime. His pleasure in thinking that someone may have given her what she deserved and dragged her away was shattered when she appeared. His large hands slammed her door shut, and Sam locked it.

The house silent, he sat on the floor of the top step. "I bought dog food, and came down here to tell you. After all the violence in our area, I thought our house was being crossed off of someone's list. I was ready to cancel tonight's show," he said holding his head in his hands.

"I was in a hurry to find Bessie Blesdin."

"Why?" He looked up.

"I need her to serve as my witness when I go to court."

"Did you get a speeding ticket?"

"No, it's for something I didn't do, and so far, she's all I've got. I'm sorry you worried. I was in a panic. I have a lot on my mind."

Drax stood at the bottom of the stairwell. His brown hair stuck out in all directions. "They found her?" His every word was filtered through gravel, and he looked as though he had just crawled out of bed, making it difficult to determine if he had been up for hours, or had just arisen.

"I'm fine. Remember when I ran off the stage two months ago for a bloody nose? I was going to clean up after I returned from an errand."

"Oh good," he said in his deep, rasping voice. He yawned and stumbled up the stairs.

Sam slumped forward on the top step, and his wavy blonde hair fell to his wrists as he set his elbows on his knees. She stripped the sheets, and ran to the basement to put them in the machine. He was still there when she lugged up a bucket of soapy water, plastic gloves and scrub brushes. He stared at her as though she was an apparition resurrected from the underworld, like the woman who randomly appeared to them for brief moments with her forlorn dark eyes and long sable hair.

Upon dumping the water out of the pail, Sam returned up the stairs, and Lexa took the food she had prepared to Roy's house. It took one ring of his doorbell to be welcomed in. She expressed her condolences for his wife's death. He saw her at the funeral, and he asked what happened at her house today. She gave a short version of what had transpired, and that she had been to the nursing home to visit Earl. She had recommended home care. He said he would encourage it also. If he needed any help, she insisted that he ask. She inquired if they could exchange phone numbers, and he agreed.

Friday January 21, 1977
Roy said he was grateful for my meal. His home is immaculate. Walls and shelves are filled with family photos, each of which tells a story. Fishing trips, a visit to

Washington D.C., standing under Abe Lincoln and the monuments, Niagara Falls, and best of all, big gatherings. Roy smiled in every shot, and his arms are huddled around everyone who stood beside him.

Our agent called this morning, and added a few more shows. When Karl joined the band a year ago, he said our schedule is like a marathon. We're booked almost solid throughout January and February, giving us no chance to rehearse original songs.

In sorting through stacks of mail, I discovered my nursing license renewal. The fee is due in a week. Maybe I should let it lapse. Wearing a white uniform, starting an infusion, wound care, and emptying a bedpan feels like a lifetime ago.

I wanted to rip up the summons for the preliminary court hearing for the twenty seventh, and toss it into the trash. It stated not to bring a witness, but I have been sick with fear, chasing after Bessie to be present.

Had I not returned, Sam, who wandered amidst a throng of armed men, may have been the prime suspect for my disappearance. They would be looking for my dead body and VW. If police are blaming Roy, I'm certain it's what the cops were thinking about Sam, who has other women in his life, and is the beneficiary of our insurance policy.

There was a silent celebration at our show. Everyone bought me a drink as if to say they were glad I was still alive.

Today ended twenty one days since my last taste of alcohol. Oh well, I tried to stop.

Saturday, January 22, 1977

As we threw our suitcases and guitars into the van to leave for the show, two men hauled furniture from a moving truck into the vacant house. Statues of bronzed warriors had come to life, and stepped down from their pedestals.

Bundled up in my coat and scarf, they wore light jackets. The younger man and I exchanged a smile. Unaffected by the snow swirling over his long silver and black mane, there was something unsettling about the older man, as if he could create a windstorm at will, or generate tremors in the earth by a motion of his thick, strong hands. His deep black eyes hold untold wisdom and secrets. If he heard our arguing over whose turn it was to drive and who got what seat in the van, I'll never know. Not once did he look in our direction.

Sunday, January 23, 1977

Life can hand you a shooting star to grant your every wish in one instant, and slam you to the ground in the next. When we are offered those star-like moments we need to use them wisely.

Julette, the woman who was poisoned by her husband in the bedroom where I sleep, appeared to me again this morning, smiled, and disappeared. A lovely apparition, her long hair is as dark as her eyes.

Earl and Bessie Blesdin are fading into the woodwork of the nursing home. I am helping her out of desperation to maintain my freedom. Maybe we both need each other.

Bessie lost her best friend Doris, and her friendship with the lady who lived beside me crumbled when she moved away to live with her daughter. Losing her two best friends may be why she has been so kind to me.

I spoke to the head nurse about home care for Earl, and she smugly laughed. She said Earl will never leave. It burnt a fire in me to get him the hell out of there. I fear that the sand in Earl's hourglass is running low.

Chapter 5

Monday, January 24 – Sunday, January 30

Monday, January 24, 1977

As sunset painted an amaranthine sky, my new neighbor set up a metal burn barrel. Shadows intensified the lines on his brow and the hollows under his high cheek bones. The creases around his mouth held onto resignation like it was the last sip of water in his canteen. If he raised his arms, the fringes on his leather jacket would have morphed into eagle's wings, to glide him across the sky and far away from this street which has fallen to robberies and murders.

Each week I stop at the post office box, and write responses to letters adding a photo if requested, deposit the band's take at the bank, pick up groceries, talk to the agents, update the show schedule, discuss equipment and truck repairs with the road crew, and care for Ebbie among many other things. Fan mail is always interesting, and at 2 am, I sealed envelopes to twenty replies.

Tuesday, January 25, 1977

On his way into the van, Ted and Sam started a snowball fight, and Ted landed a direct hit into the face of the elder dark-eyed man who moved in three days ago. Water dripped off of his golden skin and his long black and silver braids. He briefly turned toward me before walking into his house. I felt

53

a strong urge to slap Ted, and demand an apology. I opened my mouth to speak, but the wind obscured my words.

When we arrived at the club, the bartender gave me an odd stare when I asked for a full glass of a make-me-feel-happy-again drink. I told him I didn't care what he gave me, and to subtract all of the alcohol we consumed off of our paycheck. He reached for the 100 proof vodka. I didn't exactly feel happy, but then I didn't feel anything. I was unable to see straight by the end of the night when the manager counted out our cash and handed it to me. We were all impaired, and drew straws on who should drive. Ted managed to get us home. He ran a red light, a stop sign, and drove up a curb. None of us cared, and the roads were deserted.

The cold air stung my face as I stepped out of the van at 3 am. Fresh cords of wood are stacked alongside the aluminum walls of the neighboring garage. Swirls of vapor, reminders of the fire's heat, rose from the drum barrel despite the icicles hanging nearby.

Ebbie whined to be let out and fed, causing Lexa to awaken, but with a knife, an ice pick and a pair of scissors embedded into her skull, or so it felt. Grabbing her head, she was unable to open her eyes due to the throbbing. She massaged her temples, rolled to the edge of her waterbed, and onto the floor. She took two aspirin out of a bottle in the bathroom medicine cabinet, and gulped them down. She shuffled to the kitchen, holding walls along the way. Her unsteady hands spilled ground coffee onto the counter, and as she poured a cup of the strong brew, some spilled over the mug.

Sam opened the door to her lower flat, and his blue eyes perused the scene like an army drill sergeant. "What's going on? Why is Ebbie crying?"

"I don't recall inviting you down here," she said.

"I need something from the fridge, and if you can't take care of Ebbie, I will. She is my dog. Remember that."

"And mine too. Try to keep it in mind," she said.

"You will never see her again when I leave."

"Is that some kind of threat?" she asked.

"You seem to forget who wanted her in the first place."

Sam was a conductor of corrosiveness. His battery acid voice burned her self-esteem, and nothing allowed her to accept her desirability. She couldn't bear to file for divorce, and leave the one thing she could count on, the sweetness of Ebbie's unconditional love. She had nowhere to go if she sold the house, and divided their belongings. She forced a blind acceptance that Sam was not worth the anguish, and declared an unspoken truce due to their working relationship.

"Ebbie has been whining all morning," he said.

"No she hasn't. I'm not moving too well. I'm in pain."

"You complain constantly. I'll let her out."

"While you're at it you can give her some food and water. Where are you off to all dressed up in the clothes I gave you?"

"It's none of your business."

"Is it because it's one of your girlfriends? And why are you wearing something I gave you for Christmas?"

"What difference does it make what I wear? I see you made a mess all over the countertop. You probably left the bathroom and your bed bloodied up on purpose to nauseate me. You cannot keep anything clean, can you?"

"I will never be able to measure up to your mommy. Deep down it's what you really want. Maybe you can remember it's the seventies. Women want more than to squeeze your babies out, scrub your floors, cook your meals, and tell you what a perfect man you are as she hands you a warm, baked cookie. You want a concubine who'll obey your rules, laugh at your jokes and spread her legs open whenever you snap your fingers. Rub and grind against you. Moan. Groan. Tell you how hot and sexy you are. Stroke your ego."

"You're always going to hurl your ugly crap at me about how bad you think I am. Good luck finding anyone who can stand to be around some average bimbo like you," said Sam.

An anvil was pounding in her head from a hangover, and Sam had ripped out her last nerve. She threw her hot coffee at him. He gasped, and held up his arms in shock. Drenched from his neck to his shoes, he shoved her.

She struck the left side of her face on the corner of the open silverware drawer as she fell onto the floor. The swelling was immediate. She felt a burning pain, and touched her upper cheek which had minor bleeding from an abrasion.

"Get the hell out of here," she screamed. "And get your own damn refrigerator!"

She grabbed ice and pressed it onto the throbbing. Staring in the mirror, a black eye began its ugly markings, and nothing could stop it. *Why did I throw scalding coffee at him? I cannot allow him to bring out the worst in me.*

She held the cold compress on her eye socket, as trudging, banging and slamming of doors amplified downward from the ceiling into the kitchen. She needed to make travel arrangements for tomorrow's court hearing, but ten rings of Bessie's phone made her aware that she had to visit the nursing home.

In the parking lot, she glanced into the rearview mirror, and dabbed on more make-up. The ballooning of her left eye affected her vision. When she stepped into the facility, all eyes were drawn to the left side of her head. She turned away, and sprinted to Earl's room. It was cleaned out and empty. An aide informed her that he had left. She asked for a phone book, and dialed the office of Benjamin Blesdin, Attorney-at-law. His secretary said he was not available, and she anticipated that he did not plan to return until tomorrow.

Lexa dialed the listing for his home and explained who she was. Earl and Bessie were there. She hesitated, but asked to speak to Bessie. In discussing the agenda for tomorrow, her voice cracked. She cleared her throat and regained her composure. Bessie said she will be home and ready at 8:00 am but her son said that she should not attend a preliminary hearing. Lexa asked her to come anyway. There was no one else she could count on to keep her from breaking down.

Mired in anxiety, Lexa paced throughout the dark rooms of her house, keeping ice on her injury for most of Wednesday night, fearful of tomorrow's outcome.

She stood in the deep brown courtroom unable to hide her fatigue. The bruising of her swollen black eye extended down her left cheek. The judge scrutinized her from top to bottom. Distain filled his eyes as he skimmed over the documents handed to him by the prosecutor.

The officer who made her arrest was sworn in and made his incriminating statements.

"Where is your lawyer?"

"I'm innocent. I don't need one."

"In my hands is a report which states you were caught fleeing from a fire."

"That is false, and my neighbor is willing to testify."

"You did not obey police commands. Is this true?"

"Yes. I was on my way to my neighbor's house. I told police I needed to help someone, but I was handcuffed and taken to jail."

"The state's eyewitness is unfortunately out of town this morning. You have been positively identified by him. Are you aware of this?"

"No."

"How do you wish to plead?"

"Not guilty."

"There is ample evidence against you to take this to trial."

"I don't know what you're talking about. I was never given a single police report. Isn't that your job to make sure I have them?"

"No ma'am, it's not my job," said the prosecutor.

Perhaps the black eye aroused the sympathy of the judge. She remained silent as she was given copies.

"The defendant will be bound over to circuit court district five for trial. The date will be set for Monday, March 7th."

She eyed a sizeable man who made the kind of twinkling eye contact toward both men which suggested their involvement at social gatherings. Three insignia stripes were stitched below Officer Humphrey's city patch to the upper sleeves of his navy uniform when she last saw him. Today he sat in a white shirt, navy tie and slacks.

On her way out of the courtroom, Lexa nudged Bessie who had been waiting on a bench. "Psst, take a look at the beefy cop with the crew-cut, and little chocolate chip eyeballs. I saw him go into Roy's place. I think he's in charge of Doris' homicide investigation."

In the VW, Lexa shoved the police reports under the driver's seat. Bessie said the big cop had been at her house asking questions and taking notes after Earl's attack. "He made me feel like I shoved Earl down the steps even though I wasn't home. His name is officer Hum something," said Bessie.

"It's Harold Humphrey. He bends the law to his whims. He'll stop at nothing to lock me and Roy up, and not just us. It's about the power he has over others. I have a gut feeling he might go so far as to alter evidence," said Lexa.

"How did it go in there?" asked Bessie.

"Not well."

"Do you think my son could help? He's a District Attorney."

"Does he take on petty cases like mine?" asked Lexa.

"It never hurts to ask," said Bessie.

"How much longer will Earl be staying at Ben's house?"

"I'm not sure. His home is huge. He made arrangements for a nurse like you talked about and had a hospital bed set up in one of their spare rooms, but I feel like I don't know Earl at all anymore."

"He needs you now more than ever. He would do the same for you."

"When he proposed, he said he wanted to take care of me. He asked me to quit my job at the bakery in Port Washington. It's where we met. Every day he stopped in. He said I was sweeter than anything in the store. He got so jealous when other men got flirty." Outlined by dark eyelashes, her sparkling steel blue eyes exuded a soft beauty. Streaks of blonde strands wove through her thick, silvery hair. "On our wedding day, he picked me up like a pillow, and carried me from our car to the motel room. We laughed like love-struck kids. I saved the cute pink dress I wore that day, to hand it down to the daughter I hoped to have, but now I doubt if I'll ever have a granddaughter. I had several miscarriages. It's still hard for me to talk about it. Earl was at my side during each one, and each was a deep loss for me. Before we had Ben, I thought we were not destined to have children. I caught myself envying any woman who pushed a stroller. Earl has been a great husband and father, but I feel like those days are over."

"Every year, and sometimes after a life altering moment, we redefine ourselves. When we're young, time doesn't seem to matter. We feel almost invincible. Then the day comes when we discover our life will never be the same, and we think, 'Am I going to be okay?' And we transform ourselves once more."

"You should talk. What are you, twenty-one?"

"No, I'm twenty-two, and my life has been full of challenges. Whenever I drive through here, I watch for a woman who resembles me. I'm worried she's going to start another fire, and that more than my garage will be her target. Thanks for accompanying me today. It means a lot," Lexa said as she dropped her off. "Stay in touch. I know you're going to your son's house, but if either of us sees anything unusual, we have to call each other."

As much as she wanted to visit Roy, Lexa was fading and fast. She dove into her waterbed and yanked the comforter over her head. She awoke an hour later when Ebbie licked her cheek. Lexa reached over to pet the beige, soft, wavy fur. Sam knocked on her bedroom door.

"Are you ready?"

"When do we have to leave?"

It takes about five hours to get to Minneapolis. We need to leave in thirty minutes," he said, staring at her bruised, swollen face.

She had forgotten to set an alarm. Keeping peace with her bandmates who were vital to her paycheck was in her best interest. "I'm...ss...sorry about the coffee. Did you get it out of your clothes?"

"No. They're on my bedroom floor. I'm going to throw them in the garbage."

"Leave them at the bottom of the steps. I'll take care of it."

"Um...I'm sorry I shoved you," said Sam.

She soaked Sam's clothes in a basin, tossed essentials into her luggage, and got into the van just as her bandmates arrived.

"Who's awake enough to drive?" asked Ted. "What did you do to your face?"

"I fell."

"Yea, sure. Then you bumped into a wall and took a rolling pin to your eye."

"Get in everyone. The crowd awaits us," said Grant.

"I've never known you to be clumsy," said Karl. She was aware of his focus on her disfigurement.

"I'm wearing sunglasses tonight."

"I didn't say anything about your...your..."

"You didn't have to." She bit off a small piece of Ativan, swigged it down, grabbed the lever to recline the chair, and rolled onto her side.

She volunteered for the return drive, and all zipped up coats and jackets as the van was parked in the garage at 7:00 am. Thick ashy smoke wafted through the stillness of the morning.

Ted sniffed. "Someone has a campfire." As he rounded the corner to his car, he saw the steam rising from the steel container. "Does he burn something every day?"

"Shhh…Not so loud, Ted."

"He's not out here. I can say whatever I want to. What the hell is with that guy?"

The man walked out of his garage in the alleyway, and slammed his back door.

"I think he hates me already." Lexa sighed and walked into the house. Getting her head on a pillow was all she desired as soon as Ebbie trotted inside.

She felt great pity for Drax, Hound and Showey who navigated the truck over icy roads to set up equipment within ten hours on Friday night. Casey showed up, and like an overzealous roadie, he brought drinks to everyone, and assisted during set-up and tear-down. He was becoming a permanent fixture.

At 6:15 am on Saturday, the ringing phone near her bed awoke her in small increments.

"Hello?" Sobbing suffused through the receiver. Lexa sat up. "Hello?"

"This is Bessie." The weeping continued. "It's, it's Earl. I…I don't know what to…to do."

"Take a deep breath, and try to clear your thoughts."

"I can't. Earl isn't breathing right. He's making awful rattling noises. I told Ben, but he said to stop worrying; that Dad's fine and needs to rest. But all Earl's done the past four days since he's been here is sleep. They gave me diapers to put on him, and I'm not able to move him alone. They keep the bed rails up, and they keep postponing when the nurse is supposed to come. I'm worried sick."

"Did you notify his doctor?"

"Ben said I shouldn't. He scolded me because I fuss over Dad too much. I'm so confused. I don't know what to think anymore."

"Hold the phone up to Earl's mouth." His rattling breath sounds disturbed her.

"Do you hear it?" asked Bessie.

61

"Yes, I do. Earl needs to be in a hospital. Do your best to stay calm. I'm going to call an ambulance, so give me Ben's address. Put your coat on, get Earl's belongings together, and in five minutes, open the front door to let the attendants in. Do not speak to anyone. Now repeat it, just so we're clear. Good. Let me know when you get to the hospital, and I'll meet you there."

"Thank you."

"I'll see you soon." She pulled the covers up and closed her eyes, wondering why Ben was so resistant in letting his Mom get help, but Earl was gurgling, and she was certain he had pneumonia from not being moved in the past four days. She drifted to a light nap until Ebbie whined to be let out.

Three and a half hours of sleep made Lexa feel incoherent. Bessie called twenty minutes later. Earl was at Northwest General Hospital, and was being admitted to the intensive care unit.

"He has pneumonia and a pulmonary embolism. I don't think he's going to make it," said Bessie.

"I'll get there as soon as I can." Lexa stared at herself in the mirror. *I criticize my face whenever I look at it. It wouldn't matter if I had a black eye or not. I've found something appalling about my face from as far back as I can remember. This is wrong; that is wrong. Always, an imperfect face looks back at me. Why, damn it why?*

She put her long tan coat and sunglasses on, and left. As she walked outside, smoke swirled across the white ground like fog. Roy walked toward his garage, and Lexa called out to him. Exhaustion grabbed her in the gut and she choked on her words.

"Hello Roy. How are you?"

"I'm okay. Thank you for the nice meal you brought over, but I had to freeze it. I have no appetite." He gazed at the bruise on her left cheek.

"I understand. I'm going to Northwest General Hospital. Earl is there, and he's in rough shape." She sucked in a deep breath. "He was admitted to the intensive care unit a little while ago. Bessie's a wreck. It seems you've all been friends for so long."

"I've been collecting their mail, shoveling their sidewalk, and I even put some of my garbage in their cans. I'd hate for them get robbed again on top of everything they've been through."

"I'm certain they appreciate your kindness. Can I ask you an odd question? Is Officer Humphrey investigating Doris' death?"

"It's not an odd question. He is, and he seems to think I killed her. Said I'd better confess, but I ran an errand after working at my job that day. No one seems to believe me."

"Have you gone back to that place to check if anyone recognizes you?"

"I went to a gas station. It's like taking a pee in a men's stall. No one cares what the guy next to you looks like."

"He's got me pegged as an arsonist. He was in the courtroom during my preliminary hearing, giving me the evil-eye," she said.

"Why was he there? Did he arrest you?"

"No. As far as I know, he wasn't involved in any way. He may have been there to intimidate me."

"You have a right to know who is accusing you of arson. Who identified you?" asked Roy.

"I was picked out of a lineup," she said.

"Those are not reliable," he said.

"I need to ask you about…"

They stopped speaking and turned towards what sounded like a monk in a monastery during an incantation. Lexa became transfixed on the graceful way her new neighbor moved as he placed branches into the fire. His deep voice hummed in a low chant. The rising sun created elongated shadows over the snow, and gave the illusion of a fringed marionette circling a smoke stack. He opened his arms and raised his head toward the sky, arching his back. He flung his head downward as his feet and knees raised upwards.

On the land of his forefathers, he danced to thank Mother Earth for the abundances bestowed. He was now surrounded by asphalt and slate roofing, metal downspouts, concrete walkways, and streets covered by black tar. The beauty of open fields where a sunrise can be seen for miles was gone to him.

Once inhabiting vast plains which lie between two oceans, men like him tamed wild horses, and blessed everything that nourished his family. Fire cooked his food, warmed his tipi, and was lit for ceremonial dances. His fires had a significant meaning.

He was as displaced as she was. Though she had a bed and furnishings, a key to unlock the door, and the deed to a house in her name, it did not feel like a home where she belonged. She refocused when Roy spoke. He had watched the scene as though his mind was far away.

"You wanted to ask me about what?" he asked.

"I told Bessie I'd meet her at the hospital, but I need to talk to you about Ben Blesdin."

"And I need to ask how you know my nephew, Casey," said Roy.

"Who?"

"The guy pounding on your door the other night is my sister's son."

"I have to leave, but when I return tomorrow, I'll call you as soon as I'm up. I should warn you, though. I'm rarely up before noon."

She walked into the hospital room and stood near Bessie, who kept a vigil at Earl's bedside. An entanglement of tubes draped around him. The flashing lights and numbers on the monitors absorbed them. Echoes of pinging, humming and hissing filled his room. The women looked at each other, but neither spoke. They watched as a nurse checked on the medication and drip rate of the intravenous fluids, while another documented his urinary output in a catheter. A third nurse checked the monitors, secured an oxygen mask over his face, and said that a respiratory therapist was on the way.

Earl's wheezes, almost a snoring sound, were a strain to every muscle in his chest. Had he not been so strong and vibrant a man, it may have been too much for him to hang on. He fixed his gaze on Bessie, who was a reminder to him that every breath mattered.

Hope was a seed lying dormant in each of their thoughts as he struggled to expand his lungs. Though his life had been full for the seventy-six years that he had graced it, the fear of him taking his last breath, was in Bessie's glassy eyes. She had mourned during the memorial of her neighbor, Doris and was not ready to bury her husband. Through the years, her friends and family had slipped away, increasing the strain on her declining body. Earl's demise would face her in the direction of an eternal sleep.

"How's the old man?" asked Ben, who glided into the room as though he had jumped out of a magazine cover; his black overcoat flowing behind him like a superhero cape.

Bessie glared at him. Lexa felt too distressed to speak and turned away to hide her black eye. When a nurse said his dad was in critical condition, and they were taking it minute by minute, he lacked any hint of sorrow.

"Mom, I can't stay long. I'm in the middle of a big case."

"You always are."

"And what do I do for a living? Can you try to be just a little understanding for once? I came all the way out here to see how he is. I hope you can appreciate it."

The beauty in his structured cheekbones and jaw, thick, wavy brown hair and steel blue eyes diminished as he spoke.

"Code four! Code four!" A nurse yelled out. The piercing tone of an abnormal heartbeat bore through the air like a siren. The family was ushered out. Doctors and more nurses filled the room, and one compressed Earl's chest, while another inflated his lungs in a steady rhythm. An order was given to flatten the mattress, and paddles were pushed onto Earl's chest. Everyone was instructed to move away. Earl's torso heaved off of the bed as he was jolted by the shock, and the room was briefly silent. All eyes stared at the monitors. 'Please live' was written on each of their faces. Lexa gripped Bessie as she went down.

"Help me, Ben! Hold your mom." Bessie crumpled, and Lexa guided her gently onto the ground. The echoes of the doctors giving Earl a second shock resonated into the hallway where Lexa held Bessie's head off of the floor.

Ben stood motionless.

Nurses ran to Bessie, and tried to sit her upward. Ben's face drained of all color. Lexa wanted to run. She wanted to wake up and be in her apartment on State Street before Sam accidentally poisoned her, before her life began unraveling, but she was going nowhere. Surrounded by hospital staff, a doctor waved smelling salts under Bessie's nose. Nurses lifted her into a wheelchair, and began to push her.

"I'm not leaving Earl's side! Stop," she screamed relentlessly until a crowd of onlookers gawked at her. She was given an injection. Ben was void of expression as his mother was wheeled away and assisted to a hospital bed. Her moist, weary eyes stared into nothingness.

"Please tell me how Earl is," she pleaded to Lexa. "I don't trust them," she whispered.

In the intensive care unit, healthcare workers hustled throughout Earl's room. Comforted by the heart monitor beeping in a steady rhythm, she felt annoyed that his son was gone. She returned to Bessie's room, and reassured her that Earl was stable.

"Where's Ben?"

"I didn't see him anywhere. He must have left," said Lexa.

"How can a job change someone so much? I want my son back. And my husband." Her eyes drooping and words garbling, she exhaled her worries and drifted to sleep. Lexa stroked her hand along the creases of Bessie's cheek, smoothed the blankets and left.

Fatigue overwhelmed her. At a red light, the driver behind her laid his hand on the horn, and she stepped on the gas, unsure of what color the light was.

Her first words in the van were, "I need that bed." She opened her glass bottle, swigged down a bite of an Ativan, and tried to relax. She had slept for five minutes when a sharp, high pitched laugh flew out of Ted's mouth and startled her.

"Is there a possibility you might be able keep it down for a while?"

"It's not my fault if you didn't get enough sleep."

"Apparently you forgot you're in a band, not the one man Ted Lynnch Show. And perhaps you forgot that if I sing like shit tonight, it doesn't make you look good. It doesn't make any of us look good. Word Locket doesn't get rehired, and gossip gets out that we suck. Are you happy now?"

He turned away, and avoided her throughout the night, including the ride home from Marshfield through foggy darkness. Everyone took a long, hard stretch upon stepping out of the van.

In her bed, she tossed and turned under the peach comforter. The vision was distinct. She saw Karl sleeping on a sofa in a dark room. She rocked his shoulders and called out to him, but he remained unresponsive. Or was it Casey? Because of their similarities, she wasn't sure. She rolled over and fell asleep.

On Sunday afternoon, she kept her word and phoned Roy Kemke, but there was no answer. By the time she was up and running, most people had finished the majority of their errands, or were winding down their workdays. Maybe he had been to church and was visiting one of his daughters, or sitting at a grave site, holding fresh flowers.

At her kitchen table, Lexa closed her eyes. She saw him standing in the icy wind outside the doors of the Holy Cross Mausoleum where he had viewed Doris' crypt, wondering why his wife of forty years was gone and why he was accused of her murder. He had lost his best friend, and was facing the prospect of spending the rest of his days in jail. He tore petals off the flowers he had brought and watched them drift across the frozen snow.

An intermittent boom on the back stairwell, followed by thumping, pounding, and voices of Ted, Sam, and Drax shouting at each other aroused her curiosity. Ten minutes later, all was silent as Sam's new refrigerator was shoved into place.

The dressing room at Turner Hall in Watertown was brutally cold. No one spoke or made eye contact including roadies, as their night came to an end. Two days of freedom lie ahead for all. Lethargy had smacked everyone down by the end of the evening.

Sunday January 30, 1977

Has self-destruction become so ingrained into my psyche that I am unable to stop? Will my happiness always be contingent on one unattainable thing or other? Like my disfigured eye, a cut when it heals, still leaves a scar. A few cuts are easy to hide, but countless cuts become hideous.

Earl, Bessie and Roy are holding on by threads. All of our lives have been flipped upside down in a heartbeat.

An arson conviction carries a five to a twenty year sentence depending on the specifics. I have no idea what I did with the police reports, what was set on fire, how severely it burned, and how close it is to my home. I will need a strong testimony, but if Bessie's husband is gone, her incentive to come to my defense will collapse.

Chapter 6

Monday, January 31 – Sunday, February 6

It was 1:00 pm, when she got up to give Ebbie food and water, and let her run outside.

She ransacked her house for the misplaced police reports. Unable to find them, a sense of dread overcame her, and she closed her eyes. She opened the VW, stuck her hand under the driver's seat, and frowned at the document regarding Diene's Dress Shop, which was set on fire at the Capitol Court shopping Mall. The estimated time of the fire was at 5:45 pm. It appeared to have been caused by a lighter or a match. The damage was limited to one clothing rack and was estimated at approximately $1300. An alert security guard emptied an extinguisher, and pulled the alarm. Trucks arrived in five minutes. A witness had come forward to give an account and description of the perpetrator. It mirrored Lexa's appearance. His name was blacked out.

Her head reeled. It was roughly a mile from her house to 60th and Capitol Drive. She was capable of running this distance in ten minutes on that six below zero night.

The second form documented the police officers who were summoned to her alley by one of the Blesdin's neighbors, who heard the racket, and observed her battle with the gate and fence. He feared her intent was to harm his friends. A nearby patrol was dispatched. Her capture was at 5:55 pm.

She was now desperate for every last witness she could find, especially Tarick. She considered offering air fare to get him to return for her court date. Roy knocked on her door.

"You said you wanted to ask me about Ben?" His dark soulful eyes, like those of an aged stallion, were drawn to the bruising under her left eye.

"Yes, come in please. Can I offer you something to drink?"

"No, thanks. I saw Earl this morning in the ICU. They let me stay for a while. Bessie is shaken up," he said.

She led him to the living room where they sat on the sofa. "I was appalled at how callous Ben was toward his parents. He didn't stay at the hospital to see if his dad was going to be okay after the doctors shocked his heart. Was he always self-absorbed?"

"Everyone referred to him as the 'golden boy' when he was growing up for his curly, blonde hair and blue eyes like his mom. Since he was their only child, they spoiled him rotten. He got everything they could afford to give him. He was a star athlete in high school and was constantly in the papers. Now he's a hot-shot D.A., and he still makes his way into the news. He had an elaborate wedding, and married a model. I'm sick of how he brags about the new car he drives, the big house he has, his maid and his chef. He told me his watches are worth more than the car I drive."

"Could Doris have said or done something that made him angry?"

"I'm not sure. She detested how he was coddled. He asked my older daughter Marion to go out on a date when she was in high school, but Doris and I refused to let her. We had some heated arguments. Eventually we gave in, and it didn't take long for him to break her heart. When he set his sights on Melinda, we said absolutely not. So, she snuck out and kept it a secret. When she got...when she..." He stopped speaking and stared into space.

"Roy, are you alright? It has got to be hard for you to talk about this."

"You can't imagine." Tears welled in his eyes.

"Are you sure you don't want a cup of coffee? I can heat some up for us."

"Okay."

He perused the large bookshelf, fireplace, sofa, and matching tan chairs when she went to the kitchen. A large green plant stood in the window behind the sofa.

She returned with two cups. "Do you like cream and sugar?"

"No thanks." He took a hard swallow as he clutched the ceramic mug.

"You were talking about Melinda."

"Yes, Ben toyed with her too. She got…" He stared at his feet, and said nothing.

"Is she okay?"

He stared into space as though the ghost of his wife stood before him.

"Roy...are you alright?"

"No, not at all. If Ben harmed Doris…in any way, I'll kill him. He was the apple of Earl's and Bessie's eyes, and they were blind to his antics. We did our best to ignore him. Earl and Bessie are such good people." He set his cup on the coffee table and a blank stare choked his silence. "Since my wife has been gone, the ground has fallen out from under me."

"Doris was slain two days after Earl was pushed down the stairs. If Ben stopped in to see his parents, he may have seen her and had a chat. She knew a lot of people. And he was aware of it. I'm guessing that you've already sifted through her things," she said.

"Yes I have, and I can't find anything." His face glowered, and he clenched his hands into fists. "I had my suspicions about him. But I have no proof, and he could have offered someone a deal to do whatever nasty deed he wanted." Roy combed his fingers through his short, wavy, black and silver hair.

Lexa offered him a tissue.

He dabbed at the dark crescents under his eyes. "I can't let my girls and grandchildren see me this way. I have to pull myself together."

"You were going to tell me about Casey, your sister's son. Are you sure it's him?"

"I was lying in my bed when I heard punching on your back door. I peeked out of my window, and also I recognized his voice. How did you meet him?"

"He and my bandmates are becoming inseparable. One of the guys invited him to a rehearsal."

"He's a storyteller. I don't believe most of what he says."

"What do you mean?"

"He was bitter about his parents being divorced. He blamed it on his Mom. His dad had a job where he traveled constantly as a steamfitter. When my sister discovered he was having an affair, she left him, but her husband got custody since she didn't have a job. Casey didn't speak to his mom for years, and when I saw him at a family reunion, I was shocked by the horrid things he told everyone about her. I knew better. I think his dad filled his head with nonsense. What he said about my poor sister sickened me."

"I'll keep it in mind. Is anyone else helping you look into what happened to Doris?"

"No. I always used to rely on Earl. He'd do anything for me, but he is in bad shape. I've been too numb to talk to anyone else."

They sat quietly before saying their goodbyes.

In her kitchen, she stared through the window at the dismal grayness. Clouds obscured the sky for weeks on end in winter. The walls began closing in on her, making her feel suffocated. She left her house for no other reason than to rid the feeling of emptiness.

She drove to Lake Michigan, and watched the waves splash on the break wall. The crushing roars in each crash and retreat were like a lullaby. On her way home, she stopped at the sporting goods store she had frequented, and grabbed a box of 45 caliber shells. Under a sign labeled 'Just In', were boxes of night vision goggles. She picked up the demonstrator, peered through the lenses and set it down. She hesitated, snatched it up, glanced into it, and set it down. At the check-out counter, she asked the clerk to wait. She ran for the box containing the goggles.

On Tuesday afternoon, Sam stopped downstairs to remind Lexa about the 7:30 band practice in the upper flat, where his recording studio was set up.

At 7:45, Ted and Grant arrived. Casey walked in five minutes later. He pulled out his Fender Precision Bass guitar, and the gold horseshoe ring on his right hand caught the light as he plucked a melody on the strings. They waited for Karl until 8:30 and called his apartment, but got no response. Grant gripped his drumsticks and said he wanted to rehearse anyway, and Ted agreed. Within the span of three songs, haunted by her premonition, Lexa announced she was going grocery shopping.

"At 9 pm?" asked Grant.

"There are things I need and, it's not the same without Karl." She took her purse, coat, slipped into boots, and drove down the block, where she parked. She rang Roy's doorbell. He peeked through the curtain and opened the door.

"I need your help," she whispered. "Do you have Casey's dad's address? It's not like my bass player to skip a rehearsal. I'm going to try to find him."

"I haven't seen my ex-brother-in-law for a few years, but I don't think he moved. I have it here somewhere." He rummaged through a drawer and opened a small book. "Here it is. I'll write it down."

"Thanks, I'll tell you about it tomorrow."

She drove to Karl's apartment on 61st Street. The lights were off, and his car was gone.

She traveled five miles south, followed the written directions, and passed his empty Chevelle Malibu. She parked down the road, searched her handbag, and put the small scissors she used for trimming her hair, a nail file, a paper clip, and a metal bobby pin into her coat pocket. The TV was on, and no one answered to her pounding. The lock was impenetrable. She sprinted to the back door. Despite using of all her devices, it would not budge.

She ran through neighboring properties, and uncovered an unused flower pot to stand on. She turned it upside down, and fought to open windows closest to the rear door, but could not move them. To the side of the house was a narrow etched glass window, which she guessed to be a bathroom. Standing on the inverted flower pot, she pulled the frame upward, without success. Her breath frosted up the cold glass. Numbness crept through her gloved hands. The silver scissors glinted off the streetlight as she jammed them into the rotting wood between the window and the lock. She heard a snap. Using all of her strength, the window moved a half inch. She shoved her fingers into the gap, jerked it upwards until she had enough of an opening to squeeze into, and tumbled into the house, making sure to close the pane.

She walked toward the television voices, and found Karl lying on the sofa. He did not respond or awaken to his name being called, nor to being shaken. His pulse felt steady, and his skin was warm. She turned on a light, and near him on a table was an open beer. She held it up and sniffed it. A quarter of it was left in the bottle.

"How many of these did you drink?"

She had to get him out of that house, and fast. She grasped his ankles, set his feet on the floor, and tried to sit him up, but he slumped forward.

"Wake up," she said into his ear, but he did not flinch. She dabbed a cold paper towel on his neck and forehead, repeated his name, but his limp body did not respond.

"Let's get you to a hospital," she said. In a hallway closet, she found a bedsheet, rolled him on top of it, and pulled him towards the front door. "Wait. Where's your jacket?"

She left him on the floor as she ransacked the three bedroom house. She spied a prescription bottle in what appeared to be Casey's father's room. 'Seconal: take one capsule as needed.' She looked through what she surmised was Casey's room, picked up a small blue address book, looked it over, and stuck it into her pocket. She found Karl's jacket, covered his chest, and slid him out of the house. She left him lying on the snow, ran to her VW, drove up to him and heaved him into the back seat of the VW.

At 10:45, she parked under the emergency room canopy of St. Michael's hospital. Karl mumbled, and she turned around.

"Are you alright?"

His speech was garbled. "Where the hell am I?" His bloodshot eyes looked upward.

"You're in my car."

"How did I get here?"

"I dragged you. I'm going to get someone to help me wheel you into the ER."

"Why? What happened?"

"You were unresponsive. When did you get to Casey's house?"

"Maybe…it was…I think it was 6:00."

"What did you drink?"

"Just a beer."

"So when I broke in at 10:00, you were unresponsive because you had one beer?"

"It's all I had. Just one," he said as he tried to sit up. "Man, I'm dizzy. My head is in serious pain."

"I'll get help."

When they left the emergency room at 1:40 am, Karl's blood tests showed nowhere near enough alcohol in his system to have blacked out. A lump and a hairline fracture on the upper back of his head indicated he had a concussion. The doctors asked if he wanted them to involve the police to file charges against the perpetrator, but he did not. They recommended he stay overnight for observation, but he refused, and had to sign a waiver to leave.

"We have to get your car. Casey will wonder what happened to you. I shudder at what his intentions were."

"He's a nice guy. It was probably an accident."

She helped him get into the front seat. "When we get to his house, you'll have to drive your car, but I'll follow you. You should sleep at my house tonight."

"Did you say we're having a sleepover?"

"Dude, you need craniotomy checks every two hours to make sure you're okay. You're the one who wouldn't let them admit you to the hospital. Do you think I can drop you off all alone, and have a clear conscience? I'm going to set my alarm for every two hours and check on you. It's going to be a long night."

When they stopped beside Karl's car, she took his keys, started it up and turned on the heater. "Wait here. I have some unfinished business." She ran to the flower pot, returned it to its original place, and trampled up the entire property. She smoothed the snow around all the windows she had attempted to break into. Lying on her back in front of the house, she moved her arms and legs outward, sideways and down, and used her finger for the design in the center of it. She returned to Karl.

"Are you okay to drive?"

"Am I imagining things, or did you just make two snow angels and draw a heart in the middle of them?"

"I'll explain later. Let's get out of here." She followed him to her house.

"I feel woozy," he said as his feet hit the ground.

She grabbed his arm and helped him walk. The smell of fire permeated the air as they walked outside. She took in a deep breath, closed her eyes and envisioned herself standing in woodlands warming her hands near a campfire. She helped Karl into her bedroom. When he was settled on a few pillows, she went to lock the door.

Sam's feet marched down the inside steps. He appeared hostile. "You went shopping until 2:30 am? You blew off a rehearsal? What is wrong with you? I don't get you at all anymore."

"I need some sleep. I've had a long night of rough sex. The orgy was fun, but I'm a bit sore. Too bad you missed it." She shut the bathroom door, and clicked the lock. The door at the top of the inside stairs rattled the house when it slammed. She brushed her teeth and scrubbed her face. She checked on Karl, whose smile was lit by the night-light.

"You smell like Lilacs. My Mom used to set those purple flowers in a vase in our kitchen every year when I was growing up. The whole house was fragrant." He slipped his arms around her waist, and kissed her neck. "Your skin feels like a baby's."

She pulled away and sat up. "It's my shampoo. You're still feeling the effects of Seconal. What about your girlfriend?"

"We broke up. Why did you save me?"

"You coughed up ten grand and sprang me out of jail."

He stared into her eyes and stroked her legs. "I could easily fall in love with you."

"It's the Seconal talking. Don't do anything you'll regret."

He pulled on her arm. His hand on the back of her neck was warm, and he tried to kiss her. She turned away and his lips brushed her cheek."

"Don't you like me?"

"Yes I do, but...I can't. I would feel guilty if..."

"There's nothing to feel guilty about. I'm the one making the moves."

"It doesn't make it right." Karl was unaware of her affair with Grant.

"Why the hell are you being a bitch?" He frowned.

His tone returned her to her father's anger after Vietnam, feigning death when she was strangled at age fifteen, her second attack, and a classmate's murder. Each event shattered a part of her. She had no intention of exploiting Karl. He may have no memory of his skin against hers, but if he did, when Tarick returned she would be in his arms.

She pulled away. "Let's get some sleep. This will be a dream to you by tomorrow."

His eyes saddening, he rolled over and fell asleep. At 4:30 am, her alarm went off, and she woke him up. "What is your name? Squeeze my hands as hard as you can. Where are you? What year is it? Who am I?"

"I'm fine. Stop interrogating me."

"One more thing. I'm going to shine a flashlight into your eyes to check if your pupils constrict properly." She awoke Karl at 6:30, 8:30, and at 12:30 they got up. She made enough coffee for a party and poured both of them a cupful as they sat at the table.

"Do you recollect getting struck on your head?"

"Not at all. We were laughing and sipping on our beers, dis-cussing which songs we should rehearse. My eyelids began to feel heavy."

"I don't understand why he injured you after you passed out."

"Maybe I fell...but I...don't remember. What were you doing on the ground in front of his house last night?"

"When he looks outside today and sees the all the tracks in the snow, do you want him to think someone broke in and got you out, or do you want him to think that you left on your own, and drunken kids vandalized his dad's property?"

"Oh."

Sam pushed the door open to the lower flat. "You're here awfully early. Too busy to join our practice? Were you at the orgy too?"

"Huh? Orgy? What are you talking about?" asked Karl.

"You may want see this." Lexa stood up, and parted the hair on Karl's head, exposing a bloody, bruised lump.

Sam sat down. "What happened?"

"I went to Casey's house at 6:00 because we were going to drive to practice together, and he offered me a beer. The next thing I knew, I woke up in a VW outside of an emergency room. They told me I was drugged, and I had a concussion caused by a skull fracture." Karl took the hospital papers out of his jeans, and handed them to Sam.

"Who took you to the emergency room? His dad? What kind of drugs?"

Karl shot a glance at Lexa. "She took me there. Seconal is a strong sleeping pill, and she found a bottle at Casey's house."

"It's a long story. You know about the premonitions I get, like when you punctured your hand and almost sliced your shoulder open," she said.

"What should we do?" asked Sam. "We need to tell Grant and Ted."

"Can I go home now? I stink. I need a shower and clean clothes," said Karl.

"You're gonna have one more cup of coffee, and don't tell Casey how you left. When he asks about what happened to you, and he will, tell him that rowdy kids were on his lawn, and woke you up when they rang the doorbell."

"I still feel sorry for him. His mom is gone, and his dad is always traveling somewhere for his job. He was tortured in school."

"It's not okay to drug someone and give them a concussion. Please be careful around him," she said as he and Sam left.

She examined Casey's address book, and picked up the phone. The first entry, PNB was answered by a receptionist at the Primary National Bank, asking if she wanted to open a checking account. She said she dialed the wrong number and hung up. The second and third numbers, initialed as BBH and MK were answered by soft spoken females who said, "Hello", and Lexa pressed the receiver down.

She copied every name and number from the small blue book, and hid it.

As she dialed, she realized Roy's phone number was in Casey's small book. She told him what Casey had done to Karl. She asked how well Casey knew Doris, and if they got along.

"Doris didn't like him."

"Exactly how much did she dislike him?"

"To be honest, she couldn't stand him because of how he treats his mother...my sister, because of how he treats everyone. Like we all owe him something. He got vulgar when we last saw him."

"Did he have a difficult life, kids punching and hitting him?"

"The only difficult person I know of in his life is his dad, Radvick," said Roy.

"Did you say anything to Officer Humphrey about Ben Blesdin, or Casey Relmen? Someone needs to check where those guys were when Doris was...was..."

"I tried, but that cop has blinders on. He won't listen to anything I say."

"I'm sorry. I'll be in touch," she said.

She phoned Bessie who said Earl has shown remarkable improvement. Yes, Ben has visited, but he's too busy to stay long. Lexa almost fell asleep during her conversation before she hung up. *Please hang in there. I need your testimony.*

If it wasn't for the drunk who fell on top of him and got angrily shoved away, Lexa may not have noticed Casey in the crowd. Charming and attractive in his black leather jacket and jeans, his wavy brown hair hung loosely on his collar, and the girls at the bar lapped up his attention. One of the women was the cute, curly-haired blonde who refused to leave Word Locket's van after a show, and screamed she was free until she was physically removed from the back seat. Because of what Tarick had discussed, Lexa knew it was Kalie Deckler.

So, she's out of jail. Tonight I will hang out at the bar to stir up some trouble with a freaky little arsonist. And milk her for everything she'll divulge.

Lexa approached Casey and mustered up a falsely pleasant, "Hello, how are you?"

"I'm great, but you're not. Your bandmates are pissed at you for blowing off a rehearsal."

80

"Yea, but we kissed and made up."

"I'm sure you hang all over them to get your way." He brought his hand up to touch her hair.

She pushed him away. "Yea, easy me. They're all so horny, and they like how sleazy I am."

He frowned. "Easy come, easy go."

"Don't worry your little self. It all works out in the end, doesn't it?" She turned away. "So who is this pretty girl here? I'm Lexa. Nice to meet you."

"I'm Kalie Deckler." As she took a swig of her beer, her tight, white t-shirt and tighter jeans displayed her firm curves.

"Do you want to come back stage, and meet the guys?"

"I...I guess so." Her steel blue eyes widened. "I'm not staying long. I'm meeting my boyfriend later," said Kalie.

Casey set his beer down. "You were all over me a minute ago, you little slut."

"No I wasn't."

"The hell you weren't." He gave her a shove and she dropped her beer. Glass and foam splayed out on the floor.

"Let's get away from here." Lexa rolled her arm around Kalie's shoulders, and escorted her to the dressing room. "When are you meeting your boyfriend?"

"At 2:00."

"At 2:00 am?"

"It's the soonest he could see me."

"And you don't mind? Why doesn't a sweet girl like you want a guy to meet her earlier?"

"Oh, he does. And he gives me expensive things, but he can't get away."

"He isn't able to leave his job?" asked Lexa.

"No. His wife. But he's leaving her soon."

"He must be high salaried to buy you expensive things. What does your boyfriend do?"

"He's a District Attorney."

"How did you meet this lucky guy?"

"In court."

"What's his name?"

"Ben."

Lexa almost fell off her chair. "You two must make a beautiful couple. Does he like to see bands?"

"No, he prefers quiet, secluded places."

I'm sure he does. "I have to go, but you're welcome to stay here until you leave. What are you drinking? I'll buy."

"Thanks," said Kalie.

When Lexa handed Kalie two Pabst Red, White and Blue special lager beers, she appeared giddy.

Two brews ought to keep her occupied. I'll buy whatever she wants, to find out what tidbits she will divulge. How interesting that Ben Blesdin is having an affair. And...let me guess. She met him in court for her arson sentencing. Most likely her charges were reduced in exchange for sex.

Halfway into the third set, the band was distracted by a fight. Lexa interrupted a song.

"Showey and Hound to the stage, please." She continued singing as Showey and Hound pulled Kalie off of Casey, who laughed. Kalie swung her hands out of his reach.

"Folks, we're going to take a break," Lexa announced. She ran to Kalie who screamed, "You don't know what the hell you're talking about. I'm telling Ben."

Casey chuckled on the way to the bar, and ordered a drink. Two empty beer cans sat on the floor near Kalie. Her body swayed, and her eyelids drooped.

"Are you okay?" Lexa sat Kalie on a chair. She appeared agitated. Her curly blonde hair was in disarray.

"I wanna go home."

"Did you drive here?"

"Yup. I'm parked down the street somewhere," she slurred.

"Can you call Ben so he can meet you now?"

"I'm allowed to call his office, not his house. Casey's jealous because Ben pays me more than him."

"Ben pays you for what?"

"I do stuff for him."

"What kind of stuff does he make you do?"

"He doesn't make me do anything I don't wanna do." She began hiccuping, and closed her eyes. "I love him, and he loves me. Her head drooped forward and she closed her eyes.

"I'm going to get you a glass of water." As Lexa approached the bar, she heard Casey through the wall of voices.

"You live next to that dirty drunk. His wife almost left him a bunch of times. I know more about him than you ever will." He staggered towards her, and she took a step back. "He's a filthy, lying alcoholic."

"Who are you talking about?"

"You know damn well."

"You sound ridiculous when you're sloshed. Talk to me when you're sober."

"The guy who killed his wife, your sickening neighbor, Roy Kemke. The man who police used to haul out of his house, and stick in the slammer till he sobered up. But I don't need to warn you to watch out for that piece of wreckage."

She spun on her heels, and walked away.

Wednesday February 2, 1977

Both Hound and Showey took a few hits separating Kalie from Casey. He is a liar, like Roy said he was. Kalie got her water, and I ordered a vodka tonic to drown the voices in my head. The band offered to give her a ride to meet Ben, but she refused. I told her we should go out and have fun. Her phone number in my grasp ended our idle chatter as I mulled over Roy's tears, Bessie's turmoil and my own life turning inside out. Returning to jail is not an option.

I'm tired. I want to forget how Earl was pushed down his steps, and his son is an arrogant ass who cheats on his wife and pays people to do the unthinkable. I want to blink away how Karl was drugged and assaulted, but Casey has convinced him that he fell and struck his head on the edge of an end table beside the sofa.

I want to ignore the rant that Roy is an alcoholic. Just when I thought I knew who may have killed Doris, I realize I don't know anything.

Lexa called Bessie on an impulse when she awoke, and asked if she could visit. Earl's eyes tracked her petite frame as she entered the room. He was fed by a tube which extended from his nostril to a bag hanging on a stand near his bed, and he sat in a chair.

"He's doing so well he can go to the rehab unit tomorrow."

"I'm glad to hear it. Bessie, how well do you know Roy?"

"We've been friends for ages."

"Someone told me he has a drinking problem, but that isn't true is it?"

"Well…he used to, but he's been fine for years. He and Doris worked everything out."

"Did he get arrested when he had too much?" asked Lexa.

"Yes, but it was a while ago. He went to AA meetings and changed his life for the better."

"Has he been in jail recently?"

"No, let me think. He didn't drink at Ben's wedding, so it was about five years ago," said Bessie.

"Roy has a criminal record? How often did he get apprehended?"

"Well…long ago, Doris or someone called the cops when he got belligerent. We were afraid of him when he was drunk. But he's been so good that we haven't thought about it. He would not kill his wife," said Bessie. "May I ask you told this to you?"

"His name is Casey."

"Casey Relmen? I've known him since he was a little boy," said Bessie. "After his dad took Casey away from Roy's sister, Casey became as nasty as his dad."

"I questioned why he was so quick to point a finger at him, but now I understand. I have to leave for my job. See you soon."

As she drove, Lexa envisioned ways of getting into Ben Blesdin's house. Learning to break in and escape a basic structure was an art she had mastered when she was a teen. She remembered when she almost fell out of the upstairs bathroom window. A large house required more skill. A two story mansion fortified by large steel doors, opened by a special key for deadbolt locks, and most likely a complicated alarm system would be a challenge. She suspected he was the kind of person who might go so far as to have security cameras. How many dogs does he have? One shouldn't be too much of a challenge. She had to find a way to scale the house at 3 am when he and his wife are asleep.

Or, she could pick up the phone, and walk in during daylight. Roy's words were still fresh. She dialed and waited.

"Hello? Is Mrs. Blesdin available? This is a colleague of her husband." She gave her voice a deeper edge. "Hi dear, I work as a paralegal and I run into Ben at almost every day. He said you're the expert at this. I'm putting in so many hours at the job that my hubby has been on my case about why the house is a mess. I can't take it anymore. Is your maid service dependable? Ben told me to ask who you use, because my husband and kids are getting on my nerves. You can give me the name of a good chef too? Oh, you're such a doll. Ben must adore you."

As she spoke, the phone book flipped open to the papers she had copied from Casey's little blue book. The BBH entry matched the numbers for Ben Blesdin's home. BBO was most likely the office.

Her next call was to Responsible Maid Services. Their primary qualification was to be able to scour and clean well. They provided on the job training of proper procedures and their customer's preferences. *Sounds easy.* They would be able to see her today.

In the blonde wig, she submitted an application. When the manager verified the driver's license, she was so taken aback by the changed hairstyle that she focused more on questions as to why this girl would cut off her hair, than on the wrong address and name change to Lena Lymch on the document in her hand.

They determined she was qualified, and she listed Karl Slater as her reference, giving them his contact information per their request. *I'll tell him about it later.* They asked when she could start, and she told them that Monday, the seventh would be fine. Her availability was on Mondays, Tuesdays and Wednesdays. They said they paid $2.23 an hour, and insisted it was better than any of the other agencies in the city. Someone would meet her at her first assignment to review the formalities and guidelines.

At The Shuffle Inn in Madison, she informed Karl about her new job, and he promised to give her an excellent recommendation. She told him she also needed another favor, which was to sneak Casey's address book into his top right dresser drawer as soon as possible, and he assured her that he would. She had copied all of the names and numbers and had no further use for it.

"I took it the night you had your skull X-rayed."

"I figured you did. Anything interesting in it?"

"It's been useful," she said.

"Oh?"

"Take whatever info you want before you return it."

Tiny and his crew were in the crowd. She smiled and waved. What surprised her most was to see them on the dance floor until the encore, after which she ran backstage and packed up.

When she and her bandmates arrived at her house, each was consumed by varying quantities of alcohol. Grant commented that her neighborhood always smells of smoke. Ted patted on his mouth and howled, imitating an old Hollywood cowboy and Indian movie. When she asked him to stop, he laughed and wailed louder.

"Get in your car. Go home. Get out of here." He was garish enough for his shrill to penetrate a glass pane, and intrude on a dream. Brash enough to startle a quiet slumber, open tired eyes, grab a clock, and check the time.

When she awoke, she took care of Ebbie and placed a call to Tarick's road crew. She was able to get the phone number of the motel where he was staying. They weren't sure if they should start looking for new jobs. Signal Source's album had major label production, airplay was guaranteed, and the band considered renting an apartment near Sausalito.

She debated whether or not to call him, and since it was two hours earlier, he may be asleep. It didn't matter. He sounded groggy when he said he was happy she called. He asked how she was doing and when her court hearing was scheduled. He said his band was up at all hours working on the soundtrack, making everyone short-tempered. Their producer reorganized a few songs to add more punch to guitar solos and chorus parts, causing the recording process to be more stressful than they had anticipated. His band was required to do a tour after the record was released, which was expected to be next week, if all went well. He hadn't even a slight inkling as to when he could return home.

She wanted to tell him everything she had discovered regarding her neighbors and what had happened to Karl, but instead she asked him to keep in touch.

Already packed for the show, she gave Sam his cleaned clothes, and when she returned from the grocery store, everyone had arrived. The van doors were open.

The chicken wire had crumpled from the weight of the snow, allowing Ted to walk to the burn barrel, and look into it.

"Please stop. Let's get going," said Lexa. She shot a serious look into his brown eyes.

"Why does he always have to burn something?" he asked.

"How would I know? And I don't plan on asking him," said Lexa.

He picked up a handful of snow, and tossed it onto the fire. It began to smoke.

The back door opened, and a man stepped out. His sun drenched, caramel skin was draped over high cheek bones. The silver and black braids alongside his head hung to his chest, and loose white hairs near his neck rippled in the fleeting breeze. He crossed his arms over a tan flannel shirt, and stared at Ted.

"Hi. Just checking," Ted laughed.

"He's misbehaving like a little kid," said Grant, who pulled on Ted's arm.

In the man's dark eyes she saw the kind of pain that had been reflected in her own. Immovable in the icy gusts, his blinks were few, and his breathing was a pulsing stream of vapor into the chilled gray air. Though he said nothing, his body language conveyed his disenchantment. His cold, disconsolate gaze fixated on the perpetrator.

To ask Ted why was futile. Because he felt like it, because who cares – it was no big deal. All was insignificant. Five people in close proximity, the hum of an engine was masked by hostile voices inside the van.

She was awakened by the pounding of a sledgehammer onto a chisel at 7:00 am on Saturday morning. From her bedroom window she saw evenly spaced burning spots in the ground, smoke floating upward from each, and large stakes being pounded into the blackened circles. One wooden support was being set into place. The clinking persisted throughout the day until a rudimentary enclosure took shape. The consequence of Ted's actions were impervious to him, but were felt by Lexa and Sam who were sleep deprived, and in no mood to take passengers to tonight's show. They chose to meet everyone at the venue.

The hammering continued throughout the day on Sunday, until a six foot barricade assured privacy to the new family in the neighborhood. The riff-raff was now locked out. Within forty-eight hours, a wall of lumber denied her view of the snowmen that neighboring children built in winter, the white flowers of the Washington Hawthorn in June, purple and fuchsia lilac bushes, the summer orange daylilies, and the Thundercloud plum tree, which blossomed bright pink flowers in spring and hung onto deep burgundy foliage until fall. She remembered the collapse of the old, drooping willow as it broke piece by piece to the ground. The slats of an immense planked panel had given her property the appearance of a small pen.

Sunday February 6, 1977

As I looked up at the barrier, I realize this is what I have built within myself. The wall keeps out love and pain, kindness and sorrow, beauty and all of the ugly that accompanies it. It's easier this way, to feel nothing. The world cannot hurt the inanimate. I reached for a stone alongside my garage under the snow. My wet, freezing hands hurled it at the fence with every last ounce of force I could muster.

Chapter 7

Monday, February 7 –
Sunday, February 13

She tossed and turned, unable to escape her thoughts of rummaging through Ben's home, and what she would do if she got caught. Besides being fired, she would get arrested and imprisoned. Lexa wished she had a fake driver's license made, like she did in high school. Her ideas swirled as she dressed, took care of Ebbie, locked the door, and walked to the VW.

A police car was parked in front of Roy's house. She caught sight of the brown buzz-cut under the hat of Officer Humphrey, and froze. She backtracked to the front sidewalk and scowled when two cops led Roy, bound in handcuffs, to their squad. He looked at her mournfully. She ran to him, and the police raised their arms to block her.

"Roy, where did you go after you left work that day?" She followed him to the car. They opened the door, pushed his head down, and shoved him inside.

"I stopped at the Checklist Pantry gas station on Sherman Boulevard, but they don't believe me." The door was slammed shut, and his dark somber eyes fixed on her as the vehicle drove away.

Wind blew wisps of the hair under her blonde wig into her face.

A sick feeling knotted up her stomach all the way to the agency, where she received a black and white uniform, and written directions to her first assignment. It itemized where gloves and cleaning supplies were stored, and what each customer had requested for the day. Someone was scheduled to meet her at 9:30 am to check her proficiency and review the policies.

"Will I get to meet any of the other maids?" asked Lexa.

"Usually on Monday mornings we have a group meeting, but we're so busy it'll be on Wednesday this week."

"Thanks."

She struggled to change into the blouse and knee-length skirt when she got into the VW, as she did not plan to return home. She was determined to do a meticulous job in order to take on the cleaning, or snooping of the DA's house as soon as the opportunity arose. Confident that her morning instructional session went well, she zigzagged across the city to get to the four homes.

She fell onto her waterbed when she got home at 5:00 pm and woke up starving at 7:00 pm. The fridge was almost empty. She grabbed an apple, and ate it as she drove to the hospital.

She took the elevator to the rehab area, and was relieved that Earl did not become agitated. Either he was getting used to her, or his memory was failing.

She told Bessie how she witnessed Roy being taken away in handcuffs. Earl seemed to understand, as he frowned and looked downward.

Bessie held her head in her hands. "They had their share of ups and downs, and even on his worst day, he still loved his wife. He worked so hard to turn his life around, but the police don't see it that way. I don't know what I would do if Earl was gone." Bessie saw the look of sadness in her husband's worn, downcast appearance as he raised his left wrist to rub his eye, showing a band of lighter skin. "You miss your watch, don't you?"

He studied her devoted, glistening eyes, the windows to his universe. They were what drew him to her on the day they met, and now held the reason for his existence. So brilliant a blue, he lost himself in them. She would remain flawless into eternity.

"The guys from Allis Chalmers gave him a silver Citizen watch when he retired. It showed the day and date. It was taken the day we were robbed. He loved it. The inscription on the back said, 'We will miss you Earl'. Most of his former coworkers have kept in touch with him." She stroked his wrist. "He was a machinist for fifty-five years."

"Is Earl able to say anything?"

"Just a few words, but I don't know what he's trying to tell me. They've been taking him to therapy every day. I hope he'll be able to talk someday."

"Will you keep me posted on his discharge date? And please think about home care, like we talked about."

"I sure did. He's not going to Ben's house. We never felt welcome there. His prissy wife stopped to see us when we first arrived, but never again. Their chef brought food to us on a cart. The place felt cold and sterile."

Lexa stayed well past the 8:00 visiting hour curfew before leaving. Bessie promised to keep in touch.

Wednesday February 9, 1977

Cleaning duties of picking up toys reminds me of living with my parents, and caring for my sisters Candy and Abbie when they were small.

At the agency meeting today, I met Brenda, the maid who cleans for Ben Blesdin, and told her I will give her a well-deserved break since she is looking so pale and tired. She said she will take me up on the offer, and let me have a go at the snooty DA's house on Monday 2/14. Brenda said Ben and his wife are very persnickety, and to avoid being reprimanded, follow her instructions closely.

Karl says he has had a headache almost every day, and combing his hair is still painful, but he has been persuaded it was caused by a fall. The puppet master's firm grip on the marionettes is evident. He has one hand on their strings, and the other is around their necks.

Ted stared at the fence like a curious toddler who discovered something he had never seen before. Unable to comprehend the new barricade that obstructed his view of familiar sights, he said nothing when he threw his things into the van, as all got ready to leave for the Power Plant in Kenosha on Thursday.

Throughout the night, Grant, Ted, and the roadies received free drinks from Casey, who hauled more gear than usual. A fast set-up and tear down was always welcome since it gave the crew more time to party.

"Grant, what kind of power does Casey have over you? Lexa asked on their drive home. "He's a nutcase."

"He's nice to me, and he bought me a drink. He's not the bad guy you think he is. He deserves to have friends. He's been through a lot of terrible things. He never had a Mom. No one took care of him."

"He's like a slow poison. You won't know what hit you until it's too late."

Most days, she craved some form of caffeine to clear her muddled thoughts. Maybe it was the act of drinking the coffee or tea. It required a degree of coordination, and minimal aptitude. She wondered what was on Roy's tray as she ate an orange and a bowl of cereal. On her way to the jail, she plotted a way to get into Casey's house. No doubt he owned a hammer, but she wanted to scavenge for less obvious weapons. He was getting too friendly with her bandmates, and she couldn't miss another rehearsal. The repercussion would be severe.

The interlocked fence, barbed wire and armed guards instilled a sense of dread as she thought about her possible future. She signed in as requested, and was led to the visiting area.

Roy appeared ill as he discussed his preliminary hearing, which had been on Monday. His bond was set at seventy-five thousand dollars, and his hammer was taken as evidence. She told him of her plans to sift through Ben's home on Monday. He brightened for an instant, to know that someone was willing to take a risk on his behalf. Even his daughters doubted him, and kept his grandchildren away. His sister had numerous excuses as to why she couldn't visit. He knew she also questioned his honesty.

"What some lack in knowledge, they replace with opinions," she said. "Do not give anyone power over you." She wanted to make him feel a glimmer of hope. He nodded and smiled, but it was brief as the guard stepped in and led him away. His head slumped and he stared at the floor.

She raised her voice. "Believe you are able to rise above the despair you feel at this moment." Once more he curved his lips upward, and he turned towards her as he shuffled into the gray hallway. If he was innocent, the truth does not necessarily prevail, and he had a strong likelihood of facing prison walls for the remainder of his life.

She made a quick stop to see Earl. He could be in his house by Monday if home care was arranged. Lexa spoke to a nurse who said it was being set up. Bessie planned to be firm if Ben attempted to intervene. She said that her husband would improve the best in his home.

Lexa breathed a sigh of relief not to see Casey at the club in Kewaskum that evening. Skilled at placing a wedge between her and her bandmates, he had become like fingernails scraping down aluminum. The arguing during the drive home put her at ease. Buckled into her seat, she mimicked what spilled out of each mouth with a fair degree of accuracy.

She knew Ted would begin his rant about the smell of fire when he wandered outside, and Grant would add his two cents worth.

"Ted, I'm going to kick your ass for making a howling noise while you pat on your mouth." He giggled when she said she meant it. As car doors slammed, and engines revved, she surmised his wife Debra had married him for his good looks far more than his inane behavior. Ebbie, who was one of two puppies from their dog's litter, ran back and forth between her snowy boundaries after sitting in the van for the past several hours.

Floating down were minute, glowing flecks of ash. Lexa ran to catch one in her gloved hands, and like a firefly, she watched as the radiance faded. She placed both of her hands on the fence and closed her eyes.

She made her way up the stairwell, and onto to the landing to view dancing ribbons of heat. Mesmerized by the whispering, crackling flames, she felt peaceful, as though she could sleep. In the darkness, she saw eyes flickering at her, as if he knew she was there. Neither spoke.

As though she was in a snow globe, white crystals sifted to the ground, settling into layers of glistening, white gauze. Her eyes followed the streams of fire until frozen numbness pierced her skin, and wet hair stuck to her head. Snowflakes sizzled as they drifted over the intense heat.

Lexa gulped down a cup of coffee, and sipped on a second cup when she awoke, to clear away the fog that accumulated in her head through her night of scattered sleep.

The Checklist Pantry gas station was located on a busy intersection. The aisles had a variety of snacks, soda, motor oil, and washer fluid. She browsed through radios, cameras, and clocks, when a compact Panasonic tape recorder caught her attention. They also stocked cassette tapes. She paid for gas and the two items.

She asked the clerk if anyone had seen a man who was seventy six years old, about six feet tall, had black and silver hair, and was well-built, yet lean, like you wouldn't want to take a punch from him. He was there about a month ago. The day shift cashier had just started last week, and the manager was not available. She asked if he knew of anyone else who might have seen this man, and stressed that his life depended on it. The clerk pointed to a camera positioned in an upper corner, aimed toward the customers.

"Technology has come a long way. How long has it been there?"

"No one said anything about it, or how to use it, but the manager should know. He'll be here on Monday."

"Thanks for your help," she said.

As sound check ended at Zivko's Ballroom in Hartford, the silver timepiece on Karl's wrist glinted in the lights.

"Did you get a new watch?"

"Yes. Nice, isn't it?"

She took a closer look. "Yes, it's nice. Was it a gift?"

"Yup." He smiled.

"Your dad?"

"Nope," he said, and headed to the bar.

She cringed at the sight of Casey joking alongside everyone, especially Karl. No doubt his ability to make everyone laugh had given him a degree of control of these men. They were drawn to his charisma, but she saw through his ulterior motives. His dance and dialogue to lure victims into his web had been mastered. She had to get into his house, and would dress as a blonde-haired man. Tomorrow, her plan was to masquerade as a maid to search for clues to maintain her integrity. No way was she going to become a prisoner. The wig had become a valuable asset.

Sunday February 13, 1977

Sometimes it's hard to live with those who we know well, let alone in harmony with strangers who are an earshot away. I hear chanting, smell fire, see vapors, taste smoke and feel isolated from someone so close.

On our drive home this evening, I asked to take a closer look at Karl's silver watch. I flipped it over and etched on the back were the words, 'We will miss you, Earl'. My heart raced when I asked him who Earl was. He said he had no idea, but guilt was written in his eyes.

Earl's words, "He did it," rang in my head repeatedly. You may think you know someone, but all you see is a facade, and on the inside is boiling lava. You never know when it will spill over and destroy everything it touches.

Chapter 8

Monday, February 14 – Sunday, February 20

Ready to head to her second assignment of the day, stabs of fear gnawed at her . She envisioned all of the innocents around the world who had been incarcerated, and she refused to allow this to become her fate.

The freezing rain locked her out of the driver's side. As she double checked Ben Blesdin's address, the paper fell onto the snow and the ink smudged. She crawled through the passenger door, and bumped her knee on the stick shift. Her head hit the rear view mirror, dislodging the blonde wig and maid's cap. During stops, she readjusted and pinned them both. Unable to find the house, she drove through the area three times trying to read the numbers. Most were unreadable from the road. When she proceeded toward the mansion to park, her tires spun out on ice, and the VW rolled toward the street. She was stuck at the end of the driveway.

Finding the key in a lock-box, fumbling for the correct digits, and getting into the front door was a relief even though she was a half hour late.

At 11:30 am, all drapes were closed, giving a dreary dimness to every large room in the home. Following Miss Brenda's instructions, she found cleaning supplies and gloves, and emptied the kitchen trash into a larger bag, shoving all small salvageable pieces of paper into her apron pocket.

She stripped bedding off of the five beds in the upstairs rooms. She opened drapes, turned on all the lights and searched through and under dresser drawers, bathroom and kitchen cabinets, as well as the refrigerator and freezer on the first floor.

Two of the queen-sized beds had been slept in, and were in separate bedrooms. While linens whirled in the washing machine, she moved on to dusting, and vacuuming the basement.

On her knees, she checked all edges of carpeting but none felt loose. In each room, she groped under bureaus, nightstands, chairs and tables. Before she replaced the sheets, she pulled up mattresses and checked under the beds.

She dragged the vacuum to the second floor. The five bedroom, six bathroom residence had a living room, dining room, a pool table in a game room, a wine cellar in the basement, and steps leading to an outside deck and swimming pool. Nearest to the door of the game room was a hot tub. She was unaware that a District Attorney made enough for a house like this, but his wife was a model and maybe her family was well off.

At the top of the stairwell hung a large portrait of a woman who was dressed in a black ball gown, jewels flashing around her neck and ears. Long, wavy light brown hair draped to her chest. In her paltry uniform, Lexa felt twinges of envy as she peered behind the ornate frame.

In what was most likely Ben's room, she headed for the two drawer nightstand beside his bed. The rollers on the top drawer were so smooth, his Walther PP pistol and two boxes of bullets almost fell on the floor. She opened books, and shook them out, sifted through his dresser, pockets of jackets in the walk-in closet, and glimpsed at two ticket stubs to the 'Pink Panther Strikes Again' movie. She emptied the garbage in his bathroom and the bin near his bed, snatching any notepaper, and checked the back of all picture frames. Behind a

99

framed print of Claude Monet's Charing Cross Bridge, was a combination lock safe.

Bending to check the underside of a chest of drawers, secured to inner part of the leg closest to his bed was a small key, held in place by overlapping tape. She dared not remove this until she could replace it as she found it.

In another room, teal sheets and a bedspread had been left in a heap on a matching shag carpet. She dragged them to the washing machine, and returned to what appeared to be his wife's room.

As she opened drawers, she spied a photograph sitting on the dresser, of the woman from the hallway portrait, dressed in a green evening gown, standing near Ben. On the back was a date: 1/8/77. She fanned through cashmere sweaters, and took a folded, white receipt lying under a sparkling, green garment.

The large walk-in closet was full of size four dresses, designer gowns, slacks, jeans, tops and sweaters, several in each color. On racks were boots and shoes of every style and hue, size eight. Beside almost each set of shoes sat a matching handbag. She peeked into each purse, and within the dark fabric of a black Gucci bag, a silver lighter glinted.

On a nearby wall, a rack contained every shade of necklace, bracelet and bangle. A 12 inch by 12 inch black metal safe on an adjacent wall had a combination lock. *It must be where she stashes her diamonds.*

Lexa tucked clean linens and blankets into the bedframe, and went to empty trash near a mirrored vanity stand, as well as garbage from the bathroom into a larger bag. Other than an old razor, cotton swabs, tissues, and discarded make-up, most receipts were torn and crumpled. She straightened them out, and tucked them into her pocket. There were no cigarettes anywhere in the mansion, or in any of the garbage bags she had emptied.

Her tasks completed on the upper floor, she ran downstairs to the den where she hoped to find tape in a large wooden desk. On the desk top sat a Tiffany lamp, an empty ashtray, a clock, and an antique pen holder. One of the pens was labeled Primary National Bank. The top center drawer was locked. Behind the desk, a wall was lined with books, most of which involved law. She opened all of the drawers. In the top right was a Sig Sauer pistol, and pushed to the back were four boxes of corresponding bullets. The drawers below it held an assortment of pens, pencils, sharpeners, erasers, paper clips and rubber bands of all sizes, as well as bills due and previously paid bills, but no tape.

She banged the desk drawers shut and ran to the kitchen. While raiding every nook and cranny, she found aluminum foil, tore off a piece, and continued ransacking until she caught sight of the same smooth tape. The moment she touched it, a burly man entered the room, holding two bags of groceries.

"Who are you?" He demanded.

"I'm from the cleaning agency. I'm having a terrible day. My instruction sheet ripped, so I couldn't read it." She held up the remnants of the torn receipts.

"Oh, I should have known by how you're dressed. Where's Miss Brenda?" he asked.

"Took the day off." She smiled. "I'll return this in a bit."

She was told to leave by 4:00 pm and it was now 4:05, but she wanted that key. Lying flat on her stomach to reach under the dresser, she slowly removed the tape until the small gleaming metal came loose in her hand. The number 306 was stamped at the top. Footsteps creaked up the stairs, and voices were nearby. She pressed both sides into the foil and returned it exactly as she had pulled it off.

She shot up to grab the vacuum, pulled it into the hallway and passed Ben, who walked into his room.

"Where is Miss Brenda?"

"She's resting today," replied Lexa, who bent her head down.

"Oh, please give her my regards."

"Yes, sir."

She returned the vacuum to the closet, and walked toward the kitchen where the cook prepared dinner, the aroma of which wafted into the foyer. *Garlic mashed potatoes, sirloin steaks smothered in mirepoix, and fresh asparagus,* she thought. There was one final task to accomplish. She edged closer to the kitchen, and heard a female voice discuss the different techniques for searing and tenderizing meat with the chef. The woman poured a glass of wine.

As Ben's footsteps neared, Lexa grabbed her coat off of a dining room chair. He gave her a curious look as he walked into the kitchen and spoke to his wife. "Hello, dear."

"Who is that, and whose horrid car is in our driveway?"

"Miss Brenda is ill," said Ben. "I expect this maid to leave soon."

Lexa slipped her arms into her coat. Her right hand in her pocket clutching the tape, she contemplated keeping it, when the beautiful couple retreated to the den. She turned around, held up the tape, smiled to the chef, and placed it into the drawer.

"Have a good night." She ran outside into the bitter cold.

Despite rocking the VW from first gear to reverse, her tires spun, and she was going nowhere in the darkness. She pulled a blanket off the back seat, kicked it tightly under the rear wheels, put the car in reverse, tapped her foot on the gas, and freedom brought immense relief. She tossed the soiled wool covering into a heap on the floor.

Her head felt sweaty and itchy under the wig. She threw it onto the passenger seat at the first red light. The man in the car beside hers stared in amusement, as she untangled her long locks. They made eye contact before she sped off.

At home, she opened the phone book and jotted down the number and address to the locksmith she had used in the past. The shop closed at 5:00.

She changed her clothes, grabbed an apple, and drove to the Checklist Pantry gas station. The manager had left thirty minutes ago, but was on tomorrow's day shift schedule. The young man she spoke to had never touched the camera, and in the year he worked there, no employee had gone near it. No one was given the responsibility of checking it.

"What if you need the police?"

"We call them like we always do."

"Don't they ever ask to see the film?"

"Nope."

She sighed. *It is most likely there as a deterrent.* Still, she thought it was worth her while to talk to the manager. She paid for a sandwich, and headed to Bessie and Earl's house.

Relaxing in a chair, Earl said "Hello" when she walked in. His wet, freshly combed black and silver hair smelled of Herbal Blossoms shampoo. Though he needed complete assistance to wash up and dress, Bessie was happy with his progress. Both knew that recovery would be a long haul. Though ten new words were a part of his vocabulary, he was not able to form a complete sentence. Bessie seemed to understand him. She was pleased with the nurse who visited daily to teach her how to hook up the tube feedings.

"He belongs here, in his home. It's where he is happiest."

"I agree. Have you heard from Roy?"

"No, but Ben said it's not looking good for him," said Bessie.

"Have you asked him about assisting Roy?"

"He said the deck is stacked against him. Years ago, Roy had his dark side and lots of folks remember it. He had stints in jail, drinking and family problems, and everyone saw how Doris turned him around bit by bit. She's his second wife, and theirs was a love story of tolerance and forgiveness. He did some heavy drinking when his girls were in high school, and Doris had to send Melinda away because of him, but he's been the best these past five years. His daughters are happily married, and he's become a doting grandpa who babysits as often as he is asked to. Earl has been a little jealous."

"Lots of people stumble through a little hell. It doesn't mean they plan to kill someone."

"That's true. Earl had a broken nose when I met him. He's six years older than I am, and my parents didn't want me to marry him. They referred to him as the-loose-cannon-waiting-for-a-fight. Doris told me her parents cried on her wedding day."

"When is Roy's trial?" asked Lexa.

"I'm not certain, but as of now, the evidence is sufficient enough to put him away. I overheard Ben on the phone. He said the coroner estimated the time of Doris death to be roughly 4:30 pm, which is usually when Roy gets home from work, but he didn't notify police until after midnight. They think he waited because he needed to sober up, and he had something to hide."

"It doesn't make sense. You said he stopped drinking. If he cared about her, he was distraught. When I was a kid, I was heartbroken on the day my dog died. We took turns petting him and kept him overnight. If heaven forbid, Earl passes on, would you be in a hurry to get him out of your house?"

"No, not really. I think I would lie next to him for as long as I could. I believe Roy is innocent. "

"I agree. See you soon. Call me if you need anything." She buttoned her coat as her feet crunched across the alley to her house. She pulled out a number, picked up the phone, and dialed. When a woman answered, Lexa asked for Kalie.

"Hey girl, it's Lexa. When do you want to get together?"

"I'm not sure. I've been seeing my boyfriend a lot. He hates night clubs. He takes me shopping and buys whatever I want, and we go to expensive restaurants. Yesterday, we ate at Pieces of Eight, and he made sure we had a beautiful view of the lake."

"It sounds romantic. Do you see him often?"

"About twice a week, and he promised it will be more when he leaves that wife of his."

"We should go out and party."

"Are you free on Wednesday evening?" Kalie asked.

"Yes I am," said Lexa.

"A night club is fine. I haven't danced in a while."

"How about the Stone Toad? I can meet you at 9:30 pm," said Lexa.

"Okay, see you then."

Relieved, she opened a can of clam chowder, heated it up, and ate as she watched television. She set the bowl on the floor, and fell asleep.

She grabbed her clock when she awoke at 4:00 am. Still wearing jeans and a black sweater, she realized she had a couple of hours before she would have to change into the uniform and leave. She set her alarm, and closed her eyes.

On Tuesday upon leaving her cleaning assignment, she drove to the Checklist Pantry gas station and asked for the manager. A muscular young man with shoulder-length brown hair emerged from a back room. She introduced herself, and asked about the security camera. He said he never touched it.

"Why is it there? Someone must know how to use it."

"Probably the owner. He set it up."

"How can I get in touch with him? I may need to subpoena the film. It's urgent."

"You'll have to leave your number. I can't hand out our staff's personal information."

She wrote it down for him, and returned home. As she reached into her pockets to remove the contents and wash the uniform, she discovered all the receipts and papers she had stashed.

On the kitchen counter, she laid them flat, and like a puzzle, she pieced and taped the pieces together. Some were for razors, men's shirts and socks, cosmetics, clothing and accessories from Marshall Fields, each a different date. One that was legible and folded flat was from Diene's Dress Shop for an emerald gown priced at $105.00, dated January 4th, six days before her arrest. Her eyes widened, and her brows arched. She fumbled for her keys and drove to the Capitol Court shopping mall.

There were numerous apparel stores, and the dress shop was wedged between a shoe store and a book store. A short, stocky woman gave her a dirty look as she browsed the aisles.

"I already told you we will not give you a refund for a stained dress. If you do not leave, I'm going to call security."

"You know me?"

"How can I forget how badly you treated me?"

Lexa gave her a big smile. "When was I here?" Her hair was a mess from being under a wig all day, and her make-up was smudged.

The woman's gray eyes scanned Lexa up and down.

"You were here last month."

"What did I do?"

"What is going on? Is this some kind of a joke?"

"No. I have a sister who is spoiled rotten, and I often clean up the messes she leaves behind. She annoys everyone, especially me. Can you believe she sent me here today? She had the nerve to ask me to return a green gown she wore. So disturbing…a dress she sweated up, and now she wants her money back. I told her it's not my problem, but she said she wouldn't babysit my daughter anymore if I didn't. Plus, she," Lexa feigned tears into her eyes. "I can't discuss it. I get too upset." She sniffled repeatedly.

"Oh…yes she was here alright, and made quite the fuss, she did. Got all the customers riled up, and they walked out. I hope she never shines around here again."

"When did this happen? Is there a record of it somewhere?"

"I can check. She made such a scene; I'll never forget it. She's the kind of person who must be used to getting her way. Hmmm, let me see." The gray-haired sales clerk sifted through receipts and cards in a rectangular, metal file box. "She was in here on Monday, January 10th. We made a note of it because I was afraid she would try the same stunt with another salesperson."

"I think I remember reading about a fire in this mall on that day. Was it this store?" asked Lexa.

"Yes it was." The woman looked at Lexa suspiciously. "What are you saying?"

"My sister has done many bad things, and once again I have become involved," she said as she looked at the floor, and released a quiet sob.

"You think she started the fire?"

"Yes, it's something she would do, if she can't get her way. But I don't have any proof, do I? The receipt she gave me doesn't verify anything. If this situation goes to court would you be willing to testify?" A tear rolled down Lexa's cheek.

"You want me to go to court?"

"She convinced someone that I did it. If I bring a copy of her photo, can you identify her?"

"Oh, she's not easy to forget. She looks a lot like you."

"A person should pay for the bad things they do, even if it's your own sister. I need to get her to change her ways, or she may move on to committing more appalling crimes," said Lexa.

"How awful, you poor thing."

"You've been a huge help. Please write down your name, and I have the number for the dress shop on this receipt. I'll be in touch."

"Your sister needs to be punished for what she did."

"This is a courageous thing you are doing Ethyl, and I truly appreciate it." Lexa again forced her eyes to water.

"Now don't you fret about it, dear."

"It's Lexa and thank you," she said as she left. *Hopefully I can get the waitress to testify.*

Lexa wrote down the woman's information, and added it to the paper where she had copied the contents of Casey's address book.

She dialed the listing for MK. Too tired to come up with a story, she hung up, folded the secret numbers multiple times, and shoved it inside of a dictionary in her living room bookshelf. She realized it had been almost a month since she sat in the corner near the heating vent.

She fried up chicken breasts and added fresh vegetables. When she answered the phone, Tarick asked why she was never home anymore. He had tried calling her what felt like fifty times. He sounded upset. She gave him the details about the new job she had taken which began last week, cleaning two to five houses a day. He asked if her band wasn't doing well and she needed the extra cash. She said she would explain in person, when he's not paying long distance rates. If she really needed money, she would go back to work as a nurse.

He said his band was under contract to ABC-Paramount records, and though he was ecstatic, he and his bandmates had new worries. He made it clear to everyone involved on his tour that he needed to serve as a witness for her at her March seventh court hearing. He asked if she ever considered moving out west. She said she would enjoy a visit, but her family lived on a waterway in Florida and if anything, she preferred to move closer to them. His band was booked at different hotels during the tour, so he wasn't sure of the best way for her to contact him. She congratulated him for being signed to a major record label. He said he wished they were together before they hung up.

She realized how much she craved him. She found Ebbie, who had been in the living room, and pet her from head to tail. As Lexa cuddled with her pup, Ebbie licked her cheek, and they fell asleep on the copper-colored carpeting.

On Wednesday, she finished her cleaning assignments early enough to get to the locksmith. She added a flare of drama when she explained how she had misplaced the original, and was frantic about losing it. He said the impression appeared clear enough to make a duplicate key, as he poured Plaster Of Paris into the form.

"I'm glad I made that template," she said.

"I'd freak out if I lost the safe-deposit key for my bank," he said as he held a hair dryer over the white solution.

So that's what it is. "Thanks. You are an excellent locksmith," she said, mesmerized by his skillful hands which ground out the nickel silver, and designed the shiny metal device. *I may have to visit the Primary National Bank later this week, posing as Ben's wife.*

She paid him, affixed the new key onto a ring, and left with the curiosity as to what this would allow her to discover.

At home, she confirmed her plans with Kalie, and took a nap before dressing and waiting at the Stone Toad. Kalie arrived ten minutes late, and Lexa offered to buy her a drink. They sat at a table, and sipped on rum and Cokes to wait for the band.

"Does Ben visit you at your apartment?"

"I live with my aunt. At least until Ben and I get married."

"Do you have a date set?"

"No, he plans to get divorced soon. She's getting on his last nerve. He can't take it anymore."

"You said you met Ben in court. Was he your lawyer?"

"No, he was the DA for the prosecution, but he cut a deal on my behalf, and a few days after my trial, we started going out."

"It must have been love at first sight."

"Yea, he's gorgeous. And he's rich. He's going to take me out on his boat this summer."

"You said he pays you to do things for him. Is that your occupation?"

"He got me a day job at a law firm as a receptionist and typist, but he pays me to keep an eye on certain people."

"I suppose he wants to watch the people he has to go up against in court."

"No, I have to track a few people who work for him."

"Yea, I can see why he wants you to watch over Casey."

"What? How do you know Casey works for him?"

"You told me the night you saw my band. You said Casey was angry because Ben pays you more."

"I said that?"

109

"Yes. He got drunk out of his mind when he partied with my bandmates, and was banned by one of the clubs. Do you feel safe around him?"

"I don't fear anyone. I pack heat."

"You'll look sweet in orange."

"My good friend will get me off. I don't worry about it."

"If Ben can't take care of it, you'll get locked up. Don't let him convince you that you can get away with murder."

"Why the concern for me?"

"Why not? You would do the same for me," said Lexa.

"Uh…sure," she said as she sipped her drink. As soon as the band began, she stood up and walked to the stage, leaving Lexa sitting alone in her seat.

After ten minutes, a large man sat in the empty chair.

"Can I buy you a drink?" he asked.

"Tiny, what brings you here?" she asked.

"Do you know that girl very well?" He raised his blonde eyebrows.

"Not really."

"She's trouble. Don't get too close," he said.

"I take it you've crossed paths with her."

"You are correct. She has a long rap sheet and has been in and out of jail," said Tiny.

"So you're aware she is seeing the famous, pretty boy DA on the sly," said Lexa.

"Yes I do. I'm on an assignment, and I don't like what I'm seeing in either her or that DA." He squinted his dark blue eyes.

"I'll keep your advice in mind since I don't like either of them, and yes you can buy me a vodka tonic."

He got the drink for her and left. Lexa waited for ten minutes until her new friend returned.

"Why didn't you come up there?" asked Kalie.

"You never asked me. I love to dance."

"Come on, let's party."

"Sure," said Lexa as she set her glass down.

As their outing came to a close, Lexa put her arm around Kalie's shoulder and pretended to be drunk. "I'll bet you can't wait to marry Ben."

"Well, there are some things I need to do first. He wants me to behave, stay away from drugs, and go to college. He's going to pay for it because he wants a smart woman, not a dumb one like he has now."

Lexa choked on the last of her drink, and set it down. "When are you starting college?"

"I'm already taking an evening class in statistics."

"I'm impressed," she said as they parted ways. "Stay in touch."

"Yea, sure, said Kalie."

I don't care what you do. Ben was in my neighborhood on January sixth to check on his parents, the day Doris was murdered, and if she uncovered his affair, he may have gotten rid of her to keep her quiet.

Lexa wasn't amused by anything her new friend said except that Ben was going to cover the girl's college tuition. When Sam had asked her to drop out of nursing school, she refused. Why this man would pay hefty university fees for his girlfriend seemed odd. Spreading their thighs was expected, cooking was presumed, and higher education was usually discouraged. What was he up to and why did his future partner's schooling matter to him? Did he see some kind of potential in the disturbed girl?

On her way home, she realized she did not have to be up early to clean anyone's house, not even her own. She also pondered how much longer she intended to keep her mundane day job now that her main reason for doing it had been accomplished. As her mind wandered, she saw Casey in her bed looking down at her. She almost hit the brakes in the middle of the road. *What an odd premonition, and it better not happen,* she thought.

She pulled up the collar of her coat as she snuck up the outside stairwell to view the nearby fire for a few minutes. The flames danced higher than usual. Her neighbor's head was bent downward as though he had fallen asleep. She watched the blaze for ten minutes when he looked upward in her direction. She was not sure if he could see her in the dark, but she knew he sensed she was there. She tiptoed down each step, and had the first good night's sleep in what seemed like ages.

On Thursday afternoon, Lexa crossed the alley to visit Earl.

"Come in," said Bessie. "I can't believe how well he's getting along. He can button his shirts now. I'm shocked. He can pick up a spoon and feed himself and the doctor told me we can cut back on the tube feedings when he eats a little more. They want to do another swallow study, but he hasn't choked even once in the past week. I really think it's the herbs our neighbor has been giving Earl."

"Herbs? What are you talking about? Which neighbor?"

"The nice man behind our house gave it to me on Monday after you left. The one who watches the fire."

"How did you meet him?"

"I took the garbage out to the alley, and I saw him in his garage. I said 'Hello' and we got to talking. He said he was a tribal healer and he offered me some of his medicines. Earl has nothing to lose, so I mixed it into his food, and as of today, I am already seeing improvement."

"What made you trust someone you don't know?"

"His eyes are filled with compassion and kindness. He said he once had a good friend named Earl."

"This is great news. Ben must be relieved."

"He says he is, but he hardly ever stops over. At least he calls every couple of days."

"Does his wife visit?"

"Why do I feel like laughing? The only person she loves is herself and her mirrors. And her clothes, her shoes, her jewelry, her make-up and Ben's money."

"Isn't she a model? With her looks, she must pull in a generous income."

"After she married Ben, her sole focus is how to spend his paycheck."

It could be why he needs his side jobs. "Well, she must make him happy. How long have they been married?" asked Lexa.

"They met five years ago. Within four months he was engaged, and the wedding was planned so fast, we thought she was expecting a baby. Her parents wouldn't speak to me or Earl at the church or reception. Whenever I went near them that day, they turned up their noses and walked away. We haven't seen them since."

"There are many people who find a trophy to display at parties and social events."

"Yes, but he's my only child, and I miss the Ben I once knew. He became a DA shortly after he got married."

The Ben you thought you knew wasn't any nicer than he is now. "Sometimes no matter how hard we try, things don't work out the way we want them to. What's most difficult is accepting it," said Lexa.

Bessie offered Lexa a cup of tea, and as they chatted, she noticed Earl's attentiveness. He seemed to follow their conversation. He even interjected an occasional word or two.

When she left, as she crossed the alley, smoke fluted upward from the burn barrel. Through the unyielding bitter temperatures, the heat of his fire flared each day. She often wondered why he kept this constant vigil. He would not be sitting in the cold dancing over burning rubbish. It was the first thing he set up when he moved in three weeks ago. Maybe this was a practice by tribal healers, or perhaps he stoked an eternal flame to serve as a reminder or commitment to something.

Karl did not wear his new watch when the band performed. He was quieter and more distanced from everyone, and Casey did not make an appearance. She hoped he had moved on to harass another musical group.

On Friday, she contemplated wearing her best clothes, curling up her hair and walking into the bank, but she broke out in a cold sweat, fearing she could find herself in more trouble. She decided to follow

Ben's wife, and have an accidental meeting to get a perspective on what she was like.

Lexa dressed, brushed the short curls of the blonde wig, and drew a few moles on her chin and cheeks. She took her Leica Rangefinder 35mm camera, stashed the Panasonic compact tape recorder into her large tan shoulder-strap bag, and headed for Ben's house. As she waited down the street, she rested a map on her steering wheel. Her Volkswagen stood out like a bicycle in the middle of a highway. This was a neighborhood of Cadillacs, Chrysler Imperials and Mercedes, not a dull gray VW. In summer, the Porches and Corvettes made an appearance. As cars drove past, each driver frowned upon her, making her feel more edgy.

She spent an hour in the cold before the baby blue Lincoln pulled out of the driveway at 11:15 am, and she made sure to keep a reasonable distance. The large car was easy to keep in sight, and the lady she pursued drove as though she had all day to reach the Mayfair Mall. Parking far enough away not to be noticed, Lexa took a separate entrance from the woman who wore a calf-length fur coat.

The first stop was the makeup counter. Lexa pretended to look through the nearby luggage, and as she spied on her target, she watched the woman stuff a tube of lipstick into her pocket and walk to the designer dresses.

Lexa pressed the record button on the tape recorder and hustled up to her. "I'm a scout for the newspaper. We're looking for the prettiest lady in the city, so we can do an article about what her day is like. It's a human interest story. Would you like to be on the cover of the 'Lifestyle' section of the paper?" asked Lexa.

"Why yes, I'm flattered."

"I couldn't help but admire your beauty and I knew you were the perfect candidate for this story. I'll need a few photos to bring to my editors, so give me your favorite poses."

Lexa snapped six pictures. "These are amazing. You must be a model."

114

"I used to be, but my husband prefers for me not to work. We attend a lot of parties."

She stopped the tape. "Well, let's get your name and a number where we can reach you, and if my editors like what they see, we will notify you by next week. I'm Martha by the way." They shook hands. "Martha Feldschneider. Your gorgeous face is perfect for our story."

Her twenty minutes with Ben's wife gave her a good inkling of how to portray her at the bank. Almost slipping on a patch of ice as she ran, she took a few more captures of the woman walking to her car. She hurried to the developer, and asked for six 8 x 10 copies of every shot. In her VW, she mused about how to appear to be two inches taller when she went to the bank.

When her bandmates arrived, she finished packing and took her seat in the van. She had no desire to speak to Karl, suspecting he was guilty of theft. His help had been valuable, and without him the band would be fractured. Resigning from the group crossed her mind throughout the night. Her bassist a lying robber, Sam was a two-faced philogynist, Ted was an adult child, and Grant could not keep anything personal to himself. Despite their flaws, each was an excellent musician. Each experienced the elation of a packed audience that hung onto their every move as though they possessed some kind of magical gift. All had the ability to connect with a total stranger because of the universal language known as music.

She called the dress shop when she awoke. Ethyl was not scheduled to work this weekend. Lexa assembled the 8 x 10 photos in a folder along the side of her bookshelf for easy access. She checked her cleaning assignment for Monday, and mused over the five houses to be scoured. Her own home needed cleaning, and mail had not been opened in weeks. She went to the post office to collect what had been delivered to the band.

Saturday evening was almost torture. Casey slathered his toxic charm over everyone except for her, and she payed particular attention to Karl's avoidance of him.

115

"These clubs are getting old, aren't they Karl?"

"It's not too bad. At least the crowds are good, and our original music goes over well."

"What's the deal with Casey? Why does that dude keep bugging us?"

"My guess is that he wants to be first in line to be my replacement. And I've been furious about all the things he's been saying to undermine me."

"Like what?"

"He told Grant he can top my harmonies, and he can keep a better tempo than I do. Ted says they're best friends. They said they need to rearrange the set lists, and add different songs. He's become indignant toward me because I refuse all of his invitations, but I don't trust him anymore."

"Maybe we can get him off our backs by finding something incriminating in his house. We have to find a way in," she said.

"I'm up for it. When?"

"As soon as we can figure out when his dad is out of town, and when he'll be out for at least an hour." Her brow wrinkled. "We'll invite him to another rehearsal, and show up an hour late. I'm sure my brother might need a babysitter, and you could have a headache. We'll stagger our return times," she said.

"It works for me."

"His job involves sporadic day and night hours depending on what instructions Ben gives him. Living with his dad allows him to keep all of his earnings, and it accounts for why he drives a new cherry red, two-door Chevy Laguna. I'll bet he's loaded."

At the end of the evening, Casey said he was too drunk to drive home, and needed to spend the night in the upper flat with Drax and Sam. They told him he will get a sleeping bag on the floor as neither had any intention of relinquishing their beds. Lexa locked the door at the bottom of the stairwell, and fell asleep.

In the early morning, she was kicked out of a dream by a heavy presence on top of her body. She opened her eyes. A faint light streamed through the shades and curtains. Casey yanked the comforter downward as she reached to the side of her bed, and grabbed the sword. She smacked the sharp blade into the side of his neck.

"What the hell? What are you doing?" he asked.

"You should answer the same question. Where did you find the skeleton key to open the lock? How many drawers did you loot?" She pushed the sharp edge into his skin.

"You bitch! I'm bleeding." He reached for the sword.

She gripped it with both hands. "Get off of me. Why are you in my bed?"

"I thought you'd want to have a little fun."

"What made you think I had any interest in you whatsoever, you arrogant punk? You don't respect women. I've had a few chats with Roy. Your mother left your dad because he broke her heart. He cheated on her. I don't care what Daddy told you."

"Yea, whatever you say."

"Get out of here, and I better never see you here again. And you better hustle," said Lexa.

As he swung his arm to slap her, she slammed the sword into the side of his neck a second time.

"Get the hell out of here! Get away from me! Stop!" Her piercing scream whipped across the walls.

They fought for control of the sword. Blood dripped down his chest as they struggled. She rocked the waterbed side to side to throw off his balance. Both maintained their grip on the handle. He pounded on her hands, but she refused to let go. He began to choke her, and when she struck his shoulder causing another cut, his obscenities echoed up the stairwell, which drew footsteps to the base of the stairs.

Drax and Sam twisted the locked brass knob and pounded on the thick door.

Sam's kicking wafted throughout the house. "Open this damn door!"

Lexa continued to wail, "Stop it. Get off of me!"

There was a brief silence at the doorway, followed by the metal pins being hammered of out of the hinges.

When Drax and Sam caught sight of Casey in his underwear straddling Lexa and fighting for the sword, both of them grabbed his arms, and pulled him off.

"Dude, take your things and get out of here. Get out. You better figure out how you're getting home," yelled Drax who pulled him up the steps. "None of us are gonna help you."

Feet pounded up the inside stairwell, and within five minutes the upper door banged shut. Footsteps trampled downward. She got up to make coffee, and bent down to pet Ebbie, who whimpered. Lexa comforted her until she was calm, and let her outside, but kept a close watch over her before letting her in to feed her.

Sam and Drax met her in the kitchen.

"Do you guys want some coffee?"

"Sure. I didn't believe him when he said he was too drunk to drive last night. But I thought if anything happens to him, I would feel guilty, so I let him stay," said Sam.

"I did more damage to him than he did to me." Though the fight lasted only minutes, her arms felt heavy and sore.

"Oh yea, we saw the blood oozing down his neck. He's really flirty with women when he hangs out with us. He has no problem attracting them once they see his new car. He's pissed 'cuz you blew him off," said Drax.

"Be prepared for revenge," she said.

At the end of the night in the dressing room, Lexa approached Karl.

"There's been a game change. Casey won't be at any more rehearsals after Sam and Drax pulled him off of me this morning. He knows what our vehicles look like. Can you borrow someone's car for a few hours next week?"

"I'll ask my brother."

Sunday February 20, 1977

Is there a dichotomy inherent in all humans who become confused on the paths of right and wrong? Karl paid my bond, got me out of jail, and gave me a glowing job reference. Yet, he robbed a man at knifepoint, pushed him down a flight of stairs, stole a watch, traumatized him and caused a stroke. He lied to me, not that I expected him to be honest. What else had he taken during the robbery? The clothes he has been wearing look brand new.

My perception of Casey has become clearer this week. I believe he pretended to be passed out in the middle of the road, knowing one of us would approach him. It was a planned ruse that got him involved in every aspect of our lives. Most of his stories are lies, and he will stop at nothing to get what he wants. He uses anyone who is naïve enough to allow it, and I think he is taking steps to be rid of me and Karl so he can have his version of a perfect band.

Roy's colorful past includes incarceration. Why have I offered aid to someone I know so little of? Eulogies are a glorification of the life of the dead. Doris could have been a murdering psychopath, and they still would have dug up and resurrected her redeeming qualities.

Chapter 9

Monday, February 21 –
Sunday, February 27

Lexa slept for four hours, dressed, made coffee and two sandwiches before leaving for Responsible Maid Services' main office to pick up her schedule, and hand in her resignation. She explained that her last day would be a week from Wednesday, which gave them ample notice to find a replacement. They expressed their disappointment, and asked if they could keep her name on their roster in case she had any future availability. As she looped across the city, by her fifth assignment, the muscles in her arms and legs felt heavy, and as dusk set in, her only thought was to get home and tumble into bed.

She discovered the smashed window on the side entrance door as she unlocked it and stepped over the debris. Nothing appeared out of place in the rest of the house, and no other windows were broken. It would have been difficult to crawl through the small, shoulder-height opening. She swept the shards into a bag, and secured plastic where the glass had been. She could see her breath. If it was a random burglary attempt, the intruder was stopped by the deadbolt lock. Now a key was needed on the inside as well as the outside.

Exhausted, she bundled up and left to find an open lumber store. Upon her return, she nailed up four plywood boards, and caulked the gaps. She thrashed in her bed, unable to relax. Her house was being targeted. Her binoculars and camera nearby, she took extra precautions to gain an advantage on further intrusions. The 3" pin was still in place. She took the night vision goggles out of the box, and looked out of each window. Smoke fluted upward from the fence to the left. Bessie stood near her kitchen window washing dishes, holding a doleful garden of faith in her eyes. One of the neighbors staggered out of a Plymouth Satellite, and zigzagged to his doorway.

In between her cleaning duties on Tuesday, she removed her wig, brushed out her hair, and ran into Diene's Dress Shop. Ethyl Macmillan had no problem making a positive ID of Ben's wife. Lexa flipped on the recorder. "Do you mind being taped?"

"I guess so." The clerk studied the color print. "You look a lot like her. I remember her mink coat. I mean how can you miss that?"

"So you're sure that it was this woman and not me who had been in your store on Monday, January tenth?"

"That's what I said, isn't it?"

"This will go to court on Monday, March 7th. To follow protocol, I will have a subpoena sent to your home," said Lexa.

"Is that common practice in situations like this?"

"Yes, but it's just a formality, like an invitation to a party. It's a reminder of where to be, and what time to be there."

"But I have to work on Mondays."

"Your employer must honor this, and allow you to appear in court. Your testimony is valuable. It could save my life," said Lexa.

"I'll discuss it with my boss."

"I have to pay for your transportation, and any expenses."

"Okay. I guess I'll see you on March seventh."

Lexa flipped the tape off, and wrote down Ethyl's information.

At her house, she picked up the phone and dialed the number for MK. A deep male voice answered.

"Hello?" The laughter of children playing wove through his greeting.

"Hello, this is the lady who does your wife's hair, and I need to change her appointment. Her name is Mary, right?"

"No, it's Melinda."

"Oh. My apologies, sir. I'm getting everyone mixed up. We've been so busy these days. Everyone wants their perms and cuts. Some still want to look like Twiggy, some want to look like Cher, but your wife is one of our prettiest customers. She doesn't copy anyone."

"Thank you. Wait a sec, I'll get her."

Lexa hung up. It was a coincidence that the woman had the same name as Roy's daughter. Casey was her cousin. There was a strong likelihood that she was on his harassment list.

On Wednesday the twenty-second, upon finishing her maid duties, Lexa headed to the jail. Ten pounds had faded from Roy's once strong build. Weariness was in his walk, and his head hung downward. He had not shaved his beard, or combed his hair.

"I know there's no point in asking how you are," she said.

"Talk is cheap until you get an invoice from your attorney. I fired him." He closed his eyes.

"Unless you've gone to law school, you'll need legal expertise."

He cleared his throat. "I'm going to die in here. They're threatening to kill me. They serve us tasteless slop, and I'm getting weaker and sicker by the day." He spilled his words onto the floor, and watched the letters lie at his lead-filled feet. "The snoring is so damn loud; I can't sleep. They can all go to hell in here. Every last one of them. Why are you here?"

"I may be able to help you."

"Unless you have seventy-five thousand dollars to pay my bond, you're not gonna help me. No one can. I'll end up rotting in here. I don't care anymore."

"I'm about to end up in a penitentiary, and I have better things to do, but I found something that could benefit your case. Do Melinda and Casey get along?" she asked.

He blinked and looked up at her. "I…I doubt it."

"I took his little blue address book when I snuck into his room. She's one of his contacts."

"That slimy weasel. He better not hurt her."

"He works for Ben, who may have put him up to something."

"Damn it. Ben got Melinda…" He stopped speaking and stared at the wall.

"He got her what?"

"He…got her pregnant when she was in high school. Doris and I cried so hard over it. My daughters started fighting like witches. I couldn't stand being in my own house. There was no peace in my home. Then they all stopped speaking to each other. I thought about killing Ben every day, but he wasn't worth it." He held his hands over his face. "I should never have told you that."

Earl and Bessie have a granddaughter? She silently gasped. "What happened to the baby?"

"She gave the little girl up for adoption. Melinda was seventeen. It was nineteen years ago. We were never able to tell them or anyone else. You didn't do that in those days. We hoped Ben would do the right thing, but no one ever spoke of it, so we never said anything. Melinda went to live at my sister's house. We helped them financially until my sister got a job and back up on her feet. She liked Melinda. She said it's what she needed to stop feeling sorry for herself. They were supportive of each other, since they were both betrayed. Earl, now he's the kind of guy who you could count on to give you the last penny in his pocket if you needed it. It's a shame his son became a vain, disgusting, egomaniac." His somber dark eyes stared into space, as though he sat in a confessional waiting to hear his penance. It was evident he was breaking down, and his vulnerability stirred the room.

He closed his eyes, and turned away. "I wish I killed Ben when I had the chance. My life would be perfect. None of this would have happened. None of it. I would be a free man. I would be babysitting for my grandchildren, and have my wife at my side."

123

"I don't like Ben either. We need to figure out a way to get him. Are you up for it?"

"Oh, you better believe I am."

"What is Melinda's last name now?"

"It's Krenik."

"When you discovered that Doris was gone, why did you wait so long to contact the police?"

"I wanted to lie beside her for as long as I could, before they took her away from me. I also needed to know if she was raped."

"Was she?"

"No, she wasn't, and the coroner confirmed it, which is another reason they blamed me. Other than Ben and Casey, I can't think of even one person she disliked. Friends called us almost every day. Just when my life got the best it ever was, someone took it all away from me. I'll bet it was Ben. He has been sticking it to me ever since my girls grew up. It has to be him."

"As of now, your goal is to help me come up with a plan to give him what he deserves in the worst possible way."

His lips curved upward. "I've got nothing better to do. While you're in here, all you have is time. Time to think. When I find out who killed my wife, they're gonna pay."

"Don't let them get to you in here. Doris wouldn't want that. When I see you again, we'll discuss your ideas."

He smiled, and was led away.

On her drive home, she realized he was rapidly deteriorating. She parked her VW and rang Bessie's doorbell.

"Hi, I won't be long. I stopped to tell you that I'll be sending subpoenas to the witnesses who need to be present at my trial. You'll be getting…"

"Come in! You have to see this. Earl, look who's here."

"Hi…Lexa," he said.

Her eyes widened. "Hi Earl. When did your speech return?"

"To to…today…ay."

"This afternoon, I turned on the TV, and Gilligan's Island came on. All of a sudden, he blurted out their names and repeated them. Then I held up silverware and he named which utensil I had. His words are slurred, but I can understand him. It the happiest day I've had in a long time," said Bessie.

"Are you still giving him the same herbs?"

"Yes, I am. At first, I added it to the tube feedings, and now I've been sprinkling a spoonful over his breakfast every day. It's like a miracle."

"Can I see what you're giving to him?" She followed Bessie into the kitchen and took a sniff into a jar of fragrant, crushed, dried, greenery. "It smells like a combination of leaves, roots and flowers, but it's not anything I've come across before. He's a kind man to help Earl."

"Yes, he is."

As Lexa crossed the alley, she knew there was more to the medicinal ingredients her new neighbor shared. Though she did not understand his words, his incantations had significance, and she had seen him dancing near the fire. It was the combination of all, that Earl was the recipient of.

Through the door, she heard the phone ring. She hoped it was the owner of the gas station. When she picked it up, she was happy to hear Tarick's smooth voice which she felt as attracted to as much as his face and body. He had bad news. The producer was not willing to send his band home by March, because of the popularity of the songs from his record being aired by local radio stations. Three of his tunes were getting frequent airplay. He sounded distressed, but she reassured him that her witnesses should be more than sufficient to prove her innocence.

"Be happy your band is tasting success. Savor it. Don't let what is happening to me keep you from enjoying fame. It's fast and fleeting."

"I wish you were near me. I want to taste your lips and feel your skin," he said.

"You will. It's a promise, and take care." she said before hanging up.

She paced across the kitchen floor. She could not recollect the fake name she had given to Ben's wife when she had spoken to her at the store. She dialed, and was relieved when Miss Brenda answered.

"Hello, Blesdin residence."

"I'm a scout from the newspaper. Please see to it that Mrs. Blesdin gets our message."

There was a slight pause. "Okay."

"The pretty woman story will not be undertaken by the newspaper due to conflicting interests."

"Yes, ma'am."

It was 4:00 am on Thursday when an idling engine caused Lexa to peek behind the curtain of her bedroom window that faced the alley. She was unable to distinguish the features of the person who walked around her VW. *You think I'm asleep like everyone else in this neighborhood, don't you?* She held the night vision goggles over her eyes and the individual came in almost clearly. It looked like Karl, but she knew better. It was someone who looked close enough, but lankier.

She observed Casey's every move. He used a stick to push something under her car. He knelt down to let the air out of her tires, returned to his vehicle and left.

My, my, you creepy little sicko. Whatever it is that you're up to, I'll out-sick you, out-crazy you, and out-last you. The difference between us is that I have integrity, and now I'm onto you.

She grabbed her keys, opened the garage, plugged the air compressor in and filled the tires. Shining her flashlight in the middle of the undercarriage, she saw rags on the ground. A strong smell of gasoline emanated from under her car. She returned to the garage, used a rake to snag the tattered cloth out, and ran to her kitchen for plastic gloves and bags. She knew that eventually the gas would

126

dissipate. The smell nauseated her as she scooped up handfuls of snow into the sack. She tossed her gloves into it, left the wet bags open to the cold air, and returned inside. *You have no idea that I'm a raging insomniac. Thought you could get away with this, didn't you?*

When she awoke at noon, she called Karl. "We need to sift through Casey's things. When are you able to borrow a car?"

"My younger brother will let me use his beater on Saturday."

"If we're going during the day, we'll need disguises."

The gasoline smell wafted through the vents during her drive. She browsed the aisles of a thrift store, made her selections, and set the bag of clothes on the passenger seat.

Outside of the Primary National Bank, she sucked in a deep breath and opened the door. She memorized the faces of three tellers, two brunettes and a blonde, and a gray-haired man behind a desk in a large cubicle. When he looked up at her, she turned around, and left. *I'll see who's here tomorrow and prepare a spiel for Saturday,* she thought. At home she organized what she would wear on stage tonight.

The taste of blood saturated her lips when the alarm awoke her on Friday, and crimson smears dripped onto her hands. She grasped her face on her way to the bathroom sink, and pinched the bridge of her nose. The bleeding stopped within a few minutes. She showered, dressed, and headed to the courthouse for the scheduled pretrial conference.

She was informed that the original prosecutor had recused himself and a special prosecutor will stand in his place. When Ben Blesdin reviewed the reports, her not guilty plea, the name of the man who ID'd her on the evening of her arrest, and that she had no lawyer, he stifled a laugh, which alarmed her. **His mother was her primary witness, and each time she attempted to speak up, he spoke over her.**

"Where are your subpoenas?"

"I…I'm filling them out this morning. Your mother is…"

"Do it now," he interrupted. How many do you need?"

127

"Three, sir. But your…"

He tossed the papers at her; she filled them out per his insistence, and he studied the names which included the waitress at the restaurant, Ethyl Macmillan and Bessie Blesdin. The judge asked if Lexa had any questions, and she froze, feeling the heat of Ben's nasty glare. She was told to mail the forms today.

At the Checklist Pantry gas station, she asked the attendant who kept records of employee's schedules and in particular who worked on January 6th. She was told it was the owner. She left her phone number. A few minutes to spare, she met her bandmates in the van, and dozed on the way to the club. When she returned home, she threaded the safe-deposit key onto a piece of twine, tied it tightly, and it fell to the center of her cleavage.

On Saturday morning, she stared at herself in the mirror, relieved that her facial bruises had been long gone, and wore her highest platform boots. At the top of the stairwell, she asked Drax for a splash of his Brute Royale aftershave. Though he appeared confused, he handed it to her, and watched in bewilderment as she slathered it on.

Back downstairs, she curled her long hair, and put on extra eye make-up. She hung her Leica camera around her neck, and adjusted the strap so it rested on her navel. She pulled a long sweater over her head, and stuffed a small pillow under the elastic waistband of her leggings. The camera pressed against her skin. When she turned sideways, she appeared to be pregnant. She generously doused Wild Lily perfume on her wrists and neck. Her eyes watered, and the combination of the smells was repulsive. *Perfect.* She drove with the window partway down and the air vents on full blast to diffuse the overwhelming scent.

None of the previous employees she had seen were there. The older man who had sat behind the desk was replaced by a twenty-something short-haired blonde in a dark suit. She approached him to request the location of the safe-deposit boxes. He sniffed, furrowed his brow, and his face contorted. He backed away from her.

128

"I need to hurry. I don't feel well." She grabbed her stomach and let out a loud gag.

His eyes widened. "I have to look up the number of your box, so I can check if you have access."

"Well of course I have access! I have the key, don't I?" She protruded her chin and gagged loudly. The two tellers looked up, and all of the customers gaped at her. "I need a garbage bin," she said loudly. "I'm going to vomit. Right…now." She moaned and groaned. She rocked back and forth holding her bulging belly.

"I need to authorize…" His eyes widened as she heaved. He loosened his tie, and handed his garbage bin to her.

"I told my husband I didn't want to come here today because I'm sick, but NO, he wouldn't listen. Said he was too busy to come here himself. Can you believe it? What is wrong with him?" She writhed, clutched her stomach, and pretended to retch into the bin. The customers and tellers stared at her, looked at each other and at the young man as if to say, "Don't hassle her. She's going to puke again."

"Follow me, ma'am."

"Thank you." She hyperventilated, pulled two tissues out of her purse, and held them over her mouth. "I have been terribly queasy all morning." Looking back at him, she smothered a fake dry-heave, gave him a dirty look, and he left. She stood before box 306, checked to make sure she was alone, and opened it.

Four files were tied together with string. The knot would be easy to replicate, and she took them apart. One contained a list of addresses of abandoned buildings. She took three photos of each page. Another folder was labeled: Kalie Deckler. It held her birth certificate, listing the mother as Melinda Kemke and the father's name was blank, as well as adoption papers, a few grade school photos, a high school picture, and a copy of her high school transcript. A legal document was a trust fund which had been set up for her. The third file contained Earl and Bessie's will, and an insurance policy taken out on each of them for one million dollars. Ben's life of leisure was within his grasp.

129

The fourth manila folder contained a brown address book filled with contacts from A to Z. Inside, on a separate paper was a list of seven names, and corresponding phone numbers and addresses, three of which were Harold Humphrey, Kalie Deckler, and Casey Relmen. Lexa had more than ample film to get clear close-up shots.

She pulled her sweater down, held her protruding stomach, bent forward and thanked the young man when she left. "I'll be sure to tell my husband what a great help you have been."

He gave her a half smile, bent his head down and resumed working.

The VW fan on the highest setting, upon her return home, she showered, threw her clothes into the washing machine, and changed her appearance. Karl was due over at any minute. She ate a sandwich, and the doorbell rang. She slid her arms into the dark gray coat from the thrift store.

"Is Lexa here?"

"Karl, it's me."

He took a second look at the person wearing the short-haired blonde wig, combed and hair-sprayed flat, the way Sam had worn it when he was a cab driver. She wore young men's shoes and a man's coat. Her eyebrows were thickly penciled, and she had no eye make up on.

"You look like a creepy, girlish, boy."

"Maybe someone may take pity on me. And look at you, mister tan-plaid-jacket-and-brown-striped slacks."

"They're my brother's."

She took a few magazines and they left. He started up a car which spewed, vibrated and rattled at 80 decibels, more like a B-1 bomber airplane. The heat didn't work, and the upholstery was ripped.

When they rang the doorbell at Casey's house, a beefy, gray-haired, brown-eyed man in a dingy t-shirt answered. Both looked up at him.

"We're from the boy scouts. Would you like to buy a subscription to Look, Life, or Parade Magazine? We have some samples…"

"No." He slammed the door.

"Do we look like we're boy scouts?" Karl asked on the way to the car.

"Not really, but it was worth a try."

"There's a chance we look a little too bizarre for someone to purchase anything from us. We need a new strategy," he said.

In the crowd at the show that evening, glued to Ted and Grant was Casey. Wearing a loose, V-neck t-shirt, the dried scab remained on his neck like a badge he made sure to display. Most likely he avoided a truthful account of how he acquired the cut.

"Karl, I'm buying," she said. "What are you drinking?"

"Fill something up with whisky."

"That bad of a day?" she asked.

"My brother accused me of busting his muffler, and says I have to pay for a replacement. My dad believes him, and got on my case. Then he nagged me about the ten grand I borrowed."

"March 7th is a little over a week away." Fear rippled through her at the thought of her hearing not going well. "Both of us could use an attitude adjustment."

She wasn't sure which of them became more inebriated. They were glad to have Sam drive home. Karl's engine revved when she stumbled to the door. Sam overheard a loud laugh.

"What's so funny?"

"The note I'm reading," she said.

"It says, '*You are dead*'. That's not funny," he said turning the paper toward him.

"Yes it is. Casey is a moron. He doesn't scare me."

"What happened to the window?" asked Sam.

"I swept it up a few days ago. You like my repairs?"

"Uh…it's a bit messy. We should get a new door. Are you okay?"

"Petty idiots don't frighten me," she said.

The inside of the house was glacial, and she could see her breath. She was glad Ebbie traveled with them. She checked the heat settings and felt a strong draft as she walked to the door of the front entrance facing the street. The window was knocked out.

The porch light did not flip on, and jagged remnants hung where the bulb had been. Glass had shattered onto the concrete doorstep. She gathered up plastic wrap and clear packing tape, and placed several layers of tape and plastic over the opening. She hammered an old blanket to the door, turned up the heat, and gulped down an Ativan. Her suitcase containing her 45 caliber pistol, night vision goggles, and camera, was set within reach, and she crawled into the warm waterbed.

It took four cups of coffee to help her feel clear-headed on Sunday. She dropped the film off for one-hour developing, and asked for six 8 x 10 copies of each photo. She sat in her car viewing them, and contemplated on her best choices to guard the extras. Karl was trustworthy, and Tiny, who owned a safe, was not easily intimidated. Her drive to the lumber store was futile. An orange 'closed' sign hung in the window.

At her kitchen table, she wrote out instructions as to what to do with the pictures in the event of her disappearance. They were to go to any investigative reporter at the newspaper and every newsroom in the city. The DA's secrets splattered across the headlines would make a sensational scandal.

A week from tomorrow the evidence she presented would either lock her up or absolve her of a felony. She rested her head on her arms, wishing Tarick could add his testimony. She never chewed on her nails, but found her thumb in her mouth, and was biting on the last remnants of the fingernail. She rubbed her shoulders, dialed the number for the waitress, and identified who she was.

"I don't remember who the hell you are, and there is no way I'm setting foot in any courtroom."

"Lady, I've known my share of cowards and losers, and you are one of them." She slammed the phone down, took a deep breath, and dialed to speak to Ethyl Macmillan.

"Hello? It's Lexa. How are you?"

"Now listen here, I don't want any more trouble. Leave me alone. Don't you dare ever try to contact me again, or I will notify the police, and report you for bothersome behavior."

"But what happened? You said I'm not guilty." The line went dead.

The dress shop clerk, who had so eagerly been on board, jumped ship. *He doesn't want his wife in jail. They can all go to hell.* Exposing anything she had discovered in the safe-deposit box without getting chopped up concerned her. She sensed who was behind the crumbling of her subpoenaed witnesses.

She pulled her coat around her shoulders, as she took the short walk through the alley and into the unlocked chain-link fence. She rang the doorbell, and knocked repeatedly, but got no response. It was not like the Blesdins to be gone for so long. She would return tomorrow. Tonight she had to get ready for a show which lasted until the wee hours of the night.

Sunday, February 27, 1977

I live in the sand tower I've built and the winds are picking up. Someone is sabotaging my trial and my witnesses. Since both lack a conscience, Ben Blesdin and Officer Humphrey are strong candidates.

The smashed glass on both of my doors and the 'You are dead' message does not terrify me the way someone has intended. My performance at the bank has given me information beyond what I could have imagined. I must use it wisely.

Ben has used his power and influence to find Kalie. So, she's not his lover. He's keeping an eye on his daughter, who has a striking resemblance to Bessie. My guess is that she

133

discussed our night out, and he is aware of what she has said to me. Perhaps his parents have mentioned my name to where I am becoming a deep thorn in his side. I wonder if he has warned them all to stay away from me. Did he pay Kalie to get rid of Doris, or did Kalie do it on her own to protect who she believes is her rich lover - her future husband?

The improvement of his father's health will delay him from amassing his fortune, but I'm certain he plans to intervene.

When we opened the van, the cool night air was filled with the scent of pine bark. I was drawn to a fire like a moth to light. The flames are his consort, his vigil. Something is in it that only he can view. He sees his forefathers ride through plains on wild horses, and how they use the stars as their guide. He knows how nature is intertwined in their spirits, and how swiftly it is vanishing.

Chapter 10

Monday, February 28 – Sunday, March 6

She grabbed her buzzing alarm, unable to bring the numbers and black lines into focus. Four hours of sleep made it difficult to arise and function.

She picked up her assignments for the week at the main office. Today and tomorrow there were four homes to get to, and on Wednesday, three. Mr. and Mrs. Harold Humphrey's name was listed at the top of today's assignment. A sick feeling in her gut overcame her. She asked the receptionist if they were regular customers.

"No, we've never cleaned for them. Mister Humphrey asked for someone with a name similar to yours, but he described you really well. He said his friends highly recommended you."

He wants to see who shows up. "Before I started here, one of your former maids warned me about him. She said he hid in the bedroom, grabbed her, pulled her uniform off, and groped her. He threatened to get her fired if she told anyone. I am not going anywhere near his place."

"Are you sure?"

"Yes, I'll never forget his name," said Lexa.

"Do we need to advise him to take his business elsewhere?"

"It's up to you, but keep close track of who you send. I'd hate to see one of your employees get harmed or even worse, disappear."

The scheduler appeared shaken. "We'll tell him no one is available."

She feared that Harold Humphrey also knew about her invasion of the safe-deposit box. She sensed she was being tailed, and kept her eyes on the rear-view mirror more than the road.

Upon completing her work for the day, she parked her VW on the concrete driveway beside the garage, ran to the Blesdin's door, pounded, and rang the doorbell, but no one answered. Roy's home looked deserted, and his walkways had not been shoveled.

She approached her back entrance at 6:00 pm, and a note was posted.

Where are you? We need new doors. Sam's van was gone.

She walked up the stairwell and taped up her response. *I worked at another job all day making a few extra bucks to pay for new doors, X.*

She had used an X as her signature ever since she took on the stage persona of Lexa Loxx. She scraped out the last of the peanut butter, ate a sandwich, changed her clothes and left for the grocery store.

As the ignition fired up in the dark, large hands arose from behind her and clenched her neck. The grip tightened in increments. In her lifeguard training, she had seen swimmers pass out after three minutes without air. She began counting. In excruciating pain, her throat was caving in. Her lungs burned for the taste of oxygen.

Consumed by fright, she pulled on each thick, clenching finger, and tried to turn sideways to free her neck. Unable to release the massive steel prongs enveloping her, she fumbled for the 3" pin along the side of her purse, dreading the inability to find it. Obstructed carotid arteries pulsated into her temples. Dizziness set in. She was nearing blackout. The pressure inside her neck made her retch. She pulled out the pin, and carved up the flesh, wrist to knuckles, that dug into her. A deep scream pierced her ears, and she was free. An uncontrollable deep wheeze filled her lungs. The back door opened, and footsteps crunched down the alley. She sat motionless, panting, regaining her breath.

Lightheaded, all she could see in the darkness was a large male body under a bulky jacket and black ski cap. The engine still idled.

Whether he meant to scare or execute her, made no difference. She intended to even the score on her own. Her breathing heavy, she closed the VW doors, and staggered to the market. Ripples of pain in her neck brought flashbacks of when she was choked in high school.

She was relieved to see the yellow van in the garage. She took all of the bags into the house, and headed for Sam's flat.

"I've been working an extra job, but I'm done as of Wednesday."

"I picked out new doors, and someone will be here tomorrow to install them."

"I won't be here. Will you be able to let them in?"

"I suppose. I see your new job involves deep neck massage. Or mangling."

"What?" She touched her skin and it felt raw. His bathroom mirror reflected the bruises and red scratches from her chin to her clavicle. "I had no idea."

"Are you in some kind of trouble? Is that why our doors are broken?"

"Someone has been harassing me ever since I rescued Karl."

"Anything I can do to help?"

"Getting new doors is good. Do they have windows?"

"No, but they have peepholes. I think we should call the police."

"Really? After all the times they've been here, they'll see our address, and they won't take us seriously. We are not on good terms."

"What about the 'You are dead' letter?" he asked.

"The one they'll accuse us of writing? The one they'll spend the rest of the night laughing at?"

"What about your neck?" he asked.

"You know they'll blame you."

"Forget it."

"Yea, that's what I was thinking." Once in her flat, she grabbed the file from the bookshelf. Harold Humphrey's address, which she was given today, matched the one on Ben's list.

She dialed Karl's number.

"Hi. There are two places we need to get into."

"What are we looking for?"

"Murderers and arsonists. How soon can you be here?"

"Tonight? You want to go out tonight? I'm half-asleep. I have the TV on. It's cold out."

"Is your head fully healed yet?"

"Give me a half hour."

While she waited for Karl, she took all but one of the folders filled with photos, and taped them to the underside of her wash tubs beside the washing machine. She changed into a tan ski suit, and swung her small backpack around her shoulder. Karl arrived wearing all black.

"It's snowing. You'll be easy to see," she said.

"Aww, come on. I'm not going home to change. Let's go. What the hell happened to your neck?"

"I'll explain later," she said as they got into Karl's car. She gave him directions to the officer's residence. "By morning, our footprints should be hidden by fresh snow. Check your rearview mirror to make sure we're not being tailed."

They parked down the street, and cut through neighboring properties to view the back windows. The kitchen appeared spotless, and through it, she could see a dining room. Beyond that was a living room. They walked around the house, and curtains obscured their view. In the front, a narrow opening in the drapes exposed Mr. Humphrey, who sat on a recliner. His feet were elevated, and a bag of pretzels sat on his lap from which he grabbed, and chomped on. The back of his hands were bandaged. Mrs. Humphrey sat on the sofa, and both watched television.

"Let's go" she whispered. "Watch your step." In his car she asked, "Did you see the bandages on the big guy's hands?"

138

"Yea, so what about it?"

"This bungalow was on my list to clean today, but I refused. I'm guessing it didn't sit well with him. A large man hid in the back seat of my VW, and tried to strangle me. I sliced up his hands a little while ago. Guess who I think it was?"

"What are you going to do?"

"Find something incriminating. Dig up one of his secrets. Expose him. By the way, I need you to hold on to a file. If you have no idea of what's become of me, take it to the newspaper. Give it three days, tops. I wrote instructions out. Do you have a good place to hide it?"

"I can put it in a box in the locked storage area of my basement."

"Drive around this block twice, and watch the shape of the car's lights behind you. Slow down a little, and then speed up." He gave her a strange look. "Do it, please." She faced the back of his car. "And we're being followed. How fast does your Malibu go?" she asked.

"I haven't taken it past 100 mph."

"Backwards? Gun it!"

He threw the car into reverse, and the car behind them backed up. Karl focused on catching the car that had pursued him. The darkened vehicle ran a red light and narrowly escaped being hit by oncoming traffic. Blaring horns echoed into the night. They stopped and watched momentarily.

"Let's get the hell out of here." He hit the side streets at fifty miles an hour and wove through alleys until no headlamps shone near them. It was 11:00 pm when he stopped down the street from Casey's residence.

"I know how to get in through the bathroom window. Wait outside, and I'll let you in."

She opened up the back door. Karl stepped inside of the kitchen and looked around.

"Shhh...his dad is here, and he's asleep."

"Are you serious?"

"He takes Seconal. If we're quiet, he won't hear us."

"Until he pulls out his gun and kills us," said Karl.

The inside of Casey's home was in disarray. For as neat as he appeared on the outside, was as slovenly as his house was on the inside. Dried food was spilled on countertops, and grimy dishes were piled in the sink. She found two phone numbers on a folded piece of paper near the receiver, copied them on a paper towel, and shoved it into her backpack. She opened the refrigerator, stuck her hand under food, and pushed containers around.

"What are you doing? Are you hungry?" asked Karl.

"Keep it down. Look through odd hiding places; see if he stashed money, drugs, or whatever. Go check out his bedroom."

Lexa rifled through his freezer, under chairs and the sofa, his bathroom, and spare bedroom which was piled high with laundry. In the hall closet, was a metal chest containing an assortment of tools and a hammer, but it was clean. She stuck her gloved hand around the perimeter of carpeting throughout each room, except his dad's.

Karl was on his hands and knees reaching under Casey's bed. Scattered on top of his dresser, were gold chains, a gold horseshoe ring, and a silver watch. Lexa picked it up.

"You gave your watch to Casey?" she asked.

"He gave it to me, but I returned it after you read the inscription. I knew it wasn't his to give away. Earl is your neighbor, isn't he?"

"Yes. I'm pretty sure it's his watch, based on what his wife said about it." Lexa slid it into her pocket. "This puts him at the scene of an armed robbery. No wonder Earl kept repeating, 'He did it'. He thought it was you." She opened drawers, saw the address book she had taken, and seethed at finding white make-up and purple lipstick. "This explains why we thought he was dead in the road back in January." She held up a handful of M-80 firecrackers. "Either you were his target at Century Hall, or he was angry that I forgot to put his name on the guest list."

"It's plausible," said Karl.

She put an M80 in her pocket. "What is Etorphine…M99?" She examined the vial.

"It's an animal tranquilizer, and pretty heavy stuff. Look what was under his bed." He held out a notebook. "Read this."

At the top of a piece of notebook paper, a 'to-do list' was written.

1) Destroy Karl

2) Terrify Lexa - find her weaknesses - make her leave the band

3) Take Sam's guitar. Return it in a week and tell him I found it at a pawn shop.

4) Steal parts of hit songs – work them into originals at rehearsal.

5) Get Ted sick with laxatives– give him something to make him better.

6) Get Grant high. Tell him: 'Karl told me he hates you.' Repeat it often.

How to get rid of Karl:

1) flattery – be subtle

2) buy him drinks – get him drunk

3) buy new strings for his Rickenbacker bass

4) suggest new music for band

5) co-write a great song together

6) invite him over

7) serve my special drink

8) injure him

9) plastic gloves

10) large trash bags

11) <u>LANDFILL</u>

"Landfill?" They said in unison.

"Should we take this with us?" asked Karl.

"I don't think so. He'll freak out if it's gone," she said.

"No, he won't. " Karl ripped it out and stuck it in his pocket.

"Let's get out of here. I'm getting nervous."

They locked the back door, and took off in a sprint as a car pulled into the driveway behind the house, and parked in front of the white garage they hid against the back wall of. Stifling their breath, keys jingled, opened a lock, and a latch was secured.

"Did you put his notebook under the bed?" she whispered.

"I...I don't remember."

"His watch and his notes will be missing. He'll be pissed," she said as they walked to the car.

"I don't care what he thinks. It isn't his watch," he said.

"That's not what I'm getting at. It's how he'll retaliate. My front and back door windows were smashed last week. I was choked today, and I almost passed out. You had just left when I read the '*You are dead*' note. He won't trust us. Do you think he saw your car down the street?"

"I'm not sure, but I'm driving backwards out of here," he said.

"The good news is he planned to terrify me. The bad news is that he wants to destroy you. If he finds out I saw his list, then I'll get the body bag treatment. Are you going to show the page you took to the rest of the band?"

"Would they think it was something we composed?"

"Yea, probably," she said.

At her house, she gave Karl a folder which contained photos from the safe-deposit box. "Wait here. I'll get a copy of Casey's plans so we both have one."

Karl pulled the confiscated paper out of his pocket, and realized he had ripped two sheets out of the notebook. The second page had a list of addresses. His apartment was written near the bottom. "No!"

"What?" she asked.

142

"Some of these addresses were in newspaper articles about recent fires. My apartment building is here."

"Casey wants to scare you. You are now onto him." She opened her folder, and set one of the photos she had taken at the safe-deposit box on the table. Five of the addresses matched the properties on Casey's paper. "He must be responsible for these, and the others handle the rest of the sites."

"I'll hide your file at my Dad's place. If my building gets torched, I won't be doing you any favors by keeping your papers there. I should start packing."

"There is another option. I'll use Ben's index of the abandoned buildings they're torching, and I'll write in one of those places instead. I have the same kind of notepad. We'll return his 'to-do' list, and he would be none the wiser," she said. "How about tomorrow night?"

"I…guess so."

"See you later."

She locked the battered door, took a banana off of the countertop, peeled it, took a bite, and opened a drawer. She took out her notepad, set it on a thick piece of clear plastic, sat at the edge of her waterbed and positioned her bedside lamp on the floor. She began tracing the alternate address.

On Tuesday, she called Tiny and arranged a meeting for Thursday morning, the first day each had open. No one answered at Bessie Blesdin's residence. She searched for MK's listing, which she knew was Roy's daughter, Melinda Kemke, now Mrs. Krenik.

"Hello?"

"My name is Lexa and I'm your dad's neighbor. I saw him in jail, and he needs you more than ever. He isn't doing well."

"Did he give you my phone number?" She sounded annoyed.

"No, he did not. He has no idea I'm doing this."

"I'm not going to see the man who killed my mom."

"He's depressed, and he's going downhill fast."

"He's a liar. He took out a two hundred fifty thousand dollar insurance policy against her, and was chomping at the bit for that money. Everyone knows he didn't call the cops until hours after she was dead. He probably needed to sober up."

"When he babysat for your children, did he seem like a guy who might kill someone he cared about?"

"It's how people are. I see it every day in the news. They snap. His job disgusted him. He couldn't stand his coworkers, and complained about how badly the company was run, constantly. He couldn't wait to be out of there for good."

"I think Ben Blesdin, or Casey Relmen did it. There's a girl who is involved with them. There was no forced entry. Your mom would have let any of them in."

"None of them stood to gain anything by her death. Dad did."

"If Doris knew too much about Ben's confidential matters, he wouldn't want that leaked. If she told Casey Relmen off because of how he treats people, especially his mother, he may have lost his temper. He works for Ben, and he may have been paid to do it."

"Listen up, lady. I don't know where you are coming up with all that crap. Dad is guilty as sin." The woman hung up.

On the way to her cleaning assignments, she thought about Roy. *He needs a polygraph test. Why he hasn't had one makes no sense. Or maybe he is refusing to have it done. I should let this go. There is no reason for me to wrap myself up in something that is not my concern. Before his wife was killed, he barely spoke to me.*

When she returned home, she was locked out. A note was taped to the door: *'See me for the new keys'*. She walked up the stairwell.

The steps had become a portal to her neighbor's eternal bonfire. She was in awe of his mastery of it. Fire had innumerable uses. Wherever humans traveled on this planet they brought fire and language, which was a turning point in their evolution. The man below her stoked the ashes and added fresh kindling to revive the flames, as sunlight gazed over the horizon. He looked up at her, and she smiled at him. Sam let her in and gave her the new keys.

"Thanks. See you on Thursday." She walked across the alley.

Again there was no response at Bessie's home, which baffled her.

Karl arrived at 10:00 pm. "Do you have it?"

"Yes. The writing appears identical to his other paper. Your address has been replaced with another building on the list."

"You look like a creepy girlish boy again."

"It's all I've got. Let's go," she said.

At Casey's home, they knocked on the door. No one answered. They did not see his car, and fresh tire tracks had swerved down the driveway.

"Karl, stay here. I'll get in through the window."

Snoring grated loudly as she crawled into the darkened house, and closed the broken lock on the bathroom window. She tiptoed into Casey's room, and searched under his bed for the notebook. She opened it, slipped the two pieces of paper into it, and moved the dirty shoes and socks aside, which covered it. Pleased with herself, she got up to leave.

"Who the hell are you?"

She jumped and stuttered. "I'm, I'm L…Larry."

"What the fuck are you doing here?"

"Your son told me I had to put his shoes back, or he'll kick my ass. He let me borrow them. Do you hear the car? He's waiting outside."

"Oh." The man scratched his head and proceeded to the bathroom. He mumbled what weird friends his son has, and she walked out to Karl's car idling on the road.

"Easy schmeezy. Just do me one favor. Drive around this block twice, and watch the shape of the car's lights behind you. Slow down, and speed up."

"Then drive backwards?"

"Exactly."

It was after mopping the floor, scrubbing out the toilet, dusting furniture, and putting the vacuum away at the last house on Wednesday, that she felt the tethers release on her double life. Living on scant sleep the past four weeks had worn her down. She launched onto the waterbed, and closed her eyes. On the third ring, she picked up the phone.

"Hi, it's Tarick. I knew you were home. It's when I spoke to you last week."

She smiled. "You kept track of that?"

"When you're running non-stop in the string of clubs like we are, it's what's been keeping me feeling some sense of sanity. We're all exhausted. We never sleep much anymore. I have stomach pain every day, no matter what I eat," he said.

"It happens to me when I don't get enough rest, and let stress get the better of me."

"This is like a form of insanity being up all night in clubs for days on end to promote our album."

"We've had that kind of schedule, and I hope we don't have to do it anytime soon."

He elaborated on how worn down his entourage was, and everyone was homesick. The tour had become a nightmare with cords breaking, strings snapping during songs, amps going out, and equipment falling apart. The guys were drinking heavily, and getting testy with one another. He felt like he needed a break, but it was just getting started. He said how much he missed being near her, and promised to take her on another picnic at the beach. She said she was looking forward to it, and they said their good-byes. She closed her eyes.

The pain of hunger was knife-like, awaking her at 3:00 am. Outside, in the cold, dogs barked. Their howls were more agitated than usual. She peered outside, and the beam of a flashlight wove side to side in her alleyway. Through her night vision goggles, she saw who appeared to be Officer Humphrey, hunched forward at the doorknob of her garage. To catch him off guard, she grabbed her camera and ran

146

outside. She snapped two shots, ran toward the front of the tribal healer's house, around the fence, and into his back gate. She hid behind the burn barrel and closed her eyes to calm her breathing.

Footsteps tracked hers, and the stream of light shone in her direction. She picked up a piece of wood, and threw it onto the garage. The spotlight turned away from her toward the sound.

"Damn you! I know you're in here and I will find you. And when I do I'm gonna make sure you never see the light of day again."

The door opened. A large man turned on the light, and pointed a sawed-off shotgun at the trespasser.

"You have two seconds to get out."

"But…"

"One…"

"Wait!"

"Two!" He fired toward the intruder who slammed the gate, and ran into an idling car. Tires squealed down the road.

She shivered, having sat on frozen ground without a coat, and looked at the man in the doorway. Their eyes met, he nodded his head, turned, and closed the door. She knew she was no longer safe. She ran to her home, packed clothes, her gun, important numbers and addresses, one of the folders, the night vision goggles, an alarm clock, and food into her tan suitcase. She left a note for Sam to watch Ebbie.

She tossed a blanket over her shoulder, and headed to the Sound Sleep Motel, a place where the beds would not console her, being engrossed by the web in which she was tangled.

When her alarm sounded at 7:30 am on Thursday, she collected her things, and left for the one-hour photo developing store.

She requested six 8 x 10 copies. As she waited, she pulled out the two phone numbers she found while ransacking Casey's house. One was someone she had never heard of, a judge named Edward Ehlichs. She recognized the name and information of Thurston Tinsky, the man she had an appointment with in forty-five minutes. She considered cancelling, but changed her mind.

147

She examined the pictures. The look of surprise in clear focus, the back of the intruder's hands were scraped and scabbed. Casey's notepad documentation was as clear as the original.

She opened the foyer door, and waited on one of the ten chairs, the backs of which were lined up near a large window. Long streams of traffic headed in opposite directions. In the corner, a plastic green plant did little to add to the bare décor.

When Tiny invited her into his office, she looked up to a man who filled in almost the entire doorway, and would never need amplification. She had no idea why she had hired him as her bodyguard. He was as inconspicuous as a ketchup stain down the front of a white shirt. The dark paneled room surrounded them with posters of Queen, David Bowie, Jethro Tull, Led Zeppelin, The Ramones, AC/DC and The Clash. Even in the dead of winter, he wore a denim vest over a white, short-sleeved T-shirt.

"How can I help you?" he asked.

"I'd like you to keep something in a locked safe. It won't be for long. If anything happens to me, there are instructions in it of what to do," she said.

"Who did you piss off now? You get yourself into trouble, and then expect someone to bail you out," he said.

"What some lack in knowledge they replace with opinions. I hear you're keeping busy these days. Casey says you work for him."

"You came all the way out here to discuss something frivolous?"

"He blabs about everything when he's drunk, and he gets so crazy. And it doesn't matter where money comes from, does it?"

"I don't discuss cases I'm working on," he said.

"I have a photo of someone trying to break into my garage. Maybe you've seen him." She handed him the two pictures of Officer Humphrey's startled look as he held the doorknob.

"Why should I know who this is?"

"I said you may have seen him. He's got some high-powered friends in our community, like Judge Edward Ehlichs and Ben

Blesdin." I'm sure you've heard of them." She searched his face for clues. He made no eye contact.

"Everyone knows who they are. Big deal."

"Will you lock my folder in your safe? And rough up a bully?"

"What if I can? What are you asking me to do?"

"When people come to you with situations like this, don't you throw out a few suggestions? You're the one with the expertise here. I want Humphrey to leave me alone."

Tiny threw the file on his desk and leaned back. "This guy has the entire police force behind him. I don't get messed up in stuff like that." He shut his eyes and ran his hand through his wavy, chin-length blonde hair. "Anyone who is stupid enough to cross that man is dead. I'm not touching it."

"Then my time here has been wasted." She snatched up the file and slammed the door. She needed someone to help her and fast.

On the way to her car, a slow moving white Pontiac Grand Prix drove down the alleyway. She made note of the chrome bumper, body shape and square tail lights. If it had not been parked near the front roadway when she first arrived, she may not have been suspicious that this could be the same vehicle that Karl chased in reverse.

The Pontiac idled down the block, making it difficult for her to see who was behind the wheel, or if there were passengers. She was able to outmaneuver an undercover police vehicle in September, but was unsure if this driver would follow her through the Union Cemetery. The VW was able to fit through two granite grave markers when she had last eluded captors, but the recent snowfalls had buried anything familiar. Still she thought it was worth a try, to find a route which was not wide enough for another vehicle to fit through.

Though it was out of her way, she drove eastbound. In her rear view mirror, the pursuer kept a short distance. She drove in, waiting to be followed, but the white car lingered outside of the entry way. The entrance and exit were one and the same. Most likely the driver knew this, which made her escape easy. She headed towards Hopkins St., drove down an embankment, over the sidewalk, and onto the road.

At the Primary National Bank, she asked the gray-haired man for a safe-deposit box. The monthly fee was minimal, and she locked up one of her manila files. She asked where his blonde co-worker was, who worked on weekends, and is about twenty-five years old.

"Did he sit at my desk?"

"Yes. He helped me in the past."

"He is no longer employed by this bank."

"Oh…may I please have a small white envelope?"

Outside of her brother Nathan's house, she wrote directions to the bank and which gentleman he should ask for. She dropped one of the two keys into the envelope, and sealed it. He was at work, and his wife who was a hairdresser, was at her salon. On the outer envelope, she wrote out: 'I love you', and slid it into the opening at the bottom of his garage door. In the event that she might not live through this day, she knew that either he or his wife Polly would read her words, and pick it up out of curiosity.

No doubt by now, her stalker realized she wasn't visiting a deceased relative, and followed her tracks through the snow.

Her stomach growled fiercely as she drove home. She locked her VW in the garage, and ran down the basement steps to check the remaining folders. All were still held in place by clear packing tape. She untied the twine around her neck and added the second key stamped 575, and secured it to the underside of the tubs. The court hearing on Monday made her realize she had to find Bessie today.

At the Blesdin's home, Bessie answered when Lexa knocked on their door. "I'm relieved to see you. Come in. I tried calling you at least twenty times. You're never home, are you?"

"Not much," she said.

"You look worse than my old rag dolls. Sit down and have some of our left-over scrambled eggs and toast."

As Lexa ate, Bessie described how Ben invited them for a visit, but insisted that they stay. It was as though he was trying to keep them in his house. He even sent someone to pick up Earl and Bessie's belongings, and he bought them new toothbrushes and toiletries.

Bessie had more conversations with Miss Brenda and the chef than with Ben and his wife. She had never seen him so much as touch his wife in an affectionate way, nor had they slept together, as far as she could tell. He has a stunning home, but is rarely in it. She called a cab when she finally had enough, and they got home yesterday evening. Ben sounded angry when she spoke to him. He said she didn't appreciate his generosity. Over the past few weeks she is seeing a new side of her son that she had never seen before.

A V8 engine rumbled outside. Lexa's eyes widened upon catching sight of the Grand Prix.

"What's the matter, dear?" asked Bessie.

"The white car that's been following me all day is driving down our alley."

Bessie went to the window. "I'll see if I can get rid of them."

She picked up the phone, and conversed with several neighbors. Within ten minutes, the car was surrounded by men holding BB guns, pellet guns and rocks. When the firing commenced, wheels screeched down the street.

"See? No problem. The assholes are gone…at least for now."

"Bessie, you never cease to amaze me."

Earl laughed, "Me…too."

Bessie kissed his forehead, and stroked his black and silver hair.

"The closer my court date gets, the more I sense someone is trying to stop me from getting there. All of my witnesses have refused to testify except for you. We may both be in danger. Even the bodyguard I had trusted is balking. Someone has gotten to everyone I'm connected to. Ben most likely didn't want you home for good reasons."

Bessie frowned. "The way he's been lately, I don't put anything past him."

"I'm worried for you and Earl. Because of me, you're both vulnerable to someone harming you."

"I need to make some calls, and start packing. Stay here until I can give you an address of where to pick me up on Monday. Ben isn't the only one who has friends."

Lexa placed Bessie's instructions into her purse, unlocked the garage, took all of her belongings into the house, and opened a lower cabinet door while Karl's phone rang.

"Hello?"

"I'm being followed. I may be dead before my trial. I need to wear disguises. Can you drive me somewhere?"

"Sure. Give me about forty minutes."

"I'll be in the alley wearing my boy clothes and blonde wig."

She pulled out the phone book to look up the stores she intended to stop at, and in a half hour, Karl arrived.

She made her purchases, and returned home. "I'll have to be as convincing as I can that it's a ploy to help the band's mystique. We'll make announcements that someone is subbing for me."

She donned the new wig and make up. Her disguise raised everyone's eyebrows in the van.

Ted was the first to speak. "Halloween was a few months ago."

"I'm going to have a little fun with this costume for a few days. Call me Lola."

"Get serious," said Ted.

"Fans get tired of seeing the same boring band."

"Sure Lexa," said Grant.

"I should tell you my life depends on this."

Ted rolled his eyes. "Okay, Lola. Wait till Debra hears about it."

"Your wife will be fine with it."

The rest of the group listened in on the conversation, and said nothing. Karl looked at her and smiled. Sam made a guess as to why she dressed in a black short-haired wig and heavily bronzed her skin. The show went on without a glitch.

At the end of the night, she crawled into the back seat of Karl's car, and remained horizontal. "Do you see anyone following you?"

"Not yet."

"I've been meaning to apologize for calling you a bitch," he said.

"I understand. I should apologize for making you feel rejected. I should have told you I'm seeing someone."

At Karl's apartment in his second bedroom, she made a bed of blankets, and used his spare pillow.

"Are you sure you don't want to sleep in my bed? You'll be freezing on the cold floor. Don't worry, I won't touch you," he said.

She looked up at him. His eyes sparkled in the dim light, and his skin curved over his high cheekbones, the contour of which was lit by the moon through the window. His wavy, brown, shoulder-length hair shimmered, and she wanted to touch it for no other reason than to see if it was as soft as it looked. There was no doubt that he was beautiful enough to be desired, but she had no intention of starting something with him. "I trust you, Karl. I'm not sure if I trust myself."

He sat down on the floor facing her. "I don't get you."

"I hope you're not feeling unwanted because I have issues. It's a long story."

"Will you ever tell me about it?"

"Maybe, but if you knew, I don't think you'd like me, and we still have to work together."

He leaned over, and kissed her cheek. His mouth felt warm. "I hope you sleep well."

She smiled. "Thanks."

Unable to relax, at 7:00 am on Friday, she packed her things, called a cab, and gave the driver her brother's address. She picked open his back door lock, balled up on the sofa, pulled a blanket over her body, and slept.

Awakened by voices of children, she sat up. Polly gave her a confused look.

"How did you get in here?"

"I got a key ages ago, remember?"

"No, I don't, but I have a lot to keep track of these days. I see you have your luggage. Are you…"

"I got dropped off, but if Nathan could give me a ride home, I'd appreciate it, or I…I could call a cab. Hello, how are my beautiful boys doing?" Her nephews ran to give her hugs.

"He'll be home in a little while. It's not a problem."

Her evening was spent having dinner with Polly and Nathan, until Nathan asked his sons to give Auntie Lexa a kiss goodbye.

On the drive to her house, he asked about the key in the envelope.

"Hide it, and follow my directions if anything happens to me. I need to be dropped off here."

"This is two blocks away. What's going on?"

"I have to go. I love you, Candy and Abbie, and Mom and Dad. Please tell them." He gave her a confused look.

As she wove around the neighborhood toward her home, she saw the white Grand Prix parked down her block. She was far enough away to cut between fences and lot lines. She hunched down at Roy's back door, and pulled out her tools to open his lock. What she found most useful were large, bent paper clips and bobby pins. If it was this easy for her, it would be just as easy for someone else to break in. She shoved the back of a chair onto the doorknob and slid the chain latch closed.

The outside street light filtered into the living room. At the front window, she used her night vision goggles to study the passengers in the white car. The two men did not look familiar, but she was certain they were on the list of seven names she had a photo of, and they worked for Ben Blesdin, or Harold Humphrey, or both.

She checked her watch, picked up Roy's phone, and called Sam. He was instructed to start the engine and open the van door so she could run inside.

"What kind of trouble are you in?"

"I already told you. Someone's been after me since I rescued Karl."

"How much longer is this going to go on?"

"Do you want me to knock on the stalking car's window, and ask the fellows who have been following me, or can you do it, and tell me what they said? It's parked down the street."

"Forget it."

"Yea, that's what I was thinking."

Other than dust that settled, the beds were neatly made in the three bedrooms. Photos documented his life. Roy in his black suit and tie held his arm around a young bride wearing a flowing white lace dress. Joyous smiles beamed on their young faces. Earl, the best man in his wedding party looked like a youthful, dark-haired Gary Cooper. Photos of babies, elementary school girls, young women, all Melinda and Marion, as well as their wedding photos hung on walls. A childhood picture of Bessie Blesdin, with her striking blue eyes, sat in a frame on a dresser.

Below the mail slot in the living room door, unopened envelopes had accumulated in uneven piles on the floor. She knelt down, and felt twinges of sadness when she saw the assortment of utility bills, bank statements, and most likely the request for his house payment lay buried somewhere in the mound. Collection agencies may have already sent notices.

A plate, fork, and coffee cup sat on the kitchen table. Coffee had evaporated, and left a dark ring inside the white mug. The eggs on the plate had curled up around the edges.

When she heard the van start up, she picked up her bag, locked the door behind her, and sprinted. Inside, she prepared her disguise.

In the dressing room, Karl asked if she was spending the night at his place. She thanked him for the offer, but did not think it was a good idea. He asked her to reconsider.

"I have a couple more errands to run tomorrow, and I've taken up enough of your time."

He stared into her eyes. "I haven't minded. Feel free to take as much as you want."

She scanned the club for the men who had been tailing her. Hound, Showey and Drax hovered over her, and no guests were allowed in the dressing room. She remained true to her new persona.

On the way home, Grant announced that the same headlamps have been following the van since he took the wheel. Ted said it was some crazed groupies, and told him to pull over. Karl and Lexa knew it was the Grand Prix. She unzipped her suitcase, and slid her fingers around her Colt Commander 45 caliber handgun. Grant stopped beside a curb. The vehicle behind them did the same. No one moved in the van, nor did the occupants who pursued them.

"This is getting old," said Grant. "Let's get to our cars. It's 3:00 am, and I'm tired."

"Just a suggestion, but let's stop in front of the police station on Thirty-sixth and Fond du Lac Ave. It's not far from here. Then lay on the horn," said Lexa.

He parked close to the main entrance, threw on the flasher, and one long blare sounded. Ted opened the door and looked around. "I don't see anyone."

"They're probably around the corner," she said. "This place is too well lit. Go south, and head eastbound on Burleigh. Let me out at the train yard."

"What?"

"Do it, please."

Grant drove as she requested.

"Pick me up at that thicket of shrubs in ten minutes." She pointed. "Check your watches. Drive around the block and park on the corner near the school on Thirty-third St."

Grant turned around and stared at her. "What are you doing with those tools?"

"Creating a diversion."

She caught sight of the white car as it idled. Two men sat in the front seat, the driver of which had the same features as Harold Humphrey. Crouching down, she looped the rope she had contrived around the back bumper, and ran for the meeting spot around snow banks, and between cars.

"Okay, time to rock and roll. They won't be far behind. I never thought I'd be saying this, but I'm glad we keep so much crap under the bed of our van."

They reached the house untracked. No doubt the other vehicle stopped because of the clamor of a 12 inch section of an aluminum gutter and a weighty, empty metal toolbox dragging on the ground, clanking into each other and creating a stream of sparks.

"Lexa, are you coming with me or not?" Karl threw his bass guitar into the trunk.

She felt safer with him. "Be right there." She got into the back seat, and did a visual search in every direction as he peeled off down the alleyway.

"Karl, they know your car, and may sabotage it in your parking space."

"Down the street is an auto repair shop. I'll park there. I'll drop you off and run."

"No, let's park now, and hurry."

When he opened his apartment door, he flipped on the light switch. She shut it off. "No lights."

"I feel like a fugitive."

"Everyone I'm connected to has become one."

157

"If you're hungry, I have cheese and crackers, grapes, apple pie, cottage cheese, or I could whip up some spaghetti in about ten minutes," he said as he bent into the fridge.

"It sounds like the Slater Restaurant menu. I'll take some cottage cheese and a few grapes. I sleep better when I'm not starving."

By the glow of a night-light in his kitchen, they sat at his table eating.

"When I first met you, I never thought you'd be this kind to me," she said.

"When I first met you, I never thought we'd be snacking together at 3:30 am. Or spending the night."

"Yea, on a cold floor."

"Not tonight, please. I don't want to wake up wondering what the hell happened to you, and if you're still alive. Take one of my Ativan. It helps you sleep."

"I don't like taking your prescription medicine. You must have problems sleeping too, or you wouldn't have them," she said.

"I should tell you one of my secrets. My daddy the doctor hands them out to me and my brother like they're candy. When we were in school, he thought we could get better grades if he gave us speed. When the teacher told him we were bouncing off the walls, he combined it with Ativan."

"Do you take it every single day?"

"Every single day."

"You won't be able to sleep unless you take a pill because your body has become so accustomed to it."

"Yes."

"What happens in five years? Will you need to double your dose of everything so you can feel normal?"

"I take my life day by day."

"Yea, me too," she said.

He got up to hand her the small white pill. She bit it in half and swallowed. He stood behind her, brushed her hair aside, and kissed her cheek. "Let's get some sleep. You can wear one of my old long sleeve t-shirts."

"Thank you for everything."

"I owe you, and you know it."

"For whatever reason, I never feel like anyone owes me anything," she said as she crawled into his bed and pulled up the blanket. The pillow felt soft.

"This is the first time I've had a female in my bed, and had to restrain myself from having sex. You're putting a crimp in my bachelor lifestyle."

"Once a boundary is crossed, there's no way to turn back. What happens when some guy flirts with me? Will you get upset? How will I feel when some chick runs her hands all over you? Because of what we do, it's inevitable."

He cradled his warm arms around her, and kissed her lips softly. "You're hypnotic."

"Do you remember I'm seeing someone?"

"Why don't I ever see you with him?" He backed off.

"He's the guitarist from the band, Signal Source. They're touring through California to promote their album."

"How do you know he's being faithful?"

"I don't. It often crosses my mind."

"I wish I had a magic love-potion to sneak into your drink tonight."

"Doesn't a potion only last a few hours?"

"Yes, but it would be incredible to savor the pleasures of the flesh." He reached over and kissed her lips, cheek, neck and forehead.

"Karl, I…"

"Yea…goodnight." He wrapped her in his arms, closed his eyes, and did not move.

On Saturday as they ate pancakes and blueberries, she informed him of where she needed to go. She wore the black, short-haired wig and sunglasses while he drove. He insisted on taking her to the courthouse on Monday, so he could make sure the $10,000 was returned to his dad. She said she needed to pick up a witness that morning.

At their first stop, she explained to the receptionist why she needed to inspect the log book of calls from the evening of January tenth, and it was handed to her reluctantly. It took ten minutes to sift through the entries, and she photographed the page of the ambulance dispatch log which documented her name at 5:50 pm. She elaborated to the dispatcher why she required her testimony at her court hearing this Monday, March 7th, and why it was too late to fill out a subpoena. She wrote out details of the case, the date, location, and time.

When she picked up the new 8 x 10's, she added them to her portfolio, and left the negatives with the developer, indicating that she may need more copies. He offered to keep them on file.

Karl took her to the post office, where she mailed two large manila envelopes, one to Ben Blesdin, and another to Harold Humphrey. Her trial played like an endless reel in her mind. She had a show to get through tonight, and it appeared that Mr. Humphrey was uncertain if the woman in the black wig was his target. No white Grand Prix was in sight. Karl parked down the street in the auto repair shop.

"Tomorrow let's warn your neighbors to be cautious, and never let anyone inside unless they are positively identified. It's hard to believe how one small ripple has expanded so far outward, that countless people may be harmed because of me."

"It wasn't you who made those men become evil," he said.

She swallowed the half of Ativan she had saved, and wore the t-shirt he had offered the night before.

Once in his bed, he asked if she would mind if he put his arms around her.

"Hugs are fine. You warm me up, and it helps me relax."

"I'll be sad after tomorrow. You'll be in your bed, and I'll be sleeping alone again," he said.

"I've watched how girls eye you up. You'll soon have some pretty chick in here, and she won't be able to control her desire for you.

"Yea, sure, I can't wait," he sighed. He closed his eyes, kissed the back of her head and neck, and pulled her body tight up against his.

She awoke to the smell of coffee, and an empty bed. She slipped into her jeans to find Karl making waffles.

"You're spoiling me rotten. Your mother taught you well."

"She's someone I don't like to think about. For all of my life, she blamed me for her failed music career. She said if she didn't have me, she would have been a star. If I wasn't born, she would be living in Hollywood. If I misbehaved, she told me how I was nothing more than the kid who ruined her life. It's no wonder my dad divorced her."

"So you don't see her much?"

"Well, she's my mom, and I see her occasionally."

"Dad gives you drugs, and Mom says you wrecked her life. How did you end up becoming reasonably rational?"

"Just like anyone else who survives childhood. I got lucky."

They readied for their show, and met at the band's usual meeting place. The disguise caused fans to ask who the new singer was, and if Lexa was returning. No one appeared to follow them.

When they returned to Karl's apartment, she made sure all of his blinds were shut, and minimal lighting was on. She paced throughout his living room.

"I should have called Bessie today, and given her a copy of the photos I took. I wish I bought extra batteries for my tape recorder. I need to review the notes I've..."

A fist pounded on his door. It was 2:30 am. Four loud bursts, a pause, and four punches whacked on his door again. They both silenced, and turned toward the banging. She tiptoed to the bedroom, where she looked down from the window, and wondered if a climb down tied bed sheets was feasible.

Karl's face was sullen as he approached her. "I hope you're not thinking of jumping."

"I have another secret." She pulled a black 45 caliber handgun out of her bag. "Shhh…"

The banging progressed to two fists pounding and a muffled, "We know you're in there!" Red lights flashed in the street, pouring slats of crimson onto walls. They peeked through the blinds as a second police car pulled up.

"They must have called for backup. There's no way in hell I'm answering the door."

Two more officers emerged from the car and rushed into the building. The bashing resumed. A deep voice yelled, "Karl Slater, if you don't let us in, we will break this door down."

They looked at each other. "Officer Humphrey tailed us. I'll bet he made a guess he can bust you for drugs. Be honest. If they get inside, how much trouble will you be facing?"

"I'll be going to jail."

"Well, stuff your pockets. When I was a kid, I got pretty good at playing hide-and-seek. I'm going to show you a trick."

She stuck her gun into her waistband, sorted through her belongings, removed the important items, and placed them on the top shelf of Karl's closet. She scattered the rest of the contents onto the floor, and left the suitcase open on its side.

"Help me grab everything from your spare room closet, and pack all of it into the one in your bedroom." She took all of his shoes and spread them throughout his bedroom closet floor. She took his blankets, balled them up, and hung sheets on hangers to cram the closet full, and tossed his pillows into the same stuffed closet floor. "Now, we crawl into the back corners, and do not move. Trust me. You'll look like clothes. My sisters never found me."

"I hope you're right."

The entrance door banged open; and voices became louder, but soon quieted. Footsteps and heavy breathing cut through the silence. Bodies bumped into walls, and cabinet doors slammed. The medicine cabinet in the bathroom crashed. Dresser drawers were rifled through.

Her heart pounded. She closed her eyes briefly as the light went on, and the closet they stood in was ransacked. She saw the barrel of a gun sift through shirts, a robe, slacks, and the long sheets which hid Karl's and her legs. Large hands pushed what had hung on the hangers to the sides of the closet smothering her. She refused to move, and opened her mouth to slowly suck air in and out.

"Fuck! This guy is a slob. I saw them enter this building."

"They're onto us. Maybe they walked through the front, and out the back."

"But his car is still in the lot of the repair shop. Someone else has to be helping them."

"You're correct. They're probably in another apartment."

"Shit! This night sucks."

"Fill out your report and let's get the hell out of here."

"No fucking report. We're not gonna look like a bunch of fools. Let's go," said the voice of Harold Humphrey.

The escapees emerged from the closet covered in sweat and peeked out of the doorway to silence. There were four distinctly different voices. All the lights had been left on.

"They broke the lock, and destroyed my door," said Karl.

"Grant has great carpentry skills. He'll help you fix it. We need to talk to him now."

"In the middle of the night?"

"They're watching your car, so we can't touch it. We need him to pick us up in the morning."

"He'll kill us if we wake him up. He won't help us."

"I don't care."

She dialed, and his hoarse voice whispered out a vague, "Hello."

"Grant, listen to me very carefully. I'm in deep trouble. I need you to write down everything I say. Set your alarm for 7:00 am. I need you to pick me up in the back of Karl's apartment building. I'll fill you in on the specifics when you get here. I'm sorry you won't get much

163

sleep, but my life depends on it." She asked him to repeat what she had said before hanging up.

They heard a faint knock on the broken door. His neighbor from across the hall, in a hooded sweatshirt and pajama bottoms rubbed his eyes. "Hello...Karl? What just happened here, man?"

"The cops tried to bust me, but they ended up busting my property."

"Like wow, man. They scared the shit outta' me. I thought we were all gonna die."

"Dude, can I take a look out of your windows? Keep the lights off." She used her night vision goggles and binoculars to scan the neighborhood, and recognized two undercover police cars. "Game change. They're going to run a make on Grant's plates as soon as he pulls up, and we'll be stopped. Are you able to give us a ride to the school down the road? Grant has to meet us there instead."

"Yea...sure. What time?"

"In four hours. We will knock in a precise way, so you'll know it's us. Do not answer to anyone else. These cops...they're dangerous." She demonstrated the knock.

Sunday March 6, 1977

Most people bring a briefcase, portfolio, or a binder into court, but tomorrow I will carry my tape recorder and a picture frame I grabbed off of my dresser, keeping my parents in view, in which my evidence is hidden, both of which I have kept in my suitcase.

My biggest fear is not making it to court. Ben is well connected, and most likely knows about the damaging information I discovered. He may also be aware that his wife set a clothing store on fire. Tonight he will be salivating at the thought of me taking the fall.

Chapter 11

Monday, March 7

The alarm buzzed at 7:00 am. Both were groggy. She closed the phone book and gave Grant the name of the school and the address of where he was to pick her and Karl up. She showered while he made coffee and poured two cups.

"Your turn." She took a sip, and combed out her hair.

He was ready in fifteen minutes. They knocked on the door of the neighbor across the hall. In the same hooded gray sweatshirt and pajama bottoms, his greasy hair reminded her of a mangy dog. He said that someone rang his buzzer and knocked on his door at 6:50 am, but it wasn't at all what hers was like. Bloodshot eyes and slurred speech were perhaps how he handled the trauma he incurred. She was glad their drive was short.

They snuck into his car as he pulled up to the back doorway, sat behind him on the floor, arms around their knees, and told him to be vigilant for anyone who may be following them. He said he wasn't able to sleep last night, and he was still too scared to relax. Karl reassured him that the worst was over, as he and Lexa exited at the crowded school.

"You may want to stop for coffee somewhere. Stay away from your apartment for at least a few hours. If you return too soon, you'll most likely be interrogated," she said.

Grant pulled up nearby, and it was apparent he was unable to find them through the hordes of children and parents. They knocked on his window, climbed into the back, and sat on the floor. She kept her belongings at her side.

"Okay, what the hell is going on?"

"Someone has gone above and beyond to keep me out of my court hearing. I have been strangled and followed everywhere. I was hiding at Karl's place, but last night, they broke his door down, and ransacked his apartment top to bottom. They almost found us hiding in his closet. I think the DA is involved for numerous reasons. If I don't get to my trial, he wins, and I go to prison. Here's the address of the witness I need to pick up. She's hopefully waiting for us."

"So that's why you wore that disguise, and we were followed on Friday night. I thought we had some crazy fans. Does Sam know any of this?" asked Grant.

"Some of it," she said.

"Has he told you about Ted and me?"

"No, he hasn't," she said.

"We gave our notice to the agents. We're quitting Word Locket. Casey, Ted and I are forming a new band. We've had a few rehearsals, and we have a new agent who started booking gigs for us."

She raised her eyebrows and looked at Karl. "So, you'll need your share of the equipment and lights soon."

"Yea, Casey is hilarious and easy to work with."

"I'll bet. What did Sam say?"

"He wished us luck. Okay, we're almost there."

She and Karl sat up on the seat, and checked the cars around them. "Drive around the block, and all of us need to be attentive. These people are vicious. I'll run up and ring the doorbell."

"Why don't I go? They're not expecting me," said Grant.

"On one condition. Ask if she or her friend have two large shawls. One for me, and one for Bessie to wear, and she has to place it over her head from the door into the car."

166

"What about me? I want to get into the courtroom," said Karl.

"Wait here," said Grant.

He walked into the house. She and Karl shivered while they waited. In ten minutes, a woman wearing a shawl, and holding a cane hobbled down the walkway, and sat in the front seat.

"I'm faking a limp, but I messed up. I'm so upset," said Bessie. "I called my son out of habit. I didn't want him to worry about Dad and me. Over and over he asked me where I was. He said he stopped at the house. I told him we were staying with my friend, and that we'd be home in a few days. He got real nasty. He said he was never coming to visit us again because we don't appreciate him. It made me cry, so I told him where I was."

"I need to tell you something you will not like. I discovered who set the fire, and if I make it to court, her identity will be revealed. I believe Ben has had someone tailing me."

"Why is he doing this?"

"His wife did it, and I can prove it."

"We're being followed, damn it," said Grant.

Karl, Bessie and Lexa turned around. "It's two men in a white Grand Prix."

The vehicle rammed Grant's bumper, which threw everyone forward. He approached a red light. The shadowing car pushed them into the intersection, despite Grant's foot on the brakes. Tires squealed, and the burning of rubber smoked up the roadway.

"Hold on tight, Bessie. Close your eyes if you need to."

"I hope we don't die trying to get there," she cried.

"Grant, drop us off at the first grocery store you see."

"What are you talking about? You have to be in court in thirty some minutes."

"Either Glorioso's or Sciortino's Bakery is open. Let us out at whichever one is open. Slow down to the speed limit, otherwise we'll have more problems."

"A bakery? We're about to die, and you want shop for pastry?"

"I have an idea."

"Oh, great."

"Lock the doors, and wait for us. We won't be long."

Grant pulled over on Brady Street. The pursuing car stalled by the curb. Karl and Lexa ran into the bakery and asked the clerk to fill a box with cannoli. She threw down cash and said to keep the change.

The driver of the white car opened his door and reached into the lapel of his long black leather coat.

"How good is your aim?" She opened the white box.

They launched the milky confections simultaneously, making direct hits on the driver, his front windshield, and all of the windows. The crisp cannoli shells broke open, and the creamy ricotta slid down and froze, leaving long films of thick, sticky paste. Several of the cherries stuck to the glass. Karl and Lexa rushed into Grant's vehicle, slammed the doors, and Grant tore off down the road.

The driver of the Grand Prix picked the shells off of his car, and jumped into his seat. The washer fluid and wipers smeared the cream into a greasy haze over the Pontiac's windshield.

Two bullets pinged off Grant's back bumper as he sped. "Damn them," he said as he wove through the city.

"Get as close as you can get to the building. Pull up your shawls, everyone." She unzipped her suitcase, grabbed her shoulder-strap purse, and shoved the tape recorder, and photo frame into it.

"Grant, I'll call you when my hearing is over."

At the steps of the courthouse, each formidable landing raised her higher and closer to the scenario that held her fate. Her insides tightened as they approached the Corinthian columns. Hurried footsteps clunked nearby. Karl turned around and covered Lexa just as a man pushed her forward. The glass in the picture frame cracked. Bessie swung her cane, and struck the man's knees causing him to fall. The out of breath passenger from the Grand Prix sat on a step and grimaced as he grabbed his knee.

They arose, and helped their elderly friend walk through the doors where equally serious faces pondered the outcomes of their trials.

Inside the wood-paneled room, Ben Blesdin glanced at the distressed face of his mother, whose anxious eyes took in the polished facade of her son. Prepared for his image to be revered in his yellow tie, white shirt, gold cufflinks and matching Rolex, arrogance simmered through his fitted navy suit. He believed his past victories were in part due to how he wove his fingers through thick brown, wavy locks, and batted his dark eyelashes through steel blue eyes. He took advantage of the good looks given to him by his parents.

Ben's demeanor angered at the sight of Lexa. Everything he had done to keep her out of this chamber had failed.

She removed her long tan coat, glanced around the large room where verdicts would alter the history of a life, and took a seat at the desk beside his. She set her belongings down. Ben turned away, and read his notes.

At 9:00 am, the bailiff announced for all to rise, as the Honorable Judge Edward Ehlichs stepped out of a doorway and entered the courtroom. It was the name on the note paper near Casey's phone. A large map which marked the sites of the fire and her arrest was set on an easel near the jury. Fear chipped away at her to where her muscles quivered, her heart raced, and a dizzy sensation overcame her. The order to be seated was given, and the case number and context was read.

Jurors were called up and questioned by Ben, who could not mask his smugness. Unable to control her nausea, she declined her right to challenge. The judge asked if the prosecutor was ready to proceed. He answered: "Yes".

When asked if the defendant was ready to proceed, Lexa arose. "Your honor, I have new evidence to present to the court." Her hands were clammy.

"Please approach the bench."

Lexa made sure her white shirt was tucked into the short black skirt she had worn over black tights and plain black boots. Her bangs were pushed aside by a plain black plastic headband. She walked to the desk, and presented copies of her photos, as well as a cassette tape recording. "I have an additional witness." Lexa stated the woman's name, and pointed to the dispatcher from the ambulance company who was seated in the front row dressed in her uniform.

"Attorney Blesdin, do you wish to review?"

Ben hurried to them, and his eyes widened. "Why wasn't this submitted at the pretrial conference?"

"All of this was discovered after that date."

The judge stated that he would allow the new evidence, with the exception of the tape recording. She took it off of the bench. In returning to their seats, Ben shot an evil look at Lexa. Panic slithered down her insides. Her mouth felt dry. She had planned on using the recording, due to her crucial witness refusing to testify. It had been a while since she had put batteries in the recorder, and she doubted that the device had enough juice to power up.

Jurors were sworn in and took their seats. The judge explained their roles, the specifics and laws that apply to arson, and asked if they understood. He rattled off the counts against Lexa as well as the facts pertaining to the case.

"We'll hear from Attorney Blesdin on behalf of the state. Mr. Blesdin, you may begin."

Ben smiled as he sauntered to the jury, and opened his arms as if to embrace them. "Dear ladies and gentlemen, may it please the court and honorable judge, good morning. We are here today because on the evening of Monday, January tenth, Lexa Lynnch committed a criminal offense. The evidence will show that she attempted to burn down a clothing store and possibly a busy shopping mall, but this was stopped by a perceptive security guard. She chose to destroy Diene's Dress Shop's most expensive evening gowns. Why did she do this? Because she is an arsonist, someone who deliberately sets fires for revenge or gratification. In this trial, you will hear from the gentleman who watched her run from the scene. He made a positive identification of her in a lineup the following morning. You will also hear the testimony of the officers who arrested her. This woman will not escape the law. You will no doubt imprison her for this heinous offense, because the evidence supports a guilty verdict."

"Thank you, Mr. Blesdin. Ms. Lynnch, do you have an opening statement?"

"Yes, sir." She stood up, stumbled on her first words, and cleared her throat, feeling smothered by the eyes which fixated on her. "Ladies and gentlemen of the jury, I will prove with my witness' testimony and the evidence I have collected, that this is a case of mistaken identity, and I am not guilty of arson, or for any other crime. Thank you."

"The state would like to call Officer Simon Skarva to the stand."

The clean shaven, statuesque man who took the stand and was sworn in wore a navy uniform decorated by a silver badge on the left side of his chest. His long sideburns and black hair glistened. He answered his specifics as requested, and he sat down near the judge.

"Is this your police report?"

"Yes, it is."

Ben faced the jurors. "It establishes the arson on the evening of January 10th, at the Capitol Court shopping mall, and in particular, the $1300 in damages to Diene's Dress Shop which were incurred at approximately 5:45 pm. Did you speak to any witnesses?"

"Yes sir, I did."

"Who did you speak to?"

"I took the statement of Mr. Orson Smyth, who states that he saw the suspect run out of the Mall." The officer pointed at the man.

"What did Mr. Smyth tell you?"

"He reported that he got a very good look at a woman who ran. And he made a positive ID of her the following morning in a lineup."

"How were you able to find this woman?"

"She was caught approximately ten minutes after the fire started, breaking into someone's fence, and trying to flee from the law."

"That will be all, thank you," said Ben.

The officer stepped down.

"Your honor, the state would like to call the officer who made the arrest. Officer Bernard Glenkaz."

He whisked through the formality of swearing in as though he had done it a thousand times. He was asked and complied with the request to introduce himself, identify where he worked, how long he worked in this capacity, what area he patrolled, and where the event occurred. When he was asked to identify the suspect, he raised his large arm, pointed sternly, and stated what she was wearing.

"Officer Glenkaz, please inform the court about the circumstances of this arrest on January tenth of this year," said Ben.

"Yes sir. My partner and I apprehended the suspect as she climbed down a fence and ran through an alley which was a mile from the shopping center. She refused to stop when she was told to do so. She continued to flee, and my partner chased after the woman. She refused to comply with our request to raise her hands. We asked several times. When we questioned her, she stated she was going to give someone a pill of some kind."

"So to clarify, you're saying she fled?" asked Ben.

"Yes, she ran away. We screamed at her to stop."

"Did she comply?"

"No sir, she did not."

"At what time was she arrested?"

"It was approximately 5:55 pm."

Ben asked and was given the address of the arrest. He asked how the officers were notified of the suspect's whereabouts, and was informed that the police had received a phone call to report an attempted break in. A nearby patrol car was dispatched.

Ben glided to an easel on which rested a large map of the location. "Is this where you made the arrest?"

"Yes sir, it is."

"How far away is this from the crime?"

"Only about a mile."

"Can a young person run this distance in ten minutes?"

"Yes they can."

"You may step down. Your honor, I would like to call the state's next witness, Mr. Orson Smyth."

A balding, slightly hunched, thin man in a dark gray suit, stood up, raised his right hand, and was sworn in by the clerk. His black rimmed glasses almost hid thick black and gray eyebrows. He was directed to the seat behind a gated wooden panel, in the front of the courtroom and asked to speak up, so everyone could hear him discuss his background.

Ben rose to approach the man. "Good morning Mr. Smyth. Were you at the Capital Court shopping mall on the evening of January tenth?"

"Yes sir, I was."

"And what did you see?"

"I saw that woman, Lexa Lynnch." He pointed at her solemnly. "She ran out of the mall and across the parking lot."

"Did you see anyone else running?"

"No sir, I did not."

"Were there many people around her?"

"No, she was alone."

"At what distance were you from the subject?"

"I was about twenty feet away."

"Were you stationary, or driving?"

"I saw her out of my car window as I left the parking lot. I hit the brakes."

"Tell the jury about the lighting."

"They were those tall, bright street lights. I got a real good look at that woman." He pointed again.

"What drew your attention to her?"

"She ran down 60th St. towards Capitol Drive. Then I saw fire engines heading to the mall, so I pulled over. I saw them drive into the lot. They dragged hoses inside the building. She had no idea I saw her. I've never seen a woman run out of a mall like she did. It startled me. It's why I went to the police. I gave an impeccable description, because they caught her right away. Her face was fresh in my mind the next morning when I picked her out of a lineup."

"What time did you witness this event?"

"I looked at my watch. It was 5:45 pm."

"Did you see her get into a car?"

"No sir, I did not. I watched the fire engines, and I did not follow her."

"Thank you. That is all." Ben turned and walked to his chair.

Lexa stood up. "Your honor, I would like to cross-examine the witness.

"Proceed," said the judge.

"You said you saw me. What was I wearing?"

"You had on a long furry coat."

"Jury, please make note of this coat description. Was it a mink, or a wool coat?"

"It was too dark to tell."

"You cannot identify the kind of coat she wore, yet you are certain you saw me. Was the fur dark, or light?"

"Um…it was a medium brown."

"How long as it been since you last saw an eye doctor?"

"Objection! It is irrelevant," droned Ben.

"Sustained."

"Okay, I'll rephrase. I see you wear thick glasses. When did you get them?"

He stared in Ben's direction. "Two years ago."

She sorted through the photos, and picked up the ones she had taken of Ben's wife.

Lexa smiled. "Does this woman look familiar?"

"Uh…hmmm. I'm not sure." He looked at the judge, and turned toward the DA.

"Does she look somewhat like me?" asked Lexa.

"Hmmm…I…maybe a little."

Ben squirmed in his seat.

She walked to the jury box to assure that each had a clear view of the 8 x 10" shots she had enlarged. "As you can see by her smile and waving hand, she has given permission to be photographed. Does this woman look similar to me? She's wearing the medium brown fur coat he described. He saw her under tall street lights, and yet he cannot tell us if it was a mink or wool coat. But I'm willing to bet that all of you can identify this fur."

Ben stood up. "Objection. Insufficient authentication. Strike that from the record."

Lexa stifled a laugh, and instead smiled. "Fine, your honor." She knew the jury got more than an adequate imprint of the photos, and as a result would question the witness' testimony. "Thank you."

"Attorney Blesdin, do you have any additional witnesses or evidence?" asked Judge Ehlichs.

"No, the state rests its case," said Ben.

"The defendant may now present evidence," said the judge.

I would like to call Bessie Blesdin to the stand."

Bessie trembled as she was sworn in. She was asked the same personal questions, and sat in the designated seat.

"What is the make and color of my car?" asked Lexa.

"Objection. Relevance," said Ben.

"Ms. Lynnch, you had better quickly tie this back to your case. I'll allow it for now. Ms. Blesdin, you may answer the question."

"You have a gray Volkswagen Beetle."

"Yes, I do, and if I go anywhere, have you seen me run or walk?"

"No."

"How long have I lived near you?"

"For about two years."

"Have you ever seen me wear a fur coat?"

"No, I have not."

"At what time did you call my house and ask for my help on the night of January tenth?"

"It was at 5:50 pm."

"Did we have a conversation?"

"Yes."

"What did we discuss?"

"I told you something was wrong with my husband. You said you were going to call an ambulance and come over right away."

"Are you sure it was me you were talking to?"

"Very certain. I know what your voice sounds like. An ambulance arrived in about ten minutes."

Lexa unfolded and held up a copy of the Milwaukee Sentinel dated Monday, January 10, and pointed to the weather on the front page. She held up an 8 x 10 photo beside it. "Mrs. Blesdin, can you please read this to the court?"

"The weather report states that the temperature in our area was minus six degrees, and the picture is taken of the Vital Sign Ambulance dispatch log of January tenth. Your name, Lexa Lynnch is listed at 5:50 pm requesting emergency services for Mr. Earl Blesdin. My address is listed on this form with the company's name and logo at the top."

"Thank you. That will be all."

Ben stood up. "Your honor, I would like to cross-examine this witness."

"Proceed."

"If what you say is true, what time did she arrive at your house?" He faced the courtroom, and crossed his arms.

"She never made it because she was arrested."

"Did you see her get arrested?" He floated across the floor, his stage, his personal territory, where he commanded the lights and action.

"No, I didn't have to. I read the police report. I'm certain you have a copy."

His haughtiness washed away, and his face darkened. "Do you wear a watch in your house, or check a clock every few minutes? You could have phoned her at 5:30 which would give her ample time to start a fire, sprint to her house, and speak to you."

"Don't twist what I have said here. I picked up my telephone, and called her at 5:50." This may have been the first instance she stood up to her son, and she appeared to relish in it. "Almost every night my husband and I eat dinner at 5:30. We do the dishes together, and then we sit down to watch the evening news. Ten minutes before the news started is when my husband appeared confused and couldn't speak, and I called her. The ambulance arrived when the news began."

After a long pause, Lexa said, "This witness is excused."

Ben turned away, and reached for his notes.

"Your honor, I would like to call my witness from the Vital Sign Ambulance Company," said Lexa.

The blonde woman in the navy uniform arose, took the stand, was sworn in, and gave her pertinent data.

"Hello. Thank you for being here today."

The woman smiled and nodded.

"Will you please inform the court what your log book states?"

The dispatcher reiterated all that had been previously discussed. Whispering commenced throughout the room.

"Thank you. That will be all."

Ben's face soured.

"Lastly, your honor, I would like to discuss the copy of one of the police reports. This one states the fire began inside of Diene's Dress Shop. I went to this store in mid-February, to do a little investigating, and one of the clerks thought I was the woman who tried to return a stained green gown. We had a discussion, and several days later, I showed her these same photos of the woman in the fur coat. She made a positive ID. Though she received a subpoena, she refused to be here.

This is relevant because it further demonstrates that not me, but another woman was involved in this crime of arson."

"Objection your honor. That is inadmissible."

"Sustained."

"Will there be any further testimony?"

"No, sir."

"Any additional evidence?"

"No, sir."

"The judge turned to the jury and said, "Both parties have now finished presenting their evidence. We are ready to hear closing arguments, and will begin with the prosecution. Mr. Blesdin?"

The 6'1" DA glided toward the group which was fixed upon him. He pursed his lips, turned his head skyward, pulled his hand to his face, and slid his forefinger and thumb down each side of his chin. He furrowed his brow, and gave a serious look to all who viewed his handsomeness. "May it please the court, judge, ladies and gentlemen of the jury, do not be fooled by this female who has mustered up her convoluted and confusing evidence. She has gone so far as to dress like a young school girl to fool you into thinking she may stand a chance of being pitied."

He paced, took a deep breath, and made intense eye contact. "A fire was intentionally set at a busy shopping mall, which incurred $1300 in damages. It had the potential to have been far more severe if it was not for a fast acting security guard to use an extinguisher, and call for help. A credible witness fortunately got a good look at the perpetrator, and did his duty as a concerned citizen to report it to the police in a timely manner, thus bringing her to justice. She ran from the scene, hid her coat, and she could have driven her vehicle and been at her house by 5:50 pm. She tried to escape from the police. When she was apprehended, she was told to stop and did not, and had to be chased. She was detained and taken to jail that very night. Other than the phone call to the ambulance company, she is unable to prove her whereabouts for the evening of January tenth. She was identified in a lineup the following morning. Ladies and gentlemen, it is up to you to make the right choice. Think of your responsibilities as upstanding good people who will not tolerate the evil behavior that has been perpetrated by this woman, and find her guilty of this crime. Thank you."

Lexa stood up, stepped forward, and faced the jury. "Each of us is guided by morals which have been taught to us by family, friends, peers, and mentors. You sit here today, holding the power to decide my fate. Within your conscience is where that power lies, and where you decide right from wrong. Do you think you will be able to make a valid decision despite what I am wearing today? Will your verdict be tainted by how I look? Will it be affected by my age? By my gender? I have presented substantial testimony, the newspaper and photos to prove my innocence. I stand before you to ask that you adhere to the state laws, and to seek the truth, justice, and to do what is right. A police report states that I was not wearing a coat when I was placed under arrest. It was minus six degrees that night. I have never owned a fur coat, like the woman you saw in the pictures. I shivered all the way to the police station. Why was I not wearing so much as a jacket? Bessie and I are neighbors. She called me on January tenth at 5:50 pm, and told me her husband, Earl was in serious distress. I called an ambulance, and ran to offer help, not thinking about where my coat was, but how Earl was. My main concern was for his life, not who was shouting at me to stop. I had no idea who those men were. Because the gate was frozen, I never got the chance to help her husband. Fortunately, emergency personnel arrived to assist him. I have provided photos, most especially a dispatch log which shows my name as a caller at 5:50 pm. It's impossible to have started a fire, run out of a building at 5:45, and been in my home which is over a mile away within five minutes to call an ambulance. There was another woman out that evening, who has a strong resemblance to me. I can understand how our identities could be mistaken, especially in the dark. I'm certain that the mink-dressed perpetrator of this crime was in

179

her car, and far away from the area altogether, not outside freezing in an alley trying to find a way into someone's house. Several witnesses would have been willing to testify that I have never owned a fur coat. Hopefully my evidence will facilitate your finding the truth today, most especially to me being falsely accused, and for you, ladies and gentlemen, to find me not guilty. Thank you." She turned and sat down.

"The court will adjourn while the jury deliberates." The judge gave explicit instructions to the jurors, struck the gavel, arose and slipped through the door behind him.

She pushed the black 'play' button. Ethyl MacMillan's voice was like a haunting echo. The courtroom silenced upon hearing, "You look a lot like her. I remember her mink coat. I mean how can you miss that?"

"So you're sure that it was this woman and not me who had been in your store on Monday, January tenth?"

"That's what I said, isn't it?"

Though Ben was reaching for her, she did not look up when she pressed 'stop'. Many of the jurors gasped before being led away. *Well, I guess the batteries are still good.* She shuffled the remaining photographs which she did not show the court, returned them to the broken picture frame, and shoved everything into her shoulder bag.

Ben made no eye contact with either her or his mother. He crossed his legs, swung his right foot, and checked his watch. The man who had given her so much anguish sat at arm's length. She wondered how many innocent defendants he had put away to maintain his almost unblemished record, to use as a stepping stone to a higher appointment.

People in the courtroom whispered amongst themselves as they sauntered out. She stood up, and joined Karl and Bessie.

The jury deliberated for almost an hour when court was called into session. The bailiff stated, "All rise." The judge re-entered the room, the jury foreman read the verdict of 'not guilty', and the misdemeanor charge of fleeing was also dismissed. She smiled and turned toward Ben. He felt her icy stare boring through him.

His face reddened, his teeth clenched, and he fled through the doors, clutching a dark brown briefcase.

She took a deep breath, and released the weight of her worries. Karl and Bessie joined her, and she used a pay phone to call Grant who said he would pick them up near the doors of the museum down the street. "I want to get as far away as I can from this building. Ben should have never taken this trial. I wonder if the jury made the connection of his and your last names," Lexa said to Bessie.

"He was such a sweet child. I had my doubts when he was a teen, but now I don't like him so much, and he's my own son. I've had a sense of purpose since Earl got sick. I found strength in me that I never knew I had. It's as though everything looks and feels different. It's like I'm hearing my voice for the first time."

"Sometimes, an out of the ordinary circumstance reminds us of the courage we've had all along," said Lexa.

"He wanted you to take an arson rap, and he believed he would get away with it," said Karl.

"He'll do what's necessary to keep his wife out of jail," said Lexa.

The trio walked the half block toward the museum, and the white Grand Prix pulled up near the entrance doors. The passenger rolled the window down, gripping a black handgun in his opposite hand. The barrel was aimed in their direction.

"Get in." He motioned to the back passenger door.

"No, thank you. We already have a ride."

"I've had enough of this." He stepped out and grabbed Lexa.

Trailed by Karl and Bessie, she broke free and ran into the museum. "You and your pal are parked on Wells St. There will be at least fifty witnesses who will be able to provide a description of the make and plates of your car. Do you intend to abduct me in a place where all these people can give a composite sketch of you?"

"I said get in the car, now." He pulled her arm.

181

At the ticket tellers' window, the eyes of the two women widened. They pointed at the man in the black leather coat, and one picked up the receiver. The people in line scattered.

"Officer Harold Humphrey, leave me alone," she screamed, even though he was not the man holding the pistol.

The dark-haired man became jittery and backed away. "Shut up. Shut the hell up."

"I want people to hear the name of who is responsible for my kidnapping. I'll go with you, but this better be fast. I've had enough of this too." She gave her bag to Karl, who stood immobilized in shock and fear.

She crawled into the back seat, and the car sped westbound on Wells St. The men in long black coats did not speak. The powdery, musky smell of Brylcreem, which glued their dark hair in place, filled the car.

"So, is this your idea of a grand tour of the city? I see you got your car cleaned up."

They remained silent as they drove to a deserted area and parked under a bridge.

The driver turned around. "Okay. Who are you working with?"

"Excuse me? I don't work for anyone. My job is a musician. I was set up by someone to take the fall for an arson rap, but the person who did it must think everyone else is stupid. It didn't take much to put it together. Is that what you're referring to?"

"Who has been helping you?" asked the driver.

"I have friends, just like you do. My good buddy Ben Blesdin, he's not the brightest bulb in the pack. He's been one of the easiest people I have ever figured out. And it helps to know his parents. He's long overdue for a good spanking. You've been tailing me for at least a week, and you better stop, or things for Ben and Harold are going to get ugly. They should be getting copies of my letters and pictures in an envelope by tomorrow. What a shame I had to dig up their dirty details. The things I found out weren't pretty."

Both men turned around. "What do you mean?"

"I discovered a few flaws in their schemes. I'd like to live in peace, and the photos in those envelopes should be my guarantee."

"What pictures are you talking about?"

"The ones all my friends have in case something happens to me. I mailed copies to Ben and Harold on Saturday. Don't do anything foolish. Your bosses better review those incriminating deliveries first."

They looked at each other. The driver picked up his CB radio. "Break 1, 2, Break 1, 2. You got your ears on? We been reading the mail. We got 10-12. Repeat, we got 10-12. Come back?"

"You have your orders. Proceed as instructed." A squelched voice pierced the small speaker.

"Well if it isn't my friend Humpty. He's going to be ruined real soon if one hair on my head gets ruffled. You may want to mention that to him."

"Your instructions have to wait until tomorrow," said the driver.

"10-9, repeat?"

"It has to wait till tomorrow. There are circumstances we need to discuss."

"10-4. I'll see you in one hour."

"10-4." He turned around. "Lady, this is your lucky day."

"And yours. So…are you going to get me back to my friends?"

"Go to hell." The passenger opened the door and attempted to grab her.

"Do not touch me." She flung her arm at him. "I'm capable of getting out."

"You'll be hearing from us." The driver revved the engine, which thundered under the bridge.

"I'm looking forward to conversing with such courteous gentlemen." *No I'm not, you assholes. And I have no idea how I'll get home. I haven't a dime to my name.* She slammed the door. Spinning wheels ripped up treads in a cloud of exhaust. She stuck her cold hands into her pockets and frowned.

Chapter 12

Monday, March 7 – Tuesday, March 8

Above, a murky sky wallowing in shades of gray, denied sunlight to endless stretches of concrete and dank tar roadways. Her black leather boots were designed for style, not for warmth. In a thirty degree climate, frost bite was inevitable. Dressed to impress a courtroom, not for a winter tour of East Walker Street, she picked up her pace toward a familiar landmark: the Allen Bradley Clock, and the request to use a telephone. Running past factories and parking lots, she crossed 1st Street, when the white vehicle veered toward her. The passenger slapped a hungry stare at her. The euphonious roar of the eight cylinder engine rumbled down asphalt, and echoed off the thick dampness. She raced into the first door that opened.

The red brick building had numerous windows which allowed her to see the car drive to the back alleyway. She asked the first person she saw where she could use a phone, and was directed to the main office. Grant, Karl and Bessie were not home, and Sam's line rang ten times. Desperate to get out of that building, she dialed Tiny's number.

"Dependable Security, how can I help you?"

"Don't hang up. It's Lexa."

"Why would I hang up?" asked Tiny.

"I need you to pick me up as soon as you can. I'm being chased by two creeps in a white Grand Prix, and I'm in the Schaefer Brush Company on First and Walker Street."

"What the hell are you doing there, and where is your car?"

"My car is in my garage. I got a ride to the courthouse, since I preferred to get there alive. I'm here because those jerks pointed a gun at me after my trial, and abducted me. They dropped me off near here, but they're following me again."

"I don't have time for this," said Tiny.

"Damn it, I'll pay for your gas."

The young man who directed her to the office stared at her nervously.

The receptionist backed her chair away, and her eyes widened. "Do ya want me ta call the cops?"

"That's the problem. They're with the cops. Tiny...hey are you still there?"

"Yea, hold your horses. I'm on my way."

"What is the make and color of your car?" She hung up after his response to watch for a dark blue Chevy El Camino.

"Listen lady, we don't want any trouble here. I'm calling the police."

"Good luck. Where I'm concerned, they're not going to help you."

She asked the young man to escort her out of the building, but upon leaving the office, she changed her mind. She was intrigued by all the large windows. Taking a tour through an area where she could view the alley was her best option to watch for the rats who pursued her. "My name is Lexa. What's yours?" She smiled and shook his hand.

"I'm Ma...Ma...Mel...Melvin," he stuttered.

"Can you show me where you keep scrap metal and wood from the brushes your company makes? I also need an empty box."

"I don't think so."

"Your help would mean a lot. I'm in a bit of a jam."

"I...I don't want to get fired."

"I have to hurry. I'm in trouble and I really need your assistance."

"Well, maybe…"

"You are doing the right thing for a desperate person. You're a great guy, Melvin."

"Don't tell anyone I helped you," he said.

"I promise. Do you have anything that's roughly the weight of a bowling ball?" She followed him to the scraps, grabbed a cardboard box and filled it up. "Have you been here long?"

"I've been here for almost nine months."

"Then you know the building well enough to show me where the highest open window facing the alley is. I need your help to carry this box."

He furrowed his brow and hesitated. "I…I don't want to get fired."

"Don't worry, we're going to get some nasty men away from here, and keep us both safe. You need to get to your car after work, right?"

"I don't have a car. I take the bus."

"All the more reason to keep you safe. Where is that place you said you would show me?"

He led her to a window which she opened. She set the box on the ledge, and watched the Grand Prix drive around the block. "You don't have to wait. As soon as I'm done, I'm leaving."

He directed her to the entrance, and she thanked him for his help. The cold air sent a chill through her, as she waited for the perfect moment. She opened her hands, and the heavy box dug into her target with a boom. Battering the roof, it crumpled inward. The vehicle lurched at the instant of impact. The cardboard box splattered open. Metal scraps slid down on all sides. Both the driver and passenger got out to examine the jagged dent in the roof. Just before they looked upward, she ran for the exit.

Almost unrecognizable in a black knit cap which covered his blonde wavy hair and a turned up ski jacket collar, Tiny's dark blue Chevy El Camino idled near the front door. She got in and bent downward.

186

"Get as far away from here as you can, and fast. I've made a declaration of war with the garbage bomb I dropped on a white Pontiac. Those snakes won't leave me alone. I should head to the newspaper today, and find out if an investigative reporter would be willing to do a probe on all the names I have."

"Whose names?"

"The names of the men who received insurance payouts for setting big fires in this city. I'll give you every piece of information I have. The plate numbers of the Grand Prix, and the men driving it. I have proof that Harold Humphrey and Ben Blesdin are involved in the building burns and the payoffs."

"How did you get that?"

"I did some snooping, and it was in the folder I tried to give you."

"I hate those two, and my friends hate them worse than I do. I got in over my head on a case. I came across a heap of dirt on a couple of the men who burnt downtown businesses. They got hefty payments. I got threats to back off. They vowed to shut me down by torching my place. Each morning my partner and I wake up wondering if our office is standing. We hid all our files in a rented warehouse. Nothing of value is in the office."

"Is that why you didn't help me when I saw you?"

"I wasn't sure to what extent they bugged my building."

"I'm certain someone is listening in on my calls," she said. "Everything we need is at my house, but I'm being tailed like a fugitive. I don't feel comfortable going there in daylight. I've been staying with Karl, but they broke in and ripped his place up. I hope my home is still in one piece."

"So where am I taking you?"

"To Karl's apartment." She directed him. "You saw the two photos I took of Humphrey breaking into my garage, but you didn't see the ones I got in the early afternoon of the same area, to give a clear image of where he was. I think he intended to plant something in my car, and get some of his cronies to stop and search me. I'd be in prison, and out of his way."

"Unless he was searching for something."

"Getting me busted seems more like something he'd do. He's still unhappy about not being able to pin the murder of Shane Zadrik, the club owner on me last year. I understand why you don't like the DA, but why the warning to stay clear of his daughter?" she asked, referring to their conversation at the Stone Toad.

"His what?"

She realized her slip. "You warned me to stay away from Kalie and Attorney Blesdin."

"I didn't say anything about his daughter."

"Let's move on, shall we? We discussed the DA."

"His wife hired me because she believes he's having an affair. That's why I was at the Stone Toad. I gave Mrs. Blesdin the low down, and got paid well."

"What did you tell her?"

"I took a few snapshots of Ben and Kalie, and she believes she has proof of his infidelity. Ben may have recruited Kalie to start fires also. Her rap sheet includes arson, retail theft, drug possession, disorderly conduct, forged checks, unpaid parking tickets, and assault."

"And oddly enough, she's not in jail," said Lexa.

"He posted her bond, and keeps a close watch on that gal."

"Do you know she works as a receptionist and typist at his law firm?"

He smiled. "This has been quite informative. We should do more business together."

"I'll give it some thought."

"Is this the place?" he asked.

"Yes, wait here. I'll get your gas money."

"It's on me." He smirked and pulled his ski cap off. "Damn, that thing is hot." His hair was covered in sweat and stuck to his head. He unzipped the ski jacket and threw it on the passenger floor. "See you around."

She rang the buzzer to Karl's apartment. He met her down the stairwell. His eyes were reddened, and a sad, worried smile formed on his lips. As he held her, she felt him tremble.

"I'm fine, really. I had some help. How are you?"

"Not so good. I…I…thought you were dead again. I have all your things."

"Did the police show up at the museum?"

"I have no idea. Bessie and I got out of there as soon as Grant pulled up."

"It looks like he helped you fix your door."

"Yea, but I have to get a locksmith out here to install a better lock."

"I can give you the name of one. I'm so hungry," she said.

"I have plenty of food. Sit down, and tell me what happened."

An hour later, she asked him to take her home.

"I don't think you're safe there."

"I have to change clothes. I'm not safe anywhere, really. Look what they did your place."

When they got to her house, her back door was ajar. "It was locked when I left."

Inside, the rooms were in disarray. Food and cookware had been pulled out of cabinets and strewn across the floor. All cupboard doors were open, silverware drawers were exposed, and the contents scattered. Books had been ransacked and left to lie in heaps on the plush copper-colored carpeting. The four bottom cabinet doors of the bookshelf were open, and the contents looted. The tan sofa was askew, and the matching two chairs were on their sides. Dirt had been pulled out of the plants near the front living room window, and was trampled into the carpet fibers.

Footsteps ambled down the inside stairwell, and the door opened. Sam appeared pale and shaken.

"The police barged in this morning, and demanded to search your flat. They took something out of the bookshelf, and said they were keeping it as evidence."

"How many men were here?"

"Four of them."

"Was one a big guy with a crew-cut and small brown eyes?"

"Yes, why?"

"He was here when you called for help a few weeks ago. He searched my flat when he thought I killed someone last year. He and his buddies tore Karl's place up. I believe he plans to make my life as miserable as he can."

"What are they looking for?"

"Probably copies of whatever I used today to prove my innocence for the arson charge.

"Arson charge? What are you talking about?

"My hearing was this morning. Maybe they think they have something important, and will leave me alone, at least for now."

"So that's what's been going on. Some guy by the name of Tarick stopped by early today, looking for you. I told him I wasn't sure where you were. He asked me to call if I heard from you. He flew in from L.A. He gave me a note to give to you. I wanted to help you put things away, but I don't know what goes where."

"No problem. Thanks for telling me what happened." She put the slip of paper in her pocket.

Karl knelt down, picked up books and pushed them into the bookshelf. "You can redo this later."

She looked for the dictionary and found it on the floor of the dining room. Inside was the paper which she had folded several times and taped to a page. It remained intact.

While Karl rearranged the sofa and chairs, and organized the dining and living rooms, Lexa cleaned up the kitchen, followed by her bedroom, in which every item of clothing was thrown onto the floor. *That guy is really unhinged,* she thought.

190

Karl joined her in her bedroom as she folded and hung her clothes up. "So, is Tarick the guy you were telling me about?"

"Yes."

"You're married to Sam, and you have a boyfriend. I'm just a number to you, aren't I?"

"What are you talking about?"

"I need to put some distance between us," said Karl.

"Am I not good enough to be your friend?"

"No, that's not it."

"Do your friends have to fit a certain criteria?"

"That's not why I'm freaking out. I'm not sure if I can work with you anymore. I want more from you than you can give me."

She hung her clothes up as she spoke. "Whether you think so or not, I do understand. I'm sorry that I can't give you what you need, but I am thankful for your help." She turned toward him. "You are the best friend I have right now. I may not be alive if it was not for you. You must know I care about you, and I worry about you."

He curled his head downward and rubbed his temples. "I'm so damn tired, I can't think straight."

"We both need some sleep."

"Yea, I need to go."

She walked toward him, but he turned away. "If I led you on, it was not my intent. You let me hang out for a few days, and I'll try to figure out how to repay you."

"For what? For making me feel happy? There's nothing to repay."

Her eyes felt as though they were soaked in sand. She wanted to talk to Bessie, but her body was shutting down. "We both need some rest. It's been a stressful day."

"What about your boyfriend? He's waiting for you."

She slipped under the covers. "Loosen up. Take off your jacket. You look wiped out."

He tossed his jacket on the floor, and crawled beside her. "Other than my sister, no other girl knows me as well as you do. You don't judge me. And it's hard to keep my eyes off of you."

"When I first met Sam, I thought he was perfect for me. Look how that turned out."

"So, are you afraid to get close to anyone now?"

"I'm not sure if I can trust any...bod..." She fell into a sound sleep.

They slept for an hour. She awoke to his hazel eyes fixated on her.

"How long have you been awake? She yawned and stretched.

"For about five minutes," he said.

"Do you recall when I told you about the dark-haired woman who was poisoned in this bedroom by her husband? She haunts my house on occasion, but she's harmless. I dreamt that she and I sat at my dining room table. She told me to have a séance, because she has something important to tell me."

"Don't you find it a little odd? Why didn't she give you a message in your dream?"

"Maybe she wants others to witness what is said. Whatever she said while I slept, I might think was a meaningless dream. But if she speaks during a séance, there will be others who will validate it, and make it more believable."

"One more question. Can I kiss you?"

"Yes, if you attend the séance."

He smiled. "I'll be there." He leaned over, balanced on his elbow and stroked her face. They stared into each other's eyes.

He kissed her forehead. "You should get going. I'm going to see what my friends are up to. I need some distraction." He took his leather jacket, waved at her and left.

She changed clothes, jumped down the basement stairs, and on the underside of the rectangular wash tub beside the washing machine, she pulled off tape, and grabbed one of the folders containing photos and instructions. She made sure the twine and safe-deposit keys had not been tampered with.

192

She slid on her coat, and stepped outside. The white vehicle idled in the alley. She backtracked, grabbed a dozen eggs, rushed up the inside stairwell to Sam's flat, and knocked on his door. He did not answer.

"I know you're in there. I need your help. Get your clothes on. Stop whatever it is that you're doing, and help me." She heard clinking and movement.

He opened his door a few inches. "What?"

"Do you see that car in the alley? It's the one I've been telling you about. I've been tracked for at least a week. I'm sick of it. I can't go anywhere until they're gone."

"What do you want me to do about it?"

"Take one of these, and aim for the windows."

"No. I have a guest."

"Screw that. If she can throw, she can help me." She pushed the door open with her leg. "Quick, take one." She handed one to Sam, and one to his girlfriend. "Hurry." She opened his outside door, and launched one at the car, but missed it.

Sam and his female friend threw an egg, and both struck the windshield.

Lexa made another attempt. "Leave…Me…Alone!" she screamed as the egg landed on the hood, broke open and splashed onto the windshield.

The driver stepped out, and aimed a gun at them.

"Damn them," she said as they ducked into Sam's kitchen.

Two gun shots struck the upper doorway and the railing. She ran downstairs, slid her hand around her Colt, and opened a kitchen window. Bending under it, she fired toward the Grand Prix. When the vehicle roared out of sight, she rushed to her VW, and headed to Tarick's house.

She checked her watch and knocked on his door. *In five hours this day will be over, and I will lie in my bed alone, wishing he was beside me.*

In jeans and a blue cashmere sweater, the sparkle of his iridescent opal irises reminded her of what it would be like to open a treasure chest, and gasp. She smiled, touched his face, and kissed his cheek.

"I got here as soon as I could," she said. "I've been hiding out, and had no idea you planned to come into town. You said weren't able to get away."

"I couldn't concentrate, knowing what was happening to you. How was your hearing?" he asked. "Sam didn't know anything about it."

"The prosecutor tried to grind my face into the legal dirt, but ended up falling into the hole he dug for himself. He made every effort to keep me from getting to court, including ripping up my bass player's apartment, and my place. It hasn't been a good week. I need to ask a favor. Please hide this folder in the safest place you can. If anything happens to me, instructions are inside."

"What kind of instructions?"

"Simple steps to follow if I'm missing. Not to worry."

"What are you talking about? Why would you be missing?"

"I found damaging information on some high profile people. I've been harassed ever since."

"Oh, I'm sorry. Is there anything I can do?"

"Not that I can think of. They'll get over it."

"I had so many plans for us." He lifted a bookshelf and hid her folder under it. "Look what's in my wallet." He showed her the receipt from the Glass Rainbow restaurant.

"The DA would have done his best to disprove our dinner together. The wife of the man who had the stroke and the ambulance dispatcher put his accusations to rest. It took the jury an hour to deliver their judgement."

"My flight leaves in three hours. Can I offer you a glass of wine? When I arrived yesterday evening, I bought some Pino Noir for us. Better late than never, I guess."

"I might need a few glasses of wine after this day."

As the Pino Noir swished in his glass, he smiled at its scented bouquet, and sipped. "Nice." He handed one to her.

"How are you getting to the airport?"

"My parents."

"Let me take you," she said.

"I like that idea. I'll tell them." He left the room for five minutes, while she sat on his sofa, sipping on Pinot Noir.

"They weren't happy about it, but they understood. Have you had dinner?"

"No."

He pulled out a variety of cheeses, crackers, grapes, strawberries, spreads, plates and silverware. "When I browsed the aisles yesterday, I wondered what you might like." He sliced up the cheeses, set them near the crackers, added fruit, and offered it to her.

"It's delicious. What is this?"

"My mom gave me her recipe. I sauté onion, add toasted walnuts, and cooked lentils. Add a few spices, and blend until creamy."

"I'm wowed by the taste, and by the fact that you made it."

He smiled. "Here's to winning your trial." He raised his wine glass to hers tapped it, and they sipped. He kissed her wet lips, moistened by the earthy liquid of her drink. Deep and penetrating, he ran his hands along the sides of her head and rubbed her hair as he pulled her to his chest. His fragrance filled her with longing, like underbrush in a forest craving sunlight. He embodied all that was sensuous to her.

"I think about you incessantly," he whispered into her ear.

Her eyes still closed, she drew in a deep breath, and held tightly to the velvet feel of the skin on his neck. She wrapped her arms around him. Voices, sounds, and worries melted away, and time momentarily stood still. The match was struck, and in a matter of seconds, heat raged around their interlocked bodies.

He grabbed his suitcase, and she sped to the airport.

"A few years ago, my life felt so uncertain. I played the field, and sowed every last wild oat I had, but I got tired of it. I'm in LA recording because it's my future."

"I understand. My life won't always be like this. And yours will also change. Once your album takes off, your agents will want hardcore touring throughout the U.S., and Europe." She felt doleful at the thought of rarely seeing him.

"I hope distance does not become our adversary." He caressed her, waved, threw a kiss, and ran.

There was a gravitational pull between them that neither had control of. If by some chance they were separated for years, she knew that with the merging of their paths, this magnet would draw them together, to reconnect them.

Though the scent of Tarick's body, the pine, lime, leather and vanilla was still strong on her skin, it dispersed like the smoke fluting upward from behind the fence, lingering in the air around her as she walked to her door.

She quietly stepped up the outside stairwell. A battle-scarred face in the light of the rolling flames, she realized her neighbor had witnessed the screaming and gunshots. No doubt he thought of her as a criminal, a troubled woman. Though a curtain of thick wood slats kept her and her menacing friends at a distance, he offered help when she hid near his home, and she did not comprehend why.

His dark eyes reflected the light of the writhing flares. Amidst tires screeching on asphalt, exhaust fumes, sputtering of engines, and sirens wailing, fire returned him to the elements of his ancestors. It was his meditation, his ability to travel into the past. His confined space once spanned for untold miles of trees, lakes, rivers, mountains, and valleys.

Despite her silence, he looked toward her. She sat on a step, and did not move. They had become kindred spirits who found solace within vaporing sparks which glowed under a moonlit sky.

It was midnight when she set her keys on the kitchen countertop. Her thoughts ruminated on the feel of muscle on skin, legs on thighs,

196

flowing, moving, and gliding. Three and a half hours she had spent with Tarick, yet it felt like she had known him in another lifetime.

Though exhaustion hovered over her, sleep would not visit without the powder of a Nembutal capsule. She envied anyone who could whisper to slumber, to have it arrive swiftly, and without a potion, pill or serum to induce it. *Someday, I won't need this.*

Monday March 7, 1977

Bessie is no longer the meek woman she had been. She has become self-assured and confident.

Sometimes when we look for the truth it finds us. Though I hid it, my knees shook as I pleaded for my freedom. My palms were damp when I displayed the photos. While the jury deliberated, my composure faltered until I imagined myself in the midst of ocean waters rolling over me. I swam into the current. The sizzle of waves crashing into sand calmed me. It is what reminded me to breathe, as I awaited my sentence.

Tonight my heart was reawakened by the flame which ignited it, like a wick which awaited a match. Love is a fiery conspiracy which holds us captive.

Her eyelids opened; coffee lured her, and she responded with two cups. The kitchen, brightened by the three windows, gave her a reasonable view of her neighbor's homes and garages, and the fence from which fumes billowed. As she ate a bowl of cereal and a banana, she saw no vehicles. Using covert utensils, she snuck into Roy's house, called the telephone company, and asked for a new, separate phone line to be installed. A technician was expected to arrive tomorrow. She threw on her coat, and walked through the alley.

"Come in, my dear. Earl and I worried about you all night. When I had spoken with my son a while ago, it was about helping you. Not to defy you."

197

"I've never been to one of his trials. Possibly he went easy on me," said Lexa.

"I doubt it. He threw a temper tantrum on the way out. I didn't raise him to have such disregard for others. He's not using his power wisely."

"How did you get home yesterday?" asked Lexa.

"Grant took me to my friend's place. I got Earl packed up, and I drove us home."

"I don't suppose you've heard from Ben."

"No, I haven't. Earl and I decided we need a break from him."

"I wonder if you became involved in my defense to discover a quality of your son you hadn't seen before."

"I began seeing it when we stayed at his house after Earl's stroke. It almost seemed like Ben wanted his father to die."

"Somerset Maugham once said, 'Money is the string with which a sardonic destiny directs the motions of its puppets.' He isn't the first, nor will he be the last person who loves his finances more than people."

"That boy of mine never saw one day of hardship in his life. He has had everything handed to him since he was a baby."

"He can change. Nothing is constant. Don't give up hope for him yet. Look how much Earl has improved."

"I...think...the...herbs...made...me...better. I...take...them every day." His dark eyes mirrored the sunlight filtering through the white lace curtains.

"Our new neighbor is so good to us. He told us he took care of his parents. His father taught him about combining medicinal parts of plants. He learned which ones were poisonous, and which ones could heal," said Bessie.

Lexa gave Bessie a hug and expressed her gratitude. She opened the door, saw the white Pontiac, knelt on the ground and inched her way around a tree. Uncertain if they saw her, she wove around houses to reach her home. The roof remained caved in, and pock marks riddled the exterior. She was to blame for it all, and they deserved every dent and scratch.

She knew the car was registered to Harold Humphrey. She called the seventh district Police station where he worked, and reported a suspicious vehicle to the dispatch officer. "A white Pontiac Grand Prix has been driving up and down my alley, circling through here all morning. I think they are planning something. This neighborhood has already had a robbery and a murder." She gave Bessie's address, and hung up.

She took her camera and ran outside. At the driver's window, she snapped three photos at close range of two men sporting primped dark hair, and wearing long black leather coats. On the passenger side, she snapped two more photos, and took off running behind the car, around garages and through a neighbor's garden. Her childhood game of hide-and-seek paid off. She snuck around her house, and ran into her side entrance.

Her phone rang as she opened the door. "Hello?"

"Hello, this is the owner of the Checklist Pantry. I have been trying to call you for weeks, but you are never home."

"I'm glad to hear from you. I hoped you may have some video footage of my neighbor, who is in serious trouble. He insists he was in your store on January sixth. You could help prove his innocence."

"My security camera uses labor intensive magnetic tapes. I used to thread the tape through the recorder onto an empty tape reel daily, but it is expensive and unreliable. It sits there for show now."

"Thanks. I appreciate your assistance, but I have one more favor to ask. May I have a roster of the employees who worked on that day? Maybe one of them saw my neighbor. I can provide a picture of him."

"I'll look it up. Can I call you later?"

"Yes, please do. I'll give you an alternate number if I'm not here. Please ask for Bessie, and tell her you need to leave some information for me."

"Yes, ma'am."

It was after she hung up, that she saw it. The room was ablaze, but no heat was emitted. Something dripped onto the floor at her feet. As she reached out, the flames vanished. Her thoughts of fire diminished upon realizing the flashing red light was from a police vehicle. She stepped outside and viewed two men being questioned near the Grand Prix. Both were in handcuffs.

She left to get groceries and a new phone for the second line. She would soon have a new number to memorize. At the photo shop, she asked the gentleman to make six copies of each negative, and a close-up copy of Harold Humphrey's surprised face.

Back in her kitchen, she called Karl as she put food away.

"Hello?"

"Is there any chance you'd want to take a joy ride?" she asked.

"What are you talking about?" he asked.

"The Pontiac that chased us all over the city is sitting empty in my alley. The men who occupied it were taken away in handcuffs. I'll bet their gun was confiscated. If you have a friend who has hotwiring skills, we could park it in a busy shopping mall.

"Like Capitol Court?"

"Yes, but we have to hustle," she said.

"Anyone can hotwire a car."

"Wear sunglasses and a ski cap. Tuck your hair under it." She hung her head upside down, pulled an old black knit cap on, and waited.

He arrived in fifteen minutes.

"You have talents I wasn't aware of," she said as they walked to the deserted white car in the alley.

In her VW, she followed him to the mall, where he parked the Grand Prix between two station wagons. "I'm sure Harold will appreciate our nice gesture. How was your night out with the guys?"

"It was just great. Are we done rehearsing together?" he asked.

"I have no idea. If Sam is home, we should discuss it."

They walked up the inside stairwell, knocked, and were let inside. Sam had spoken to the agents who were setting up club dates for

Grant, Casey, and Ted, who had informed Sam that his new band stood to make much more income and insisted that he join them. He refused, and did not to allow as much as a cord to be taken until the last show. "We have a month's worth of venues to fulfill. On our itineraries, we'll announce our last date, and promote it as a big party."

"Sounds good. See you tomorrow night," she said.

In her kitchen, she turned toward Karl. "Are you hungry?"

"Yes, a sandwich would be fine."

"Do you like grilled cheese?" As she opened the refrigerator, he put his arm around her neck, and pulled her into his chest.

"Can you feel how fast my heart is beating? That's what happens when you're near me."

"You're feeling the rush from hotwiring, and joyriding someone's car. To me, it felt exhilarating, even though I wasn't behind the wheel." She took out the frying pan, buttered it, and heated the bread.

"Don't you get it? I want you…and no one else," he said.

"Someone once filled my head with promises, and broke each one until there was nothing left to break. The truth was devastating. I don't think I'll ever trust someone the same way again." She pulled strawberries and grapes out of the fridge.

"All men aren't like Sam. My parents had horrible issues. When we heard about the crap my dad told my mom during his affair, I wasn't sure which of them to hate more."

"Are you saying you want to be my boyfriend?" She set the food on two plates, which she placed on the table, and took a bite. The cheese was warm and gooey.

"I don't like that term. I'm not a boy, and I want to be more than a friend."

"What about Tarick?" she asked.

"You have no idea if he is faithful to you."

"I saw him last night. I'd like to believe otherwise. I wish you and I could hang out and have fun. No strings. Soon you'll be able to distance yourself from me, and you can make a fresh start. I've noticed how girls look at you."

"It doesn't matter. When I don't know where you are, I feel hollow no matter how many women are around me," he said.

"Try to keep in mind that someone is trying to kill me, so all the more reason I'm not a good girlfriend for anyone."

"We should show the guys your photo of Casey's to-do list...of what he planned to do to us," he said.

"No, they'll think it's a fake, and worse, he'll find out about our break-in. They're the best of friends."

"Yea, they'll be inseparable until they kill each other."

She checked her watch. "I need to visit Roy. I have some info he'll be interested in. Despite all the evidence stacked against him, I think he was either set up, or is a victim of circumstance. Things tend to happen to me for a reason. Being unjustly accused of a crime changes one's perspectives about everything you believe in."

"Are you getting one of your intuitive feelings about him?"

"Yes."

They were interrupted by the ringing phone. "Hello?"

"It's Bessie. The owner of the Checklist Pantry called. There were three people working on the evening of January sixth. He says they're still employed, so you can find out when they're in, and speak to them." She spelled out the names.

"Thank you."

Karl's sad eyes glanced at the alley, and down the street. He smoothed her windswept hair, hugged her, and told her to be cautious.

At the jail, she showed a photo ID, and waited almost fifteen minutes. Severely hunched forward, shackles on Roy's ankles gave him an awkward shuffle. A black and gray beard had aged him ten years, and his eyelids drooped. He stumbled into a chair, and sat down hard.

"What the hell are you doing here?" he asked.

"I stopped by to give you an update," she said.

"I'm locked up." His speech was slurred, and his head bobbed downward.

"Locked up?"

"In in…solitary mostly."

"Why?" she asked.

"Fighting…but hey, they started it. They got on my last damn nerve antagonizing me day and night…day…night. Roy, Roy, the murder boy."

"I have the names of a woman and two guys who worked at the gas station when you stopped in. I'm going to talk to each of them to see if they recognize you."

"Ha! It's not going to happen. It was two months ago, and I'm invisible."

"Describe who waited on you that day. I'll focus on that person."

"Some guy…who had brown hair, or maybe it was black."

"Was he short or tall?"

"Tall, I think. No, my height, six feet," said Roy.

"About what age was he?"

"He was youngish."

"Who is your lawyer?" she asked.

"Who the hell cares?" His laugh was snide and condescending.

"Why did you take out a two hundred fifty thousand dollar life insurance policy against Doris?

"None of your fucking business. Stop this bullshit."

"I'm trying to get you the hell out," she said.

"She told me to! It was her damned idea, so the girls would be taken care of. We both had policies on each other."

"Have you heard from your daughters or sister?"

"Fuck them. Fuck everyone…everyone."

"Snap out of it. I need to tell you something," she said.

"Get out of here, and let me rot, like they say I'm gonna. The murder boy, my ass."

"You are not going to rot in here."

"Yes I can, and I will."

This was not the man she had seen inside the borders of a white picket fence, the planks he had nailed together on a spring day. He painted each board white, coating it top to bottom, gliding the brush to create a perfect gloss because it made Doris happy. Their babies would be safe. A man whose thick jet black hair had never been out of place, the man who dressed in casual neatness, like he shopped alongside his wife and valued her thoughts, desires and opinions, sat in a dull gray chair, falling apart. Bloodshot eyes, deep red and blue marks on his wrists, he drooled onto his orange jumpsuit.

"Don't let the guilty win. They're not worth it. They never are."

"Guard...guard get me the fuck out of here," said Roy. Strangled by mental and physical pain, he hobbled behind a uniformed man.

Keys jingled in each leaden footstep. Unable to give him the news of her trial, she doubted he could process her offer of help to find a witness for his defense. She needed to know when his court date was scheduled, and the name of his lawyer.

Ebbie greeted her at the house, and as Lexa bent down to pet her, she pulled the phone to the floor and dialed while she stroked soft, off-white fur.

She called the gas station and inquired about the three names on her list, and when they worked. One of the employees was there until 10:00 pm. She slipped into Roy's house, took one of his recent photos, got into her VW, and was standing at the register within twelve minutes.

The young woman who had worked that day could not identify the face of the man in the picture. Nothing stood out. She searched her memory, but came up blank. "He looks like an actor I've seen somewhere."

"Yes, I agree. And if he continues to take punches to his face, no one will recognize him ever again." Lexa was unable to mask a pitiful frown. She thanked the girl, read the other two names, and asked when her coworkers were in. One worked on Thursday, and the other on Friday.

Sam met her down the stairwell upon her return. "The police just left. They asked if I had seen a Grand Prix. The one we egged up."

"And?"

"I told them I had no idea where the vehicle was, or where you were. But I did say that the car they're looking for has been following our band, and hanging around the neighborhood for a while, but I couldn't remember for how long."

"Was one of them Mr. Beefy-buzz-cut?"

"Yea, the stalker was here. Why do you ask?"

"Did he give orders to search my flat again?"

"No."

"A friend of mine looked up the license plates. The car belongs to him, which is why he is interested," she said.

"Do you happen to know where that Pontiac is?"

"Why should I keep track of where he keeps his car?" She turned her back as she spoke, and reached into the refrigerator for strawberries. "Would you like some?"

"Sure, thanks. Well...see you tomorrow, Lola."

"I'm done being Lola. No one believed it anyway. Thanks for keeping me updated."

"We never talk much anymore. Why didn't you tell me about all the trouble you were in?"

"When you said that if I get thrown into jail, don't even think about calling you, what did you expect?"

"Oh, well I might have helped you."

"Yea, you might have. See you later." As she reached to pull down her kitchen shades, nearby smoke clusters drifted upward and twirled into the wind. She opened the window, and heard a low chant, but the words were inaudible. She took another folder, placed all of the same photos into it, and sealed it in a large, clear plastic bag. In the dark, she reached over the six foot fence, and let it slide down into the snow. Four folders were now dispersed.

Tuesday March 8, 1977

Long before the compass, men like my neighbor were guided by constellations. Under their light, he remains close to nature. Away from it, he knows a man's heart will harden, and lack of respect for growing, living things leads to disrespect for others. He sees a sky which is shared with enemies and friends, the just and the unjust.

His thick, weathered hands brush over smoke as though he commands the rolling clouds to bow to his control. His stance could withstand a hurricane, yet he seems weightless as air.

I looked upward at the twinkling dots of light, and wished I knew more than that the big dipper lies within the constellation of Ursa Major, the third largest constellation, and has seven stars.

Roy has taken a closer step into an inferno. I have two more potential witnesses to speak to. Two more times I will roll the dice, and hope he can be recognized. Because of the scab across the bridge of his nose, dark circles under his eyes, bloodied lip, and his mind heavy with questions and despair, lifting his head was agonizing. The darker his reality becomes, the farther he drifts from this realm.

Chapter 13

Wednesday, March 9 – Sunday, March 13

T hough she did not sign them, the letters which were sent to assure her freedom, would heat the flames of her enemies. She questioned if she had made the right move in exposing her discoveries. Written before her trial, she had no idea what the outcome would be. A loss meant imprisonment and pointless words. She kept a copy of each letter, and the corresponding 8 x 10's which she had taken. Harold's included the unflattering photos of him.

It's done Harold. Get over it. You have inflicted enough of your wrath on others. Obviously you have forgotten something. You started this. You began the process for which you are now experiencing the CONSEQUENCE. Enjoy the ride, but feel free to hop off anytime. You may think you are a knight, but you are merely someone's pawn.

Do you like the pics of you breaking into my garage? I'm certain your wife and coworkers would like one. Take a close look at the gouges on the back of your hands. There's more of where that came from.

Five friends of mine have copies of this. They have instructions to send them to the newspapers, and to newsrooms, if you cause any harm to me again. We are watching you.

Ben's letter went through four versions, the first one being extremely vile. She had contemplated whether or not to send the photos of his spouse. It was a hard decision. Then again, if his wife hadn't started the fire, Lexa would never have had to put her life in danger to prove she did not deserve to be incarcerated. She included a copy of the clerk's recording at Diene's Dress Shop, and all the ones of his wife. Of course he knew she was guilty. It made perfect sense to give him proof.

Ben, don't cry too hard over losing. Somewhere in your dark, self-centered heart is a place where you have memories of the people in your life who have cared for you. Sometimes something as wicked as the truth will prevail whether you want it to or not.

There are many who get away with the evils they bestow onto others for their own gain. Today it ends for you. To keep these photos tucked away you will:

1) Tell your parents they have a granddaughter.

2) Be kinder to them than you have ever been.

3) Do not set another building on fire.

4) You will help Roy Kemke. You will find out who murdered his wife and assist in his defense in any way you

208

can. He has been a good friend to your parents and to you.

5) Harold Humphrey is to stay as far away from me as possible.

Your dear wife keeps a lighter in a black Gucci purse. She wants you to know how easy it is to start a clothing store on fire.

Do you like the pics? Five friends of mine have copies. They have instructions to send them to the newspaper and television newsrooms, if so much as a harassing event happens to me. We are watching you.

At noon, the doorbell rang, and the service technician asked where she wanted the new phone set up. She directed him to the bedroom.

"Why do you want two lines? You're gonna have to pay two bills."

It won't be wiretapped. "That's fine. When my Aunt visits from out of town, she has the receiver glued to her ear all day long. She talks, and talks. She'll pay for it."

"A separate unpublished line? Well okay then."

When he left, she placed a call to Tiny's office, but there was no answer. Her intention was to ensure that a folder was in his possession. She slathered a piece of toast with peanut butter, honey, and cinnamon. In between bites, she sipped on coffee, and from her window, saw the usual plumes swirl and disperse behind the wooden wall. Bessie raked leaves, and Earl in a jacket, sat in a lawn chair. It pleased her to see him stand on his own, lean on a cane, and walk inside of his chain-link fence.

She threw on a jacket, and walked through the alley.

"Hello, I have never seen anyone improve as quickly as you have, Earl."

He smiled. "I…am…getting…stronger…every…day. The…nurse said I don't need her…anymore. I can lift…five…pounds…and…I'm working on…ten."

"When we were young, we went to the beach all summer through fall, and he gave me piggy-back rides for miles on the sand. He said it kept him strong," said Bessie.

"I…have…been…reading…the paper. It's supposed…to get…in the sixties today."

"How nice. I saw Roy yesterday. He is not doing well," said Lexa.

Earl frowned. "I…owe …my…life…to…him. He…saved me from a fire when we were in high…school. He broke…the…window and…helped…me…get out but he stayed behind…to help the…others. The…fire…scarred his…legs…up."

"You went to high school together?"

"Yes, in…Menom…on…ee…Falls. Our…school…burned down. When he married Doris…it was the…happiest…day…of…his…life. I…wish I could bring her back. Bring…her back. I…wish…I… " He grabbed his head.

"What's the matter, Earl?" asked Bessie.

"My…head. Pain…in…my…head."

"Should I call our doctor?"

"No…wait…a…little bit."

"I'll get my blood pressure cuff." Lexa ran into her bedroom, and back to Earl.

As he sat in the lawn chair holding his head, she wrapped the cuff around his arm and pumped. "It's 180/100. Did he take his medicine today?"

"I…I thought so," said Bessie. "I'll check." She ran to her kitchen, opened pill bottles, and returned to her husband's side. "Here, Earl, take this. Can you swallow?" She held a glass of water.

"Yes…I…I…can."

"Put it under your tongue, and let the pill dissolve. Then drink the water. Try to relax, and take deep breaths through your nose. Can you smile? Now lift your arms, and squeeze my hands." He followed Lexa's instructions.

For fifteen tense minutes, two apprehensive women sat at each side of him. He took a deep breath through his nose, and said he was feeling better. His blood pressure was 150/90.

"Don't forget to take your pills." Lexa patted his shoulder. "I know the herbs are helping, but the meds are important."

She rechecked his blood pressure in fifteen minutes, and it was 140/80. "I have to go, but I'll check on you tomorrow." When she returned home, she dialed Tiny's office, and left a message for him to call. As she packed her bag, the phone rang. She hoped it was him.

"Hello?"

"Is this Lexa?"

"It depends on who you are."

"We have your friend, Karl."

"So?"

"We have a gun to his head, and we're gonna blow his brains out unless you destroy all the photos and the negatives you sent to Ben Blesdin and Harold Humphrey. Every last one. You will call everyone who has them, and they better rip them up."

"I need some proof that he's okay. He'd better be able to speak to me," she said.

"Lexa, it's Karl. They…"

"There. He's a dead man unless you do exactly what we say."

"If you hurt him any way at all, we don't have a deal. Do you understand? He better be perfectly fine."

"We have some questions. How did you get the receipt for the green gown?"

"What are you talking about? What makes you think I have it?"

"Someone told us."

"My, my, you brilliant men are gullible," she replied.

"Listen chick, we know you have it. How did you find Ben's wife?"

"My neighbor has her son's wedding picture on her wall. I looked up his address in the phone book. It was easy to follow her," she said.

"Other than this schmuck here, who is working with you?"

"I already told you. No one. He isn't working with me. Are you going to abduct all of my friends?" she asked.

"Lady, you better follow our instructions. Now get busy."

"Okay, give me a number to call when it's done."

The phone muffled for a few seconds. They gave her the number for Karl's apartment.

They did not plan this out well. She dialed Tiny's office, and his partner answered on the fifth ring.

"Dependable Security, how can I be of assistance?"

"Thurston Tinsky, please."

"Hold on a minute."

"Hello?"

"It's Lexa. The bassist of my band is being held hostage. I'm told there's a weapon at his head unless I scrap all the photos I had told you about. Are you interested? It's probably who is threatening you also. What they don't know is that I have a pretty good idea of what their names are."

"What do you have?" asked Tiny.

"Hold on a sec." She opened a folder, and found the list she had photographed. "It's possibly Lydel Lurante, Jerry Cabalski, Ellis Ehlichs, or Gordon Shills."

"Lydel...spell it. I'll see what I can find out about him and Jerry. Ellis and Gordon don't do grunt work. I'll give you an update in about ten minutes."

She gave him the new number to use. He said he would keep it safe. Logic simplified the determination of their names. *I suppose I should call the two dimwits.* "Hello, is this Jerry or Lydel?"

"How do you know who we are?"

"Your names are on the list you want me to rip up."

"You're lying."

"Why are you working for someone who doesn't give a damn about you? Maybe it's what they want, so they don't have to pay you anymore. You may want to get in that Pontiac, and drive as far away as possible."

"That ain't gonna happen."

"Tell Benny and Harry I don't do business with losers."

"Then both of you are gonna die."

"My friend better call me in three minutes, and tell me he's okay, or when you get to your car, it will be on fire, and you'll be walking home. I have your phone numbers, license plate numbers, and your addresses. Don't believe it? Let's see…does 3026 North 13th St. or 2750 North 10th St. sound familiar? Someone is on their way to your houses to break in, so take your time, and give them a chance to rip your places up. Your employers leave too much information lying around."

Their connection went dead.

In five minutes, Karl called to tell her he was shaken up, but fine. She told him what she had said to get the thugs out of his apartment.

He said they jumped him as he exited his car, stuck a pistol to his head, and dragged him up his stairs. He was anxious to check his car for signs of sabotage. If there was any reason why he could not be at the show this evening, he promised to keep her posted.

The phone rang on the new line, and Tiny rattled off a long laundry list of crimes on the men.

"So, long-rap-sheet-one, and long-rap-sheet-two are on the streets doing business. You and I had a discussion about collaboration. I can deliver something to you in fifteen minutes."

At his office she gave him the portfolio, under the condition that he stored it in a vault. He thumbed through it, and smiled. "This is making my head spin. Harold, Kalie, Lydel, Jerry, Casey, Ellis Ehlichs, and Gordon Shills. Their addresses and phone numbers. Sweet. The investment broker Ellis, the evil, manipulative brother of the judge, and Gordon Shills, the president of the Primary National

213

bank have been my biggest threats. Apparently their day jobs don't pay enough. They live large and lavishly. Are you going to tell me how you acquired this?"

"No."

"I didn't think so. It will be extremely valuable."

"If you're interested, I have a few suggestions to stir the pot," she said.

"What do you have in mind?" he asked.

"Show the gorgeous, young Mrs. Blesdin a few more photos of Ben out with Kalie. Tell her you continued your investigation and discovered that he's all over her like Velcro. And he's spending a fortune on her. What were you planning?"

"I'm going to let the air out of his tires, and a few days later, siphon the gas out of his tank, while he's at the office, so he can't get home."

"I'll show Harold's wife the pictures I took of him, and tell her I caught him stealing my bras and panties."

"Okay, I'm in."

"One last question. I have been curious as to why Casey requested your services."

"It's nothing serious. He wanted any dirt I could dig up about your bandmates."

"I figured."

"He also wanted a list of your weaknesses. I made stuff up to throw him off."

"I'm not surprised. In the meantime, we'll follow our list of dirty deeds, and see what happens."

On her way home, she took an extra-long route, and watched her rearview mirrors so closely she almost struck a parked car.

During the show, Casey made certain everyone noticed him, and spoke to his new bandmates during their first break. Lexa took the camera out of her suitcase, and approached them at the bar.

"Well guys, I wish you all the best. It's a bittersweet moment. Can I get a picture?"

"Sure," said Casey, who placed his arms over Grant's and Ted's shoulders.

She took three photos of them. "Casey, can I buy you a drink?"

"Yea, I'll take a Kamikaze shot."

"Make it two," she said to the bartender. "Cheers! To the best of luck and success."

"What, no hard feelings?" asked Casey.

"Why should I be bothered? I don't want Ted or Grant to stick around if they're unhappy. If you all have a better chance of making it, more power to you."

"You're not as bad a chick as I thought you were."

She fumbled out a compliment. "I really like how your horseshoe ring catches the light. It looks great on you." It had been on his dresser the day she and Karl raided his room.

"Thanks. Elvis Presley used to wear one almost like it. I'm a big fan of his."

She smiled. "See you later." *A twerp like you might succeed, but it won't last, and you're nowhere near Elvis' league.*

Throughout the evening, she made several announcements as to whether anyone in the crowd was familiar with conducting a séance, or if they knew of anyone who was. If so, they were to approach her or Karl during a break. No one came forward.

On Thursday, she took the new photos to the developer, and asked him to enlarge the one of Casey from the waist up.

She paid the clerk for the four pictures and said she planned to pick up the rest of her film and photos another day. She knew it was the safest place to keep them.

She knocked on Earl and Bessie's back door. They were having a lunch of ham sandwiches and potato chips. She explained to Earl that she had a picture to show him, which may make him feel anxious.

215

"Let him finish his lunch first," said Bessie. "Can I get you anything?"

"No thank you."

"I...want...to...to...see...see...it," said Earl.

"It may distress you to see him, so I'm warning you to try to stay calm."

Earl studied the face and demeanor of the young man on the paper. He twisted in his chair. "It's...him...him. It is...who...pushed me down...the...stairs."

"When you said you thought it was someone in my band, I thought of this guy. I believe he is capable of hurting someone, and I don't trust him."

"What...what...should...we...do?" asked Earl.

"If you want to press charges be aware that he may retaliate. I don't put anything past him."

"No...it...won't do...any...good...and...I...I...don't...want to see Bessie harmed in...any way."

"So, you're sure this is who pushed you?" asked Lexa.

"Yes...yes I'm sure. He...yelled...into...my...face...to...give him money or he would kill...kill...me. He swung a...knife...at...me. I...fell...backwards down to the bottom of...the...base...basement. Other than...my...watch...I...still don't know what...he...took."

"I forgot to tell you. I have your watch. I found it while I was snooping through his room. I'll have to check where I put it. One more bit of bad news. He is Roy's nephew, Casey Relmen which is most likely why he was in the neighborhood. Roy has no idea he did something so terrible to you."

"We haven't seen Casey since he was a child at Roy's and Doris' parties. When he was little, his dad gave him such a short crew-cut; we weren't sure what color his hair was. He doesn't look the same now that he's an adult. I don't recognize anything about him, but I'm certain he remembers us. He may have killed Doris. We should call the police," said Bessie.

"No…no…no…we…can't…can't…do…that," said Earl.

"But…"

"No…Bessie…no…please…"

Bessie was dismayed, but did not want to upset her husband, and did not press the matter.

Lexa stopped at the Checklist Pantry gas station, and asked for the second employee. He had chin-length, light-brown hair and was at least four inches under Roy's height of six feet. She asked if he had worked the late afternoon of January sixth. He insisted he was there, but the man in the photo had made no impression on him. A twinge of fear eating at her, she hoped for a better interview tomorrow.

The nearby charity store had an assortment of bras and underwear in her size. She purchased five colorful, lacey items. At home, she removed the tags, sprayed perfume over them, and stuck them into a paper bag.

At their show that night, she made several appeals for a medium, or anyone who knew how to conduct a séance, but again received no response.

The van in the garage, everyone filtered out and fired up their engines as she walked to her house. Smoke dispersed above the partition. Each step upward widened her scope of all that surrounded her. The barricade became a small dividing line.

Sitting in a wicker chair, a worn man sustained the whirling and billowing plumes. Though his head was bent downward, his whispers resonated skyward. "May I be ready to return to the earth with eyes which have admired beauty in nature, ears that have heard truth, hands which have shared with others, arms that have worked hard, feet that have tread many miles, a mouth which has spoken kind words, lips that have tasted passion, and a heart filled with love."

Her grandmother once pointed at the peak of a fire, where the heat disappears into space, the shimmering, mirage-like place and said,

"Infinite beautiful things exist in this world which are meant to be admired, and never touched. Remember it always."

The white steam of breath floating around each of them was as transient as each rising and falling flame. Both became quiet observers of clouds circling the moon. Immeasurable light years away, stars speckled through the darkness.

Thursday, March 10, 1977

The man who watches the flames sits outside in solitary, holding a branch over the fire like a wand, prodding and stoking the flames as if he commands it to rise. As if a formless apparition will emerge and speak to him. He sees more than flames in his fires, he sees someone who made beautiful promises in his past which can never be kept, and his world no longer feels the same. He misses someone who once lit the fires inside of his heart.

There was a time when he was indestructible, like the stars that twinkle in the eyes of a child before constraints of the world have dulled them, before loss and disappointment has had a chance to grab ahold of the innocence and stomp it out.

Awakened by a ringing phone, Lexa was startled out of a deep sleep. As a rule, she set no alarms. Her voice was hoarse when she answered. It was one of Tarick's bandmates.

"Tarick is in a slump. He's not singing well. The guys and I got to talking and wondered if you could come out here for a few days."

"I want to go, but I can't. Where are you?"

"Right now we're in LA. We'll be heading to San Diego and up the coast to Seattle on our tour bus. Have you heard our single on the radio?"

"I'm sorry I haven't, but I'll listen for it. Where is Tarick? Can I speak to him?"

"He stepped out."

"Do you expect him to return soon?"

"We're not sure. He just left."

"Tell him I've said hello, and I wish everyone well."

"Sure."

She glanced at the kitchen clock, and realized she slept for six hours. She pet Ebbie, let her out, and got dressed while coffee percolated. She wasn't sure whether to visit Harold's wife first, or stop at the gas station. In the event Mrs. Humphrey had errands, she headed in that direction.

On her head was the blonde wig, and under her arm was the bag of fragrant lingerie, which included the picture of Harold's surprised face. She knocked on the front entrance door. No one answered. She rang the doorbell, and pulled her coat collar up to brace against the wind. She rang the bell, and still no answer. *Perfect,* she thought. She took a quick sweep of the area, knocked and rang the buzzer. When she was certain the house was empty, she broke in, and found what looked like the bedroom shared by the couple. She placed the bag of undergarments under the bed, and left.

She dreaded the drive to the Checklist Pantry. If this person could not identify Roy, it held grave consequences for him. She found the brown-haired young man who fit the description, and introduced herself. She showed the black and white photo to him, and he appeared baffled.

"I'm sorry. We have so many customers. Unless his hair was orange and purple, or he wore a bathing suit in the snow, I'd never give him another thought."

"Okay, thank you."

"Wait!"

"Yes?"

"Does he speak with an Irish accent?"

"No."

"Oh. He's not the guy I'm thinking of."

"Thanks, anyway. If anything comes to mind, here is my number."
She did not hold out hope for a call from him. In her VW, she
slammed her fist on the steering wheel.

Inside of Roy's house, dust accumulated on the counter tops,
silverware, and the table. The liquid had evaporated in the cup, leaving
dry scabs. She tossed the egg into the garbage, and washed the
dishware. She returned the borrowed photo into the frame which
contained six assorted family memories. Earl and Bessie smiled in
one. *They are all so young and beautiful. Their friendship has spanned
many years,* she thought. She picked up the childhood picture of
Bessie to see what year it was taken. The vivid color struck her as
unusual, and a copy of it was in the safe-deposit box, but no writing or
name was on it.

Pictures from that era were sepia, or black and white. She took the
photo out, and read the back: 9/20/1964, Kalie Deckler, age six. She
almost dropped it in her distraction of wondering why they would
have this, until she realized it was Doris and Roy's granddaughter.
*How did a friendship last for decades and something like this remain
silent? Sometimes, the longer a secret is kept, the harder it is to tell.*
She removed the garbage bag from under the sink, and underneath it
were extra trash liners they used for the plastic bin. Under it all was a
half empty flask of vodka. She locked the door behind her.

Tiny called as she arranged stage wear for the evening. He said that
toying with the beautiful couple had become like a sip of a milkshake,
sweet and so cold. Ben's wife became irate when he showed her
several new photos of her husband with Kalie. He said he flattened
Ben's tires a few times, and siphoned out the gas tank.

"Here's another suggestion if you're up for it. Stop at his house this
Monday the fourteenth. He and his wife are usually gone at 3:45, but
his chef, and the maid, Miss Brenda will be there. Show her a badge,
and say that you are with the Drug Enforcement Agency. Hint that
Ben has been using drug money to pay his staff's salary. Ask her if she
has seen him selling drugs, or if he tried to sell her anything. Of

course, apologize for upsetting her. Make sure the chef hears that Ben may go to prison. But here's the caveat. Don't do this unless you're up for a haircut and a shave, and you're willing to dress in a dark suit."

"I'll think about it," said Tiny. "Just to get even with that jerk, it may be worth it."

"I'm looking forward to your report."

The drone of engines wafted into the room. She took her bag, and Ebbie trotted to the van. As she stepped past Karl to sit in the chair beside him, he pulled her onto his lap. She lost her footing and fell onto him.

"We need to replace the carpet in here. It's so lumpy; I keep losing my balance." She sat in the empty chair, and smiled at Karl. "Well guys, a few more weeks, and we'll all be calling it a day."

"I can't wait," said Ted.

"Have you decided on a band name?"

"We have, but we're not telling anyone yet."

"You're all coming to my séance, aren't you? I'll have good food and it should be fun. It's on Monday, since we aren't rehearsing anymore. I'll have plenty of booze."

Grant, Karl and Sam glanced at her, not certain if she was serious or not. She looked confident. As she sat back, she realized she hadn't checked the yellow pages directory, where she was sure someone provided the service she desired.

At the club, Lydel and Jerry sat at the bar, but when the first set ended, they were gone. She told Showey, Hound and Drax to keep one of the cast iron mic stands near the sound board, and explained why. They were happy to keep a few items nearby just in case. Though the duo did not return, she planned to show their photos to the crew tomorrow.

On Saturday morning, she thumbed through the telephone directory. There were three names from which to choose. It was an easy decision. Any Medium who was free on Monday evening was perfect.

Relieved to secure a booking, she took a sip of coffee. The séance was in two days. The deceased woman who appeared to her on occasion needed to relay something significant. Even if this clairvoyant was just out to make a buck, and had no idea what she was doing, the voice from the past had a message.

She dressed and headed to Harold's house. She wondered what his wife's reaction to the photos might be, and her story about him stealing her underwear.

On his street, she proceeded slowly and drove around the block. There was no alley behind his home. It was 10:00 am, and she waited for any activity. She wove in and out of his neighborhood, passing his house until 11:00 am. Unless she got out of her VW and walked, there was no good way to get a clear view of his residence. She wanted to speak to Mrs. Humphrey, but had no idea what she looked like, having a brief view of a darkened facial profile and short brown hair from the outside of a window.

She felt a warm liquid trickle into her mouth, touched it, and knew it was blood before she saw her hand. A nose bleed had started. She parked the car, and pinched the bridge of her nose. No tissues were in her purse or glove compartment. It brought her stalking to a halt for the day, and sent her home. Glad that she was not on stage or in the middle of a conversation, she contemplated on seeking medical help, but hating doctors, she chose to wait until she had no other option.

In her bathroom, she washed her face, hands, and the front of her coat. She changed her clothes. When she stuck her hand in the pocket of her jeans, she pulled out a silver watch. The inscription read: 'We will miss you Earl'. She took her blood pressure cuff, and went to his house.

Bessie opened the door.

"I want to make sure you get this," said Lexa.

"Please come in. Earl will be so thrilled." Her clear blue eyes brightened the low, gray clouds overhead. "Look what Lexa found."

He bent forward, struggled a bit, arose and walked to the kitchen using his cane. "I…never thought I would see…this…again." He held it for a moment, smiled and slid it onto his wrist.

"I took it from Casey. If you see him, do not tell him you have it. Most likely he thinks he lost it. Let's get your blood pressure." She pumped the cuff. "It's 130/76."

"This…has been…a…great…week…for me," he said, working hard to speak. "I went…to thank…my…new…neighbor…for helping me. I…told…him…his fires reminded me of when my high school…burned…down. He said it's…what happened to his high school too. When he told…me…his…name, I…was shocked. I always wondered what became of him. We were once…the…best…of friends, and then his…family moved away. And my…my folks…moved. We didn't have cars or…or…phones, and…we lost track of…of each…other. I wish I could…tell Roy. The three of us were inseparable…years…ago. I wish…" He frowned and turned away.

"The three employees who worked on January sixth, when he went to the gas station don't remember Roy. He's falling apart. I hardly recognized him when I saw him on Tuesday."

"We all…worked…so…hard…our…whole…lives, and this…is what it comes to." He bent his head down. "I'm…going…to…help him. I'll be…his witness. I saw him that day," said Earl.

"You were unable to go to his hearing because of your stroke, right?

Earl did not speak. Bessie went to comfort him. Lexa bade them goodbye. She had a show to prepare for.

At the bar, Lydel and Jerry waved at her. Jerry, in a yellow plaid shirt, and purple bell-bottom slacks sat beside Lydel who donned a green turtle neck and blue plaid trousers. Both had dark, slicked back hair. Without black overcoats, their mystique had vanished.

Showey knocked on the dressing room door when the first set had ended, and asked Lexa if she was willing to speak to these men.

"Sure. Whatever you want to say to me will be said here and now." Though the men were large, Showey was taller and wider. They looked up at him.

"Officer Humphrey wants to talk to you."

"Tell him where to find me. He can stop acting like a baby, and take care of his own business. You don't need to hold his hand or change his diapers anymore." She slammed the door.

Two hours later, Harold sat at the bar alone, wearing a black turtleneck and jeans. She approached him when the set had ended. "From what I'm told, you want to speak to me," she said.

"My wife found lingerie and a photo of me in a bag under our bed, damn you. Just when I thought about letting this ordeal go, you pull that stunt." He stood up, and stepped closer to her. "Because of you, I changed all the locks on my doors."

She backed away. "I have no idea what you're talking about. I'll bet hundreds of people dislike you. I'll make an announcement about your new locks when I'm on stage, for anyone who cares."

"You can go to hell!" He took a swing at her, and she arched backwards. The tip of his fingers brushed against her cheek. The bartender and road crew rushed to subdue him as he reached for her long hair. "Get the hell away from me, all of you," he snarled. He exuded anger and hatred for her. "You little bitch."

"In war, no one wins. Deeds get uglier and more vicious. Mine can match yours. It stops when you decide it will." She was surrounded by the road crew and Karl who walked up to the scene.

"Lady, who the hell do you think you are? You're gonna be sorry you ticked me off." He stormed away.

"That went well," she said.

"What is that guy's problem?" asked Showey.

"I've tossed a lit match into a pool of gasoline."

Karl offered to buy her a drink. "I'll have whatever you're drinking." She took a large gulp of iced Gin and tonic. She squeezed the lime wedge into it, and took another sip.

Karl helped her walk to her door. The four drinks played havoc in her brain. She was unable to walk or see straight, and had no fear of anyone. She grabbed onto him to keep her balance, and could not get the side door opened. He took the keys, opened the latch and helped her up the stairs.

"I discovered something about this drink. It obliterates every last worry and care. It also makes me feel horny."

"I've never heard you say that before."

"I hope it's not why you bought me four of them." She grabbed a glass and filled it with water. Her equilibrium was off, and she teetered, as she took large gulps.

"Are you okay?" asked Karl.

"Other than not being able to focus my eyes, or walk, I'm fine, and you'd better go before I make a fool of myself. Good night and thanks for your help." She held the stove and walls to get to her bedroom. She fell onto the waterbed.

He stood in the doorway watching her. "Lexa," he said.

She pretended to be asleep.

"Hey, your door won't be locked if I leave."

She kept her eyes closed, and said nothing.

"Don't you want to take your coat off? You're gonna wake up sweating."

She rolled over to face him. "I'll take my coat off, and lock the door when you leave. Thanks again for your help."

"Where are your keys?" he asked.

"I think I left them on the table."

He locked up, returned to her bedroom with her things, and helped her take her coat off. He took off his jacket, pulled the comforter over both of them, and remained motionless.

"Karl...did I tell you that the photos the police found when they ransacked my place were two 8 x 10's of Ben Blesdin's wife? They didn't find the two folders I still have hidden."

225

"No, you didn't tell me."

"I'll bet your dad was happy to get his ten grand."

"Oh, he was."

"You're not going to be able to sleep. You didn't take an Ativan."

"It's outside in my suitcase."

"In your car? And your Rickenbacker is within reach of someone who could grab it," she said.

"If I leave, will you lock me out?"

"Maybe."

"Then I'm not moving."

"I won't be able to sleep. I'm too hungry. Get your stuff in here and let's eat."

He smiled. "Promise?"

"I don't want to break Tarick's heart, and I don't want to cause you any anguish. But, you're tempting me like you can't imagine. Stripping you naked would be a distraction for my starvation."

"Hold onto that thought." He arose, walked down the steps, turned the knob, and opened the door.

A large angry face stared down at him. He swung the door to shut it, but the man had a firm grip on the handle, and pushed inward with his massive leg. Karl was too drunk to match the man's strength. The wrestling was vicious. Lexa reached for her pistol. On all fours, she crawled to the darkened entryway.

"Stop! Stop or I will kill you," she screeched.

The bodies of both men banged into the hallway wall and door. Karl was rammed to the ground. She fired one shot into the wall behind them. The man ran outside. Karl lay motionless on the ground.

"How badly did he hurt you? Should I see if Sam is in any shape to take you to an emergency room?"

She turned on the hallway light. Blood trickled down his nose, lips and chin.

"It was Harold," he said wiping the red ooze off. "You don't need to take me anywhere."

226

"If we press charges, this vendetta will get really ugly." She dumped ice into a plastic bag, got a washcloth, and handed it to him. Knuckles rapped on the doorway of the upstairs stairwell. "Yes, Sam," she said as she opened the door.

"What happened? It sounded like all hell broke loose down here. I almost called for help."

"Karl took the worst of it. I fired my gun to stop an intruder." She let out a deep sigh. "It was the guy who took a swing at me this evening. He's unhinged. See you tomorrow."

Sam closed the door.

Karl ran the bathroom faucet. "This nosebleed won't stop."

She asked him to sit on the floor, rest his head against the wall, and pinch the bridge of his nose for five minutes. Not that it would work, but at least give it a try.

When the bleeding stopped, he took in a deep breath.

"Don't move. I'll get your stuff, and get some food out." She held onto the walls, every corner and doorway.

They ate, and he brought his belongings into her room. "I never knew being in a band was so dangerous," he said, as they nestled their heads on pillows.

"Everything I do has been hazardous these days. It's what I get for hanging around the wrong crowd." She turned a night-light on, and the lamp off.

"It comes with the territory. How often has someone come into the dressing room handing out uppers, downers, cocaine, or some kind of hallucinogen like it was candy? Now we've attracted a team of criminals," he said.

"Yea, but in a few weeks, it will all be over."

He stroked her hair. "You, Sam, and I can find a drummer."

"Sam will be relieved to be as far away from me as he can get. Possibly he has something else lined up. He hasn't said one word to us about staying together."

"We have poured so much time, work, and energy into this project, and I'll have nothing to show for it." His face saddened.

"I don't have a strong enough belief in my abilities. You have real talent. There is a successful band waiting for a musician like you."

"So you're going to give up?" he asked.

"It's probably for the best." She loved music. She closed her eyes, and all she could envision was smashing her Telecaster guitar to the ground.

When they awoke, she made coffee and French toast. Karl had little to say, other than that he would see her tonight, and attend the séance tomorrow.

Guilt provoked her to call Harold's wife.

"Hello?" The woman's voice was eerily soft.

"Is Harold home?"

"No, he's not."

"This is the woman who left lingerie under your bed, and I want to apologize. I should never have dragged you into the issues I'm having with your husband."

"Are you having an affair with him?" the woman asked.

"No. I think he's a disgusting bully. He enjoys hurting people." Sobbing suffused through the receiver. "I'm sorry. I hope I didn't cause problems for your marriage, said Lexa."

"We've had trouble from the start. I'm always scared. He has a fierce temper, and when he's angry, he lashes out. I never know what sets him off, or when he'll attack me."

"Is there any other place you can stay?" asked Lexa.

"I've thought about it a lot. I would have to grovel to my friends in Russia. They'll gloat and remind me daily that they told me not to become a mail order bride."

"Isn't it a better option than being beaten?"

"It would be if I wasn't so afraid he would kill my brother Jack, and I would be next."

228

"I'm sorry. Don't give him permission to have power over you. If he bruises you, take pictures, and keep them in a safe-deposit box. Make sure your brother and a good friend are aware of what is happening and give them each a key."

"My husband doesn't let me have friends," the woman said through her sobs.

"Mrs. Humphrey, if I gave you my phone number could you memorize it? I may be able to help you."

"Please call me Aleeya. I will try to remember."

Seething in anger, Lexa dialed Ben Blesdin's office. A receptionist answered, and informed her of his unavailability.

"Please leave him this message. The newspaper would like to discuss the fascinating story he has regarding the arson cases. And Mr. Humpty has fallen off the wall again. Thanks." She had to repeat it.

An hour later, her phone rang.

"What the hell is going on?" asked Ben.

"Keep Harold away from me."

"He's not my responsibility. You of all people should know that."

"Then bask in the ugly publicity when news agencies get copies of the material I mailed to you. Harold breaking into my house last night was the last straw."

"Why do you think I can control what he does?" asked Ben.

"He's on your payroll. Cut him off," said Lexa.

"What did you say? My what? Where are you getting this?"

"How long do you believe you can get away with all the crap you've got your hands in?" she asked.

"Listen here. I'll make sure you're sorry you ever crossed me."

"Be careful dude. I have friends you do not know about. And…do the names Bessie and Earl mean a damn thing to you?

"What have you told my parents?" Ben asked.

"I don't need to tell them anything. They have been through enough. Your Mom takes good care of your Dad, who could have another stroke at any minute. They have lost some of their best friends. I have no intention of putting them through more grief. Are you that self-absorbed? They gave, and you took. It's all you know."

"That's bullshit. They don't appreciate what I do," said Ben.

"Be sure to write up the guidelines they need to follow for their golden child, and give it to them. See how that works. In the meantime, the pictures go nowhere if you're a good boy, but perhaps it's too much to ask." She hung up.

Showey, Hound, and Drax mocked the startled look on the faces in the photos given to them of Lydel and Jerry. Three solid, cast iron mic stands stood near the sound board during the night. It was a relief to have an uneventful evening. She reminded her bandmates about the 6:00 pm event tomorrow as they went separate ways, and all planned to be there.

Sunday March 13, 1977

Adversaries force us to make choices we may never have made. We think about where we stand in our lives, and the outcome of our decisions. Sometimes it's hard to step out of our element of comfort, and speak out on who we are, especially when those who have louder voices, bigger hands, and bolder personalities can so easily overshadow us if we allow them to.

I'm feeling more than a brotherly attraction to Karl. I tried to tell him about the affair I had with Grant a year ago. What I thought would never matter has trickled my way and is making a surprising impact. When I first met Karl, I saw us as acquaintances only, but he has seeped into my life, and his friendship has become the glow of a light in darkness. Though he is caring and kind, the insecurities and demons each of us battle would destroy a relationship. I hope he can accept me as his friend, as that is all we can ever be.

Chapter 14

Monday, March 14 – Sunday, March 20

When she awoke at noon, six hours remained in which to get to the courthouse, grocery shop, and be ready for a séance.

Her first stop was the register of deeds office, where she looked up the addresses of burned down properties which were owned by Benjamin Blesdin. She found it peculiar that no news media viewed this as suspicious. She questioned the depths to where his hush money went.

In the clerk of circuit court's room, she acquired Roy's court date, which was in two weeks, and his public defender's name. A gnawing fear arose in her stomach. He was a withered tree, splintering apart branch by branch, being destroyed by a storm over which he had no control.

At the grocery store, she lingered in the bakery aisle. The cannoli caught her eye. Today she purchased them to serve as a dessert.

She called Tiny on the secured line as a batch of chocolate brownies baked. "Are you aware that twelve of Ben Blesdin's buildings have been torched? I looked it up today. Why this hasn't been publicized makes me wonder if his high-powered news agency friends are suppressing this story. He has no fear of my letters and photos."

"You could be right," said Tiny.

"Did you consider visiting his maid as a DEA agent?"

"Yes I have. Ben's cohorts threatened to burn my business down. I was in a bad state of mind when you first came in. I was ready to give up. Your folder has been a royal treat. Gordon, Ellis and I had a little chat, and we called a truce. Apparently they don't want their places in ashes either."

"I spoke to Harold's wife yesterday. He beats her up on a regular basis. She's terrified of him to the point of telling a random stranger during our phone conversation. I stumbled on what to say to her. She thinks he'll kill her if she leaves," she said.

"When he patrolled the streets, I lost track of the speeding tickets he gave me. Once he charged me with reckless driving. He said I was twenty miles over the limit. I knew I wasn't. It cost me plenty. I hated him. Humphrey is out to get you because he doesn't have the same kind of power over you like he has with everyone else."

"Maybe...make sure you're out of Ben's house by..."

"Yes, I know. 3:50," he said.

She prepared fresh vegetables, whipped up a creamy dip, and placed them on a silver tray. An assortment of fruit was set on a large red platter. The warm brownies were sliced and arranged, as well as a variety of sliced cheese and crackers. On a colorful plate, she lined up the cannoli. Six white candles and a matchbox were set on the dining room table, and she blew up three white balloons, which she left on the floor near the table. Ebbie gnawed on a bone nearby.

She had finished a bowl of fruit when her guests arrived. Karl, Grant, Ted, and his wife Debra entered the kitchen, and selected appetizers. Lexa greeted everyone including Sam, who opened the door at the bottom of the steps. The front doorbell rang.

Dressed in purple satin and almost lost in the fabric, the woman introduced herself as Dorothea. She removed her coat and held it in her arms like an infant. Her artificially deep black hair, eyes and eyebrows were offset by her pale skin. Lexa welcomed her in, and offered her a choice of Merlot, Pinot Noir or Chardonnay. She opened her red mouth to reveal a hoarse voice from either age, or constant use, and declined a drink until the session ended. She placed a brownie and fruit on her plate.

Ted brought a six-pack of Blatz beer, sipped on one, and heaped desserts on his dish.

"Please join me in the dining room," said Dorothea. She lit up the candles, and asked what the balloons were for.

"Being lightweight, they move easily. I have seen them float upward here for no apparent reason." Lexa wondered if the pallid woman also got glimpses into the future, or if her primary skill was the ability to connect with deceased souls. "I hope to connect, or speak to a specific spirit. Her name is Julette Zadrik. She lived here many years ago, and randomly appears in different rooms in this house."

The woman's deep, smoky voice was filled with assurance. "Everyone, please be seated." Her dewy crimson lips glistened in the dim candlelight as she spoke, and her purple dress glimmered. "Please join hands, and let us take deep breaths in, and deep breaths out. Breathe with me, a rhythmic, steady inhale and exhale. See the balance of light and dark, day to night, dawn to evening, as we breathe together, synchronous, harmonious. Though our planetary rotation is swift, and vibrational energy encircles us, we feel stillness. Sun, sand, and Chronos the serpentine from a timeless place, the eternal surrounds us on this finite realm where we are all travelers. Let the earth fall away for these moments, and let the door be opened between our worlds. Surround us with light, and let us be of service to souls who may be in need."

Lexa felt tingling on her skin. Karl held her right hand and Debra her left.

"Julette, we are aware of your presence in this home. We call upon you to join us tonight. Again we shall breathe together, and repeat the name, Julette. If you are near, please move a balloon or blow out a candle."

The dining room was mildly electrified and eerily silent.

233

"Julette, we invite you to be a part of our session. We wish to hear your words. I will gladly speak for you."

As the clock ticked by, the restlessness in the room increased.

"When a spirit is hesitant to join us, it is for a reason."

Ted let out a loud belch. "This is a joke." Debra smacked his arm.

"Feel free to wait upstairs in the studio," said Sam. "You can use my guitar and amp."

Ted arose, popped a beer open in the kitchen, and jumped up the steps.

The group rejoined hands, and Dorothea repeated the reason for all to relax and deep breathe. It was about five minutes later, when her voice changed to a lighter, clearer tone.

"It is the school...you must visit....Casey...his school knows." A pause of silence ensued for ten seconds, and the woman grimaced. "Fire...erupts...will consume Lexa. Beware the needle. Flames submerge her...asleep. Casey...has a ring...crowbar...Earl. Doris death no accident...unforgivable."

One of the white balloons ascended to the ceiling, and lingered there long after Dorothea thanked Julette for her message, and requested the door between worlds to be once again sealed. Long after she was paid and left, and Ted returned to the group to hear everyone's version of the session, a small white ordinary air filled balloon remained affixed above them.

Debra slapped his arm again. "You should have stayed."

"Dude, you missed it," said Grant.

Drax snuck down the steps to grab a few desserts.

All of the guests filtered out except for Karl. "I'll help you clean up, if that's okay."

"It's really nice of you." She didn't mean to sound stiff and formal. But she wasn't sure how to treat Karl anymore, especially after two glasses of wine, which melted her moral code.

"What's your take on the messages we got?" he asked.

"I wasn't sure if the woman was a fraud, but I'll take her words seriously. I'll make some calls to find out where Casey went to school. If Doris' death was no accident, and Earl is involved, I'll try to piece it together before Roy's court date on the 28th."

"And walk the fine line of Earl's fragile health."

"Maybe he's ready to talk about it."

"Especially if he thinks he doesn't have much time left." Karl wrapped up the remainder of the brownies and set them on a shelf. He placed the corked wine in the refrigerator, as though he had always known how her kitchen was organized. "I forgot to ask if you wanted anything to drink before I put it away," he said.

"No, I've had enough, thanks."

Sam's door slammed outside, and footsteps pounded a steady rhythm down the stairwell. The garage door let out a low hum as it closed, and his van revved. Drenched in the excitement of some luscious woman who awaited him, he would tell her the story of his evening, and enchant the warm body he held.

She felt twinges of loneliness. If the streets were safe to run in, she would sprint for miles to raise her heart rate, and invoke a sense of calm. Karl stood close to her, almost like a child waiting for a mother to validate his good behavior. She turned to face him. "So, where are you headed off to?"

"I'm going home to have a sandwich."

"I can make some for us. There's a lot of leftover fruit also."

"Can we have grilled cheese? It was so good."

"Sure." As she flipped the bread, she felt his breath on her neck. He said nothing as he watched her. He had already opened up about his feelings, and repeating it was pointless.

"Let's eat in your bedroom, and watch the Tonight Show. It's usually funny," he said.

"Okay."

He turned on the TV, and they laughed with Johnny Carson. He melted into her eyes and stroked her arms. She looked at his hands. Both jumped at the sound of a loud bang emitted in the alleyway.

"It was either a gunshot or a car backfiring," he said.

"Should we sneak outside?"

"So I can get wailed on again?" he asked.

"What if someone shot at your car or popped one of your tires? What if someone is breaking into Roy's place or hurting Earl and Bessie? I'll take my gun, and you can use my civil war sword."

"We should see what's going on, but I hate this," he said.

She clutched her pistol and night vision goggles, and reached alongside of the wall. Karl grasped the sword, and they headed outside.

"Let's take the stairs. We'll get a better view," she said.

All appeared quiet. Bessie peered out of her bedroom window, her neck reaching side to side as if it created a better survey of the landscape. Roy's house appeared undisturbed, as did Karl's 1970 turquoise Chevelle Malibu. Below them, the untended steel drum carried smoke into the vastness of the clouds above.

"We're so on edge; we're overreacting to a misfiring car." He rested his head onto his hand. "I'd better go." He handed the sword to her, and took each step as though he waited for her to stop him. His eyes gazed at her like river stones in moonlight, pausing as though he was certain she would ask him to stay. An ambulance wailing like a lone coyote in the distance gave her a pang of worry as his car drove through the alley. She sat on the cold step for five minutes, watching hot embers light up, sizzle, and sparkle.

Monday March 14, 1977

To start a good fire, there are simple guidelines. Like everything else in life, rules must be followed to attain success at any task. Generating a flash above ignitable fibers causes heat particles to nestle and imbed it. Continued

236

friction arouses sparks, which burrow and penetrate deeper into the tinder nest. Sustained stroking causes the temperature to rise until the heat of combustion ignites into an eruption of flames.

Small twigs which burn the brightest and most intense become cinders in a matter of minutes. The lingering hot coals will ignite anything that touches it. To keep it alive, it must be cultivated. Lavish new kindling into it generously; add fuel to keep it strong. The greater the attention given, the grander the fire will be. What had been powerful and combustible can subside and fade.

Those who do not learn how to nurture a fire will be left with scorch and ashes which will scatter into the wind. One must know when to enrich, when to step back, but also when to run.

Karl Jung once said, "The difference between a good life and a bad life is how well you walk through the fire."

I say, 'when fires erupt around us, we can either be consumed, or we can conquer them with knowledge and insight.'

Almost an hour of her morning was spent checking off schools listed in the yellow pages. She asked each secretary about a student named Casey Relmen. No one had heard of him. When she spoke to the receptionist at Lincoln High School, she leaned back on her chair relieved, and took a sip of coffee. She asked if she could schedule an appointment with the principal. No she was not a reporter. He listed this high school on his job application. Yes, of course he used them as a reference. Why did the secretary argue with her? A meeting was arranged for Thursday morning.

She walked to Earl's house. He let her in, and said that Bessie had left to run some errands.

"I dropped by to make sure you see your doctor as soon as possible. You will need a certificate to prove that you are mentally capable to take the witness stand. He may refer you to a psychiatrist, and it must be done by the following week."

"Can…you…write…this…down…for…Bessie?"

"Yes. I also have the name of the public defender you need to contact. He has to be aware that you plan to testify. Should I tell Roy you plan to go to court on his behalf, and you saw him that day? He'll be able to pull himself together if he has hope. Right now he has none."

"I…didn't…see…Roy…that…day. He…will…know."

"What do you mean? I thought you said you saw him."

"I…went…to…see…Doris."

"Was she still alive when you saw her? Do you remember what time it was?"

"It…was…at…about…4:00. She asked me…to…do…a…favor."

"You went to help her? Doesn't Roy usually get home at 4:30?"

"She…asked…me…to…open…a large…antique wooden box she got at…an estate…sale. It…was nailed shut. I took my crowbar. She didn't…want…to…to…bother her husband. I…said it shouldn't take more than…five…minutes, and I would be done before he got home."

"It was nice of you to help her."

"I found…a…a picture…she didn't want me to see."

"What picture are you talking about?"

"I…wondered…where…she…got…a a…color…picture of Bessie when…she…was…young, that…I…had…never seen. I took it out of…of…the frame…to…look at…the back of it. It…wasn't my wife."

He saw the photo of Kalie. "Are you able to tell me who it was?"

"It…is…my…my…granddaughter. Doris said…said it was none of my business. Can…you believe it? My…granddaughter…is…none of my…business? Bessie lost a piece of…of her heart, a belief in…her…dreams every time she had a miscarriage. Five times we…went…through…it, and we resigned from ever having a child.

238

When Ben was...born, it took the sting...out...of...the next lost pregnancy. She got up to...four...months...with...that...one. For nineteen years, we were denied the...knowledge...of...of...a granddaughter. Nineteen ye...years. Wh...Why? My son never told me. No one...told...told us. I was so angry." His eyes became the shiny red ornaments she had seen when she first visited him. Rueful droplets fell off of his cheeks, and streaked his tan corduroy shirt.

"Was she alive when you left her house?"

He sat at the kitchen table in a daze, staring through the window. "Every day, I...can see their...their...house...from...this...window. Every day. Roy...saved...my...life."

"Was she still breathing?"

Saltwater seeped down his weathered face. He sat motionless. His once strong hands were bent, veined, and spotted. His grand view of life had diminished. "I pushed her. I...I struck...her...with the crowbar. I...picked her up and carried her to her bed."

"Please show Bessie this note. And you must tell her all of this before you get into the courtroom."

He did not speak as she left.

Her blood was boiling as she opened her door. She dialed Ben's office, and asked for him. She was told he was in a meeting. She said this was life or death urgent.

"Hello?"

"Asshole! Your father knows about Kalie. Just because he hasn't said anything to you, doesn't mean he's an idiot. You have some serious amends to make." She hung up.

Her heart raced, and she hyperventilated. She slipped into her boots and a jacket, leashed Ebbie, and they ran until she was unable to breathe. She ran until her legs ached, and the muscles in her stomach stabbed her. Doubled over, she stopped to catch her breath, and the duo walked home, Ebbie intermittently looking at her.

She dialed Tiny's office. "How was your visit with Miss Brenda?"

"It was entertaining. The chef stood in the doorway listening. They both looked...they looked..."

"Mortified?"

"Yea. I was there for five minutes. Any longer and I couldn't have kept a straight face. And I called my buddies. The three of us have some business to tend to regarding Harold. He deserves the full treatment."

"Somehow, I don't think he'll change."

"We use a special cure. It hasn't failed me yet."

"You're going to beat him senseless?"

"Hell no. He wakes up dressed in women's clothes, lipstick and make-up. We paint his nails. Drop him off downtown, and let him go. We use up a roll of film. His co-workers get a copy. If he still doesn't behave, we drop him off in a pink tutu. Everyone gets a photo, including his mom and dad."

"Is there a third time?"

"Most definitely."

"I won't ask."

Though Tiny's dialogue brought her mood up, she still felt distraught. She wished it was as easy to console the men whose friendship had spanned decades. She started up her VW.

At the jail, she paced as she waited for Roy, deep in thought.

It startled her to see his clean-shaven face. His eyes returned to their dark clarity.

"I realize you never knew me well, but I have to tell you something. Today, I told Ben his dad knows that Kalie is his granddaughter. Earl found out when he saw her childhood photo at your house, and he feels betrayed."

His deep gaze had seen the worst, and his speech appeared constrained. "I should have told him about Kalie years ago. How do you tell a man his repulsive son screwed my daughter for months, and dumped her as soon as he found out she was pregnant? Of all the girls who clamored over him, I always wondered why my child became his victim."

"They lived in close proximity. It would have been easy for him to sneak away with her, and have a rendezvous. But that's not why I'm here. I don't want to upset you, but I need to ask what your wife's post-mortem report showed."

"Why does that matter to you?"

"I had a conversation with someone who told me she was hit by a crowbar."

"A crowbar. Who told you that?"

"Earl admitted to it."

"He was at my house that day?"

"Doris asked him to open a small wooden crate."

He gave her a long stare, and was silent for a minute. "She... she." He choked, and stared downward for a few seconds. "She died from..." He let out a sob. "There was blunt force to the left temporal lobe. She also had a hematoma on the top of her head." He turned away. "Blood was pooled to the back of her skull." He sat in silence for a minute. "They also discovered she had an enlarged liver due to excess alcohol consumption. She never let on. I never knew."

"I'm so sorry, Roy. But, if they're accusing you of striking a hammer to her head, it would leave a different mark than one from a crowbar. Don't you see? It should prove your innocence."

"I'll never believe he killed her. He cried so hard at her funeral."

"He discovered Kalie's picture, and went into a fit of rage. Doris told him it was none of his business, and they had a heated argument. He was in your house at the time of her death. A new autopsy must be done right away. It shouldn't be too hard to remove her from a Mausoleum. Put up a fuss, and do whatever you have to. When this comes out in court, it's going to make a lot of people look incompetent."

"Have you had a polygraph test?"

"No."

"It's one more thing for you to demand. I'm disappointed in your public defender. Call him as soon as I leave. You may already have this, but here's a copy of his number. I can verify everything if necessary. If his office stalls you in any way, tell them that someone else intends to confess."

He cleared his throat, and his dark eyes appeared to restore. "Earl and I go way back. He would confess for no other reason than to protect me."

"Ben lost his cool when I won my trial. His stomping echoed down the hallways. Today I told him he was an asshole."

Roy smiled. "I've wanted to tell him that for ages."

"Before I forget, Earl discovered that he and our new neighbor went to the same high school. The man we saw dancing near the fire. His herbal remedies have helped Earl tremendously. He said the three of you were once best friends, and your high school burnt down."

Roy's moist eyes flickered. "I remember him. He said he was going to become a doctor. When his family moved, we lost touch. All of our lives changed."

"What do you mean?"

His head hung low. "Earl got into a fight and almost killed someone. He sat behind bars for a while, but I'll never believe he would harm Doris. I started drinking, and did a little time myself." He raised his eyes toward her, his face filled with sadness and apprehension.

"I'm sorry to hear that. I know your old friend would like to visit you. See you soon," she said.

"I want to thank you for your stopping by, and for your help." His voice was soft and tight, as though he held back tears.

She had not seen him smile since the beginning of December when she watched him and Doris from her kitchen window, as they struggled to get an evergreen off of the top of their car and into the house. The ground was white, and flecks of snow blew around them. Doris slipped, and his gloved hands dropped the base of the tree to help her. He picked her up under her arms, like a mother would to a child. When she regained her footing, he kissed her lips as the snow melted onto their hair and faces. Love brimmed through his sable eyes while he steadied her, and they regained their grip of the branches. They laughed as they slid the evergreen into the doorway.

On her way home, Lexa stopped at the park where she and Tarick picnicked last summer. The winding path twisted toward the beach. The roar of the waves amplified off of the profusion of trees, and concrete walkway. She paused to watch the whitecaps gnarl their watery fingers toward her and recede into calm, ebb and flow. The forces of wind, the gravitational pull of the moon and sun as it had done billions of years ago, swirled before her. In her mind, she floated out into the distance questioning if she had the strength to make it back to the shore.

Though the sound of the TV was like a friend in her bedroom, she was far away, deep in thought as to what she would do when her band ends. She dwelled on both Roy's and Earl's revelations. A life unexpectedly ending, broken friendships, and a betrayal exposed, innocent bystanders became wound up in the conflict.

She awoke in Wednesday's daylight to a ringing phone at 11:30 am, and Tarick's voice.

"I've awoken you, haven't I?"

"Yes, but I'm glad to hear from you. Where are you?"

"We've been zigzagging all over the state. A few weeks ago, we were in Chula Vista, and we worked our way up through Anaheim and Bakersfield. We've toured through Fresno, San Francisco, and today we're in Oakland, but we must have hit thirty some other clubs on the way. Almost one club a night."

"Are you enjoying it?"

"For the most part. The crowds have been multiplying because of the airplay of our record. We've been getting a lot of hype on the radio."

"The bigger the crowds are, the bigger your paycheck will be."

"We have a huge overhead. We pay a bus driver, bus rental, roadies, catering, stage crew, a sound engineer, a merchandise manager, and an agency. We're already worrying about recording our next album."

"I often wonder if I really want the scrutiny of stardom. Tabloids don't harass nurses."

"There really isn't any way I can explain how it feels to have thousands of fans screaming for you. It's a major high."

"I understand the high of which you speak. Were there any glitches at the studio?"

"The engineer seemed to know what he was doing, but since the sound on a vinyl record depends on the mics, the converters, the preamps, and the acoustic environment, I'd say it went as well as it could for our first shot at it."

"All recordings alter the material it tries to preserve when you convert the sound onto another medium," she said.

"Anything that gets sampled at a frequency in the same or adjacent order of magnitude will lose some vibrancy," he said.

"True, but when the DJ pipes your music through everyone's radios, people will remember the groove, how good the vocals come across, and how the song makes them feel."

"I miss you." His voice was transmitted through the simple device she held in her hand. "No other girl gets it like you do."

She wished he was beside her. "I miss you too."

As she rested the receiver in its cradle, she realized she did not like his last statement. 'No other girl gets it like you do.' It spoke volumes. She closed her eyes and imagined who he was referring to, and felt a burst of sadness as her imagination conjured up the gorgeous woman. She knew the old adage; a band's popularity is directly proportional to the number of groupies. He may have wanted to break it off, but she sounded too pleasant, or he enjoyed her banter and knowledge. Perhaps she was overthinking.

One more call had to be made, as she took a sip of coffee.

"This is your dad's neighbor, and I have something important to say. Don't judge; just listen. Your father did not take your mother's life. Someone else confessed to me, and I'm unable to discuss this. It will come out in court."

"So?"

"So, your mother's body will be exhumed. A new autopsy will be done. Your dad is demanding a new medical examiner, and is taking a polygraph test. If he's telling the truth, this evidence will help him."

"And what about the insurance policy he took out?"

"If you or your sister had spoken to him, you would have no doubt it was your mother's idea. She wanted you to be taken care of if anything happened to her. I hope you tell Marion."

The stillness of guilt cut the air of silence between them. A quiet sob heaved from her burdened chest. The tragic loss of her mother looked to find blame, and her father had become an easy target. "I miss her in a way you can't imagine."

"I'm terribly sorry, but don't desert your dad. He needs his girls more than ever. Earl discovered he has a granddaughter four days before his stroke, so I'm not certain if he told his wife."

"Did the coward finally come clean after all these years? He used me to restore his reputation." Lexa heard weeping. "I moved in with my dad's sister to have the baby, but my life wasn't the same. I had to go to another school near my aunt's house after she was born. Every day I think about the child I gave up."

"Ben is in touch with his daughter. He gave her a job."

"How did you find out?" asked Melinda.

"Because of the friends we have in common, we've conversed on several occasions. She looks a lot like Bessie, doesn't she?"

"I wouldn't know. I haven't seen her since she was six years old."

For her appointment Thursday morning, she wore a below the knee black skirt, a white sweater with a black lace design, black heels, and

245

she combed her hair into a bun. She held a yellow steno pad of paper under her arm when she greeted the principal, and she thanked him for meeting her.

She sat in a tan chair, facing a large brown desk stacked with separate piles of papers, and said that she wished to inquire about the young man she had mentioned who applied to be her bodyguard. She asked if she could record the conversation.

"Sure. So, Casey used us as a reference on a job application? I find it hard to believe. He left a lasting impression here. He was most unusual and we had to let him go."

"You let him go because he was unusual? Many kids have insecurities because a curriculum forces them to do something they can't. Schools ostracize kids who don't do an assignment the way a teacher expects. I had teachers who tried to regiment my views. Everyone processes differently."

"Calm down, Miss. That wasn't his problem. His IQ is higher than most other pupils. We determined he has psychopathic tendencies. He burned his textbook during math class, and grinned throughout the entire reprimand. He set flash powder off in the hallway, and smoke consumed the school. He laughed when he was disciplined. When he attacked the girl who sat next to him in Chemistry class with a Bunsen burner, and started her clothes on fire, he was permanently expelled. There were many more incidents with classmates and teachers. They were all afraid of him. That includes me. I'm not going to sugar coat it for you, Miss Lynnch. I would not give him a good recommendation as a bodyguard."

"Was he persecuted in any way by his peers?"

"No. He victimized them. He bullied anyone who got in his way mercilessly. We have always questioned if his actions caused one of his fellow students to commit suicide."

"He wants to work with my band. What should we expect?"

"I suspect he has ulterior motives. He's been kicked out of several schools and two that I can think of are St. John's Cathedral High

School and Kemper Hall High School before he ended up here at Lincoln. This was his last chance and he failed it."

"Thank you for your assistance."

She got it all on tape. The validation she wanted to present to Ted, Grant, Hound, Showey, and the Band's agent was in her safekeeping. On the way to the show tonight, she would pop it into the cassette player. Sam, Karl and Drax needed no persuading.

The clubs scheduled for this weekend were within a thirty mile radius. Everyone decided to drive to the venue separately. She and Sam had driven to Waukesha in the van. Edginess hung over everyone that evening, especially Karl, who drank heavily. By the end of the night, his eyelids, like fleshy rolls of skin, almost covered his eyes. He refused her offer to drive him home. She asked again, and he refused.

"Give me your damn keys, Karl. I'm driving whether you want me to or not."

He fell asleep on the way home. When they arrived at his apartment, she wrapped his arm around her shoulder, and he stumbled up the stairs. She opened the faucet, filled a glass half full of water, took an Ativan, and handed it to him.

"Take this, so you don't wake up in rougher shape than you're already going to."

His pink eyes looked upward, and he drank. She took his clothes off, and tucked him in. He snored lightly as she brushed her teeth, pulled her hair into a ponytail, and changed into one of his long-sleeved t-shirts.

Blades of sunlight streamed under the blinds into his room as he awoke curled up behind her. He sat up, rubbed his eyes and looked around.

"What...happened? Last night is a blur. Did we...?"

"You were in a foul mood yesterday evening. You said you were done. Do you remember saying you were leaving us, and you couldn't stand any more bullshit?"

"Yes. The last memory I have is when you yelled at me for my car keys." He looked as though he had lost something, but could not recollect where it was, or what it was.

"Why did you get so drunk?" she asked.

"The craziness of my life got to me." He held his head in his hands, and did not speak. "I'm about to lose my band and your friendship."

"Don't be too hard on yourself," she said.

He looked up. "Where are my clothes?"

"Hanging on the knobs of your dresser. I'll make some coffee."

In his kitchen, as they ate eggs and buttered toast, she asked him if he wanted to keep the band together, because if he did, she could play the tape for everyone tonight in the dressing room. It was severely damaging to Casey. Otherwise, she would keep it as a souvenir in her bookshelf.

"Even if we play the tape, if Sam has other plans he'll leave anyway."

"I guess we'll see. We could work harder, get our game on, and prove to him that we're worth him staying for."

Prior to the show, Karl corralled everyone into the dressing room. "Listen up," he shouted. "This will take ten minutes."

The start button was pushed, and the reel began. A man's clear voice silenced the room. Some glanced at each other; some looked downward. When the tape ended, no one spoke. Showey and Hound had already made up their minds, most likely because Drax had told them about throwing Casey out of the house. Ted and Grant faced each other.

"Is this why you had the séance?" Grant's thumb and forefinger stroked his chin. He did not hide the fear in his face. "I'm not sure how to get out of the gigs we have. We already signed contracts."

"No one said you shouldn't honor any current obligations, but I thought you might want to know this before you begin working with him. I highly doubt he would ever tell you."

When Casey showed up, he was met by icy stares and suspicious looks. The road crew refused his offer of drinks and equipment assistance. Lexa moved her belongings behind the stage to keep a close watch on them. Karl, Sam, and Grant followed suit. Ted's usual relaxed friendliness stiffened, and Grant's smiles were contrived.

Casey sensed this, and was quieter than usual. He shot an evil look at Lexa, and left before the last set ended.

She returned home in Sam's van. "Did you have something else lined up?"

"I've had a few serious meetings and some interesting offers, but I wasn't sure how things were going to play out," he said.

"If something better comes along will you tell us?"

"Sure," said Sam.

She thought of the conversation they once had about honesty, about his broken promise of telling her if he desired someone else. Now their relationship was a charade. It would be as hard to confess their separation to their families as it had been for Roy to tell his secret to Earl. The truth now held dire consequences for both of these men. She was drawn to the smoke when the van door opened.

Friday March 18, 1977

Above wooden panels, a splash of soft gray streaks floated upward, whirling to the tips of trees like blossoms in one moment, and vanquishing in the next. I crept up the stairwell until I could see the man's black and silver hair gleaming in the light.

When settlers who poured into the South during the 1800's began moving westward, tribes who inhabited the land were considered an obstacle. Settlers petitioned the government to remove them.

The dimness of the fire accentuated his cheeks which were hollowed out by the forces of oppression that he and those like him had withstood in their lives.

The U.S. Government used treaties to displace Indigenous people from their rightful land, which was strengthened by the Indian Removal Act of 1830. Indirectly, this shaped the displaced man he had become. The government had violated both the treaties and Supreme Court rulings.

He gazed upward, as if he knew I was there.

The death of more than four thousand Cherokees who were forced out, called their passage the Trail of Tears. To peel back our fragile flesh is to show the same tissue, veins, muscles, and bones which reside in all of humanity, the DNA design by which we all live.

And below me tonight sits a man who is as imprisoned as Roy is.

At her white table, her breakfast of cereal and a banana was as unsatisfying as lying beside Karl, and not touching him. Through Earl's wire fence, she saw a police car park, and two uniformed men walk to his front door. Anxiety struck her like a slap to the face. She dropped her spoon, grabbed her coat and ran to his house. She hit his back buzzer again and again.

"Lexa, I can't speak to you now," said Bessie.

"I need to talk to you and Earl."

"Not now. He's talking to the police."

"Did you get the message I left for you? Did he see a psychiatrist?" They overheard Earl ask where Bessie went, and Officer Humphrey repeated Bessie's name.

"I'll be right there," she said turning away. "No. Why does he need that? He's not crazy."

"Oh, no, no, his doctor must evaluate him to make sure he is competent to stand trial. There is a competency test that needs to be done to make sure Earl is of sound mind, otherwise, the prosecution can throw out his testimony. Whatever he says right now is inadmissible."

"I had no idea."

"What does he plan to tell them?"

"He thinks he killed Doris, but I don't believe it."

"We need to find out what's in the new autopsy report. I should have spoken to you. Interrupt him, and tell them that he cannot tell them anything right now."

Bessie walked into the room. "I'm sorry to have bothered you, but what my husband says can't be used in court. He had a stroke, and I'm certain you must know it causes a degree of damage to the brain. I need to take him to his doctor before he can discuss this."

Earl frowned. "I know what I'm talking about."

"Dear, don't forget that legally, they can't take any statements from you."

Harold Humphrey bent his head down and rubbed his temples. "Now maybe you can both calm down, and tell us what happened. Where were we?" His grip tightened on his pen.

"I said he cannot talk to you. I'm sorry we wasted your time."

Lexa hid in the kitchen. Earl appeared baffled by it all, and his face was reddened, but not as much as the faces of the two large men who had come to hear a confession.

"Are you sure?" asked Harold.

"Yes, we're sure. Right, Earl?"

He was silent.

"Right?"

"Y…yes."

The house shook when the large hand of Officer Humphrey slammed the door.

Lexa explained to both of them the reason the doctor's visit was needed, and most likely he would recommend a specific test from a psychiatrist, which was typical protocol. "You said you had a crowbar in your hand, and you pushed Doris. Did the metal bar strike her head?"

"He frowned. "I…don't…remember."

"What were you going to tell the police?"

"I...killed...her. I...did...it...not...Roy."

"Was she breathing when you left her?"

"I...I'm...not...certain."

"Would you have called for help if you thought she needed it?"

"I don't...know. I was...so...angry. All those...years...lost to...us. All those...years...we...had...a...a...granddaughter. How callous she...was...toward me after everything I have done for...for them."

"Have you spoken to Ben recently?"

"No...I...hung...up...when...I...heard...his...voice."

"Oh, he banged the phone alright," said Bessie. "Over and over. I thought he was going to break it."

They promised to make an appointment the first thing on Monday, and Earl agreed to avoid any official statements until Roy's court date on March 28.

Lexa showered, dressed, and as she organized this evening's stage wear, she saw Casey's face encircled by flames.

She watched his mouth open and form words. He spoke, yet she was unable to comprehend him. She felt his arms under her as he carried her somewhere. He dumped her onto filthy wooden flooring. As her head struck the boards, she curled up on the ground, and the warmth of blood trickled down her nostrils onto her cheek. She dared not move. He stuck a gun to her head, but the bleeding had become fierce enough for him to believe she was dead. His words began to register, but it was as though both were under water. "She said she was done paying me. She treated me like I was a beggar. I hated Doris." *You hate how everyone treats you*, she thought.

Her doorbell rang. Outside, a red Chevy Laguna had parked by the curb. She tucked her pistol into the waistband of her jeans, ran up the inside stairs, and knocked.

"Drax, I'm so glad you're still here. Please answer my front door. Casey's banging on it, and I don't want to answer."

He swung the entrance door open. "Yea?"

"I need to talk to Lexa."

"What do you want, dude?"

"I need to tell her something."

"I can give her a message."

"Fine. Tell her she's about to become a corpse for meddling in my life."

"How about we beat you senseless first? I'm sure you'd enjoy it. Do unto others."

Casey's laugh was deep and evil as if possessed by some demonic force. He cackled down the walkway to his car, and slammed the shiny, scarlet door. Eight pistons fired up on the crankshaft as though an amplified beast bore down the road.

"Thanks, Drax. He knew I was within an earshot."

"If he comes near us, he'll feel the wrath of our iron mic stands."

"Whatever you do, watch your every move. Warn Hound and Showey. He's dangerous."

"We had him pegged ages ago."

It did not surprise anyone that Kalie showed up, and danced close to the stage. What did catch everyone off guard was the way she wriggled in front of Karl. Her blatant eye contact up and down his body let him know she wanted him. She was his, whether he desired her or not. It was difficult to erase the van incident where she was picked up by every limb and thrown out.

The last chord resonated, and the instant he stepped off the stage, she attached her curvaceous softness to him. At the bar, she stroked his back, waist, and buttocks. She laughed, and whispered into his ear.

Lexa approached them. "Did you and Ben break up?"

"The guy refused to kiss me anywhere but on the cheek. I got sick of it."

"Do you still have the job at the law firm?"

"Yes. Now leave us alone."

Karl's eyes widened at Kalie's abrasive tone, but he said nothing. He pulled out his wallet and flagged a bartender.

"So he hasn't told you why you're out of jail, or why his eye color is the same as yours, or why he gives you fatherly hugs."

"What are you saying?"

"You're not very observant. He buys a petty criminal expensive gifts, takes you to classy restaurants, and meets you at all odd hours of the night. You're as arrogant as he is."

The girl's nostrils flared. She threw her head back, and widened her eyes. "You're a liar."

"And you live by Neanderthal rules by which you navigate your simple life, expecting hand-outs, pity, and now sex from a stranger."

Kalie stepped closer to Lexa. "You bitch. How dare you."

"There, there. Do you feel better now? Such a limited vocabulary you have."

"Get the fuck away from me!" She dove at Lexa, and Karl brought his arms up to restrain her. He took a scratch to the cheek which was not intended for him.

"I take it you're not happy to have met your biological father. Your grandparents would have loved you so much."

Kalie's eyes reddened, tears filled her eyes, and her hand wiped away the array of emotions which bubbled and dripped down her cheeks. She blinked hard. Her body shook. A void had opened inside of her as if the floating pieces of her life had joined together for the first time. People at the bar backed away from her to avoid anyone who dared to rain on their party.

She stared at her feet, the floor, and everything below her as she deeply sighed. Her shoulders heaved inward as if she had been defeated by everything she had ever believed in. She ran through the club and out the door.

Karl stood motionless clinging to his wallet, uncertain as to how to process the scene.

"Are you still getting a drink?" asked Lexa.

"Um, I guess so," he said.

"Order something for me too. I shouldn't have lost my cool, but she'll get over it." The cash in Karl's hand reminded her of the premonition she had earlier. Casey's garbled words of how he hated Doris. She doubted that Roy had any knowledge of a portion of his paycheck being used to silence his nephew. Whenever she closed her eyes to envision the demise of Doris Kemke, she saw Casey standing over her, not Roy or Earl.

In the dressing room as everyone organized guitar cases and changed their sweat soaked clothes, Karl was silent as he packed. He looked at Lexa. "If I didn't know better, I thought I heard a tone of jealousy in your voice. You got rid of that woman in the matter of a minute."

"I don't feel very good about myself right now. I owe her an apology. I snapped."

"The same way I did two days ago?"

"I guess we all have our moments. I hope you can forgive me for my bad ones," she said.

"On one condition. I feel like I'm breaking apart. I need to hold onto someone tonight. I was desperate enough to use that girl. We don't have to…"

"No problem. Get your things. I need a change of scenery."

A light snowfall feathered onto them as they walked to Karl's Chevelle Malibu. He started up the engine, turned on the wiper blades, and got out to brush off the windows.

The heat flowing through the air vents blew across her face as Karl closed the door, slid his hands behind her neck, and slowly pulled her close. He cradled her head. The warmth of his mouth perfused a light tingling across her face, and immersed her in the buzz of an indulgent voltage.

Her grandmother had often told her to never turn her back on a raging fire, and Karl's was intense.

"It's the subtle, spicy, musk of your scent, the shape of your body, the smoothness of your skin, the way you part your lips. The way you say my name like a whisper, the tone, the sound of your voice," he said. His hazel eyes blinked into hers. His moist kiss trailed down her forehead, cheek, and to her neck. He turned to the wheel, and advanced the drive shaft.

As the tires rolled, ice on the black roadway crunched and crackled. The wheels spun out as he hit the gas, and the whirr of the engine filled the car. In his assigned spot behind his apartment, they pulled out their guitars, took them up the steps, and into Karl's apartment.

"What are you hungry for? The Slater menu specials include left over baked walnut encrusted salmon..."

"That's fine. Who taught you how to cook?"

"Despite all her faults, my mom insisted I learn how to cook and clean. She hated what a slob my dad was."

"This is delicious," she said.

He moved up against her, kissed her mouth, cheek and shoulders. He brushed her hair aside, and kissed the back of her neck. His warm lips brushed against hers.

His hair was as soft as she had imagined it to be. She gave him a suckling French kiss, twisted her tongue around his, and lightly bit his lower lip.

As his timepiece ticked into her ear, she had become what she shouted to the unsuspecting girl at the bar, one of the many cave-dwelling Simian creatures who fulfilled primal physiological desires throughout the ages. A breath of air, a sip of water to quench thirst, masticating, swallowing of nutrients to alleviate hunger, panting, like two runners, beads of dew glistening on them in the night. Soon they would sleep.

Lying beside each other, calf against shin and leg to thigh, the conduction of heat swirled between their bodies. Outside of their cave, distant shrieks stirred amidst thick foliage, branches, and darkness.

Her eyes closed, and she pictured them walking in a forest.

It was 11:30 am when the frying of eggs and coffee percolating drew her to the kitchen.

Karl smiled. A stream of sunlight slashed across his white t-shirt. "Are we still okay…I mean friends?" He poured and handed her a cup of coffee.

"I hope we are." She added a splash of milk.

"I don't want to ruin anything…between us, I mean." He had become uneasy and cautious. He looked at her more intensely.

"So, we've crossed a boundary. I guess we'll have to see how it goes. I think we'll be fine. Can you take me…?"

"Home? Sure." He finished her sentence.

"Relax. It won't be a problem."

"I hope so," he said.

"I need to apologize to that girl," she said in the car.

"You saved me, really. For all I know, she might have harassed me when I took her home, or worse, stalk me if I don't want to see her again." He stopped at a light and looked over to her. "Last night was great."

"You're not going to tell anyone about it, are you? If you had been with someone else, you could boast to all of your friends. I don't plan to tell anyone. Maybe never."

His face became doleful, and he remained silent until he walked her to her doorstep. "See you tonight."

She dialed Kalie's number. As the ringing began, she scrambled to find the right words.

"Hello?"

"I'd like to tell you about your grandparents." Click. The line went dead. *I guess she'll talk to me when she's ready.*

She looked at her clock. There was ample time to visit Roy.

In a plastic and metal chair, she waited. He appeared in a baggy orange jumpsuit. His dark stubble made him appear weathered and drawn.

"You look a little better today. Are you getting nervous?"

"I'm sick to my stomach. I can't eat or sleep. Even if I was at home, I don't ever want to sleep in my bed again. I shared that space with one woman for so long, it's not right without her. I miss her so much."

"I'm sorry. How did your polygraph test go?"

"I told them a zillion times it would be fine, and they finally believe me."

"When do they expect Doris' new autopsy report?"

"They assured me it would be ready by Friday."

"What time did you get home on January 6th? Earl said he left at 4:15. He was there for about fifteen minutes."

"You sound like my public defender. I got home around 5:15. Doris asked me to stop for milk on my way home. It was going to snow that night. She always worried about running out of things. She wasn't breathing when I found her on the sofa. At first, I thought she was taking a nap, but her color looked so bad, I touched her. She was clammy and cold. I knew she was gone."

"Were you and Doris giving Casey payments to keep him quiet about Melinda's daughter?"

"Not that I know of."

"Were there any unusual withdrawals on your bank statements?"

"My wife said she would take care of the cooking, cleaning, and checkbook, if I did the outside work, the snow shoveling, and maintenance on the cars. I rarely used the checkbook. She balanced it."

"Your nephew was getting money from your wife."

"How did you find out?"

"I…I overheard him." *I get premonitions.*

"My Melinda called me, and said she was sorry…that she'll talk to Marion. She stopped in this week. I was so glad to see her. I'll ask her to check our finances."

"You don't deserve to be here. I'll be glad when you're home. Your friends must really miss you."

"Yea, my fair weather friends."

"Don't be too hard on them. A lot of people are like that. I'll see you on Monday in court."

His eyes closed, and his head dropped to his chest. "I can't wait until this is over."

Though she knew she was overstepping her bounds, she called Melinda to plant the seed of her cousin's interference.

"Have you spoken to Earl and Bessie about Kalie yet?"

"Why do you care?"

"It would help them understand what happened, and why they were never told."

"That damn Casey has been blackmailing me for years, and said he would tell them if I didn't pay him."

"He may have done the same thing to your mom. If my hunch is correct, the proof would be in your parent's checkbook. Your dad rarely used it."

"How do you know so much?"

"I've had many conversations with Roy. I think he's innocent, and I've walked a similar mile in his shoes. Kalie knows who her birth father is. She'll find out the rest soon. You don't have to lose another cent."

"I don't know why I let Casey control me all these years."

"Warn your husband and your friends to watch out for him. He threatened to kill me for interfering with his plans."

"I'd like to meet you. When I stop at Dad's place on Tuesday, will you be home?"

"Sure. What time?"

There was a wall around Karl during the night. He made little eye-contact with anyone. When she approached him he turned away.

"Are you having a bad night?"

"I thought about what you said." He faced her.

"Which thing?"

"About never telling anyone about us."

"And…that's bad because…"

"No matter what I do, you'll never be my girlfriend."

"Hmm…I gave some thought about breaking up with that other guy. We work together, so we have to see each other. I think eventually we'll end up getting on each other's nerves. Flirt with anyone you want to. I promise not to be jealous."

"Yea, but I will be. And that sucks."

She sighed. "You can let a fire consume you, or you can conquer it."

"What the hell is that supposed to mean?"

"It means you don't know me." She walked away, and kept her distance from everyone the rest of the evening.

Sunday March 20, 1977

Jealousy is like wearing an anchor around my neck and having no control of it. It has loosened the glue from my seams and twisted my self-control. I do not understand why my aversion spewed for the girl who came onto Karl, unless I'm attracted to him more than I want to admit.

In nature, when something breaks apart, we consider this beautiful; clusters of leaves blowing to the ground nourish the soil. Fallen trees make homes for insects and animals. Humans think they're some kind of invincible creature not meant for falling apart in any way. How wrong we are.

Karl is distraught, and does not have the same support system Grant has. I regret my lapse in judgement. Karl never had the good relationship that Grant has with his mother, and both relate to women differently. There is no way to turn time backwards to erase my words or actions. I hope I have not created another enemy.

Chapter 15

Monday, March 21 – Saturday, March 26

G rant called during her breakfast, concerned as to why there was so much tension between everyone, and asked if it was his fault. She told him he was not responsible for the behavior of others, and reminded him to guard his belongings, especially beverages.

"Do you think everything will get back to normal once I'm done with the other shows?"

"There is no normal when it comes to rock and roll. There never has been, and there never will be."

"Yea, I get it. See you later."

Her phone rang within the minute. The Responsible Maids' receptionist asked if she was interested in cleaning the home of Mr. Ben Blesdin. Miss Brenda had quit, and no one from the agency was up to the task. She explained that she had another job, and was unable to, but thanked them for keeping her in mind, as she may consider something in the future.

She dialed Tiny's office. "It worked."

"What are you referring to?"

"I was asked to clean the Blesdin's home. The agency is desperate. I guess the beautiful couple will have to pick up their own messes," she said.

"And the delightful woman has been formally charged with arson for her dirty deed at the dress shop. She's facing a ten thousand dollar fine and a year in jail. On top of it all, she filed for divorce."

"She'll look fabulous in an orange jumpsuit."

"She's probably sharpening her fingernails as we speak. Apparently a store clerk developed a guilty conscience and went to the police. She described the two men who threatened her. Lydel and Jerry are in jail," he said.

"Again? They might catch a chill without their leather coats. I remember that clerk. Are you and Harold having your outing soon?"

"It's planned for later today," he said. "Gotta go."

Her next thought was of Kalie, who identified the law firm, herself and title.

"I need to apologize. I took the anger I have for your father out on you, and I regret having lost my cool. There are people who would be ecstatic to meet you."

There was a brief pause. "I was too stunned to handle what you said to me on Saturday. I went to Ben's office this morning. I slapped his face so hard; he'll have a handprint for a week. I asked him when he planned on telling me who he really was. No, I screamed it. The whole office heard it."

"You have step-brothers and sisters, and cousins also."

"I want to meet them all. I feel like I have something to look forward to."

"I'll let you go since you're at work, but I had to tell you how sorry I am for what I said."

"The truth would have come out sooner or later. Not knowing anything about where I've come from has always been unsettling to me. I'm able to put the pieces together now. I want to meet my birth Mom, and my grandparents."

"I'll let them know. They'll be relieved and happy."

"Thanks."

The facts about Ben's daughter were leaking like water from a broken faucet, each drop splashing into eager ears, and swishing through a basin of thoughts. Expanded by vivid imaginations, it poured from open mouths.

The majority of her afternoon was spent on the phone. She spoke to Bessie, and Earl's appointment to see his doctor was scheduled for tomorrow. She reminded them the latest he could see a psychiatrist to have his written report would be Thursday, in order to give it to the attorney by Friday.

She spoke to the band's agent to get the schedule for April, and hand printed it along with a design on a blank postcard. At their favorite Mexican restaurant, she met up with Debra, who would take the original to the printer to make five hundred copies. She would then place address labels on each one while she watched TV, and take them to the post office to be mailed. She liked having the extra cash. After a few margaritas, Debra divulged all the details in which Ted annoyed her, and why her marriage was not going to last.

They parted company at 11:30 pm, and Lexa locked her VW in the garage at midnight. Prior to touching the outside knob to pull the door shut, she saw a dark brown liquid saturating it. Deep red drips streamed to the door of the house, and onto that handle also, along with what appeared to be hair at the base of the door. She took the front entrance, flipped on all the lights, inspected the untouched rooms, walked to the side entryway and turned on the porch light. It was unclear if the long strands were human or from a wig, and whether the red liquid was human or animal blood.

She ran for gloves, a bucket of hot water, and a scrub brush. In her basement she emptied the murky water into the wash basin. It was deep pink, and smelled of blood. She closed her eyes, and knew who had done this. What worried her was if someone had been harmed, or if the hair had been taken from the floor of a beauty salon. The brown strands measured fifteen inches long, and when she broke a few, each curled at the center. She wrapped the tresses tightly in a rubber band, placed it in a plastic bag, and hid it along the wall beside the sword and her waterbed. She flipped through channels on the television.

At 1:00 am her doorbell rang several times. She turned down the sound, and kept all the lights off. Her goggles viewed two police officers rapping on the front entrance. She observed flashlights waving back and forth through her property to the garage and back, for fifteen minutes. Finding nothing, they left. She knew what they had come to investigate. Her night of sleep was fitful.

At 11:00 am, she answered her door, and was aware of who it would be, but not what the woman would look like. Her wavy, almost black hair and brown eyes had been her father's gift, and her small nose, high cheekbones and full lips were her mothers.

Lexa invited Melinda inside, and offered her something to drink. She requested tea.

"I'll have a cup of tea also. We can take it to your parent's home while you sort through mail. Will Marion be joining us?"

"She said she isn't ready to set foot in the house. She wouldn't be able to hold herself together."

Melinda's childhood was unlocked by the key in her hand. When her mother had given it to her at the age of ten, she was told she must keep it on a cord around her neck. Waiting for her had always been Lucky, her small tan mutt, who squealed for joy, upon hearing the latch turn. Smothered in kisses, she let him run free inside the boundaries of the white picket fence. She spent many hours caring for him for fourteen years. Lucky now wagged his tail beside her mother.

As the lock rotated, Melinda turned away. "I can't do this." She looked upward and blinked hard as tears streaked down her face. "I can't."

"There are no magic words to stop your pain. It may never go away. Time may soothe it, but you'll always feel her loss."

A faint voice called out to them. They turned around, and saw Bessie waving. She crossed the alley, and opened the gate. "Melinda, how are you, my dear?"

"Terrible." Their sobs shook their embrace.

"I'm not well either. Earl is deteriorating. I'm worried he'll have another stroke. He thinks he killed your mom."

"What do you mean?"

"He came over to help her, and they got into an argument on the day she died. Let's go inside. I'm freezing. What are you ladies drinking?"

"Hot tea, but it's cool now." Melinda opened the door.

"I'll make some more for us. I'm at my wits end. Earl is so distraught."

"You're like an aunt, and he is like an uncle to me. Since I was a baby, you have both been a part of my life. You've been my parent's best friends. Earl wouldn't hurt us."

"He knows about your child. Yours and Ben's I mean." She filled a tea kettle, placed it on the stove, and turned on the heat. "He hasn't gotten over it. He refuses to speak to Ben, and he hardly says a word to me."

"Oh no, that's horrid. Mom and Dad never knew how to handle my pregnancy. They felt hurt and embarrassed. They sent me away to have the baby. I was seventeen. I was too ashamed to say anything to anyone. I truly hoped Ben would tell you. He never cared for me."

"Why would you say that, dear?"

"My husband told me. Just before the high school state final football game, he and a few guys witnessed a touchy feely incident in the locker room, and your son's teammates blasted him. The ridiculing stopped when they all found out I was pregnant. I was head over heels in love with your son, but when he said I was a cheap slut, I felt devastated. I took my anger out on everyone, even you, Bessie."

The water came to a boil, and each poured a cupful.

Bessie took a sip. "May I see the picture my husband found?"

Melinda went into the bedroom. She came into the kitchen holding a 4 x 6 inch frame. "Her name is Kalie Deckler."

The moment she saw it, Bessie's eyes moistened. She covered her mouth, and used her shirt sleeve to wipe away tears. "She's beautiful."

"While I investigated my arson charge, I found out she was related to you. Would either of you like to meet her? She's nineteen, and I'm sure she'd love to meet her family," said Lexa.

"Of course we want to meet her," they said in unison.

"I have to check on Earl. When I saw you ladies, I had to stop in and say 'Hello'. It is so nice to see you again, and I can't wait to meet Kalie. I'll let myself out," said Bessie.

Both women gave her a hug. They glanced through the window as she walked through the alleyway.

"Do you have any idea where your parent's checkbook would be?"

"Dad hasn't told me where it is, but I remember where they used to keep it," said Melinda.

"Somewhere in the pile of mail on the floor of your front entryway are bank statements. I'll separate them from the rest of the mail, while you scour though the check ledger," said Lexa.

"I still don't get why you want to help us."

"There is almost no worse feeling than knowing you're innocent, and the rest of the world thinks you're guilty."

Melinda understood the seriousness in Lexa's face. They sat near each other in the living room. The black-haired woman studied dates and money flow.

Lexa sat on the floor, and sorted mail into piles. She admired the antique wooden chest that Earl had opened on January sixth. The distressed wood was sanded to a smooth flat finish, and on the top sat a glass lamp. It appeared that Doris wanted to use it as an end table.

"This must be the crate Earl opened for your mom. I can see why she liked it." Lexa saw the holes left behind by the nails.

"It has an interesting character to it. Mom was always rearranging the furniture. She often gave this room a new look when she got tired of it," said Melinda.

"Is the lamp new also?"

"No, it's old. Mom would put them in boxes in the basement, and rotate them fairly regularly."

"Earl told me he opened the trunk, but who put the lamp on it and placed it beside the sofa?" She removed the lamp, and opened the wooden lid. Inside she saw a gift wrapped in blue paper, and a large blue envelope. Roy's name was handwritten on it. "When is your dad's birthday?"

"January ninth. We had planned a large party to celebrate his seventy-sixth birthday, but instead we all sobbed while we worked on Mom's funeral arrangements."

"Do you think your mom did this? Because if she did, she was alive after Earl left. Your dad said he found your mom on the sofa, and Earl said he carried your mom to bed after he struck her."

"Dad has never mentioned anything to Marion or me regarding a card or gift, but I intend to ask him." She examined the envelope and package, touching it as though it was a fragile treasure, and her mother's last breaths were contained therein. She knew it was the final task her mom had undertaken. Melinda set it on her lap, lowered her head, and covered her face. Her anguish poured into her broken heart. She sat motionless for a few moments, looked up with troubled, crimson eyes, and took several deep breaths.

"I never liked that my dad put Mom in a mausoleum. She said she wanted to be cremated."

"Could it be one of the reasons you felt so much anger toward him?"

"Yes, probably. I hadn't thought much about it until now." Still clutching the box, she drifted far away, as though a memory had overcome her. "My parents gave me the best childhood a girl could have. My sister and I had more Barbie dolls and clothes than any of my friends." She remained silent for about ten more minutes before she reopened the checkbook, and reviewed the entries. "Every week, a check was written out as 'cash' for fifty dollars. She paid her hairdresser, groceries, the utilities, the house and the car payment all with checks. But that much spending money each week makes no sense. Mom was too frugal. It wasn't like her. Casey wanted fifty bucks a week from me ever since he was sixteen. For the past seven years, I have felt nothing but hatred for him. I have four kids to worry about. I was always afraid he might hurt them. They had to do without things. No music lessons, no dance lessons, and the toys I wanted to get for them."

"Since he was sixteen?"

"When Casey's dad stopped in to see his ex-wife, my aunt, he saw that I was pregnant. I tried to avoid him. My family was always afraid of who he would tell."

"This bank statement shows a withdrawal on the day she died for one hundred dollars. She must have gone to the bank after work. Maybe she asked your dad to get milk because she wanted to keep him away a little longer. Earl was pushed down the stairs two days before your mom died. Earl positively identified Casey as his attacker from the 8" by 10" picture I have of him. Could he have threatened your mom, or frightened her into giving him the hundred?"

Melinda looked up, a blank stare etched on her face. "I would stake my life on it. Every Wednesday he took my money, and every Thursday, my parent's. If I find him, I'm going to kill him."

When the wail of an ambulance filled the room, they stared at one another, arose and walked to the back door. Neither spoke. Outside, they shivered as they watched three men wheel Earl outside on a stretcher, covered by a blanket. Bessie beside him, their neighbor was pushed inside, and the doors were slammed. The vehicle sped away, red lights flashing, sirens blaring. Drizzle collected around them, and onto their cheeks, making neither one question whether tears or mist clung to the sadness in each of them.

"I need to leave for work," said Melinda.

"If you have access to a copy machine, get these bank records to your dad's lawyer. I need to give you something." Lexa ran to her house. Out of breath, she handed Melinda a folded piece of paper over the white fence. "If you need to reach me, please call this number. I'm glad we made progress."

"I hope you're right. I can't think anymore. Thanks for your help."

As Lexa turned around, smoke dispersed above her like a low hanging cloud. She had a fleeting thought that the man's previous home was set on fire with stray ash, as if some gust of wind blew a tendril of heat to the rooftop, and ignited it. Red flecks, like fireflies blew in swirls. At her usual spot on the stairwell peering down, the space beyond the fence was deserted.

Earl's home was empty. It seemed hopeless that he would be able to offer any help to his friend. She had to find out if it would be the last time she would see him alive. She took her purse and keys before buttoning her jacket. The phone rang.

"When someone beats his wife, rules with an ugly iron fist, makes false accusations, and treats folks like lowly servants, what do you do?" asked Tiny.

"Uh…give them a pat on the back…then cripple them."

"You're onto something. You slip a Nembutal and a Seconal in their beer at the bar. It's what he gets for being so jumpy when someone bumps into him. That nice combo makes them feel real tired, so you follow them to their car. Wait until they're snoring like a baby. Outfit them in the flashiest ugly purple and green dress you can find, the largest high heels, fish net stockings, jewelry, make-up, and give 'em the works. Make sure they don't have a wallet or car keys. Take a roll of film to a one hour developer. Pin the pictures up all over their office before they get to work, and watch the fun begin."

"Were you in the building when the entertainment started?"

"You betcha. We overheard a few choice names, like Sugar Plum and Beef Cakes."

"It suits him. Did he show up in a dress?" she asked.

"No, we followed him to a drug store. He must have begged some poor kid to use the phone. We watched his wife pick him up, so she probably took him home to change into his uniform, but he loved the 8 x 10 photos up all over the precinct, and the catcalls from his co-workers."

"He may need a few more spa treatments."

"We plan on it," he said.

What kind of wig did you find?"

"It didn't fit on his head. We left a green pillbox hat on his stubble.

"It sounds like his outfit was well coordinated. I was about to leave for the hospital to see Ben Blesdin's father."

"Yea, Ben's house is up for sale, his boat is up for sale, and he may have to let go of his property in Miami," said Tiny.

"How do you know all this?"

"A buddy of mine applied and was hired to be his chef. He'll be getting fired any day now. He can't cook to save his life."

"Either Ben figures out how to use the oven, or he'll be living on sandwiches," she said.

"Either that or stove top pizza."

"One of your favorites?"

"You betcha. Gotta go."

Lexa walked through hallways and up the elevator to the intensive care unit. The nurses recognized her, and they nodded to her as she entered the room.

"Melinda and I saw the ambulance."

Bessie held her head in her hands. "They said he has symptoms of another stroke. I couldn't keep him calm. I should have called the doctor. He needed to be sedated. I should have asked you to take his blood pressure. It's all my fault. It's all my fault."

"It's easy to take the blame when something goes wrong, but I believe you did your best. Give yourself credit for that much, and take this hour for what it is. Beating yourself up won't make him better. Have you told your son?"

"I'm too upset to speak to anyone right now."

"I'm sorry." Lexa sighed deeply.

"What a shame to finally find out we had a granddaughter, and Earl may never get to meet her." Bessie looked upward.

"I'll tell her what happened. It's up to her if she wants to visit."

"Why are you here? You don't owe us anything."

"You've become like family to me. If it wasn't for you I would be sitting behind bars."

"Helping you was the right thing to do."

Lexa pulled up a chair as close as she could get to Bessie, and squeezed her hand. They swallowed hard, and blinked back tears as they watched Earl snore in a deep coma. Hospital staff came and went throughout the day, to check his lines, monitors and catheter.

"Would you like me to give you a ride home? The nurses will take good care of him."

"Maybe I should. Sitting here watching and waiting isn't going to change anything," she said as she arose. "I never called his doctor to cancel his appointment today. What's worse is now he won't be able to do anything for Roy." They walked down the hallway.

"It's so hard to see each of them suffer so much. You live your whole life the best way you can, and one day it all gets pulled inside out," said Lexa as she drove.

"The morning the school caught fire, Roy took his chair and smashed as many windows as he could and helped get his classmates out. Earl said he begged him to leave, but he wouldn't. Roy ended up in the hospital for a few months, nursing third degree burns on his legs. He was in a wheelchair for a while. Our new neighbor was once a close friend to both of them. When I see him, I'll tell him about Earl's setback," said Bessie.

"I'll let him know about Roy also. Who knows, he might want to visit them." She let Bessie out at her gate before pulling into the garage.

Tuesday March 22, 1977

Youth holds a sense of invincibility, a shield from which one can rebel and rise above all the harm that has been inflicted. Then one day you wake up and all your wounds are on fire, and you aren't sure how to extinguish them.

When my life rains down shards of charcoal, I need to collect enough to build raging flames to heat up my empty heart, and find a happy place. Time zips by at light speed. Some childhood memories are so vivid, it seems like they happened yesterday.

I sat imprisoned for one night. In finding keys, locks, and clues to search for the truth, I was able to live a life of freedom. Roy has made his share of mistakes, but none so severe as to be caged for the remainder of his years.

On Friday, a major piece of evidence will be released. It will either exonerate or damage him, despite what we found out about his hateful nephew.

What I saw in Casey's hands on the night Karl and I found him on the road and dropped him off near his car was either money, a knife, or both. He had taken $20 from me when I believed his lie about the M-80. That same day he took $100 from Doris, and collected $50 from Melinda and Doris each week.

Earl's fragility has left him lying on a pyre that could devour him at any second.

Ever since the poisoning incident by the previous neighbor, Lexa kept a close watch on her pup, and this dull gray morning was no exception. Ebbie was not a barking dog. She licked someone's cheek when she wanted to be let out, and preferred to speak in as human-like sounds as possible. The food and water bowls were a heavy pink solid plastic, and clattered loudly when she slapped her paw on them to be fed. When Ebbie returned to the kitchen, she dug into her crunchy breakfast. She ate standing up most of the time, but on occasion, she would lie on her stomach, paws splayed in front of her, and eat while watching anyone who was nearby.

Apprehensive about speaking to the man who wore his hair in chest-length braids, she finished a bowl of fresh fruit and yogurt. Accompanied by Ebbie, she walked up the stairwell. Spirals of gaseous cotton wove into the overcast skies. "Hello. My name is Lexa."

He nodded and returned the greeting.

"Our neighbor, Roy Kemke is in jail. He is accused of murdering his wife. I don't think he did it, and he may end up in prison for a long time."

He stared upward.

"The man you have shared your herbs with, Earl is in the intensive care unit of Northwest General Hospital. I thought you might like to know about them, since you had once been friends." She sat on the step and pet Ebbie. "Thank you for helping me a couple of weeks ago."

"You're welcome." His gritty voice echoed up the stairwell.

She smiled. "I know they would both like to see you, although Earl is in bad shape. You gave his wife hope that he could become well again."

He returned the smile, threw several more logs into the fire, said he would see her later, and entered his house.

She sat on the step petting Ebbie for another minute, wondering if Sam was home. Two of her bandmates would be at another venue this evening. She feared for their safety. When her phone rang, she hurried inside.

"Dad said he didn't know anything about his birthday card, or a gift. It means Mom was still alive after Earl left. A more detailed autopsy will be ready in two days. I hope it gives us some peace of mind," said Melinda.

"Please call me when you get the result. I've vested so much time into helping your dad, I'd like to know the outcome."

"I will."

She picked up the receiver a short while later to Tiny's voice.

"You up for some good news?" he asked.

"Always."

"Ben and Harold's tight knit circle is unraveling."

"Aww…how atrocious. So, how do you know?" she asked.

"Their chef has been fired, but not before he bugged Ben's phones. A week's worth of burnt steaks, charred potatoes, and half raw vegetables was all Ben could stomach. His conversations have been interesting. He and Casey seem to have a thing going on."

"A thing?"

"They get cuddly. Need I say more?"

"Not really. Casey uses and manipulates people. He wouldn't be involved if there was no monetary gain, especially now that two of his income sources have dried up. And the band he was counting on to be a success will be ending soon."

She explained the ledgers in the checkbook, the bank statements, and the details of her meeting with Roy's daughter before they hung up.

Her coat was on, and she headed outside when ringing caused her to backtrack and pick up the receiver.

"Last night was murder. I can't do this anymore," said Grant.

"It didn't go well?"

"No. Every muscle is killing me from lifting all the gear. Casey acts like he's my best friend. It's weird."

"Did you tell him you're quitting?"

"I'm telling him tonight."

"He retaliates on anyone who crosses him. Let him make the decision. If you really want to be rid of him, pretend you're drunk, drop sticks, play as badly as you can, and act like an idiot. Tell him you have diverticulitis, and spend an hour talking about your bowel and gas issues.

"Diver what?"

"Tell him you have intestinal problems."

"Okay…sounds easier."

"Elaborate on the fungal infection on your feet, and all of your bodily disorders. Good luck."

"What are the symptoms of a fungal infection?"

"Make something up. He won't know. I'll see you on Saturday."

She looked up Kalie's number, and dialed. While explaining what had happened to her biological grandfather who was hospitalized and gravely ill, the voice on the other end became quiet. Lexa gave directions to the hospital, and was soon heading there.

Wednesday March 23, 1977

I spent most of my day with Bessie, and said nothing about her granddaughter, who did not visit. Since Bessie has no desire to speak to Ben, he is not aware of his father's condition, and his mom knows nothing of his house being up for sale.

When I explained what Melinda and I discovered to prove that Doris was alive when Earl left, Bessie was relieved, but she was burdened that Earl may never know. He may have injured Doris, but he did not cause her death.

It has taken two months to converse with my new neighbor. The lines on his face are a map of his travels, a reminder of his seventy-six years. His thick, black and silver mane is woven evenly along his shoulders, revealing the meticulous way he measures the healing herbs which he shares to revitalize anyone who is fortunate enough to know him.

Her first errand of the day was the grocery store. She often glanced at the bulletin board for postings of items for sale, and saw two pictures near the entrance, of Harold Humphrey dressed as a woman. The caption read: "Have you seen this person?" There was no reward or number to call. She made a guess that his photos were plastered all over the city.

Shortly after she put the groceries away, Melinda called the untapped line that Lexa had given to her.

"I felt my usual revulsion when I saw Ben the day my mother died. I didn't think much of it at the time, when I thought Dad was responsible for what happened. Mother would have let Ben in. He had a motive. He was worried she would tell his family and prissy wife about his daughter. Maybe he feared his parents would disown him for keeping the truth from them all these years.

"What time where you there?"

"I was there at about 3:45. I was on my way home from work, and I stayed for about ten minutes."

"Did she seem anxious or nervous?"

"Not that I recall."

"I don't think we'll be able to find any evidence to place him at the scene. Your dad cleaned everything up, unaware of what he should be looking for. The police made a sweep of the place long ago. In January, it's cold out. Ben wouldn't dare step outside unless he had gloves on," said Lexa.

"I'm going to see if I can find anything we missed."

"Okay. I'm going to see Earl in a little while. He's not doing well."

When Lexa got to the hospital, she sat beside Bessie, who kept a vigil at her husband's bedside, her head in her hands, exhausted by waiting, and not knowing if she would soon be living alone. Earl snored soundly.

"Has there been any change?"

Bessie looked up. "No, he hasn't opened his eyes once. I'm watching him fade away, and I can't stand it."

"Does your son know?"

"Yes. He found out, and said he was stopping by later today."

"I told your granddaughter Kalie about Earl, in the hopes that she would visit. They work in the same building. Have you had lunch? I can bring something up from the cafeteria."

"A sandwich would be fine."

She returned with the food, and remained until visiting hours ended." Call me if you need anything."

"I'll be leaving soon."

Lexa flipped the light on in her bedroom, changed into jeans and a sweatshirt, grabbed her coat and keys, and headed out.

She approached the club entrance. Music blared, voices shouted, glassware clinked, and about thirty people mingled near the bar. She pulled the hood of her sweatshirt up, and ordered a beer.

Red, blue and yellow lights flashed onto the stage, and the rest of the club was so dark, she almost tripped on the worn flooring. She watched her bandmates Grant and Ted perform with someone who she had lost all respect for. The PA amplified Casey's smooth vocals as he sang, 'The Boys are Back in Town', by Thin Lizzy. A few people danced. As she took a swig, she was approached by Debra.

"When did you get here?" asked Debra.

"A few minutes ago," she shouted. "They sound pretty good."

"Yea, but my friend and I think they're not as good as Word Locket."

"Is Ted happier?"

"Not really. He hates hauling equipment."

"What are you drinking? I'll buy you one." As she approached the bar, a young male chatted to a friend. Though his back was to her, a shaved spot along the side of his head of long brown hair caught her attention. She approached him.

"Interesting haircut. You're setting a new style trend."

He pointed to the stage. "The bass player bought a chunk of it. The band sounds great, don't they? Do you want to dance?"

"No, but I'll give you ten bucks for a small snip of your hair."

"Are you joking?"

"No."

"How weird, but whatever," he said.

She took out her silver scissors, and cut at the left side of his scalp where the rest of his hair was missing.

"That's not much."

"It's perfect, thanks." She handed him the money, but he refused it. "How long have you known him?" She took a swig of her beer.

"For a few years. He knows how to make his friends laugh. You look familiar."

Before she could block his arm, he pulled her hood down, and hair flooded around her shoulders.

"You're like…ice crystals, beautiful and unique, but like black ice, too dangerous to set foot on," he said.

Her body felt the singe of his fire, as his eyes bore through her.

"Do you want to know my name?"

"I won't remember it," she said.

"It's Jack, as in the ripper."

She shivered at the gory images it conjured. She turned towards Debra who tapped on her shoulder, and Lexa recognized the woman beside her instantly. A sickly sensation poured into her like a broken dam, and a knife-like pain shot through her chest and into her back.

It was Janie, whose flesh Sam had found so desirable when she lived in the upper flat. Perhaps Lexa's marriage was destined for failure, but staring at her was face of inevitability, the face that took up a comfortable spot in her house and dissolved her vows. Lexa set her drink down. "I don't feel good." She sprinted to the door.

Debra gave her a confused look.

As she approached her VW, she bent forward, with dry heaves. She leaned against the driver's door and struggled to get the key into the ignition through the welling in her eyes. Of all the ugly things transpiring around her, this one bore intense weight, and cut into her bones, shredding her. Moments ago, her sense of judgement was affected by varying degrees of betrayal, and she did not want to trust anyone, not ever again.

"What the hell is Debra doing with that damn woman?" she shouted as she pounded the key into the lock at her house.

She kicked the door which lead up the steps into Sam's apartment, and secured the chain latch. Ebbie backed away. At the bottom of a kitchen cabinet, she pulled out a bottle and poured a quarter glass of whisky, and took a long sip. In her room, she pet Ebbie, held the newly acquired hair over the clump she had saved, and breathed a sigh of relief. *Well Mr. Ripper, it seems to be yours.* The color and length was identical. Her kitchen phone rang repeatedly at 1:30 am. She refused to answer, and unplugged it.

When she awoke on Friday, she pulled out milk and cereal, and plugged the phone in. The ringing was immediate.

"Hey, I have a question." She recognized Grant's voice.

"So do I. Did you call me last night?"

"No. Why?"

"Curious."

"He wants to know more about my fungal infection. Do you think he doesn't believe me?"

"It's possible. What did you tell him?"

"My feet burn and itch."

"You can also mention that it's contagious and give him the Limburger treatment."

"The what?"

"Smear Limburger cheese on your feet, and rub some on your wrists for added effect. While he's getting a good whiff of you, tell him you didn't have time to take a shower."

"It's worth a try," said Grant. "Thanks.

Ten minutes later, she took a call from Melinda, who had been given the updated post-mortem medical examiner's report.

"My sister and I aren't doing well. We cried for most of the day yesterday. My mom had liver inflammation caused by alcohol consumption. None of us knew. If it wasn't on paper, I wouldn't believe it. Her death wasn't caused by a hammer blow. She had a u-shaped mark imbedded in her left temple. She also had a bruise on the top of her head, which I'll bet was what Earl did to her."

"The initial report said blunt trauma. There was no mention of a specific mark near her face. I wonder if Harold Humphrey got to the first examiner. It's a good thing she wasn't cremated."

"Yes, it is."

"Now is a good time to discuss your mom's wishes with your dad and sister. Was there speculation on the cause, or the force of the strike?"

"It said there was an inertial loading of the neck with head contact. Like whiplash. Death was due to direct impact with the temporalis, and rupture of the temporal artery." She paused and sobbed. "The medical examiner is willing to testify," she wept. "My...my poor mother's skull had a twelve millimeter indentation shaped like a tiny horseshoe. I discussed it with my sister Marion."

"I'm so sorry, and thank you for calling. I'm certain your dad is not responsible."

"Yes, we know."

She remembered Roy's conversation about maintaining the car, and wondered if one of his wrenches could have been used on Doris. She thought about breaking into his garage, and now was as good a time as any. She selected her equipment, stuck it into her pockets, and zipped up her jacket.

On the way, she swung her keys, as if one would open the garage. It was as easy as getting into Roy's house. Maybe it was how someone got in on Doris' last day, and she never answered the door to her killer.

To the right of the doorway, rows of shelves were built into the wall beside the light switch. Organized together were various flashlights, screwdrivers of several lengths, widths and styles, sockets, pliers, and a car jack, but no hammer, which she assumed the police had taken. What caught her eye was a dog bone wrench. It could have left a u-shaped mark. She wanted to measure the opening. Picking it up in gloved hands, she heard the engine of a car pull up. She relocked the door, and glanced out of a small curtained glass pane. It was a patrol car, and two officers. *Ben and Harold have a copy of the new autopsy.*

She edged around a parked car, and unlocked a small window facing her house. Cracking it open, she tossed the wrench out. She climbed onto the hood of the car, pulled up the pane, and jumped outside, just as the door knob was twisted, and the door shook. In a matter of seconds the glass on the door was smashed, and it sprinkled onto the concrete.

Though she shook, she ambled down the sidewalk, strolled into her kitchen, and held a ruler to the wrench. It was almost identical to the 12 millimeter mark. Using a magnifying glass, she could not find any hint of blood. Police were still in Roy's garage. When she caught sight of Officer Humphrey heading toward Roy's house, she ducked below the sink.

She possessed a potential piece of evidence. Not intending to be accused of aiding and abetting a criminal, she hid the dog bone wrench against the narrow opening beside the wall and waterbed. Possibly Roy used it, sobered up, scrubbed it down, returned it to the garage, and then called police. Perhaps he did belong behind bars. *Three days from now he'll be facing a jury who will be as confused as I am.*

She phoned Melinda to inform her that her parent's home has been occupied by two officers for more than an hour, so if she expected to find anything incriminating, most likely it would be gone.

"Damn them," I'm going out there as soon as my shift at Gimbels ends. I've been working at the jewelry counter for the past seven years, and there's no one to replace me at the moment."

"I'm going to visit Earl, so I won't be here."

At the hospital, Bessie explained how Ben's visit turned into a nasty argument. Though she was not surprised to hear about his divorce, she was upset that his wife would get alimony and half of his estate when she gets out of jail, as she had already spent so much of Ben's earnings pampering herself throughout the marriage.

Her charming son would never admit to his stockpile from side endeavors, or that his marriage might have been a charade in order to become elected to his position.

"Did he and his wife take trips to Miami?" asked Lexa.

"She disliked hot weather. They spent vacations skiing in Vail, Colorado. She wore her mink everywhere."

"Did she like boating?"

"Anything that messed up her long hair annoyed her, so I doubt it."

"Have you been on Ben's boat?"

"What are you talking about? He doesn't have one," said Bessie.

"Oh, for some reason I thought he did." *So, he didn't tell you. What a shame. You and Earl might have loved it.*

A nurse entered the room with a syringe on a tray. As she was about to inject the solution into the intravenous tubing, Lexa asked what it was."

"I'm following the doctor's orders."

"I'm not questioning the doctor; I'm asking what you're giving him. Would you like me to ask your supervisor instead?"

"It's 10 milligrams of IV Diazepam."

"How long has he been getting it?"

"Since he got here."

"How often?"

"Every eight hours."

"He's not the least bit restless. You can tell the doctor, and document that the family is refusing to allow any more IV Valium, unless he is visibly agitated."

Bessie looked at her, and Lexa's gaze was firm. "He is not to have this. Do you understand?"

"Yes, ma'am." The nurse stormed out.

"What just happened?"

"They're over-sedating him. That's why he's been snoring for the past three days, and doesn't respond. No one questioned a drug that should have been stopped two days ago."

"Are you sure?"

"Ask the doctor for a medicine list. They need to get Earl up and moving. Hopefully by tomorrow, he'll wake up, and they'll be able to see what cognitive abilities he has."

"I hope you're right." Exhaustion had gripped Bessie's face.

"I'm sorry if I upset you. If he was my father, I would have said the same thing."

Bessie revealed a weary smile. "I'm so tired." She rubbed her temples. "It's over for me and him. We lived in a bygone era." Swirling through her mind was the prospect of more days spent in hospitals and rehab facilities. The strained relationship with her son, and the uncertainty of her husband's fate was breaking her into small pieces that she was losing hold of. She faced the floor, and appeared to drift far away. Whether she was immersed in the better memories of her past, or if she realized that she had no control of any aspect of her life was irrelevant. She knew that whatever the outcome, it would not be good.

"Hello?"

They both looked up as Kalie walked into the room. Bessie looked stunned. She opened her mouth but did not speak.

"Hello, said Lexa. "I'm glad you could visit. I'd like to introduce you to your grandparents. Your grandfather is sleeping, and this is Bessie."

Kalie smiled, held out her hand, and hesitantly approached her grandmother. Both women stood in awe of each other, as though they looked into a mirror viewing similarities. As if the love for each other which was imprinted in their souls since birth had awakened.

They clasped one another, and sobbed. What had been one of Bessie's darkest hours, brightened in increments. They backed away from each other.

"You have no idea how much I've wanted to meet you. Promise me we'll talk about your childhood and your adoptive parents sometime. I want to hear it all."

"You won't like it. I'm not on good terms with them."

"Do you have any brothers or sisters, dear?"

"I have an adopted brother, but I don't see him much. I have a friend that I'm close to, and his name is Casey."

"Wait, is it the same Casey who fought with you the night I invited you backstage?"

"We have our quarrels, but we hang out a lot."

Lexa almost fell off her chair. "Have you met his dad?"

"Yes, he's a heavy drinker. No one likes to be around him."

"I should leave. You two have some catching up to do. Bessie, let me know if you need anything."

"I will, and thank you for introducing us."

The cold air felt good on her face. It was bittersweet to see Kalie meet the family who had long awaited her. Though it was where she belonged, Lexa felt pangs of fear that this young woman may harm her kind-hearted grandparents. She wished her neighbor had also visited Earl, and offered his healing herbs. She walked up the stairwell to see his son tending the fire, and she introduced herself. She asked him if his father had mentioned how he had known his neighbors.

"My father was involved in a serious accident this afternoon on his way to visit a friend, and is in a coma. My wife and I just got back a short time ago from Northwest General Hospital. After we eat and make sure our teens are alright, we'll return to dad's bedside."

"I'm so sorry. I was just there visiting Earl, who is unconscious in the intensive care unit."

"It's where my father is also. We'll try to stop in Earl's room, if they let us." He waved as he gave her a sad smile, and walked into his house.

On his way to visit a friend. Maybe he was on his way to the jail or the hospital, she thought. Her throat clenched. Twinges of guilt crept up her spine. She told him where his friends were, and now he was critically injured. She took another breath of the cool darkness, and opened the side door. The soundless rooms closed in on her. Sam and Ebbie were elsewhere.

She opened her lower kitchen cabinet, and reached for one of the open liquor bottles. The first sip burned going down. She took the drink to her bedroom, turned on the TV, and fell asleep. The street entrance doorbell rang. She took another sip, and refused to move. Knocking, and several more rings ensued. She pulled out the night vision goggles. There was no mistaking Harold Humphrey. He had been in Doris' home asking about Earl in January, and was strong enough to leave a dent in anyone's head. He may have seen her walk into her house through Roy's open garage window earlier today. And worse, he may think that she tampered with evidence.

Her side door rattled, and she turned the TV off. The deadbolt lock was one of the more pricey ones, but had proved to be worth it thus far.

She grasped her Colt Commander, realizing she had not shot it in a while, and sat in the dark on a kitchen chair aiming at the door. Her mind vacillated on what she would do after the bullet struck him, and where she should aim. As far as the law was concerned, she was a criminal. She did a mental check of how much plastic wrap, how many large garbage bags she might need to wrap his body, and how far she needed to drive to find an open store at this hour.

Five minutes into the scraping, it stopped, and began again at the front entrance. She tiptoed to the living room, and sat on the floor, pointing her weapon at the door. *Damn, he'll make a bloody mess on my carpet.*

Silence followed for three minutes. Scratches and clanks on the window to the right of the fireplace sent her flying to her bedroom closet when a loud snap caused it to open. She closed her eyes, and clasped the gun. *Relax, take big slow breaths.*

The floor creaked in the living room. Two minutes later, the window closed. The engine of a vehicle faded down the road.

She shut all the drapes, turned on the lights, pulled out her flashlight, and ransacked her bookshelf, but found nothing. She waved the light beam into every corner, under chairs, and the dining room table. In the back of the sofa, were three large plastic bags of white powder, and six large, square wrappings of what appeared to be marijuana packed tightly. *This would get me put away for life.*

She ran to the kitchen for a large trash bag, and threw all of it inside. She pulled on a sweater, slid into boots, dragged the heavy sack, and dumped it into Bessie and Earl's garbage bin. Within the minute of returning home, two squad cars pulled up. As soon as she heard ramming on her front entrance, she turned on the porch light, and opened the door.

"Hello, can I help you?"

"We have a search warrant." They stormed into the house.

"I think you have the wrong address, but make yourselves comfy." She masked her fear with a wide smile. "So, am I entitled to see this warrant?"

There was no reply. Four officers left no cabinet or drawer unchecked. One of them ordered her to sit on a kitchen chair, and stood beside her. He refused her offer of a drink of water. They asked about the upper flat, and she explained that she lived in the lower unit, and did not track the whereabouts of the man who resided upstairs.

"That door is locked, and I do not have a key."

It was midnight when their hour of searching proved futile.

"Someone lied to you, and sent you here as a deterrent. It's too bad. Your valuable time could have been better spent elsewhere. This neighborhood has become dangerous. My neighbor was murdered, and shortly before you arrived, someone banged on my door at this late hour. I hope you keep a better patrol in this area."

The second the door closed, she flipped on all of the lights, and examined the window used to gain entry. *He broke the damn lock.* She took a long nail and pounded it into the wood frame.

Harold was already irate over his unsuccessful attempts to harm her, and most especially now due to the contraband not being found, the street value of which could add up to a hundred grand. Garbage pick-up would be on Monday morning.

She stuck her tongue onto a Nembutal, and swigged it down. She turned the TV on. The Tonight Show with Johnny Carson had ended. Possibly the Bob Hope movie, and snacks from the fridge might help her relax.

Steeped in anger, she sat up. Sick of Harold's constant harassment of her, she questioned what he had done in the two hours he spent in Roy's house. She thrashed, and stirred when Sam bounded up the back stairwell. Every noise, slam of outside car doors, and dog bark echoed into her room.

The glow behind the shades opened her eyes on Saturday morning. She arose, tended to her usual tasks, and gathered supplies. In the basement, she found an old soda crate, placed it beside Roy's fence, climbed over, and rigged her way into his house.

A circular imprint on the blue paint above the sink where Roy's clock had been was visibly darker than the rest of the wall. His glass cookie jar was no longer on the counter, and as she stepped into his living room, there was not one picture or photograph anywhere. His small bookshelf had been emptied out. Two bedspreads were gone, and the mail was removed.

She picked up the phone to inform Tiny of the events that occurred the previous evening, and asked if he wished to possess large amounts of highly illegal substances.

"It would be a shame for it to end up in a garbage dump. I was set up last night. Humpty must be going bonkers. He knows I have it somewhere. I'm willing to bet he's spying on me at this moment. Are you interested?"

"I...I why in the hell do you do this to me? I shouldn't let it go to waste, but I don't know. I need to have a plan, and find a good hiding place. I'll wait until tonight. My heart is racing."

"Think it through. Humphrey is usually home with his wife by 6:00. I'm sure you know how to track his whereabouts."

"Yes, I do. Make sure you keep that Colt I sold to you handy. If need be, I'll help you clean up the mess."

"Thanks." *I almost needed you last night.*

She returned the old wooden soda crate to her basement, changed clothes and headed to the hospital.

Through the glass walls of the intensive care unit, she saw the couple who had recently moved in. He and his wife tearfully hovered over a sleeping man who was surrounded by an entanglement of intravenous lines.

A large white sheet covered his legs, and a ventilator pushed air into and out of his lungs. A wide white dressing was wrapped around his black and silver hair.

Her stomach tightened. When she got to Earl's room, Bessie stood up, and hugged her. Earl was alert, and was able to speak.

"He's not as bad as they thought he was. You were right. They were giving him too much sedation. The paramedics gave him something that knocked him out, and he's been tranquilized ever since. The doctor apologized, and said Earl could be transferred to a regular floor."

"Ben must be relieved."

"He doesn't sound like his usual self."

"Did you have a nice visit with Kalie?"

"She's a little rough around the edges, but all she needs is a little loving from her grandmother."

"Do you know our neighbors are down the hall?"

"Yes. They stopped by and told me they saw you yesterday. What happened…is terrible." Bessie frowned. "Someone ran a red light. His dad had to be extricated from the car. He has fractured ribs, punctured lungs, a broken arm, and breaks to both legs. He's in critical condition, and they're taking it minute by minute."

"I told him where his friends were. It's my fault he's here." Lexa remembered her grandmother's words: 'Guilt is like microbes multiplying in the bloodstream which become lethal if we allow it.' The ugly self-worth killer known as guilt poured into her veins. She crumpled downward, and tried to clear the tightness in her throat.

Bessie turned to her. "What was it you told me? Beating yourself up won't make him better." She rubbed Lexa's back. "You're wound up tighter than a torsion spring."

The touch of another human felt warm on her skin. "It never stops. When I wake up, I wonder what awful thing is going to happen today."

"Always look for the light in the clouds on bad days, and there will be more of each than we care to count."

"Have you ever felt like getting in your car, and not stopping until you reach some beautiful sunny place?"

"Even people in the land of sunshine have their struggles," said Bessie.

She was hoping for words which could reset her heaviness into wings. She drew in a breath. "Every choice has an outcome."

"Yes, it does."

"I have to work tonight, but I'll try to stop by tomorrow."

"Kalie said she would visit. I hope she can make it," said Bessie.

"No one is better for her than her family. I'd better go."

Though their show was at the Palms in Milwaukee, everyone except Sam traveled in the van due to the lack of available parking. She sat in her usual seat behind Ted, who drove. In the passenger seat, it was hard to miss Grant's black eye.

"Do you feel like talking about it?" she asked.

"Casey and I got into it."

"What infuriated him this time?" she asked.

"He said I was lying about my health issues, and kept repeating how much I stank. He called me Grant the 'gross-guy' into the mic. Then he criticized my drumming. I couldn't take it. I told him to shut the fuck up, and he smacked me."

"He's a good fighter," said Ted. "It's like he was trained. He was fast, and ducked all of Grant's punches."

"I hope he leaves us alone. I'm sick of him. I miss our roadies. I'm buying them drinks tonight," said Grant.

Karl's smile seemed forced. She wasn't sure. It had been six days since she last saw him, and what they had done had an impact on their working relationship. She smiled back. "How was your week?"

"Perfect. People tell me they saw my brother's band. It's what Casey tells everyone."

"I've been visiting my neighbors. The one who put up the fence and the one who lives behind my house are at Northwest General hospital."

"If it wasn't for this show, I'm not sure if I would know what day it was," said Karl.

"Why bother to find out what day it is? It's only going to change again tomorrow," said Ted.

"And yet you remembered to be here. Let's not challenge his fragile mind. We don't want his brain to explode," said Grant.

To be heard above the amplification of guitars, drums, and vocals, the four hundred people in the club were as loud as usual. Showey,

Hound, and Drax were glad the band did not break up. Lexa was relieved to have tonight's cash, as the roadies received the same pay whether they hauled gear or not.

When the last encore song had ended, the band ran backstage, and hung out until the crowd thinned down. The dressing room at the Palms was at the opposite end of the club, up a flight of stairs. Her bandmates went to the bar for drinks, while she lingered in the room behind the stage. She turned to see a figure in a dark gray sweatshirt, the hood pulled up and tightly tied. A familiar voice breathed down upon her.

"Lexa Loxx, do you have a boyfriend? I never see you with anyone."

"Nothing I do is any of your business."

"There's gossip of you being a lesbian. Or, are you ambisexual?"

"I have no intention of discussing any aspect of my life with you."

"So, you kept your band together. How did you convince them? You're not like any whore I've ever met." Casey sat beside her. She arose to face him, and moved away. His eyes became sullen. He held something in his hand, and lunged at her. His horseshoe ring glinted, and she realized what had crushed the side of Doris' head. She backed away, but the sharp tip dug a four inch cut into her arm. His eyes bore through her as he thrust a syringe toward her a second time. "You won't ever fuck with me again. Some M99 will take good care of you."

"Is that how you handled Doris?"

"I was sick of her bullshit. She said I wasn't worth another cent. Said she'd give me a hundred bucks, then decided to keep it. When she called me a few disgusting names, I had enough. She had it coming, and I found the cash."

"What did she have coming?"

"A good hard smack to her face, to knock some sense into her, but she turned her head. That bitch pissed me off."

She wished she had stolen the Etorphine when she had the chance, but he would have found a replacement. As she turned to run, his stride exceeded hers. He stabbed her upper arm. The pain was intense as the needle hit the bone. She fought for consciousness, to tell someone what caused the imprint on her neighbor's temple. She drifted into a trance when he picked her up and carried her out of the back door. She wove in and out of a dull sleep as he drove. His words, "I need to burn that damn place down anyway," rung through her head.

Her body became like the trunk of a tree being dropped on a gritty floor, and her bloody nose was immediate. The red wetness trickled under her nose and onto her lips, along the side of her face, into her hair, and onto the ground. The barrel of his gun pushed into her cheek, and the click of him cocking the hammer was clear, but he did not shoot. The heavy bleeding caused the appearance of death, and he was satisfied. His footsteps pounded on the wooden planks, and the air smelled of gasoline.

A lit match thrown on the ground created plumes which expanded around her, becoming a bright yellow winged creature snapping with a ravenous appetite.

As smoke seeped into her, she was awakened by a dark-haired man, that much she knew. A loud crack shot through buckling dry-wall. In a piercing pop, walls became engulfed in golden flames. She had walked through this inferno before, in the premonition in her kitchen, and in too many dreams to count. Burning up inside, she attempted to open her eyes. Unable to inhale, the conflagration surrounding her intensified. Charged with static, hair blew over her face and around her head. Enveloped by the crackles of crumbling plaster and particle board, she coughed and choked. Fumes rolled, billowed and expanded. Doom hung above her like a black halo. Dancing, writhing and scribbling its destructive limbs, smoke and Etorphine paralyzed her attempts to move.

Lying on floor boards, panting in shallow breaths, she thought about her brother, young nephews, her sisters and parents who she would never see again. She would become a missing person who vanished without a trace. Scorching pain seeped into her pores, and exposed flesh became deep pink. The magma-haired man watched her through shimmering waves of heat. It was one of her visions, the brief glance into another realm, only to be zapped to the reality of her cremation.

His arms opened as he stepped closer to her. Through wavering, mirage-like air, he swaddled and guided her to a doorway. The heat scalding her, she could not fathom how he was able to stand upright. Through an open portal, the cool night beckoned, and a deep gasp of ordinary air became a cherished gift. Perplexed, on all fours, she watched the cataclysm take the large structure to the ground. It was the kind of light that opened a curtain in the blackness, to display barren trees and empty hills for miles.

Grateful for his quick recovery, she looked around to thank him, but he was gone. She did not expect him to speak to her anyway. He never had much to say to her. She had no idea how he found her, but none of it mattered. He saved her life and she was indebted to him.

The near freezing temperature and scattered snow mired the field from being engulfed. As the brilliance of the blaze diminished, no stars, no moon, and no navigational tools would guide her. She had no coat to warm her. The cold sting on her bare arms made this dream real, and hypothermia was lying in wait. Shivering and disoriented, vapors flung through the air from her every breath. She took a patch of icy snow, rubbed it into her face, and walked down a gravel driveway, following muddy tire tracks. She ran through a checklist to test her ability to remember basic information, and it seemed intact. What she could not recall was the sequence of numbers for either her brother Nathan Lauden, or Karl Slater. Her insides were seizing, and she wanted to collapse. Her lungs burned.

Casey's red Chevy was parked on the path. She opened the door, finding it odd that his keys dangled in the ignition. Her toes and fingers felt numb. She had no guilt taking the vehicle of a murderer. He deserved to walk. The half full gas tank should get her to a filling station or phone. She had no idea which way to steer at the end of the roadway, and guessed at a left turn. She faltered at the next intersection and steered right. Turning onto a larger road, a sign came into view, and Fredonia, Wisconsin was three miles away. The countless drives through the state did not help her navigate through the scrambled heaviness in her head. Two lanes separated by white lines stretched for miles, but there was not one house. For all she knew, she was headed toward Canada.

Chapter 16

Sunday, March 27

She blasted heat through the car, and maintained a speed of 45mph to conserve on fuel. She wanted to make a collect call, but could not find an open gas station, or remember any phone numbers. As she concentrated on staying on the road, the sunrise peeking over the hills brought the realization that she would not get home in time to inform Roy's public defender that she was a witness for his trial. The murder weapon was a gold ring, and a punch with enough volatility to render a death blow.

Through trees embossed by morning dew, a white farm house came into view. It was too early to awaken the occupants. She pulled into the driveway, and left the engine running. The mirror was brutal. Her long, light brown hair was stuck together by hardened blood, her face was blackened by soot, eye make-up had run downward in streaks, and crusts of the nosebleed had stuck along her chin and cheek. She pushed the seat downward, closed her eyes, and fell into a catatonic sleep.

She awoke to the sound of banging on her window by a blurred uniformed man, who wore a gray brimmed sheriff's hat. The door opened at the same time as her eyes. Her body felt the pit of emptiness, hunger, and a chill dug into every cell. Her vision was hazy, and she wanted to ask what day it was.

"Your license, ma'am."

"I…don't know where I am. I was kidnapped."

"I need to see your license, and registration."

"I have no identification. Someone tried to kill me last night, and this is not my car. I need to call someone for help, which is why I parked here."

"Are you saying this is a stolen vehicle?"

"No, I'm saying I borrowed it so I wouldn't freeze to death."

"I'll need you to accompany me to the police station for questioning."

"Do you have a blanket?"

"No, I do not."

"Will you allow me to make a phone call?"

"Yes."

The glimpse of her reflection in the glass made it apparent as to why he wanted to get into the car. The ghastly human wearing high-heeled boots, black spandex slacks and a one-shouldered tank top in the driver's seat appeared dead. He sat her in the back seat of his squad, and closed the door.

He filled out forms, made several calls, and acquired the owner's name of the red Chevy. When he asked her about a Casey Relmen, she insisted that he allowed her to use his car. There was no report of a stolen vehicle, and he accepted her clarification of how she and her friend got lost after attending a party, and she fell onto her nose, which bled profusely. Her coat and purse got left behind. She planned to return her friend's car today. No, no one tried to kidnap or kill her. It was a dream he had awoken her from. Her friend found another ride home. *Maybe someone followed them.* Yes, someone took him home, because he was drunk.

He queried the address of where the party was held. She affirmed that her friend drove, and she did not pay attention.

"I was given the keys, so if someone can return me to the car, I'll leave, but I need directions to steer me southbound."

He allowed her to use a restroom. She used damp paper towels to wipe her face as best as she could.

"Make sure you keep your driver's license on you."

"Yes sir."

At 4:30 pm she banged on Sam's door, asking him to let her in. She told him and Drax she didn't have her things, and judging by the look on their faces, it wasn't a problem. They stared, but said nothing.

The shower felt like a glorious, enveloping, warm embrace. The stench of ash on her skin swirled down a drain, along with sweat, blood, and the sting of embers. Water streamed along her spine. The burns on her body would eventually heal.

Sam knocked on the hallway door, and she opened the latch.

"What happened?"

"I don't want to think about it, let alone talk about it. Have you seen my purse? And my coat, my guitar, and my suitcase?"

"I dunno. The roadies probably have it."

"No one noticed I was missing?"

"I left as soon as I got my stuff."

"Now that you know I'm still alive, we can call it a day.

"If you're going to be like that, I'm never asking you again."

"Are you trying to satisfy some morbid sense of curiosity? I said I don't want to talk about it. I'll ask Drax if he knows where my things are, as soon as I get some food in me."

He slammed the door behind him and she made a sandwich. A few minutes later, Drax knocked.

"Hi, come in."

"You looked like you were brought back from the dead. I hear you're being a bitch again."

"I'm sure it comes from a reliable source. Do you know where my things are? If it's still at the club, I need to get over there. Tonight's band will have no problem emptying my wallet."

"He's right. You are acting testy. Your guitar is in the truck."

"Any idea where the rest is?"

"I haven't a clue what your purse looks like."

"Okay, thanks for stopping by." Her next option was to try Karl, and keep her fingers crossed, but he did not pick up, and there was no answer at Grant's place.

When she last aimed her Colt 45 caliber handgun at someone, not one shot was fired. Seven rounds remained in the magazine. She slid it into a compartment of her largest purse, hung the strap over her shoulder, and locked up.

Garbage would be collected in the morning. The goggles brought her darkened neighborhood into view from Sam's porch. It seemed quieter than usual. She picked up the lid to Earl's metal cans beside his garage. *Empty. I'm sure I'll be hearing from Tiny.*

In her VW, she sat quietly for a moment. She drew in a deep breath, and envisioned where her belongings were. Karl had them, and she fired up the ignition. She pulled out of the garage, parked Casey's car inside, and locked it.

She rang Karl's doorbell, and waited a few minutes. His Chevelle Malibu was in the lot. Fear jabbed at her, and she buzzed several more times. She stood at the door like a lost child waiting for her mother. If he had a woman upstairs, she preferred not to intrude, and walked toward her car when the back door opened.

"Uh…hello?" He appeared haggard, red-eyed, and impaired.

"Hi, are you okay?" she asked.

"I'm fine, just numbing myself to dull the pain."

A broken man stood before her, and the combination of their brokenness was a bad match. She felt conflicted toward him. He was a desirable man. She feared if she got too close it would ruin their working relationship like it had with Sam, yet she needed his help to move a car. His body was too limp to offer aid to anyone. "I wondered if you have my purse and coat."

"I do. I couldn't find you anywhere. Why did you leave the club so fast?"

"I was drugged and kidnapped," she said as they stepped upwards.

"What?"

"Remember the Etorphine we found?" she asked.

"Casey used that on you? I want to mangle him. How badly did he hurt you?"

"I stole his car, but I have to figure out how to get to his house, preferably tonight."

"How did you steal his car?"

"It was parked near the end of the driveway where he tried to kill me. The keys were in the ignition. Bizarre, isn't it?"

"Yes, it is…I'll…I'll…hel…help…you." He opened the door to his apartment.

"You can hardly walk," she said.

"I had to stop the sick feeling. It was chewing me up. My heart was racing, and my mouth felt dry. It got the best of me."

"I know how it feels. I'm sorry."

"I'll make some coffee, shower, and change clothes. Don't go anywhere," he said.

Barefoot, his lower half wrapped in a towel, his hair was dripping wet. In the kitchen, he poured coffee into a mug, dropped a couple of ice cubes into it, and chugged it down. Ten minutes later, he was dressed. "Let's go."

She started the engine. "Thank you for everything."

"I haven't minded. If I had a real girlfriend right now, we'd probably be bored, sitting on my sofa watching TV."

"And wearing towels."

He smiled. "Maybe."

"I just realized this VW doesn't have an eight cylinder engine like your car has. If we're followed…"

He turned around. "How long have those same headlights been behind you?"

"Since we left your apartment."

"Damn it."

299

"I'm taking a detour, so, brace yourself." She drove eastbound, and made a right turn on Teutonia Ave.

"Why are you in a cemetery?"

"It's how we're going to escape." The tires whirred as she veered off the slick gravel. The ground below them gave away. Thick, wet mud thumped against the undercarriage. The VW shook side to side, as the car hobbled over the sludge. Though she gunned the engine, her speed dropped as the vehicle dug deeper into the mire.

"They're still behind us."

"No, no, no, no…"

The wheels spun harder and harder until the VW became submerged in muck. They made eye contact, and Karl hopped out to push the car.

"Gun it," he yelled.

The car behind them had sunk into the wet slop, tires spinning and screeching. The VW rolled up out of the trench as Karl pushed.

"Get in, hurry!"

He slammed the door. She drove down the embankment, onto the sidewalk, off of the curb, and onto the street, leaving the four door tank behind.

"I've given this trusty hunk of steel its share of beatings." They reached her home at 8:00 pm. "Casey's car is in my garage. Why do you think he left the keys in it?"

"Someone was supposed to pick it up," he said.

"Maybe Jack the ripper."

"Who?"

"A friend of his. I met him at the bar where Casey, Grant and Ted had a show. Was his name ever mentioned?"

"No."

"I'll check the listings from his address book," she said.

Roy's house was lit up. *I'll bet his daughters are taking more of his things.* Again, guilt chipped away at her for not getting her new found facts to Roy's attorney sooner. She wanted to attend his hearing tomorrow, and surely his lawyer would listen, even though she had no tangible proof.

"You drive my VW, and I'll drive the Chevy Laguna. I'll wipe it clean."

"But I'm full of mud," he said.

"It's okay. I'm glad you can help me."

By 8:45 the red vehicle was parked in its usual spot, and they were in her kitchen. The lights were still on at her neighbor's home.

"Do you want to hang out for a while?" she asked.

"You better tell me what the hell happened last night." He kissed the burns on her hands.

"You should see my knees. My black slacks are ruined."

She divulged the mayhem of the previous evening, and went into detail about being set up for a drug bust. As he was about to kiss her lips, the doorbell rang. Answering it had not had a good outcome as of late. The peephole revealed distorted, darkened features. When the bell rang again, she flipped on the porch light, which gave her a better view of a man who had Roy's features. She opened the door.

"I thought you'd like to know I'm home. Melinda and Marion are visiting."

"You're...you're...they...let you out of jail before your court date tomorrow?"

"No...no. They released me. I'm a free man again. Remember the girl you questioned at The Checklist Pantry?

"Yes, I do."

"She told her mom about your conversation and how sad you looked, and they got to talking. Her mom was at the gas station the day I was there, because her daughter didn't have her license. Whenever her mom took her to work, she usually picked up a few groceries. On January 6th, her mom took a snapshot of a dark-haired man who she thought was Robert Mitchum. She had seen his movie 'Midway' a few months back. It turned out to be me. Her daughter remembered me when she saw the snapshot. They showed it to the guy who thought I was Irish, and he recalled me too. Three people said they would serve as eye witnesses. They called me at the jail, I told them who my attorney was, and the girl's mom got the pictures to him. There's more to the story, but there isn't going to be a trial. The judge demanded the paperwork to get me the hell out of there."

"I am so relieved."

"Can you believe it? Me? Robert Mitchum. I owe you one."

"The resemblance is uncanny. It seems we all view the world through the distortion of our own lens. You're an actor to one person and from Ireland to the next.

"I was messing with that kid. Once in a while I break out in an Irish accent."

"There is a small favor you can do for me, Mister Mitchum."

"What is it?"

"Will you go to the hospital with me tomorrow? Earl is there, and he blames himself for Doris' death. He almost had another stroke. He'll be relieved to see you."

"I'd like to see him," he said.

"Our new neighbor saved my life," she said. "He was unconscious in the Intensive Care Unit, but I guess he's home already." I'm curious to know how he knew where I was. I need to thank him."

"His name is Kekentha," said Roy. "He and I go way back."

"Thanks," she said.

"After what I've been through, I'm up for anything. Being free feels sublime. I want to scream, run, and laugh out loud. My daughters and grandchildren are having a welcome home and belated birthday party for me tonight. Melinda said she thinks Doris is watching over us."

"It's the best news I've heard in a long time. See you tomorrow." She wanted to tell him about having seen the murder weapon, but his spirits were the highest she had seen since his wife's death. She turned around to see Karl at the top step.

"We have some things to sort out," he said.

"Yea, you're right. I need to clean your clothes, and you need a shower." Exhaustion fell onto her like a dead weight. She wrapped her arm around his waist. "Let's discuss whatever you have in mind under the covers. Do you mind if I close my eyes while you talk?"

"Why am I not surprised?"

In satisfying the human desire to be touched, to be exposed in the most vulnerable way, she warmed her hands on the heat of the body beside her. His breathing gave her a glimpse of Tarick, but she pushed it away.

She surmised that Casey conspired with Ben and Harold, and their car was out of the graveyard. They were hunting her down. Too drained to devise a plan, she made sure her pistol was within reach.

Chapter 17

Monday, March 28 – Tuesday, March 29

S he awoke and stretched to the smell of coffee brewing. The closed drapes gave Karl's arms and chest a satiny glow. His jeans fit snugly against the curves of his body as he sat on the wooden frame of the waterbed.

"Want a cup?" he asked.

"That's like asking if I want a backrub and a hot shower."

He returned with a steaming mug. "We haven't talked. You said want to be friends. I want you to know I'm okay with it."

"I'll be both happy and sad when you find the right girl."

"What about your boyfriend?"

"I sense he's taking advantage of the beautiful women who are fascinated by him. It feels like forever since he and I have spoken. I want something real, to be with someone who cares about me for who I am. You make a mean cup of coffee, thanks."

"You're welcome." He smiled, and took a long sip.

"I've been thinking about why we were followed from your apartment. They believe you have the drugs that were planted under my sofa. They also think I'm dead."

He stared at the ripples in his cup as though he was able to foresee some future event. "They have to be freaking out. I bet they saw you last night."

"Maybe. I wrote harsh letters to those men, but they're blowing me off. They've lived above the law for so long; it's all they know. I've been a minor disturbance, like a flea they've had to swat away."

"You've been more like a brick in the bathroom window when their pants are down."

"Every Thursday Casey collected money from my neighbor, Doris. With the racket we make when we get settled in the van, he recognized us from our pictures up in the clubs, the newspaper articles, and our song on the radio. His devious mind began spinning."

"So, he spied on us long before we found him in the road."

"His hair is cut like yours, he dressed like you, and he wove his way into all of your friendships," she said.

"I bought into his flattery, and he asked who my hairdresser is," said Karl.

"He's also on our mailing list, so he knows our schedule, but Debra and I will have a chat. I need to visit my neighbor to thank him for saving me, and get you home. Roy and I plan to visit Earl. His health is almost back to where it was. But first, let's eat." As Karl made toast, she cracked three eggs into a frying pan. The phone rang. "Hello?"

"Where is it? Do not play dumb, or you will regret it."

"Ask the four innocent officers you sent who couldn't find anything. And none of them might seize the contraband, to slip a few extra bucks into their pockets, would they? Are they aware that you can't discuss your wrongdoing without a severe repercussion? Or, perhaps they knew someone was trying to set me up, and chose to do the right thing. They didn't believe I'd be in possession of the large quantity of dope you left. It was a bit excessive. I overheard a few jokes while they tore up my house about their boss. It was something about a fool in high heels and a gaudy dress. They enjoyed the flamboyant photos of how you get your kicks."

"What are you talking about?" His voice notched up several decibels.

"Your pretty portrait is posted in my grocery store. And, speaking of regret, if you continue to harass me, remember I have friends too. It's pathetic when the corrupt feel so much entitlement. Oh, and you might want to watch what you say on this line." She slammed down the receiver, and looked at Karl. "I need to do something about that guy."

"You mean shoot him?"

"If he so much as points a weapon at anything I care about, but no." She picked up the receiver of the new bedroom phone. "Hello…do you recall what we discussed about the ballet?"

"Yes ma'am, I do."

"Nice." She hung up.

"What was that all about?"

"I'll explain while we drive."

Upon her return home, she stopped at the tribal healer's house, rang the bell, knocked, paused, and rang again, but there was no answer. She rapped on Roy's door. He stepped outside, looked up, and took in a deep breath.

"Freedom. It's like a steel chamber was lifted off my chest, and I'm able to breathe again. I ate a plateful of pancakes, drank up the coffee I made, and shoved what I wanted, when I wanted it, into my mouth. I opened my closet, and oddly, I wanted to kiss all my own clothes. I picked my favorite blue shirt and jeans to wear. I want to do odd stuff like go to a florist, and smell fresh flowers. Though I held onto a smidgeon of hope, I thought I would never see this place again."

"I'm glad you're back. Tell me about your evening on the way to the hospital."

In his bed, Earl sagged and stared blankly at the dreary sky. His gown hung on him like the mood he was in.

"I don't suppose you're up for singing that Elvis song you like," said Roy.

306

Earl turned toward his friend's voice as though a truck was about to hit him. He stared in stunned silence.

Roy embraced Earl through bleached white sheets and bedrails. The unconditional love of their lifelong friendship had planted the seed of forgiveness which blossomed in that moment. Bessie joined, and the reunion was reverent.

"Earl, I am so sorry I never told you," said Roy. "I didn't know how."

"Bessie helped…me…understand…what…happened. I'm sorry for for…what my son… did…to…your Melinda," said Earl.

Tears filled their eyes.

Lexa asked if their new neighbor stopped by.

Bessie turned to her. "He's been unconscious in the Intensive Care Unit. Late yesterday evening, his heart stopped, and he got shocked back to life like Earl did. It took them a while to restart his heart. They weren't sure if he was going to make it. His son stopped in here an hour ago, to tell us his dad woke up, and they took him off of the ventilator."

"Did he go home…then return?"

"No. He was in a coma. They almost gave up on him."

Lexa fell into a chair. "He saved my life. I'm certain it was him."

Immersed in the details of Kalie's visits, and of Earl being discharged home tomorrow, they had not heard her. She ran to the unit where her rescuer lay stricken.

The face of the dark-haired man, who had sat dutifully beside his fire, looked into her eyes. A nurse's hand pulled on her shoulder.

"You are not allowed in here."

She remained motionless in his doorway. "Thank you for being there for me."

He nodded.

In a daze, she walked to Earl's room. *Sometimes, there is no explanation for events which we cannot understand.*

"You're as pale as my husband was in the ambulance," said Bessie. "Sit down. I'll get a cup of water for you."

"Thanks," she said, and took a sip. She sat in a chair, and Roy continued to unfold the grim story of his past month.

Earl and Bessie listened solemnly, and assured him that his exoneration filled them with joy and relief. Their hugs were fervent when Roy arose to leave.

"See you soon."

In her VW, Roy asked what her plans were. When she said she had none, he asked how far they were from Menomonee Falls. He hadn't been there in ages.

"Anyplace special?"

"I want to see the rushing river and the waterfalls."

"Point us in the right direction."

The wiper blades rhythmic tempo on the windshield swept rain droplets to the road. When their destination was reached, drizzle tapped on their faces.

Roy inhaled, and smiled. "Follow me," he said. Turning around, taking in his surroundings like a young child in awe of all that was unfolding for the first time, he took a path, and slid down a wet hill between two limestone kilns. Inspecting a ruddy wall, he counted the indentations upward. He used a small pocket knife to dig into several of the holes. "They're still here, all of them. "I don't believe it," he shouted. "It's still here!" He held out nine golden rocks, which glistened in the palm of his drenched hand. His scream of joy carried into the trees and walkways. "My friends will be thrilled." Rain melted into the euphoric tears streaming down his face. "I wish Doris could be here to see this."

For fifty-eight years, the gilded pieces survived in small crevasses of a decrepit, aging wall, undisturbed by small creatures, high winds, and storms. For fifty-eight years, the elements pounded on a fortification where hidden gold waited to be rediscovered.

"I need to tell them. Can we please go back?"

Roy strode down the hallways as though he floated on air. His hands deep in both of his pockets, he entered Earl's room.

"I found it." He opened his hand. "It's a park now. It looks so different."

Earl laughed out loud. "Our...g...gold." His eyes sparkled more than the nuggets in Roy's hand. "Kekentha. It's...not...right without him."

"Yes, we have to tell him. Come on Earl, let's go." Roy pushed Earl's wheelchair down the hall to the ICU, Bessie and Lexa alongside them.

As they neared his room, Roy saw his friend lying under white sheets, the head of the bed partway up. As their eyes connected, they waved. Roy opened his palm and held up one of the rocks.

"Remember these?" he said loudly.

His bedridden friend nodded yes, and his son stood up. "Who are you?"

"I'm an old pal of your dads. I found these today. They were still where we left them."

The older man smiled, and waved them in. Kekentha's voice was weak. "Roy, it was my understanding you were in jail."

"I was, but witnesses and evidence set me free yesterday. You look pretty rough."

"They say it will take a while, but I know I will be okay."

"Well, buddy, three of these are for you. I remember our pact. We take no more than our equal share." Roy set the gold into the creases of his friend's thick, strong hand.

"I never imagined seeing these again. We kept the promise we made all those years ago," said Kekentha.

"We...did. Three...for...each...of...us. Bessie look...we...found these the day...before...our...school...burned...d...down."

"And you never once mentioned this?" she asked.

"There...wasn't...much...to say. I...never...thought...the...gold was rightfully mine. I didn't...think...I'd see it...ever...again."

309

"Well fellas, these are ours now. Let's promise to stay in touch. Kekentha, when you're feeling better, we have some catching up to do," said Roy.

The three men joined hands over the intravenous lines, heart monitors, and bedcovers. There was no separating the value of the restored friendships from the precious metals. Their youthful adventures under open skies, the walls of a small room now beheld their reunion.

"You must be the men my dad spoke of for so many years. He had missed you deeply, and especially now that my mother has passed on."

"Well, don't you worry; we'll be there for him," said Roy.

Each of their hearts beat with a renewed sense of purpose, to live their remaining days restoring friendships weathered by the ultimate tests of time and trials.

On their way to Roy's house, Lexa asked him if he planned to meet the lady who held the key to his freedom.

"I want to thank her and her daughter as well as the other attendant. My family and friends are my life now. I found out I got fired from the job I had. Heck, you put this many miles on a tire, the treads are gonna be worn down. I don't think anybody's gonna want to be with this old third wheel."

"Don't underestimate yourself. Get your rocks appraised as soon as possible. They may be worth a fortune."

She asked him to wait in her hallway, and returned holding the dog bone wrench."

"Why do you have this?"

"It could leave a twelve centimeter mark on the skull. Officer Humphrey paid a visit to your garage, but I beat him to it."

"Do you think I killed her?" He reached for it.

"No, I'm certain you loved her. Who do you think may have killed your wife?"

"May have? I know who did it," said Roy.

"Who could…"

"My nephew. My own sister's son." He shook his head. "When Melinda was cleaning up, she found a note taped to Doris' flask of vodka under the kitchen sink. It said, 'If anything happens to me, Casey took your gold horseshoe ring'. She took it to my attorney who has a copy of the autopsy. Yesterday, the police in Casey's district obtained a warrant, and guess what they found? It matches the mark on Doris' skull. Can you believe it? I asked her about the ring for years. My father passed it on to me. It all came together, the witnesses and the evidence."

"Is Casey in custody?"

"If so, I haven't been told."

"Doris must have been terrified of him."

"There are no words other than, thank you for everything you've done. Our plan was to retire on the same day. I kept a job I didn't like to put a few extra bucks in the bank. We were looking forward to traveling."

"You're proof that when one door closes, another one opens."

"Strange how it works out that way, isn't it? See you soon." Though his life would never be the same, his eyes reflected the light of a new purpose and destiny.

Finding a treasure he had left behind long ago had awoken a part of his forgotten youth. Sharing it with his closest friends, who were pulled back from the threshold of mortality, filled all of their veins with vitality, and a sense of belonging.

Monday March 28, 1977

Each awakening of our eyes, adds one more day to our lodging in the finite realm. We see one more rotation of the planetary forces, and the consciousness that guides our direction. Given to us again is a measure of time. It can be our greatest gift or worst enemy. New moments are granted to view hands of a clock spin around a dial and determine how we wish to use those valued hours.

Tarick has disappeared the same way fires do. The words of my grandmother to look but don't touch, may have referred to him all along.

To show her gratitude for someone who she owed her life to, she studied the assortment of compasses in a lit case, picked her favorite, and paid for it. One of the most valued tools on a journey, the floating needle aligned with the earth's magnetic field. The magnifier improved accuracy, and could navigate him through rugged terrain. She wrapped the box as though Doris had incarnated and explained how the blue wrapping paper should be folded and taped.

Kekentha had been transferred to a medical floor on Tuesday, and though one arm and both legs were casted, he sat in a chair. A white blanket partially covered his faded blue, dotted gown. His son, daughter-in-law, and teen grandchildren sat nearby.

"Thank you for saving me," she said as she handed the present to him. "Mister…"

"Kekentha Silverheels."

"Mr. Silverheels, open it whenever you wish to."

He held the box, smiled at her, and grimaced in pain. "You're welcome, but all I did was kick a trespasser out. Thank you for the gift."

"Dad, you are keeping stories from me again," said his son, who turned to Lexa. "When did he save you?"

She hesitated. "He led me out of a burning building."

"Wow! That's impressive. He surprises us all the time. Our home before this one was set ablaze. We saved the most important things, photos, documents and the clothes on our backs. Our herbs were stored in the garage, which was fortunate. We were discussing where we would like to move to. It's been Dad's dream to live on a large piece of land, near a lake or a river. When he gets home, we'll have the gold appraised."

"I'm happy for all of you."

The son filled the room with words and laughter. Kekentha grinned widely as his son spoke of the tasteless hospital food, his anxiousness to get Dad home again, and the activities of his teen-agers. He elaborated on what an articulate story teller his dad is. Lexa stayed for an hour.

On her way home, she drove past Casey's house, and the red vehicle had not moved from the spot where she had parked it.

She stopped at Tiny's office, and expounded the events of the past three days. The burns on her hands were evident, despite her attempts to hide them.

"I locked the contraband up. I can't tell anyone about it."

"I'm sorry for putting you in the middle of my situation, but what you have in your safe could help you do a whole lot of things you weren't able do before."

"I'm contemplating burning that stuff.'"

"Do what you think is best. I have a few things to figure out also," she said.

"Don't worry too much about Casey. I think he fled to avoid the police, Ben, and Harold, since he failed at putting you away. I bet he left town."

"It's hard to believe he didn't take his Chevy."

"He'll be harder to track without it. The guys and I plan to dress Harold in the pink tights and tutu on Thursday. We'll keep an eye on how he behaves."

In the early evening, from her bedroom she saw the lights go on at house beside hers. Though she planned on having it for dinner, instead she wrapped the warm salmon and fresh sautéed vegetables. She rang the buzzer and was welcomed in. "Mr. Silverheels, this is for you and your family."

"It will be nice not to have to cook tonight. We spent most of the day at the hospital. Dad is improving, but slowly." He and his wife thanked her. "Come in, please."

"Thank you. Until yesterday, I've only seen your dad at a distance, tending to his burn barrel."

"The fires give him comfort. He's been disheartened since our home burnt down. They suspect it was arson. Through the years, his sister and his brothers have passed on. My mother lost her battle with an illness a year ago, and we miss her terribly. Though he'll be happy to live in the countryside, it's been a great turn of events for us to have moved here…for him to have found his friends."

"They have all missed each other. It's as though he was meant to be here. I owe my life to him. No telling how Earl and Roy would be."

"On my dad's desk, I discovered a large envelope. Your name is written on it. When I asked him about it, he told me to give it to you." He returned, and handed it to her.

She felt confused as she held it. "Your father doesn't know me."

"Our fence kept out intruders, not voices." He smiled.

"Thank you." She waved as she left.

In her kitchen, she opened it. He had returned the folder which contained the copy of her letters and photos of Ben and Harold. Another page was added. Under the hanging lamp of her table she read his words:

Dear Little Cloud,

Do not succumb to the evils around you. There will always be many. Become the fire which shines through blackness. Be the light that denies complete darkness to the night.

Never allow brokenness to define you, or to govern your thoughts.

Follow the path which leads to happiness, prosperity and peace.

You must not live your life in fear. Instead live with the courage to stand for what is right, for what is true, and for what will make our world a better place.

It is you who will suffer most if you cannot find it in your heart to forgive others. If you have not acquired wounds on your journeys, you will never experience something as powerful as healing.

Do not surrender tranquility at the cost of holding onto anger. It may be anger you have no awareness of. Become conscious of your emotions, no matter how deeply seated; for the choices which you do not control, will ultimately control you.

Remember to smile when you awaken, to set the tone for your day, and smile before you sleep, to fill your slumber with sweet dreams.

In helping others find light, we forget our own failings. When we focus less on ourselves and more on the well-being of another, we lose our burdens for that moment.

Your friend, the mender of fires,

Kekentha Silverheels

Tuesday March 29, 1977
   No matter how we cup our hands, the sands of time slip through them. As the wind carries away each sand granule, we realize that we never had control of the world all along.

Though we may be able to shake-up our domain for a while, the wind will whirl up again when we least expect it to.

Karl has qualities that I'm attracted to, but Tarick makes my heart dance. Waves of excitement ripple through me when I feel his breath. Not knowing where he is brings on the words of my grandmother, 'a bird in hand is worth two in the bush'. Perhaps that was the nature of her life as well.

Casey seems to have disappeared. In the real world, criminals aren't always apprehended. Instead, they move elsewhere to wreak havoc and misery on others.

The man who led me to safety is my reminder that judging the surface of anything is destructive, and sometimes we discover that people are watching over us when we least expect it. Fire is the light in his darkness, the spark of humanity in his heart. The pops and snaps, a synchronized rhythmic beating of drums, quietly pulsate in his feet. The distant songs of his ancestors echo in crackles and sizzles of damp branches. Within the dancing flares on dissolving twigs, he finds comfort.

I had watched a warrior who, through the mastery of his healing skills was able to mend those he cared for. In helping others, he found peace.

Earl Blesdin was healed by more than a combination of Kekentha's herbs. It was his loving energy and attention, his strong will and unwavering belief that those who are broken can become whole again.

Harold is an aggrieved, desperate man, who will soon have a sparring match with me, Tiny, and those who have the fearlessness to rise against him.

Sometimes we unexpectedly make friends with the lonely stranger standing in the road who longs to hear a voice to speak kind words. Sometimes we unknowingly collect enemies, like the dust that clings to our socks when all we've done is walk on bare floors.

For every person who shrouds their life in lies, there will be another who searches for truth. For every person who strikes out in anger, there will be someone whose hands can heal another. For every individual who delves into darkness, there will be those who serve as a guidepost, a glowing lighthouse. For every person who sees the ugliness in this world, there will be those who point out the beauty, and some who can lead others to it.

We will often find ourselves in the midst of fires. Some may haunt us in our dreams. The choice to transcend them lies in each of our hearts.

Thank you to the characters in my story:

Lexa Lynnch (Lexa Loxx) – The protagonist who tends to attract trouble.

Sam Lynnch - Lexa's estranged husband, who lives upstairs from her, and is the lead guitarist of the band.

Ted Lynnch - Sam's brother, (Lexa's brother-in-law) plays guitar in Word Locket.

Grant Slanik – The band's drummer.

Karl Slater – Bass player of Word Locket.

Hound, Showey, Drax – The band's hardworking road crew.

Roy and Doris Kemke – Lexa's neighbors, live to the right of her house.

Melinda and Marion – daughters of Roy and Doris.

Earl and Bessie Blesdin – Lexa's neighbors, live across the alley, behind her house.

Ben Blesdin – Son of Earl and Bessie, is a District Attorney.

Tiny (Thurston Tinsky) – Lexa's former bodyguard.

Tarick Tagan – Guitar player for the band Signal Source, is dating Lexa.

Casey Relmen – A bass player who has a strong resemblance to Karl Slater.

Officer Harold Humphrey – Sometimes Lexa refers to him as Humpty. He has three insignia stripes stitched below his city patch.

Nathan and Polly Laudon – Lexa's brother and sister-in-law.

Oma – Lexa's deceased German grandmother.

Ethyl MacMillan – A clerk at Diene's Dress Shop.

Miss Brenda – Ben Blesdin's maid.

Kekentha Silverheels – Lexa's neighbor who lives to the left of her.

Ebbie – Lexa and Sam's small, off-white, mixed breed dog.